THE SENATOR ENTERED THE BRIEFING ROOM

"The fiasco of which I was a victim three days ago was a demonstration of the ineptitude of the American military effort here in South Vietnam. It was a classic example of everything that is wrong. That demonstration of military failure has convinced me that all I heard about Tet was true. It was a breakdown of American military policy that resulted in a defeat for our forces."

Gerber couldn't let that pass. Infuriated, he scraped his chair back and said aloud, "That is bull. I've heard enough. Tony, let's go."

"You, sir. Halt right there!" the senator ordered.

Gerber turned to face Bishop, fully aware of the trouble a senator could cause for a military man. But at that moment he didn't care.

"I am not going to listen to a man who has no knowledge of the military or the way it works malign it. The facts show we won at Tet. And if we were so bad, explain why no civilians were hurt on that convoy of yours."

Gerber spun on his heel and pushed through the crowd. At the door he was stopped by an MP. The sergeant looked into the captain's eyes, then stepped aside without a word.

Also available by Eric Helm:

VIETNAM: GROUND ZERO

STRIKE

ERIC HELM

A GOLD EAGLE BOOK FROM
WORLDWIDE®

TORONTO · NEW YORK · LONDON · PARIS
AMSTERDAM · STOCKHOLM · HAMBURG
ATHENS · MILAN · TOKYO · SYDNEY

First edition July 1989

ISBN 0-373-60503-X

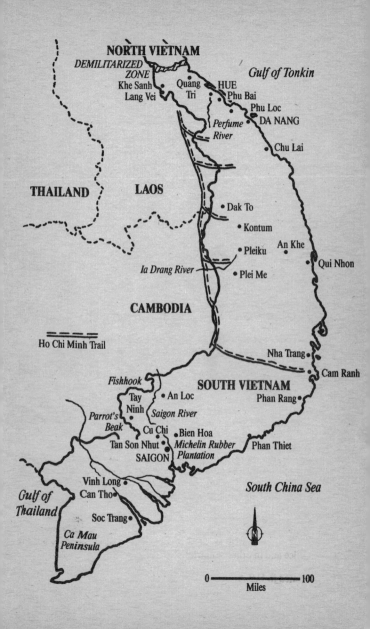

NORTH VIETNAM

DEMILITARIZED ZONE

Khe Sanh
Lang Vei
Quang Tri
HUE
Phu Bai

Gulf of Tonkin

Phu Loc
DA NANG

Perfume River

Chu Lai

THAILAND

LAOS

Dak To

Kontum

Pleiku
An Khe

Ia Drang River

Plei Me

Qui Nhon

CAMBODIA

═══════
══════
Ho Chi Minh Trail

Nha Trang

Cam Ranh

SOUTH VIETNAM

Fishhook

Tay Ninh
An Loc

Saigon River

Phan Rang

Parrot's Beak

Cu Chi
Bien Hoa
Tan Son Nhut
SAIGON
Michelin Rubber Plantation
Phan Thiet

Vinh Long
Can Tho

Gulf of Thailand

South China Sea

Soc Trang

Ca Mau Peninsula

N

0 ─────── 100
Miles

VIETNAM: GROUND ZERO..

STRIKE

PROLOGUE

It had been a long, tiring trip from his home in Kim Cuong, People's Republic of Vietnam, a trek through Laos and then into the western regions of Cambodia. Lieutenant Quang Vo Thanh sat on the soft jungle floor, his back against a smooth-barked teak tree, and drank from his canteen. The hot, metallic water did little to refresh him.

Thanh was a young man, like most of the others with him, and carried an AK-47 that had been new when he had received it. He wore a ragged khaki uniform, a chest pouch that held three spare magazines and low-cut boots that looked like old-fashioned tennis shoes.

Around him were the other members of his company, a unit drawn from his hometown and the surrounding hamlets and villages. There were men who had been boyhood friends and men who had been unknown to Thanh until they arrived in the small training compound near the Laotian border. Once there they were shown the AK-47 and learned the basics of military life, and were taught about the Americans who had invaded the land to the south and about the greatness of Lenin.

There hadn't been much training, and when it was completed, they had been led out of the camp and along the highway that took them into Laos, where they would be relatively safe from the Americans. That had been the beginning of the trek; a long, hot journey down jungle paths and trails, sometimes dodging American fighters, fleeing at the roar of jet engines and hiding in the dense vegetation, a difficult journey where the food was sometimes impossible to find, where the rains came, threatening to wash away everything around them, and where the heat threatened to bake and kill them.

Now, sitting less than a dozen kilometers from the South Vietnamese border, hidden by the triple-canopy jungle where the humidity was so thick that it could be seen hanging in the air, and where it was impossible to see more than a few feet, Thanh knew that the easy part of the journey was over. There had been dangers—from the snakes, the tigers, the elephants and the American Air Force—but as soon as they crossed into South Vietnam, the level of danger would increase dramatically. Fighters and helicopters would crisscross above them, searching for them, hoping to kill them, and there would be patrols of both American and South Vietnamese soldiers. Danger was now everywhere around them.

Slowly Thanh got to his feet. He took another drink from his canteen, sloshing the water around his mouth before swallowing it. Moving to the east no more than half a dozen meters, he could look out over the Ho Chi Minh Trail where porters, soldiers and trucks brought in supplies to keep the war in the South going.

The Ho Chi Minh Trail was nothing like the Americans thought it was. It wasn't a trail but a highway, maybe not made of asphalt and divided by a white line, but a highway nonetheless. Portions of it were paved with pea gravel on a hard-packed base of clay, the center elevated slightly so that monsoon rains ran off into ditches, leaving the Trail intact. Rivers and streams were crossed with underwater bridges designed so that the Americans couldn't see them from the air. The jungle had been carved so that the woven branches of the tallest trees hid the Trail. American reconnaissance aircraft would photograph an unbroken sea of green, while the North Vietnamese and the Vietcong moved under it with impunity like fish below the surface of the ocean.

As Thanh watched, the porters passed him, moving their heavily loaded bicycles. Each of the bikes held a hundred kilos of supplies, weapons, ammo or equipment. The porter walked beside the bicycle, a pole attached to the handlebars to help steer it and another for balance sticking up where the seat would have been. Bags, boxes and equipment were tied on the frames of the bikes.

It was an endless stream of traffic. Hundreds of porters, walking toward the South where the equipment and supplies would be stockpiled. Once his bicycle was unloaded, the porter would then begin the trip north again, heading toward another shipment of supplies and ammo.

But it wasn't just bicycles or backpackers; there were trucks, too. Many of them were Soviet-made ZILs, which were modeled after Second World War Dodges. There was also a great number of American trucks, captured in the fighting, not as many trucks as bicycles, but enough to ensure that the men fighting in the South had all the equipment and ammunition they needed to continue the war.

"An impressive sight, isn't it?" asked a quiet voice behind Thanh.

He turned and saw his friend, Sergeant Nguyen Van Ngo, standing there. Like all the Vietnamese, Ngo was a slender, small man with jet-black hair. He had a round face, almond-shaped brown eyes and a scar on his jaw. Sweat stood on his forehead and stained the khaki of his shirt, and his trousers were threadbare and dirty.

"Quite," agreed Thanh.

"They won't be able to stop us," said Ngo. "We're like the ocean, a relentless tide that will sweep them away. Maybe not today or tomorrow, but eventually."

Thanh nodded, though he didn't agree with his friend's assessment. The Americans weren't like the South Vietnamese. They were brave soldiers who knew how to fight and weren't afraid of anything.

"Tet didn't go well for us," said Thanh.

"No," said Ngo, shaking his head. "I was surprised by that. But they don't expect us to come back so soon. We'll surprise them this time."

"That's true," said Thanh, his eyes still on the flow of supplies to the South.

"We'll teach them not to underestimate us."

Before Thanh could respond, the rest of the men were on their feet, picking up their equipment and weapons.

"Looks like we're about to move out," said Thanh.

The men formed a line and began to wind down the hill toward the Trail. They weren't taking normal precautions because they were in Cambodia, where the American ground forces were forbidden to operate. The only danger was from the American Air Force, which sometimes flew over but almost never dropped bombs. Not much of a danger.

They joined the traffic on the Trail, walking along with the porters and their bicycles, other soldiers from a dozen other battalions and the trucks, all on their way to the war in the South.

It wasn't a difficult walk. The canopy cut down the sunlight, turning everything a bright green, and although the heat and humidity managed to seep through the protection of the vegetation, it wasn't as bad as it would have been under the full blast of the sun. They stuck to the Trail, stringing out along it but not talking.

No one had much to say, anyway. They moved carefully, almost as if afraid to make a sound. There was the rumble of truck engines and the crunch of gravel as bicycles rolled over it or men walked on it. From overhead came the occasional roar of a jet engine, and from South Vietnam the boom of artillery. They were getting close.

At about dusk, when they were no more than half a kilometer from South Vietnam, they stopped to rest. Thanh opened his pack and took out a bag containing rice and fish heads. As he opened the plastic, the odor of the fish rolled up and out. He breathed it in, like a man sniffing the cork of a fine wine before he tasted it.

He ate slowly, savoring the flavor, although it was the same thing he had eaten every day for the past month. Occasionally there had been monkey and once they had killed a water buffalo. Beef was a rarity, and after the meal had been consumed, Thanh had felt an inner glow of tranquillity, which had lasted until the next morning when he'd been forced to begin the long march to the South again.

Now, within sight of the destination, he felt his belly grow cold. Until that moment the war in the South had been an abstraction. It was something to be talked about at night around the campfire. It was a topic of discussion for those who had nothing else to talk about. But it was also something the future held. It was days, weeks, months away. And then, before he knew it, he was less than a kilometer from South Vietnam, and the war was about to become the most important thing in his life.

He stood there, one hand out on the rough bark of a palm tree, sweat dripping down his body, and stared into the glowing green hell of the jungle, trying to see something beyond the trees. The vegetation looked just like that which he had seen during the trip. No different. The air seemed to be the same—hot, humid and heavy. There was no difference between North Vietnam and Laos or Cambodia and South Vietnam. Everything the same, except that there were millions of men in South Vietnam trying to kill one another, and only a fraction of them belonged there.

Ngo approached and stared into the distance. "Nearly there," he said.

"Yes. That's what bothers me."

"The Americans don't fight at night," said Ngo. "They retreat to their camps and hide behind rows of barbed wire."

"There are airplanes and helicopters flying in the night," Thanh reminded him.

"But they're too high. They can't see us."

There was a noise behind them and a truck pulled over, hiding under the canopy. Thanh looked up at the driver, a young man with stubble on his chin and sweat beaded on his forehead. He didn't say a word.

A moment later the company commander, Captain Trang Huu Nhuan, came forward. Nhuan was taller than the others, and older, almost twenty-five. He was a slender man with a long, angular face, lined by his years in South Vietnam fighting the Americans and the South Vietnamese. He had short hair like the others, delicate features and brown eyes. They were hard eyes that had seen much in a very short time. It made it difficult for Thanh, or any of the others, to look at Nhuan. He was a tough man, and he scared them.

The captain stopped and stared at each of them before announcing, "We'll ride the rest of the way. An hour or two in the trucks and we'll be at our final destination."

"Won't that make us targets of the American artillery and helicopters?" asked Thanh.

"No. They'll never see us at night, and if they do, they always think it's one of their own units. We're too poor and primitive to have trucks."

"Where are we going?" asked Ngo.

Nhuan pointed into the jungle. "Final destination is our stronghold inside the Black Virgin Mountain. From there we'll begin the fight to free all of South Vietnam from the yoke of imperialist aggression and oppression."

Thanh looked east, where the company commander had pointed, but he could see nothing except the thick jungle. He hoped the Americans were as blind as he, especially if they were going to take the trucks to Nui Ba Den.

Before he could say anything, Nhuan ordered them into the rear of the trucks. As Thanh climbed into the back, he hoped the commander's assessment was correct. He also wished he had more confidence.

1

WASHINGTON, D.C.

Congressional assistant David Halpren sat in his office and looked out at the traffic that flowed past. It was slow, early-morning traffic, windshields winking orange in the sunlight. No one seemed to think of starting for work a few minutes early to avoid the rush. Instead they would get snarled with everyone else and curse the roads, the traffic lights and all the stupid people who happened to be in front of them.

Halpren was a young man, just out of college, who had found his job through family connections. He had avoided the draft thanks to student deferments and was now shirking it by being declared essential by the senator who employed him. As he sat there, he realized he had everything that was good in life, and there didn't seem to be much chance it would be spoiled by the draft.

He leaned back in his chair and put a foot on top of the walnut desk that dominated his office. Although he was a junior aide who normally would have occupied a small office with others, Halpren had used some of his family's money to buy a larger desk, rent a bigger office and install a floor-to-ceiling window, one that allowed him to see the traffic outside the building.

Halpren had caved in to the fads of the moment. He wore his hair long, touching his ears, though it was cut once a week, thus maintaining independence while not offending the establishment too much. To complete the picture he wore a Nehru jacket, dark pants and highly polished shoes. For those who didn't know him, he seemed to be his own man; those who knew him well, however, could see through the veneer.

He was a good-looking youngster who worked hard to keep his body trim and fit, and he was damned if he was going to give a bunch of Orientals in a hot, stinking country half a world away the opportunity to shoot holes in it. He liked having both arms and both legs right where they were. He ran, lifted weights, played racquetball and lay in the sun to obtain the golden look of the California surfer.

If there was a flaw in the golden look, it was his dark hair. It should have been blond; instead, it was dark brown. He had regular features, wide-set eyes and a sharp nose. He had tried to grow a mustache but hadn't liked the skimpy results and had shaved it off.

Just then there was a knock at the door. Halpren dropped his foot onto the floor, picked up a file folder stuffed with papers and yelled, "Come."

Julie Drake, a woman slightly older than Halpren, entered. She'd been out of college for a couple of years and had also used family influence to secure herself a position on a congressional staff. Thin, almost to the point of looking unhealthy, she had long, straight hair, a thin, angular face and big brown eyes. She could have put on ten, fifteen pounds and no one would have known it. Like all young women of the day, she wore a short skirt, though hers was always the shortest, showing off her long, slender legs. Sometimes she didn't bother to wear stockings, and Halpren found that erotic—just bare skin that seemed to glow with health and sexuality.

She entered, glanced out the window, then moved to one of the extra chairs. Dropping into it, she crossed her legs slowly and grinned. "What we got on for today?"

Halpren closed the file and set it in his out basket. From a stack of papers near his left hand he took a single sheet. "Nothing critical. Why?"

"Networks last night were talking about the Tet offensive again. There was a hint that it might not be the disaster everyone seems to think it is. A few things were said to indicate that our military leaders in Vietnam weren't caught flat-footed."

"So?"

Drake turned her head and looked out at the street. There were pedestrians now. Men and women hurrying along the sidewalks. Men in lightweight suits, women in dresses and skirts. Young men and young women. The workers, the drones, who kept the government functioning.

She looked back at him. "They're going to keep this thing going. More troops to Vietnam."

"The senator's talking about a fact-finding trip," Halpren told her. He opened one of the drawers and pulled out a file. As he did, he sneaked a look at Drake's legs. He had an image of them wrapped around his waist, her feet tugging at his buttocks as he pumped away. He closed his eyes tightly and forced the image from his mind.

"What good is a fact-finding trip?" she asked.

"Adds weight to the senator's words. He speaks from experience because he's been to Vietnam. Makes him a quotable source for the evening news and does away with those stupid 'how do you know' questions."

Drake shifted around, then leaned forward slightly. "I would think the senator would have better things to do with his time."

"Julie," said Halpren, "what could be more important than learning the truth about Vietnam?"

She ignored that question. "So what's on the schedule?"

"We've got a briefing by the military on the results of the Tet and how we actually won there. Then a budget meeting and finally a Democratic planning session."

"Uh-huh."

"What are you getting at?"

Drake stood and faced the window. Finally she turned around. "I want to go to Vietnam with you."

"Oh, for Christ's sake, don't be stupid."

"What's stupid about that?"

Halpren took a deep breath, exhaled slowly and tented his fingers under his chin. "This isn't going to be a picnic. We're heading into Vietnam, to the forward areas to see how the soldiers feel and think, and what we can do to bring this war to a close."

"That doesn't answer the question."

"No, I suppose not," said Halpren, "but then it's not my decision to make."

"You can support me when I make the pitch."

Halpren rubbed his eye. "Seems to me that if I help you, then you should be willing to help me."

"Of course."

"What's in it for me?"

She stared at him, searching his eyes, his face. "What do you want?"

"I see us suddenly developing a new relationship."

Drake took a deep breath, then sat down. She crossed her legs again, letting her skirt hike up. "Just what do you have in mind?"

Halpren knew he had the situation in hand. He knew from her attitude that nothing was outside the realm of possibility. She was willing to do anything, give anything to get what she wanted. And he was willing to accept the bargain on those conditions, simply because that got him into the game. "I don't think we need to worry about that now."

"No," said Drake, "we don't have to settle this now."

"Okay," he said, his voice rising slightly. "What would you like me to do?"

"Just support me when it comes to the discussion of who's going to Vietnam."

"Well, I can't promise you'll get to go, but I'll support the idea of you accompanying us."

"That's all I can ask." She got out of the chair and walked to the door.

"Oh," said Halpren, "what are you doing for dinner tonight?"

She froze, facing the door. For an instant she was angry, but then forced a smile and turned. "I've no plans."

"Would you like to eat with me?"

"Sure."

"I'll call you this afternoon with the schedule."

"Good."

As she disappeared, Halpren put his feet up on the desk and locked his fingers behind his head. He couldn't think of one thing that made his life miserable. He had it all and it seemed that they were throwing more of it at him in buckets. The only thing he had to do was rake it in.

TWELVE THOUSAND MILES AWAY, locked in a sandbagged bunker with a single light bulb hanging from a wire stapled to a thick beam, two men bent over a table studying a series of photographs. The table, a rough wooden thing cobbled together from the remains of ammo crates, stood in the center of the room, which had walls made of sandbags. There was a thick door with a lock on it, though anyone who wanted to get in could have done so with little difficulty, even if it was locked.

Specialist Thomas Coats, dressed in sweat-stained jungle fatigues, leaned forward, his elbows on the table. He studied the black-and-white photo in front of him, looking for anything out of the ordinary. When he spotted nothing, he moved on to the next and still found nothing. Black-and-white photographs shot from twenty thousand feet as the jet flashed over the countryside at six hundred miles per hour showed almost nothing, even to men trained in photo interpretation.

He pushed the pictures away. "I don't see anything here."

Lieutenant Richard Staab, a college boy who had graduated from ROTC only a year earlier, stood up. He stretched, then wiped the sweat from his face. "I didn't, either."

"Then let's call it a night, sir."

The lieutenant shook his head. "We've work to do yet." Again he wiped away the sweat, staining the sleeve of his jungle fatigues. He was a tall, thin man with pale skin and jet-black hair. Although he'd been in Vietnam for five months, he didn't get out of the bunker often and preferred it that way. Buried there, he was safe from rockets, mortar shells and stray rifle bullets. The longer he stayed in Vietnam, the more paranoid he became. Now he rarely went out, and had his meals brought in.

Coats, almost the opposite, was a short, stocky man with light hair and a round, tanned face. He had close-set eyes, a short nose and a substantial chin. Though a heavy man, he didn't look strong.

The sergeant hated the bunker: the odor of dirt and sweat reminded him of a grave and he took every opportunity to get out. Now, reluctantly, Coats sat on one of the folding metal chairs that ringed the table. He didn't move, but stared at the pile of file folders on the table. "Just what do we have to do?"

"Well, for one thing, we've got to examine those field reports to correlate the info contained in them."

"That's something we could do in the morning."

Staab sat down again and leaned forward. "You got a hot date or something?"

"Well, sir," said Coats, "now that you mention it . . ."

"Tom, we're not here on a vacation."

"But the lady's waiting at the club. She said she'd ignore everyone else if I could get there early enough."

Staab took a deep breath and exhaled slowly. He glanced at the material spread out around him. "Just a few minutes more and then we'll pack it in."

"Yes, sir." Coats picked up a file folder and opened it. He read through the report, made by a recon team that had been deployed near the Cambodian border. Lots of activity around the border, but not much of it Vietcong. Most of it NVA. Coats added this information to the reports of contact between American and enemy forces, and suddenly saw the picture clearly. "Sir," he said, "seems there are very few Vietcong left. These reports describe hard-core regulars."

Staab held out his hand, took the file and glanced at it. "This is only one report."

"Yes, sir, but if you read some of the others, you'll see what I mean. A couple of months ago we had VC dressed in black pajamas with SKSs or old French weapons. Some AKs but not many. Now we've got men in khaki and almost everyone of them has an AK."

Coats dug through the pile of documents and came up with a couple of others. All the reports were of men wearing khaki. The black pajamas of the guerrillas were gone. More and more the fighting was being done by North Vietnam-ese.

"Seems to me, sir," said Coats, "that we should head out there and look around. See for ourselves."

"Just where would you plan to go on this little fact-finding tour?" Staab asked sarcastically.

"Tay Ninh Province," said Coats. "That's the terminus of the Ho Chi Minh Trail. Close to the Cambodian border with good support available. We'd be able to see everything we wanted from there."

The last thing Staab wanted to do was leave the safety of his bunker, but then, he needed to gain the information available in the field. "All right," he said. "Tomorrow we'll make the arrangements to get into the field."

"And tonight we knock off early?"

Staab couldn't help grinning. Coats had a one-track mind and there was a girl tied to that track. He nodded. "And we knock off now."

Coats rubbed his hands together with barely restrained glee. "I've just got time to take a shower and get over to the club."

"Just be ready for duty at 0700 tomorrow."

"Seven, sir? That's awfully early."

"Then no later than eight."

Coats leaped to his feet and headed for the door. He slid to a stop and looked at the papers, maps, documents and charts spread over the table.

"Don't worry about them," said Staab. "I'll clean up in here, but you'll owe me one later."

"Yes, sir." Coats bolted for the door, stopped and added, "Thank you, sir."

ARMY SPECIAL FORCES Captain MacKenzie K. Gerber stood near the perimeter wire of Camp A-324 and looked out at the countryside. From his perch on top of Nui Ba Den, the Black Virgin Mountain, he could see for miles. To the southwest was the sprawl of Tay Ninh City, a huge metropolitan center with more than a million residents. It was the home of the Cao Dai Temple, which was filled with gold statues and had avoided the worst of the war so far.

Next to the city, to the northwest, was the American base camp of Tay Ninh. From the top of Nui Ba Den it would have been possible to lob shells into the camp, but the Special Forces had a camp there, too.

Farther to the south was the Oriental River and south of that was the huge swamp that became the Plain of Reeds. With binoculars Gerber could see the small towns that dotted the area, including Go Dau Ha with the Highway One bridge crossing the river.

By turning his head he could see the rubber plantation of Dau Tieng. The rubber trees looked like rows of giant green soldiers marching off to war. There was an American camp in the center of the plantation, while the Saigon River wound its way along the southern border, marking the beginning of the Boi Loi Woods.

"Not much going on out there, Captain," said Master Sergeant Anthony B. Fetterman.

Gerber turned and looked at the diminutive NCO. Fetterman was a small, balding man, his remaining black hair noticeably graying. He had a heavy beard that required him to shave twice a day or find himself in violation of the Army grooming regulations. A nondescript man who would have been overlooked in a crowd, Fetterman was probably the best soldier Gerber had ever seen. He could move through the jungle like a light breeze, disturbing nothing, and he had an ability, rivaled by no one, to find the enemy and to eliminate him.

"No, Tony," said Gerber. "Not much. Saw some movement along the highway, but it was an American convoy. And helicopters. Dozens of them."

"There's always helicopters," said Fetterman. He stepped close, put a foot up on a sandbagged bunker and leaned an arm on his knee.

Behind them was the Special Forces camp, ringed by barbed and concertina wire. There were bunkers and fighting positions, a helipad and commo bunker not far from where they stood. The team house, artillery, dispensary, ammo bunker and headquarters were in the center of the camp. Red dust covered everything, staining the rubberized green sandbags a rusty color, which made them appear as if someone had bled all over them.

But the camp had its advantages. They could watch the countryside all around them, seeing far into Cambodia and nearly to Saigon, which was fifty miles away in relative safety. It was cooler on the mountain. Heat and humidity sometimes invaded the camp, but more often the humidity was trapped on the side of the mountain, and although the camp might not be that much cooler than the surrounding jungle, rice paddies and swamps, it certainly seemed as if it were.

Gerber sat down on the sandbags and looked at Fetterman. "I think we've learned about everything we can up here. We should start thinking about returning to Saigon."

"No one's going to get me mad by telling me I've got to go back to Saigon."

"It is better than being in the field," said Gerber.

For a moment both men were quiet, each lost in his own thoughts. Then, before they could say anything else, the commo sergeant appeared. He saw them, lifted a hand as if he was going to wave, then turned toward them. "Got some news," he said as he approached.

"I don't like the sound of that," said Fetterman.

"No, when they come up and announce they have news, it's always bad," agreed Gerber.

The commo sergeant stopped and looked at Gerber. "Message in from MACV-SOG. We've got a couple of MI types flying in tomorrow. They want you two and a squad of strikers to escort them out toward the border."

Gerber nodded, then grinned. "Any reason Sergeant Fetterman and I were selected for this task, other than that we happen to be here?"

The commo sergeant shrugged. "Captain Gallagher thought you'd like the assignment."

"No," said Fetterman, "I don't think we'd like it. I think we'd rather go back to Saigon where we can chase women, drink beer all night and sleep without worrying about mortar rounds falling on us."

"Sir," said the commo man.

"Sergeant Fetterman's right. We'd much rather go back to Saigon, but if you need someone to cover this, we'll take it."

"We're a little shorthanded," said the commo NCO.

"Everyone is," agreed Gerber. "I suppose I should get together with Captain Gallagher and see what this is all about."

"No need for that, sir. Just two MI guys coming who want to look at the border area and maybe sneak a peek at the Ho Chi Minh Trail. They're interested in learning if the enemy's stepped up infiltration."

"Sounds fairly routine," said Fetterman.

"Oh, it is. Nothing to it. Five days in the field to learn what's happening and then back here."

"Okay," said Gerber. "Tony, you think we'd better go look at a map?"

"Sure, Captain. And you can buy me a Coke."

"There a reason I get to buy you the Coke and not the other way around?"

"You make the big money."

"And have to pay taxes on it. You don't have to pay taxes and therefore make more than I do. You should buy the Cokes." Gerber stood up.

"But you get a tax break, and besides, you're supposed to be a leader of men."

"You win, Tony. I'll buy the Coke."

"Not possible, sir," said the commo man. "We're out of Coke. We've got some Kool-Aid and some warm beer. That's it until the supply chopper arrives in the morning."

"Now why doesn't that surprise me?" asked Gerber. He turned and stared eastward, where he could see the glow of Saigon now that the sun had fallen below the horizon. They could see Saigon, but they couldn't get supplies.

2

INSIDE NUI BA DEN
BLACK VIRGIN
MOUNTAIN

In the month since Quang Vo Thanh had arrived at the camp hidden inside Nui Ba Den, he hadn't done much. The trucks they had boarded in Cambodia had driven them across the border and right into the side of the mountain. They had driven over roads paved with American asphalt and guarded by American MPs and had had no trouble from American helicopters, jets or soldiers.

The first cavern was a huge truck parking lot that looked more like the interior of a giant warehouse than the inside of a cave. The walls had been smoothed until they looked as if they were made of concrete. The floor had been compressed by years of use so that it too seemed paved. Light came from the headlights of the trucks and from electric lights strung along the ceiling.

The widened passageways of the cavern were packed with boxes, bags of equipment, ammo and food. Many of the crates were stamped with the names of U.S. manufacturers; they had been sent to South Vietnam to aid the villagers and soldiers fighting the Communists. The main corridor jogged to the left, narrowed, then jogged back to the right. If the VC had to defend it, the twists and turns would make the task easier.

Eventually the passageway climbed upward by way of steps carved into the rock of the cavern floor. A switchback path took one to the approximate center of the mountain. Here there was another huge room that had once been part of the cave but that was now used as a dormitory. A few hammocks were strung where possible and the floor was littered with sleeping bags and straw beds on which a hundred men tried to sleep. Thanh, Sergeant Ngo and his platoon were bivouacked in this room.

The waiting got on Thanh's nerves. No one seemed interested in them, or in the fact that they were sitting around day after day. Men would come in. Dirty men who talked among themselves of fights with the Americans and South Vietnamese. Tired men who cleaned their weapons before they disappeared to take showers or baths and dress in clean clothes. A spirited bunch who didn't care that there were more men in the cavern with them, down from North Vietnam to support them.

Finally, after a month of inactivity in the cavern, while men came and went, men who fought the Americans, Thanh's ordeal came to an end. Captain Nhuan, the company commander, arrived and said, "I want you to go out with a patrol and learn what to do."

Thanh sat there, surprised for a moment, then replied, "But I know what to do."

"No, you've learned in a classroom how it's done. That's not the same as doing it in the field. There are things to be learned there that aren't taught in the classroom."

Thanh thought about it and realized the company commander was right. He did need to continue his education. "When do I go?"

"Get your weapon and come with me."

Thanh gestured to the right. "What about Sergeant Ngo? He'll need training, too."

"You'll be required to provide it for him later. Now it's your turn."

Thanh got to his feet and picked up his rifle. He grabbed the chest pouch that held the extra magazines, his canteen and a pistol belt taken from the Americans. Putting on the khaki-colored pith helmet with the red star in the center, he said, "I'm ready."

He followed Captain Nhuan through the labyrinth to a large room cut into the side of the mountain. The stone walls showed marks from picks and shovels. There were grooves cut in the floor to carry away water dripping from the ceiling. A lantern sat on the floor, the glow from it filling the room with a harsh brightness.

"Lieutenant Thanh, this is Comrade Sergeant Vinh. He'll be in charge of this patrol. Stay close to him and learn what he has to say."

Thanh bowed slightly. "Comrade Sergeant."

"Comrade," answered Vinh, also bowing.

Thanh studied the other man. He was a youngster, like so many of the men fighting the war, a tired, skinny man with short hair, the sides cut so short that the white of the scalp showed through. Vinh's face had been prematurely lined by the tension of war and the lack of sleep. Dirt was ground into his skin, and a week of scrubbing would be needed to clean it.

"I'm in your hands," said Thanh.

Vinh nodded, turned and looked at the men in the room with them—a ragtag bunch in dirty uniforms who were working on their weapons. Uniforms wouldn't stop enemy bullets, but a well-maintained rifle might save a life. They knew the priorities and were taking care of them.

He glanced back at Thanh. "You'll stay close to me, and I don't want you making any noise."

"Of course."

"If you're ready, then."

As Vinh spoke, the men got to their feet and donned their equipment. None of them took much—a canteen for water, a small plastic bag containing a little food, and their ammunition. They didn't waste time carrying medicine because none of them would know how to use it. If wounded, they would be left behind for the Americans to capture. Caring for the wounded man would slow the American pursuit, and afford the VC an opportunity for survival.

The men lined up and Vinh inspected each of them, examining their weapons and ammo. Dirty ammo would jam a weapon as fast as anything. Satisfied, he nodded and looked at the company commander. "It'll be morning before we return."

"I'll be waiting," said Nhuan.

With that, Vinh moved through the door and led the men along another dark passage that took them down and through the mountain. They stopped to rest in a huge cavern with a pool of clear water at one end. Water dripped into it, the sound echoing through the chamber making it sound as if the flow was constant.

Thanh walked over and looked down. Light filtered in through the passageways that led into the chamber, but there was nothing overhead. Crouching, he reached out and touched the surface. The water was numbingly cold.

"It's very good," said Vinh as he dipped his canteen into the pool. It bubbled quietly. "That's why we come this way."

Thanh shrugged, dumped out his water and refilled his canteen. He drank from it and felt the cold water move down his throat and pool in the pit of his stomach.

"See?" Vinh said.

A few moments later, when everyone had had the chance to fill his canteen from the cold, clear pool and to rest, they moved out. The men talked quietly among themselves, ignoring Thanh. They were a unit that had operated together for a long time. Each man was aware of the others and knew how each would react in a firefight. They could count on one another. Thanh was the unknown man, the one who might get them all killed, or who might run off and leave them. He was the question to which there was no immediate answer.

They came to a darkened cavern and Vinh stopped. He moved toward Thanh and whispered, "We're close to the surface here. We must be very careful and not display a light."

"I understand."

They moved into the final chamber and hesitated. One of the men worked his way forward, then stopped at the wall. There was a single dark hole that led up to the surface. The men spread out and waited.

"Go ahead," ordered Vinh.

The man disappeared into the blackness. He was followed by another and then another until only Vinh and Thanh were left. Vinh stepped close and whispered, "It's your turn. Follow the tunnel and be careful."

Thanh nodded, aware that Vinh would not see the gesture in the dark. He reached into the blackness then, felt the edge of the tunnel and crawled up into it. He felt his way along, the odor of dirt filling his nostrils. As he worked his way forward, he tried to convince himself that it wasn't the smell of an open grave that frightened him. He tried to talk himself into believing that he was only scared of being wrapped in darkness where there were no sounds and only the odor of freshly turned earth. But somehow he just didn't quite believe himself.

Then, suddenly, he came to the end of the tunnel. Over him was the charcoal of the night, the sky visible through the opening, showing him the stars overhead.

He stood up and felt the clean evening air on his face. For the first time in weeks he smelled the tropical air, the humidity, the freshness of it. He let the light evening breeze blow into his face until he felt hands on his shoulders as the men tried to drag him up out of the tunnel.

Once clear he rolled into the deep grass on the sloping ground. Below him, in the blackness, he could see lights, the glow reflected in rice paddies about a hundred meters lower. Not far away was the brightness of Tay Ninh City and the American base on the edge of it.

"Now we climb down, find a good hiding place and wait for the Americans," Vinh whispered. He was still standing in the tunnel, only his head and shoulders visible.

One of the men stepped out, at first distinct only as a dark shape walking through the grass, and then he vanished. A second man followed and Vinh climbed out of the tunnel. Two of the men replaced the cover that hid the tunnel entrance from American recon planes and helicopters.

That finished, they all moved off, walking slowly down the mountain toward the fields below. In the distance they heard the boom of artillery, impossible to hear when they were buried in the caves and tunnels that riddled the mountain. A helicopter came close and the men scattered, diving for cover among the bushes and grass on the mountainside. The noise grew and a dark shape loomed over them, but then it broke away, flying off to the south. When the sound of the engines faded, the patrol began to move again.

Slowly they descended, walking carefully so that they didn't make noise. They spread out two or three meters from one another, close enough to see the man in front, but far enough so that they wouldn't all be hit in an ambush. The

Americans had patrols out, too, though few of them ever got close to the slopes of Nui Ba Den.

They came down off the mountain and walked out into a forest, not a heavy jungle with two-hundred-foot trees and a dense undergrowth, but a forest with palm, coconut and banana trees, a light undergrowth and no canopy to hide them. They found a game trail, a narrow pathway through the trees barely wide enough for one man.

Vinh stepped close. "We normally don't use any paths. The ones used by the farmers are often booby-trapped and sometimes guarded by Americans. Many game trails are overlooked by the Americans, but sometimes the big cats wait for a victim. It's best to move cross-country, away from the trails and the paths, but I'm in a hurry tonight."

After a short hike, the sergeant stopped them. Thanh was grateful for the rest. The weeks of inactivity in the caves had sapped his strength. He found himself breathing hard and sweating heavily. The muscles of his legs ached and his chest hurt. If someone had told him that he was out of shape, he would have argued, but now he knew the truth. When he returned to the cave, he would begin a program of exercise to help himself and his men return to the strength they'd had before the leisure of the cave.

When Vinh was sure that no one was following them, he ordered them on again. They moved through the forest carefully, pushing the branches of bushes out of the way, sliding around ferns and avoiding wait-a-minute vines. Stepping carefully, trying to leave no sign for the Americans, they discovered the trail and tried to follow it back up the mountainside.

Again they stopped, and Vinh spread his men out along the side of a trail. He put one man behind them to watch their rear just in case the Americans got curious, then crouched in the bushes and grass himself, not far from

Thanh. When everyone was set and the sounds of the insects began again, Vinh moved slightly and whispered, "We'll wait here. Stay awake."

Thanh nodded but didn't speak. So far Vinh had shown him nothing he didn't already know: move quietly, don't leave signs and stop frequently to determine if the enemy is near. Thanh shrugged and got down on one knee. He touched the chest pouch to make sure it was still there, though he knew it was, touched the safety of his weapon to make sure it was off, then began to memorize the landscape around him. Nothing looked dumber than to shoot up a bush that you thought was attacking.

For an hour he knelt there, studying the ground around him and listening to the sounds of the night creatures. Insects buzzed near his face, sometimes landing to bite, but he ignored them. There was a rushing in the vegetation around him, a quiet sound of tiny claws as animals searched for one another, just as the men did. Thanh remained stationary.

Then, from far to the west, came the steady pop of rotor blades. Thanh turned to look. A searchlight stabbed out, illuminating the ground. There seemed to be nothing behind the light. It was a death ray that grew out of the sky and played across the ground, showing Thanh farmers' huts, bits of road, rice paddies and bunkers. Nothing moved in the light as it orbited to the west, seeming to come closer all the time.

The sound built until he heard the roar of the turbine engines and could see the dark shape behind the light—an American helicopter with lights inside it, shining down, searching for Thanh and his men. He watched in fascination and then in horror. The light was coming closer, and in minutes he would be in the center of it.

When he had picked his cover, he had worried about men on the ground seeing him, so he had elected to kneel behind a bush. In the darkness he would be a part of the bush, but there was nothing to protect him from above. When the light reached him, he would be visible for all to see. The Americans would swoop in and kill him as surely as he had walked all the way from North Vietnam. Months of hardship—rain that threatened to drown him and sunlight that threatened to bake him, days of hunger and nights of terror—all for nothing because he didn't know the Americans had lights in the night sky.

As he stared up into the charcoal, the light came closer. It was as if the pilot knew that someone was hiding below him, knew almost where Thanh was, and was making sure the enemy wouldn't get away. The light, brighter than the sun at noon, flashed across the ground, revealing everything. Nothing would be able to hide.

Slowly Thanh brought his rifle up toward his shoulder. He didn't want to move fast, afraid he would give away his position. Then he glanced at the light, thinking he would be able to put a couple of rounds into it, knocking it out. Without their light the Americans would go away. That was the thing about the Americans. They seemed to be afraid of the dark; everywhere they went they took light with them.

The roar from the helicopter increased as it came closer. On the ground the light passed over another hut and then a water buffalo, which was frightened by the noise and light. The animal pulled at the stake in the center of the field and bellowed its fear.

Now the light had reached the edge of the forest, no more than a hundred meters away. In the brightness Thanh could see bushes, ferns, coconut trees. They were all easy to spot because the light was so bright. The noise from the helicopter dominated everything else. The little sounds that had told him they were alone in the forest were gone. The animals, the insects, all creation had fled from the noise.

Thanh raised his weapon to his shoulder and aimed at the center of the light. He stared into it, blinked, then pulled the trigger, feeling the kick of the rifle on full-auto. The light suddenly went out.

So much for learning something from Vinh, he told himself.

The sound of the aircraft retreated for a moment, then came back. Vinh dived out of the gloom and knocked Thanh over. "Never shoot at them," he yelled. "That's what they want."

Almost before Vinh had finished speaking, the air was filled with the sound of angry bees. A bright red line stabbed out and the forest around them exploded. Bullets snapped by as the red ray raked the trees, ripping at them. A man screamed, his voice rising, then stopping abruptly.

"Don't shoot!" screamed Vinh. "Don't shoot!"

The light from the helicopter came on again, now no more than ten meters away. Thanh looked up into the night. The aircraft was obvious now. A red light flashed on it. A machine gun began to chatter, the tracers coming down nearby.

Just outside the circle of light the ground erupted in an orange ball of flame and smoke. Shrapnel rattled through the trees, tearing at the leaves, at the bushes, stripping bark from the trunks. Thanh threw himself to the ground and wrapped his arms around his head.

There was more screeching now. A man shouted for his mother, his voice unnaturally high. Another shrieked in terror, the words making no sense.

"Don't shoot!" ordered Vinh again. "Lie still. Don't move."

The light went out and the forest blew up. Shrapnel rained down, tearing at everything. The sound of bees came again, this time louder, as the minigun in the helicopter fired. The muzzle-flash was dazzling, a wall of fire that lit up the bottom of the helicopter.

Thanh risked a glance, then pressed his face to the ground. He smelled the rotting vegetation, the dirt, the mustiness of death. He heard screaming around him, but he didn't move.

Overhead the helicopters circled like vultures eyeing a corpse. Rockets exploded, the concussions washing over Thanh like surf on a beach. Hot air, filled with death, pressed him into the ground. And when that stopped there was the hammer of machine guns and the roar of miniguns. Thanh rolled to the right and tried to crawl under a bush.

The bright light from the chopper seemed frozen over him. He didn't want to move, yet felt that everyone could see him. The skin on the back of his neck crawled as he waited for the white-hot impact of the bullet that would kill him. The ground shook with the vibrations of machine-gun rounds, and the air was alive with the roar of helicopters.

And then suddenly it was dark. The helicopters retreated, as if driven off by a superior force. Thanh didn't move, suspecting a trick, but Vinh was on his feet.

"We must go," he said, "before they can return."

Thanh didn't want to go. He felt safe right where he was, hidden under the broad leaves of a bush, hidden from the sky by the shadows that now offered protection.

But Vinh wouldn't have it. He was on his feet, pulling at his men, kicking at them. "We have to get out," he insisted. "They'll come back."

Thanh felt someone kick the sole of his foot. He tried to ignore it, then decided he'd better heed the summons. He'd already made one bad mistake.

Scrambling from under the bush, he stood and looked into Vinh's face. The younger man was angry. He shoved Thanh once and screamed at him. "Never shoot at the lights! Never!"

The men assembled quickly. Vinh counted them. "Where's Van and Doung?"

"Dead. Killed by the helicopters," one man answered.

The sergeant shook his head. He glanced over his shoulder and then at the men in front of him. "We'll return to the cave. Now. Trung, you take point. Hurry."

"Why?" asked Thanh. "Why do we have to run now that the Americans are gone?"

"They'll come back. They always do."

Trung took off at a run, dodging through the forest as he tried to get away from the spot where the helicopters had shot at them. The men hurried off, following him. Thanh wasn't afraid now; he was certain they were safe. In the distance he heard the faint popping of rotor blades and knew then that Vinh was right. The Americans were coming back.

3

**SENATE OFFICE
BUILDING
WASHINGTON, D.C.**

David Halpren and Julie Drake sat in the spectators' section of the Senate Inquiry Room and watched as Senator R. Turner Bishop entered from a doorway hidden behind the raised desk. He stepped up and took a position at the middle of the desk, from where he would chair the investigation.

Bishop was a man of medium height who had acquired additional bulk during his years in the Senate. He had to attend countless dinners, and luncheons larger than many of the dinners. To top it off, a Senate dining room, which Bishop couldn't resist, provided excellent meals for a small fee. Although he was only five foot ten, he weighed more than two hundred pounds. Like his fellow senators, he had voted the appropriation for a gym on one of the upper floors of the Senate Office building, but somehow he never managed to find time to use it.

Bishop had black hair trimmed short and slicked down. His face was pudgy and rounded and there were black circles under his brown eyes, not because he worked hard but because he had trouble sleeping. He sat up at night watching old movies on TV or reading spy stories. And now, though it wasn't warm in the chamber, he was sweating heavily. By late afternoon even his jacket would be stained with perspiration.

As he sat down the other two members of the committee entered, each carrying a black leather folder embossed with the symbol of the Senate. Carbon copies of Bishop, they sat down on either side of him and waited for their chairman to call the session to order.

Bishop lifted his gavel and cocked an eye at the rear of the room. Halpren nodded, a signal that told Bishop he had all the information he needed. Confident, Bishop banged the gavel down once and glanced at the secretary sitting to one side. A young woman in a summer dress, a stenographer's machine sitting directly in front of her, she held her fingers poised, ready.

"I call this session to order," Bishop rasped. The huskiness was the result of too many speeches, too much alcohol and too many cigarettes. He banged the gavel sharply.

Before he could say more, one of the other senators spoke up. "I want the record to show that I protest this inquiry as premature."

"Exception noted," said Bishop. Then, to prevent the others from agreeing, he called the sergeant at arms and said, "Please inform General Tucker that we're ready to see him."

Like everyone else in the room, Halpren turned to watch the general enter. Tucker was a tall, slender man with a shock of white hair. He moved with the ease of a man who was in good shape. An older man, on the verge of retiring, Tucker commanded attention with his ramrod posture. His tailored uniform fit as perfectly as a thousand-hundred-dollar suit. Row after row of ribbons adorned his breast pocket, most of them combat awards, not the service decorations that covered so many other uniforms. His two stars gleamed impressively.

Tucker moved to the railing and stopped, waiting for one of the other officers with him to open the gate. After a captain leaped to do it, Tucker moved through and took his place at the table, facing the panel of senators. A colonel sat beside him and the other officers took places behind him.

"Senator," said Tucker, "I'm ready to proceed."

For a moment Bishop sat quietly, taken aback. Tucker had wrested control of the inquiry from him easily, naturally, and Bishop wasn't ready for that. Halpren leaned close to Drake and said, "That was a pretty good performance."

Bishop banged the gavel once again and peered down at Tucker. He locked eyes with the man, trying to stare him down. Ten seconds later the senator turned and picked up a sheet of paper. "This morning we're going to look into the defeat suffered by the United States Army during the recent fighting in South Vietnam."

Tucker leaned forward, his lips inches from the microphone set in the desk in front of him, and said evenly, "There has been no recent defeat of American forces fighting anywhere in the world."

"General, I'm afraid no one here is going to accept the premise that the United States didn't suffer a setback during the recent Tet attacks."

"The facts speak for themselves," said Tucker.

Bishop nodded then and rocked back in his chair. "Why don't you fill us in on the facts of the situation? I'm sure it will be enlightening."

"Thank you, Senator," said Tucker. "I'd be happy to do so." He held out a hand and the colonel put a file folder into it. "As was mentioned repeatedly by various members of the general staff and various intelligence agencies, we were aware of a major buildup of enemy forces in South Vietnam.''

"Oh, come on, General," interrupted Bishop, "this is Monday morning quarterbacking of the worst order."

"Excuse me, Senator," Tucker said, "but we have the facts to back up the statements. For example, in December of last year General Westmoreland warned that the North Vietnamese were preparing for a major effort in the new year. That would be the Vietnamese new year, not ours. General Wheeler later warned the public of this in a speech in Detroit that was ignored by the local media."

Tucker flipped a page, then added, "On January fifteenth, General Westmoreland claimed in a military briefing that there was a better than even chance the Communists would launch some type of major strike around Tet."

"Warned or not," said Bishop, "the enemy still came out in force, attacked literally everywhere at once and drove back American forces."

"They made initial gains," Tucker agreed, "but within a week these had for the most part been reversed. The army sent against us was smashed at a great loss to the enemy."

"*Time* magazine of the ninth of February, General, claims that this showed the enemy could materialize anywhere, could strike all over the country at will. The suggestion is that we were powerless to stop it. That's the real problem."

Tucker nodded, as if thinking about Bishop's words, but then said, "I don't suppose *Time* suggested that we allowed the enemy to form for the assault."

"That's a ridiculous statement, General."

"No, it isn't." Tucker fell silent for a moment, then said, "For two years we've been waiting for the Vietcong and the North Vietnamese to come out and fight. We've chased them through the jungles of Southeast Asia, searching for them and their bases, hoping to engage them in an open fight. Our intelligence estimates suggested the enemy was massing for an assault. Why search for them when they are going to come to us?''

"All right," said Bishop, "let's talk about those intelligence estimates. According to the figures being reported to the Administration and to the Senate, the enemy couldn't have mounted the attack. Those estimates suggested the enemy didn't have the manpower.''

The colonel leaned forward and whispered something to Tucker, who nodded. The general grinned broadly. "Well, we've gotten into an accounting area. It comes down to the question of who is a military resource and who isn't.''

"Please clarify that, General.''

"Intelligence estimates are tricky things. Who do you count and who do you ignore? A rice farmer with a rifle might be considered a guerrilla, but is he an effective soldier? Do you count all the men in an unfriendly village as hostiles, or just those of military age? What if you know the enemy has a force of one hundred poorly trained individuals in the region? Do you count all of them? And if you know there are only twenty-five bolt-action rifles for those one hundred supposed soldiers, do you count them as twenty-five or one hundred?''

"The point, General.''

"The point is, the accounting system changed at the first of this year. The poorly trained, badly equipped guerrillas were no longer counted on a one-for-one basis. A new formula was devised to account for the shortage of weapons and the lack of training of those guerrillas. It was those numbers that were leaked to the press and that gave the press a false sense of what was happening in Southeast Asia.''

"You're blaming the press for the disaster in South Vietnam?''

"No, sir," said Tucker. "There was no disaster in South Vietnam, except for the Vietcong."

Bishop took a deep breath and glanced at the men on his right and left. "Please explain to me how you can call this a disaster for the enemy."

"I haven't finished explaining the new accounting system and how it gave false numbers that were immediately reported in the national media. We reported the number of soldiers and not the number of men that could be pushed into the field."

"I want to clarify your last statement. How do you call this a disaster for the enemy?"

Tucker turned and snapped his fingers. One of his men put a sheet of paper into his hand. "The Tet offensive was launched with a force of one hundred thousand enemy soldiers—"

"Soldiers that you said didn't exist."

"No, sir. I didn't say that. We knew the enemy had a large force in South Vietnam. The numbers of effectives had been reduced, according to intelligence estimates, but we never said the enemy didn't have a large force in South Vietnam."

"Please," said Bishop, waving a hand, "tell us about the disaster for the enemy."

"Simply stated, they attacked with one hundred thousand men, had some initial success, but within a week, ten days, more than half the men were dead, wounded or captured, and almost every one of the enemy's gains had been reversed. Notably there was still heavy fighting around Khe Sanh and in the imperial capital of Hue, but much of that started after Tet."

Bishop shook his head. "I'm afraid I just don't understand this."

Tucker was silent for a moment, then said, "We wanted the enemy to come out and fight. They threw everything they had into that fight and found themselves stopped at every turn. Preliminary figures show nearly half the force killed and ten percent wounded. We captured more than a thousand crew-served weapons and more than seven thousand individual weapons.''

"Crew-served weapons, General?"

"Yes, sir. Weapons such as heavy machine guns that take two or more men to use effectively. Antiaircraft guns and small pieces of artillery.''

Bishop smiled and nodded. "Certainly impressive figures.''

"It's the sort of thing not being reported in the press. It's being ignored in favor of stories that suggest we were caught off guard and that the enemy has the ability to defeat us in the field.''

"But you don't think that's true?"

"Senator, if we study the facts objectively and forget about the student protests and the media's misinterpretation of the facts, we see that the enemy was badly hurt by Tet. The Vietcong as a fighting force has virtually ceased to exist, and almost all activity is now being generated by the North Vietnamese.''

"General," said Bishop, controlling his anger and choosing his words, "I find that assessment objectionable. You're suggesting students have no right to protest and the media has no right to publish.''

"No, sir," snapped Tucker. "I'm suggesting that the Administration, worried about pressure from the antiwar movement and the press, has buried its head in the sand. I'm suggesting that we in the military are aware of what the enemy is doing and that we're hamstrung by regulations and orders that effectively prevent us from doing our jobs.''

"The Secretary of Defense—"

"Is a civilian manager and not a military leader," Tucker interrupted, a hard edge to his voice.

Now Bishop's voice rose in anger. "Are you suggesting, General, that we suspend the Constitution?"

"No, sir. I'm merely pointing out that a civilian whose expertise comes as a manager in a civilian corporation may not understand military leadership. There is a difference between a civilian manager and a military leader."

Bishop wiped a hand across his face and stared down at Tucker. Again he looked away first, losing the contest of wills. He fumbled with the papers on his desk, then said, "We're getting away from the subject here. What we want to learn today is how the military could have so badly underestimated the size of the enemy force fighting in South Vietnam."

Tucker shook his head. "I'm afraid we've covered that ground. Warnings about the offensive were given repeatedly, and ignored by the Administration. When the offensive was launched, as predicted, the Administration responded with shock and the media picked up on that surprise. No one, not the Administration, not the media, not Congress, thought to ask the soldiers in the field what was happening."

"We had film of the enemy in the American embassy."

"No, sir," said Tucker again, "you had footage of dead sappers on the embassy grounds. You had no footage of sappers inside the embassy itself. A very different thing."

"General," said Bishop, "your splitting of hairs has given us some interesting insights into the way the military mind works—"

"Senator, I'm merely relating the facts. Let me draw a parallel for you. In December 1944 almost all intelligence reports suggested the German army was defeated. It was merely a question of pushing into Germany and forcing the surrender. Then, suddenly, an army no one thought existed roared out of the forests and pushed back the Allies, forcing retreats. Within two weeks the fighting eased, and the Battle of the Bulge became an American victory. How is that different than what happened at Tet?''

The room was quiet for nearly thirty seconds. All eyes were focused on Bishop, who sat as unmoving as a stone Buddha. Finally he said, ''We're not here to discuss history. We're here to examine recent events in Vietnam.'' He turned, looked pointedly at the junior senator to his right and asked, ''Do you have any questions for this witness?''

The younger senator opened his folder and read over a page of notes. He looked down at Tucker but didn't speak.

''I think we can get out now,'' Halpren whispered to Drake.

''No,'' she said. ''I want to stay here and listen to all of this.''

''Not necessary.''

''I know that.''

Halpren shrugged and settled back into his chair. He noticed a couple of reporters sitting just behind the military officers. One of them scribbled notes periodically, but the other just sat there, listening and nodding, as if he agreed with what Tucker was saying.

The inquiry continued for another hour, but the nature of the questioning changed. The junior senator seemed to have a prepared list of questions, and Tucker answered as if he had seen the list in advance. They worked their way through the script, letting Tucker again talk about the restrictions placed on Americans fighting the war. Tucker suggested that the sanctuaries provided by international borders allowed the enemy to mass for the Tet offensive without having to worry about American interference. The supply lines that should have been hundreds of miles long were only fifty miles long. Bases, depots and assistance given by the locals reduced the problem even more. Tucker suggested that the elimination of those bases would strengthen the American effort.

When the junior senator finished, another man took over. All the senators were allowed a few minutes to question General Tucker. Some of them were hostile, asking questions with anger in their voices, almost as if they believed Tucker was lying. Others asked their questions in such a way that it seemed they had been rehearsed. There didn't seem to be anything impromptu about the session.

Finally Bishop banged his gavel and announced that their allotted time had expired. He thanked Tucker for his assistance, then added, "But, General, I warn you. I'm going to Vietnam to learn exactly what's happening there. I'll be looking for proof that your information is less than, shall we say, candid."

Tucker stacked his papers and tapped the edges to straighten them. "You'll find that my information is accurate."

Bishop stood and made his way to the door. As he disappeared through the doorway, Halpren was up and moving. He left through the same door and stepped into the hallway. There were dozens of people moving through it, each looking as if he or she had an important destination. Halpren, with Drake following in his wake, worked his way through the crowd until he reached another door. He tapped on it, then opened it.

"Ah, David," said Bishop, "come on in. What did you think of that performance?"

Halpren waited for Drake to enter, then closed the door. The room was a small library with only a single desk and two chairs. Bishop sat behind the desk, a small light centered on it. Behind him were floor-to-ceiling law books.

"I thought the general handled himself well."

"And you believe him?"

Halpren shrugged. "He certainly had the facts and figures. I've noticed that these guys tend to dance if they don't have good information. The general thought he had good information and certainly presented it forcefully."

"Well, that just means we'll have to go look for ourselves," the senator said, pulling out a handkerchief and wiping his face with it. "Once we get over to Vietnam, we'll see exactly what's going on."

Drake mumbled something and Halpren turned to look at her. She raised her eyebrows and waited.

Bishop looked from one to the other. "What's this all about?"

"Julie wants to go with us to Vietnam," said Halpren.

"I don't know about that," said Bishop.

Now she moved forward. "I checked with the military about it, and they said they weren't set up to accommodate a woman. Sounded like a lot of bullshit to me. There's no reason for me not to go, if that's what you want, Senator."

Bishop looked at Halpren and then back at Drake. "It's not going to be an easy trip. There are going to be hardships on it. You sure you want to put yourself through that?"

"Senator, until we, meaning women, are allowed to do everything that men are, we'll never have equality. All I'm asking is for the opportunity to do my job."

Bishop grinned. "With that attitude, how can I refuse? I'll inform the people out at Andrews that you'll be going with us and that I don't want to hear a lot of crap about it."

"Thank you, Senator."

"David, you're going to have a lot of work to do in the next few days getting everything ready. Keep me advised. And since Julie feels she should be included, you can use her as your aide in preparing this."

"Yes, Senator."

"If there's nothing else, I'm going to return to the office. You two had better get to work."

Halpren left the room, followed by Drake. In the hallway they stopped. Drake glanced at all the people in the corridor and then leaned against Halpren. "I want to scream," she said, "but it wouldn't look right."

"Why scream? You got what you wanted."

"But it was so damn easy. I thought he'd fight the idea because I'm a woman. Can't take our women into battle so we have to leave them all home, that sort of thing."

"You know what sold him?" asked Halpren. "I think it was the fact that we'd checked with Andrews, and the military had balked at the idea. That's what sold him. It was another opportunity to stick it to the military."

She nodded as she thought about it. "Yeah, that makes sense to me, and now I want to scream even louder."

"Tell you what," said Halpren, "I'll buy us a bottle of champagne to celebrate."

"And I'll help drink it," she said.

"But first we'd better get some of the arrangements made or neither of us will be going."

"I can't wait," she said. With that, she started down the hall, leading Halpren toward their office.

4

SPECIAL FORCES CAMP
A-324 ON TOP OF
NUI BA DEN

Gerber stood just ten yards from the edge of the helipad, a smoke grenade in one hand and a strobe light in the other. The sun, rising over the South China Sea, would determine which one he used. In a few minutes it would be too bright for the strobe and he would toss the yellow smoke.

Fetterman stood slightly behind Gerber, a weapon clutched in his right hand. He held his left hand up to his eyes, trying to spot the chopper that had reported itself inbound a few moments earlier.

"There," said Gerber. "Eleven o'clock low."

Fetterman turned and stared. "Got him. He's going to have to climb to land here."

Gerber looked at the chopper, now about a klick off. He flipped up the grenade and caught it, then put the strobe light in the side pocket of his jungle fatigues. As the chopper climbed toward them, its lights flashing brightly, Gerber pulled the pin on the smoke grenade and tossed it into the center of the pad. Then he turned and retreated toward Fetterman.

The noise, which had only been a low buzz in the distance, built slowly until it was a roar that filled the air. The blades began to pop as the chopper, now higher than the mountain, began descending, its landing light stabbing out once before being extinguished.

Gerber turned his back and put a hand on his beret as the helicopter neared the pad. A sudden rush of wind tore at his clothes and peppered his back with dust and dirt. He closed his eyes but could smell the dirt swirling around his head.

Then, quickly, the chopper settled onto the pad, and the pilot pushed down on the collective. The roar of the engine died and the blades began to slow, as the pilot shut down the turbine.

Gerber turned and saw two men leap from the back. One of them, carrying a CAR-15 and wearing a pistol, came forward. The straps of his steel pot hung down so that he looked like John Wayne in a World War II epic. He wore a flak jacket that looked new and even had on an olive-drab T-shirt, which indicated the man didn't get into the field often.

"I'm Lieutenant Staab."

"Lieutenant," said Gerber. The sound of the turbine wound down, and it was suddenly quiet on the mountain. "I'm Captain Gerber."

"Yes, sir. I was told we could stage out of here and that a patrol would be standing by."

"First," said Gerber, "I think I'll want you to brief both me and Sergeant Fetterman. After that, we'll be able to figure out exactly what we need to do."

"That seems simple enough. We want to look at the Ho Chi Minh Trail."

"That's in Cambodia," said Gerber. "Cross-border operations aren't authorized."

"Yes, sir," said Staab. Another man approached, stopping short of Staab. "Captain Gerber, this is Sergeant Coats."

"Sergeant." He held out a hand. "Tony, let's head for the team house."

"What about the flight crew?" Fetterman asked.

Gerber turned and saw that the men were in the rear of the chopper. One of them was lying on the troop seat, using his chicken plate for a pillow. Two others were lying on the deck of the cargo compartment, and the last was sitting behind one of the machine guns, reading a paperback novel.

"Looks like they're happy," Gerber said, grinning.

Fetterman turned and moved away from the helipad. They crossed between two bunkers, both of them low so that they weren't silhouetted against the skyline.

Entering the team house, they descended into the dim interior. It was a small building with a tin roof that looked as if it was partially buried. There were sandbags along the walls, and although they couldn't see them, sandbags were hidden under the rafters. The tin of the roof would detonate mortar rounds and rockets, and the sandbags would absorb shrapnel. Such precautions provided some protection.

The interior looked like the inside of most team houses. There were several tables, each with four chairs. A metal napkin container, a salt shaker with rice in it to absorb moisture, a pepper shaker and a sugar holder were in the center of each table.

"Coffee, Captain?" asked Fetterman.

"All the way around, Master Sergeant."

"Yes, sir."

They sat down to wait. Coats picked up the sugar and spun the container in his hand, watching the sugar as it shifted.

"This your camp, Captain?" asked Staab.

"Nope. I'm with MACV-SOG out of Saigon. I was out here on a special assignment when your call came in. Since they're shorthanded, Sergeant Fetterman and I decided to take the mission to help out."

Fetterman returned with empty cups and a full pot. He put the cups on the table and sat down. As he poured the coffee, he asked, "Now, just what's going on?"

Staab looked at Gerber, who nodded. "We've seen some interesting things lately in the photo recons and thought we should take a closer look."

Coats took out a map and spread it on the table. He glanced around and saw that they were alone in the team house. "We've got indications of heavy traffic along here, crossing the border and moving into Tay Ninh Province. HUMINT sources suggest another assault on Saigon. Charlie wants to prove that the first attack wasn't a fluke."

"There a real need for us to go look?" asked Fetterman.

"If we can confirm that Charlie's moving more people, new people, into the area, we can move to stop him."

"And," said Staab, "we've got a theory that more of the war is being taken over by the NVA. The VC were pretty well chopped up by the Tet offensive. Their replacements are regulars, not guerrillas."

"Well, I suppose we can find that out."

"We don't want to make contact with the enemy," said Staab. "We just want to confirm some stuff for ourselves. And we've got a report that a firefly team took some fire not far from here last night. Thought we'd look at the site and see what we can learn from it."

"Saw that last night, Captain," said Fetterman. "Watched the choppers working about a klick or two away."

"They take fire?" asked Gerber.

"One guy," said Fetterman. "They hosed down the area, so I suspect there were more down there, but only one guy was dumb enough to shoot."

"I'd like to see the site," said Staab.

Gerber looked at the map. "You're going to need choppers for that. We sweep the area where the firefly was, we'll need airlift toward the border. It's too far to walk."

"I'll coordinate that," said Fetterman.

"No need," said Staab. "I've got a flight standing by. As soon as I give them the word, they'll be here."

"Breakfast?" asked Fetterman.

"We've eaten," said Staab.

"Well, we haven't," said Gerber. He pushed his chair back and walked to the bar that bisected the room. Behind it was a set of shelves stocked with canned goods and dry food. "You got a preference, Tony?"

"Cornflakes."

"Jeez, Tony, you could have anything—Cocoa Puffs, Frosted Flakes, Cheerios—and you want cornflakes?"

"Well, sir, then I'll have some Frosted Flakes, though I thought we wanted to maintain an image here. Didn't know that we'd let the legs see us eat kiddies' cereal."

Gerber grinned. "Hell, I'll even offer the legs some of our kiddies' cereal."

Staab held up his hand. "No thanks. We had a big breakfast before we left."

"Suit yourself," said Gerber. He carried a box of Frosted Flakes to the table while Fetterman poured powdered milk into cold water and stirred it. As he walked to the table, the master sergeant said, "I really don't like this powdered shit. It doesn't taste anywhere near the real thing."

Gerber took the pitcher and poured the ersatz milk over the cereal in his bowl. "It's better than nothing."

"I'm not sure," said Fetterman. "Sometimes I think nothing would be better."

They ate in silence as Staab and Coats watched. Gerber hooked a thumb and said, "There's orange juice in the refrigerator."

"Real?" asked Staab.

"No, powdered, just like everything else. Can't get the real stuff in here."

"I drank real orange juice before I left."

"You know, Lieutenant," said Fetterman, setting his spoon down on the table, "I could get real tired of hearing about everything you had before you got here."

Staab grinned. "Sorry, Sergeant."

Gerber finished his breakfast. "Why don't you whistle up your choppers. We'll get the strikers together and ready to move."

"How many are we going to take?"

"Two squads," said Fetterman. "Twenty men, plus the four of us."

Staab stood and picked up his weapon. He glanced at Gerber, who then said, "Tony, why don't you and Sergeant Coats get the strikers. I'll take the lieutenant over to the commo bunker."

"Yes, sir."

Gerber picked up his weapon and moved to the door. As he opened it, two NCOs assigned to the camp came through. They nodded, then moved directly toward the refrigerator. One of them opened it, pulled out two beers and looked at his friend. "What are you going to have?"

"You let them drink beer for breakfast?" asked Staab.

"It's not my team, and they're capable of deciding if they should have beer or not. This isn't high school and we don't have to watch them."

"Yes, sir."

They left the team house and moved off toward the commo bunker. It was a large structure made of rubberized green sandbags. On the top was a forest of antennae, though with the base's position on the mountain, the extra twenty feet they afforded made no difference. They entered, walking down the steps made from planks. The interior was dark and cold, and the only light came from the faces of the radios stacked in the corner. Glowing reds, greens and ambers cast an eerie glow in the bunker. A man sat behind one bank of radios, paying no attention to them. In front of the radios was a long table covered with maps. On the walls were more maps, barely visible in the half-light.

"Lieutenant needs to use the radio," said Gerber.

"Yes, sir." The sergeant moved off, letting Staab have access to the equipment.

Staab sat down, glanced at the radios, then reached out for the Uniform. He dialed in a new frequency, waiting for the radio to cycle itself, then used the microphone. "Black Hawk Operations, this is War Cloud Two."

"Go, War Cloud Two."

"We'll be ready for pickup in two zero minutes at the primary location."

"Roger, Two. Understand at primary location in two zero minutes."

Staab looked at Gerber. "That's got it."

Together they left the bunker and walked toward the helipad. Fetterman and Coats were already there, the strikers lined up near them. The master sergeant was slowly moving among the troops, checking their rucksacks, pistol belts and weapons. He made sure each man had his share of squad equipment, from spare batteries for the radio to extra ammo for the M-60s and M-79s. It was also important that each man had enough ammo for his own weapon, had the water he'd need for the day, food for his noon meal and his first-aid kit. Each man also carried hand, smoke and CS grenades. Finally they all had pistols and razor-sharp knives. They were ready to fight.

When he finished inspecting them, Fetterman turned and walked back to where Gerber waited. "When the choppers arrive, we'll be set."

A moment later one of the men from the commo bunker appeared. "Choppers inbound. They want smoke."

Fetterman tossed a grenade into the center of the pad. Billowing green, it was caught by the light early-morning wind and swirled around. "Never get the flight in here," he said.

Gerber nodded. "They'll land two, we'll load them, and then the next two. It'll take us a little longer." He turned to Staab. "You and I will get on the first chopper. Tony, you take trail and Coats. You'll be on the lead ship of the second element to land here."

"Shouldn't we stay together?" asked Staab.

"And if one chopper has to abort, the whole mission goes down the tubes. Spread out the leadership and we won't be caught without a team leader in the field."

"Makes sense."

Gerber turned then and saw that the first of the helicopters was on final approach. He crouched down, his hand holding his beret tightly. Closing his eyes to protect them, he listened to the sound of the helicopter as it slowed, then landed. "Let's go," he yelled as he ran across the helipad, ducking low. He put a hand on the floor of the cargo compartment and vaulted into the rear of the chopper.

Staab and six of the strikers joined him. As they did, the aircraft became light on the skids. It lifted to three feet, hovered there for a moment, then began a shallow climb out. Through the cargo compartment doors, Gerber watched the camp drop away, and then as they began to descend from the mountaintop, the camp drew upward, finally disappearing from sight.

As they descended toward the level land below, Staab perched between the pilots, his map out. One of the men was looking at it and nodded once, holding up a thumb. Staab returned to the troop seat, and over the roar of the engine and the pop of the rotor yelled, "First stop is the site of last night's firefly success."

They orbited in a wide, lazy circle, fifteen hundred feet above the surrounding territory, fifteen hundred feet below the top of Nui Ba Den and well away from the slopes. Gerber saw two choppers lift above the Special Forces camp, climb over the bunkers and perimeter wire and fall away, descending to join them. Three minutes later the last of the five ships did the same thing, and once the flight was joined, they began to head for the landing zone.

The crew chief looked around the corner from the well where he sat. "We're about two minutes out."

Gerber nodded and glanced at the men with him. The Vietnamese didn't seem to be worried about anything. They sat quietly, their weapons all pointed straight up.

Satisfied that the men were ready, Gerber took off the beret he wore, rolled it up and stuck it into the top of his rucksack, then pushed the sack over his left shoulder again. Then he withdrew the boonie hat and put it on. He now looked like thousands of other GIs who walked the jungles and rice paddies of South Vietnam.

They began their descent, a rapid dive at the ground that left his stomach somewhere behind them. A couple of the strikers grabbed at the troop seat or the fuselage, holding on, suddenly concerned. Outside, a single chopper, loaded down with machine gun and rocket pods, flashed past—close air support just in case the enemy was lying in wait.

They approached the ground rapidly, falling toward it like a stone. The nose of the chopper came up quickly, obscuring the forest below them. Gerber rocked forward as the aircraft leveled and dropped into the tall grass. As the skids touched the ground, the captain was out of the cargo compartment door in the blink of an eye.

He crouched in the grass, one hand securing his boonie hat as he scanned the tree line fifty yards away. One of the gunships shot along it, the skids only inches from the treetops, but it drew no fire.

A moment later the choppers lifted with a hurricane of swirling rotor wash that tugged at and tried to snatch away everything that wasn't fastened down. Almost before the aircraft were off, Gerber was on his feet, waving the men forward. They spread out, sweeping toward the trees as the sound of the helicopters faded and disappeared. When the choppers were gone, silence descended, a complete silence that wasn't punctuated by normal sounds.

Gerber moved carefully, hurrying toward the trees. He lifted his feet high over the grass, putting them down and twisting them slightly to break the razor-sharp blades that slashed at his uniform and boots. Stepping over a rotting log, he crouched and surveyed the jungle. A single bird broke from the top of a tree, swooped, then climbed. Now, with the choppers gone, Gerber heard jungle noises—animals calling, birds whistling, monkeys playing.

Fetterman moved forward, leading the way. Gerber stood and moved forward, too, his eyes on the trees. He turned once and saw the trails cut by the men as they walked from the landing zone to the trees—dark green areas through the gray-green grass.

Gerber reached the trees and stopped short. He turned and looked to the rear, but there was nothing to see. He entered the forest and slipped to the right, where Fetterman stood. "Not that much farther to the site."

"No, sir."

"Let's take a break here. Get security out and see if the enemy's around."

Fetterman turned, pointed at three strikers and ordered them to go another thirty feet. They moved on, then stopped and crouched. Fetterman looked at Gerber. "We're set."

5

WASHINGTON, D.C.

Halpren sat in the wing chair that faced the open window and stared out into the night, where the lights of Washington sparkled like a field of freshly fallen snow. Then he stood and went to the window, pulled the curtain aside and watched the lights of cars and trucks as they moved along the highway below him. The ice cubes in his glass rattled as he lifted it and took a drink.

"I'll be out in a sec," called Drake from the back of the apartment.

"Don't hurry. I'm fine."

He turned away from the window and crouched in front of the television. Hoping to find some news, he turned it on, but found only commercials—lots of commercials trying to sell him lots of things he didn't want. In disgust he turned off the set and returned to the chair.

Drake appeared then, coming from the back of the apartment, her hands over her head as she tried to clip her hair up. She grinned at him. "Ready."

Halpren looked at her. She wore a knee-length skirt and a white blouse with a red tie at the throat. He glanced at himself and held out his arms as if surrendering. "You look good, but I'm not sure I belong with you."

"A suit and tie," she said. "What's wrong with that?"

"I look shabby compared to you."

"I'll take that as a compliment," she said, moving toward him. She stopped, her hip against his, then tilted her head, kissing him on the lips. "Thank you."

"For what?"

She turned so that she was facing him, her body only inches from his. "What do you think, silly? For helping convince the senator that I should go to Vietnam with you."

Halpren shrugged and was about to say that he hadn't said anything to the senator. Their boss had seen her going as an opportunity to screw the Army, and had taken it. But before he could speak, he realized she didn't know that. She knew the senator relished shafting the military, but she still thought Halpren had helped her cause. Why tell her otherwise?

"Well, we co-workers have to stick together." He kissed her and put his hands on her shoulders. "After all," he said quietly, "it's them against us."

She responded immediately, slipping her arms around him, pulling him close and forcing her tongue into his mouth. Halpren slid his hands down her arms, his thumbs out to touch her chest. He stopped, felt her nipples and heard her moan low in her throat. He broke the kiss and stepped back as she opened her eyes.

"It's not necessary for us to go to dinner," he said.

"No," she agreed, "it's not necessary." She reached up and pulled the pins from her hair, shaking her head. Her light brown hair spilled over her shoulders. "I'm not hungry now. Not for food, anyway."

Halpren took the words as his cue. He stepped in and kissed her, his fingers fumbling with the top buttons on her blouse. As they popped open, he kissed her chin, and as she lifted her head, kissed her throat, drawing his tongue down over the soft skin of her neck. Bending his head, he kissed her chest, opened another button and kissed her between her breasts.

As he did that, he reached down and found the button on her skirt. He unfastened it and worked down the zipper. The skirt slid over her hips and fell to the floor, pooling at her feet.

Halpren touched the inside of her thigh with his fingertips. He felt the softness of her skin over the tops of her stockings. She sagged against him, holding on to him, breathing hard.

"Let's go to the bedroom," he said.

She ignored that and sat down on the floor, finished unbuttoning her blouse and shrugged it off so that she was wearing only her bra, panties and stockings. Halpren knelt and kissed her. He reached around and unhooked her bra. Then, as she let it fall, he kissed her again between her breasts. With his tongue he traced a line to her nipple.

"Yes," she breathed. "Yes."

As she stretched out on the carpet, Halpren ran a hand along the inside of her thigh. She was ready for him, more than ready, but Halpren didn't want the moment to end. He wanted to savor it, playing her body like a fine instrument, taking her higher and higher until she was unable to think. He wanted to tease her until she was begging him to finish it.

Halpren lay down beside her, his lips on her as she tried to suck in air. He lifted her hands over her head, stretching her out. He held her hands there, over her head, as his lips tasted her. With his free hand he rubbed her stomach, his hand dipping lower and lower. She was moaning repeatedly now, her breath coming in short bursts.

Now Halpren found himself succumbing to his own lust. His body ached and he was losing control of himself. He released her hands, and they were immediately on him. She tugged at his belt, opening it, searching for the button on his fly.

"Hurry," she said. "Hurry."

Halpren felt the tension, too. He pulled at her panties, trying to rip them off. Then, brushing her lips with a kiss, he looked at her. Sweat had blossomed on her forehead, beading at her hairline and dripping down her face. She rolled her head to the right so that she could see what she was doing as she forced his pants over his hips.

"Hurry," she whispered.

The flimsy cloth of her panties gave way. He wadded them into a ball and tossed them away. Then he kicked off his own pants. As they came free, she reached out, trying to drag him to her.

"Now," she said. "Right now."

For an instant Halpren thought about making it last, taking her a little higher, making her wait a little longer. But then it was out of his hands. He couldn't wait as he looked down at her naked body. She wore only her garter belt and stockings. Sweat glistened on her, highlighting her body. That was too much for him.

After they finished the first time, they moved to the bedroom. Drake stripped off the bedspread, folded it and put it on a chair. The sexual edge had been dulled a little by their activity in the living room. Next she arranged the pillows, lay down on her back and looked up at Halpren. "You going to join me?"

Halpren shook his head. "I just want to stand here and look at you."

"Don't be silly," she said.

He climbed into bed, rolled onto his back and laced his fingers behind his head. "You know, if we hurry, we could still go out to dinner."

She shifted around so that she was lying on her side, her head propped on her hand. "You want to go out to dinner now? I'm not dressed for dinner."

He glanced at her. Somehow they had never gotten her stockings off. Halpren thought she looked even sexier that way. "I don't think I want dinner."

"Good."

LIEUTENANT QUANG VO THANH didn't have the restful night Gerber and Fetterman spent on the surface of the mountain, nor did he have the kind of fun Halpren and Drake enjoyed. Instead, once he reached the safety of the interior of Nui Ba Den, he sat up most of the night and cursed himself. He'd let fear rule him, forcing him to shoot at the lights, thinking his weapon would be able to chase away the helicopter and the enemy.

No one had spoken to him as they'd fled the field, running back the way they'd come. No one had spoken to him as they'd worked their way up the mountainside and found their way back into the tunnels. And no one had spoken to him as they'd walked through the tunnels and chambers that led into the main camp area inside Nui Ba Den.

Once the patrol had ended, and each man had cleaned his weapon, they had drifted away, moving to their own areas. Thanh, feeling the sting of being ignored, and knowing he had screwed up, had stayed where he was.

The words he'd spoken before the mission still echoed in his head. He'd said he didn't need a training mission because he knew how to operate in the field. That had been terribly wrong, fatally wrong. But no one had been there to berate him, either.

Just then Captain Nhuan loomed out of the darkness at one end of the cavern and squatted near him. "You had some trouble last night."

"We were attacked by helicopters," said Thanh, knowing he hadn't told the whole story with such a simple statement.

"Men were killed?"

"Two, maybe three. I don't know for sure and I was afraid to ask."

The commander nodded wisely. "How do you feel about this?"

"No one told me about helicopters with lights on them. It was almost as if the Americans wanted us to shoot at them."

"That's exactly what they want. If you shoot, you give away your position, and other helicopters, those you don't see, attack you. It's a trick they've used many times."

Thanh shook his head. "There are so many things to know, so many ways the Americans can kill you."

"Yes," agreed the commander, "they have many tools, many weapons, but they don't have the internal fire. They don't burn with the desire to free their land from oppressors. They don't understand this."

"Sometimes fire isn't enough," said Thanh.

"Sometimes it's all you have."

"I made a bad mistake last night," said Thanh.

"It's a mistake made by all of us. You weren't told not to shoot at the lights. I knew it, the patrol leader knew it, but no one told you."

Thanh looked up. "Men died because of that."

"It's the way that men die in battle. Someone makes a mistake. Maybe it's you, maybe it's me, maybe it's the man who dies, but it's someone. We can't bring back the dead. We can only learn so that it doesn't happen again."

"A very costly lesson."

"Yes, especially for the men who have died. But that's the way of the world and the way of war. We resolve to do better next time. Maybe something you learned last night will save the lives of your men later. It balances out."

Thanh nodded, not sure the logic was sound. "I'll try not to make those mistakes again."

"Good. Now you'll have the privilege of returning to the ambush site and recovering the bodies of the heroic men who died for the freedom of people everywhere."

Thanh nodded. "How soon?"

"As soon as you can get a patrol together. Do you know how to get to the site?"

"I believe so, if someone will take me to the point of departure."

"I'll arrange that."

Thanh got up then and followed Nhuan into the main chamber where his men waited. All were awake, sitting on their cots or on the cavern floor, talking quietly, playing cards or sharpening their knives.

Thanh realized he had no idea what time it was. They had all entered the cavern during the night and were so far from the surface that no sunlight penetrated. The only time he had been outside it was dark. It was dark when he had entered again, and they had worked their way deeper without waiting for the sun. His life was now wrapped in darkness, the only lights from lanterns, fires or flashlights.

He found Sergeant Ngo sitting by himself, whetting his combat knife with a stone. "Good morning, Comrade Lieutenant," Ngo said as Thanh approached.

"Good morning, Sergeant. Are you ready for a patrol?"

"You mean an opportunity to enter the world of the living? A chance to get out of this grave?"

"Yes."

Grinning broadly, Ngo said, "I'm ready."

"Then find a squad of our best men. We'll leave in fifteen minutes. Have the men ready then."

"Certainly."

Ngo got to his feet, bowed, then hurried off, touching the shoulders of the men he wanted to join them—those who were the best shots, the most disciplined, and those who were the toughest. He selected twelve men and each of them started to get ready for the excursion outside.

Thanh watched for a moment, then returned to his cot. He cleaned his weapon quickly, making sure there was no dirt to foul it. He didn't bother to change his uniform, figuring the dirt and mud that smeared it would only help conceal him when they got outside.

The men gathered near the exit. Thanh saw them as they filtered over there, forming a line near the wall of the cavern. Ngo inspected the men, checking their weapons and ammo. As Thanh walked up to them, the sergeant said, "We're ready to go, Comrade."

Thanh nodded and moved so that he was centered on the line of men. They looked at him as he stared into their faces and marveled at their youth. "We've been given the task of reclaiming the bodies of our comrades killed last night. It will be a short patrol with very little danger. Each time we leave the protection of our caves, there's danger, but today there won't be much."

He looked at his men and knew his pep talk was falling on deaf ears. Men about to travel into a war didn't want to hear that there would be no danger. They wanted to believe the enemy would be all around them, that the danger was everywhere and that only through bravery would they survive. But then each was secretly hoping the enemy would be long gone. They wanted the opportunity to be brave, but they didn't want danger. It was a strange feeling—wanting to meet the enemy and wanting to avoid him.

Thanh shook his head. "We'll have to be alert for the American helicopters. They'll be all over the sky like flies around a dung heap. They'll be our greatest threat. Don't shoot at them unless I order you to."

He wanted to say more but didn't know what it should be. Everything sounded so lame, almost cowardly. He finally shrugged. "Sergeant, are we ready?"

"Yes, Comrade."

"Good."

He stepped forward and saw the company commander returning with Sergeant Vinh. They stopped short and Vinh asked, "Are you ready?"

"Yes."

"Then follow me."

Before they could move the company commander said, "You're only to go to the site of the battle and then return. I don't want you exploring beyond that point."

Thanh nodded. "Yes, Comrade."

"Follow me," said Vinh again. He turned, entered the tunnel and began a rapid descent.

Thanh and his men spread out behind Vinh, hurrying to catch up. As they walked through the tunnels, turning left, then right, Thanh remembered some of the route. He tried to memorize the path so that he wouldn't be lost inside the complex tunnel system, but there were so many tunnels, both false ones that led to traps and good ones that led to other levels and chambers, that he would have been confused if not for Vinh.

They finally came to the mountain exit. Vinh pointed at it. "Let me have five minutes before you open it."

"Why?"

"In case there are Americans watching."

Thanh stared at Vinh, then nodded. "Go and hide then."

As Vinh disappeared down the tunnel, Thanh moved forward to the trapdoor that would allow them to exit. Pushing on it, he felt it shift easily. "Wait here," he told Ngo. "I'll open it and go out first. You follow in a moment unless I warn you otherwise.''

"Yes, Comrade.''

Thanh pushed on the trapdoor, lifting it slightly. He peeked out into the brightness of the Vietnamese morning. Fresh air blew in, seeming to cool the interior of the chamber. The lieutenant shifted around, trying to see in all directions, but he couldn't see anything hostile. There was no noise, either. The Americans, if they were in the vicinity, were well hidden.

Carefully Thanh opened the trapdoor fully. He let it drop behind him and ducked, expecting someone to open fire. But nothing happened. Then, standing, he slowly turned. He could barely see over the grass and bushes that concealed the trapdoor. Convinced there were no Americans around, he climbed out of the tunnel, stood next to the hole and looked down at the flatland below him. It looked quite different in the daylight.

When he was satisfied that the Americans were nowhere to be found, he moved off and waited for the rest of the men to join him on the surface. When the last man was out, he closed the trapdoor.

"Where do we go now?" asked Ngo.

Thanh studied the surrounding territory. None of it looked the way it had in the dark. Now he could see the tree lines, the farmers' huts, the rice paddies. Things that had been vague lumps in the dark were structures now. Far in the distance, where before there had been the glow of lights at night, was the spread of a city filled with trees.

"Down there," said Thanh, pointing at the rice paddies to the south of where they stood. He wasn't sure of the exact path but knew they had walked in that general direction. He hoped when he got down there he would be able to remember something or would see something that would give him a clue. If that didn't happen, he would just have to wander around for a while and then return to the mountain.

"How far out?" asked Ngo.

"Only a couple of kilometers," said Thanh. "We didn't walk long before we came to the site."

"And then?"

Thanh shrugged. "I'm not sure. We entered a tree line and moved inside it for a few hundred meters. There was a path and we were close to a farmer's hut."

Ngo turned and formed the men. They stayed low, kneeling in the grass until it was time to move. Thanh took point, leading them down the mountainside, dodging right and left to use the best cover. It took them only a few minutes to get off the mountain and into the trees.

As they entered the forest, Thanh felt suddenly safe. The Americans, if they flew over, wouldn't see them now. Thanh and his men would see the enemy long before they could get into a position to see them. And even if he couldn't see them coming, he and his men would hear them. The helicopters would alert Thanh and his men to the presence of Americans, which would allow them to dodge through the trees and hide. It was just a question of using all the skills he had learned while in the North.

"We'll find our dead and get out quickly," Thanh said, suddenly filled with confidence. He stood and moved deeper into the forest.

6

SOUTHWEST OF
NUI BA DEN

After a brief rest at the edge of the tree line, Gerber ordered the men to sweep forward through the forest. Fetterman, along with Sergeant Coats, moved out on point, weaving their way through the thin, scraggy vegetation and avoiding the farmers' paths and game trails. The strikers fanned out, moving silently, following Fetterman and Coats. Gerber stayed in the rear, covering the men. He fell back ten, twelve yards, searching for signs that the enemy was on their trail, but found nothing.

They moved rapidly through the light scrub. The stunted trees had short branches and small leaves and didn't provide much of a canopy. Sunlight streamed through, baking the ground and men alike. After moving only a couple of hundred yards, Gerber was bathed in sweat. In some ways the forest was worse than the thick triple-canopy jungles.

After twenty minutes they halted, the men forming a loose circle with everyone facing outward. Gerber caught up with them and moved into the center, where Fetterman crouched with Coats, examining a map.

"I make it about another klick," said Fetterman. "At the minimum."

Coats took the map, turned and tried to spot some kind of landmark to tell him where they were. Gerber stepped close, grabbed his hand to hold the map steady and looked at it. From the location of Nui Ba Den, the edge of the Boi Loi Woods and a slight rise they had climbed, he knew exactly where they were. Landmarks in the jungle or in the forest were subtle. It wasn't like trying to drive through a town with plainly marked streets and individual buildings that had numbers and names on them. It was a question of ridge lines, shallow streams and river bends. It was a question of rice paddies and rubber plantations, hamlets and villages and, of course, Nui Ba Den.

"At least a klick," Gerber agreed.

Coats looked at the captain and shrugged. "How...?"

Gerber started to point, then remembered it wasn't the smartest thing to do in the jungle. Snipers, watching a unit move through the trees, waited for someone to point, figuring he was an officer. Instead, Gerber faced north and said, "If you look at the map carefully, you'll see there's a slight slope. It bends back to the west and then up to the north. Check the forest and you'll be able to see it."

"Yes, sir," said Coats.

"Tony, I want you to scout around."

"No problem, sir."

"Fine," said Gerber. "Hold here for five minutes and give me a chance to watch our back trail."

Gerber found a place in the ring and crouched, kneeling on the soft, rotting vegetation that made up the forest floor. Through gaps in the trees he could see out across the rice paddies and open fields. There was no evidence that anyone was following them.

As the circle of soldiers collapsed, Gerber stood. He fell in behind them, moving carefully, stepping over small plants, setting his feet down gently and rocking them backward, searching for triggers to booby traps. Keeping his head moving, he searched the trees and ground for trip wires and pressure plates. He looked for vegetation that didn't quite fit, for plants that were dying and turning brown, for anything that was out of place.

They all moved slowly, working their way through the forest. Gerber glanced up and noticed that Fetterman had called a halt. The captain dropped to one knee, his attention focused on the area in front of them. Slowly he worked his way forward until he reached Fetterman. Leaning close to the master sergeant, he whispered. "What's going on?"

Fetterman glanced at Gerber. "I've got some movement in front of us. Not farmers. They're trying to stay concealed."

"Have you seen anyone?"

"Not yet."

Gerber glanced right, then left. The strikers had all stopped moving and had taken cover. He could see the side of one man's face, but the rest of the squad had disappeared in the shadows of the forest.

"There," rasped Fetterman. "Movement about fifty yards to the left. Near that single coconut."

Gerber turned and stared at the patches of shadow and sunlight. There was a flash near one of the trees, but when he glanced at it, there was nothing to see. He kept his eyes moving, searching for the enemy.

Then, near a tree trunk wrapped in shadow, he saw what looked like a human head. As he watched, the head turned so that he could see the face. The pattern of sunlight shifted and the red star in the center of the pith helmet flashed once.

"Got them," said Gerber.

"Do we take them?"

Gerber touched his lips with the back of his hand. The question was whether they could take the enemy. A company-size unit could easily overwhelm Gerber's tiny force, but it was unlikely that a company would be working in the relative open of the Boi Loi Woods. Besides, the unit hadn't made much noise and they hadn't seen many of them. A large unit would have given themselves away.

A second man appeared, the sunlight flashing from his shoulder and the barrel of his AK. Like the first man, he was dressed in khaki.

"They're hard-core regulars," whispered Gerber.

"Do we take them?" Fetterman asked again.

"Let's move toward them and see if we can determine their numbers."

Fetterman nodded, pointed at one of the strikers and motioned him forward. They moved then, sticking to the shadows and the cover of the trees, watching the North Vietnamese in the distance.

Gerber stayed back, waiting for the enemy to make another move. Slowly the strikers, along with Coats and Staab, dispersed stringing out behind Fetterman, everyone trying to stay out of sight.

For ten minutes they followed the enemy unit, keeping them in sight as they worked their way through the trees. When the enemy stopped, Gerber's men did the same. As he crouched there, using a huge bush for cover, Staab squatted beside Gerber and whispered, "We've got the opportunity for an intelligence source."

Gerber nodded but didn't speak.

"I think we should take them," Staab said.

Fetterman doubled back then and, kneeling near the two officers, said, "There aren't more than twenty enemy soldiers out there."

"Can you get in front of them?" asked Gerber.

"They've stopped for the moment. I should be able to head them off."

Gerber peeled the camouflage cover from his watch. "Take five minutes to get into place. You and five men. I'll take the rest and we'll see if we can't slip up on them. A mobile, L-shaped ambush. If they move before five minutes are up, pull back and let them pass."

"Yes, sir."

Fetterman moved off then, disappearing into the forest. He made no sound as he worked his way forward. When he was gone, Gerber got up and pointed at the men on either side of him. He signaled them forward, then motioned with his palm down, telling the men to keep low.

They filtered through the trees, moving their feet carefully, trying not to make any noise. Around them animals roamed, slipping and sliding among the trees, crashing through the branches. There were calls from birds, the screams of lizards and the buzz of insects, tiny noises that covered any sounds Gerber or the strikers might make.

After three minutes Gerber stopped. He could see a single soldier, crouching, facing away from him. The captain waved his men down, telling them to get ready. Then, watching the second hand, he waited for the five minutes to elapse.

The last few seconds ticked off. Gerber pulled a grenade, yanked the pin free and threw it as far as he could. As the grenade crashed through the light vegetation and exploded, Gerber dropped to the ground. With the sounds of the detonation still echoing through the forest, he was up, shouting, "Open fire. Open fire. Open fire!"

He raised his weapon to his shoulder and pulled the trigger, firing short, controlled bursts, aiming low into the forest where the enemy had been. For an instant there was no return fire. Then off to the right a single AK opened up. The rounds snapped overhead, stripping leaves from trees, ripping bark from trunks. More AKs joined the first. M-16s and M-1s fired, too. The sound rose and fell and then rose again until all the shooting combined into a single drawn-out detonation.

There was shouting. A voice yelled something in Vietnamese, and firing erupted from there, AKs ripping through whole magazines. A man screamed, his voice rising like a siren, then stopped abruptly.

Gerber got to his knees and glanced around. Movement caught his attention. He turned and squeezed off three quick shots. One round buried itself in a tree trunk, shaking it. The second flashed off into the distance, while the third struck home. The man stood up suddenly, his pose rigid. Blood splashed the front of his uniform. He tossed his weapon away, grabbed at his chest and fell.

Now more grenades detonated. Shrapnel tore through the forest, followed by a heavy rain of leaves and bark. The fusillade increased, many of the weapons firing on full-auto. Gerber dived to the right, rolled and came up beside a tree trunk. He stood and aimed but couldn't see anything. Smoke from the weapons and dust from the grenades hung in the air.

"To the right," shouted one man.

"To the right," repeated a second voice. Then, "I've got him. I've got him."

"Coming at you."

"Shoot him! Shoot *him*!"

Gerber saw a single soldier, his head down, running at him. He aimed and fired. The man stumbled but didn't stop. He raised his weapon, holding it in front of him for the little protection it offered.

Again Gerber aimed. He pulled the trigger, felt his weapon fire and saw dirt fly from the front of the enemy's uniform. The man screamed and threw away his weapon. He straightened, his hands on his chest, blood spurting, covering his face, turning it into a gruesome mask. He fell then, disappearing.

More shooting erupted—AKs on full-auto. Bullets ripped through the air and whined off into the distance. There were muzzle-flashes in the shadows. A few tracers, the glow washed out by the sun, lanced across the battlefield and tumbled into the sky.

Gerber turned and saw one of the strikers hit. The man dropped to his side and rolled over once, a hand clapped to his shoulder. Sounding like a wounded animal, he screamed in short bursts. His eyes were closed and he cared nothing for the battle. He had forgotten everything he had been taught.

Gerber leaped over a fallen log and rolled to the man. He jerked him toward cover and pried his hand off the wound. There was a ragged, blackened hole in the cloth and the skin underneath. Blood was pouring from it, but it didn't spurt. Gerber shook out a field dressing and pressed it against the wound. The striker, his face pasty white and covered with sweat, opened his eyes.

"Hold it there!" ordered Gerber. The man stared up at the captain but didn't look as if he understood. Gerber grabbed his hand and pressed it to the wound. "Hold it there."

The captain grabbed his weapon and moved to the left. He leaned against a tree and straightened. Checking his weapon, he pulled the magazine out and examined it, then shoved it back in and glanced around the tree.

He saw movement behind the trail where the enemy had been hiding. Gerber aimed and fired. The movement stopped abruptly. A moment later there was return fire. The rounds slammed into the tree. Gerber ducked, dropped to one knee, poked his weapon out and fired again. Two, three, four shots. The man leaped up. Gerber saw his face as he spun to run. A young face. The man bolted to one side. Gerber fired again and knocked the NVA off his feet.

The firing began to taper then. Only a couple of AKs could be heard on both single-shot and in short bursts. Gerber moved again and found a striker lying facedown in the dirt. His weapon was clutched in his hand. Blood stained the back of his uniform and soaked the ground under him. Without touching him, Gerber could tell that the man was dead.

He pressed on, saw movement to his right, but didn't fire. Instead, he dropped to the ground and waited. One of the strikers appeared, walking slowly back along the line.

"Get down!" ordered Gerber.

The man fell to his stomach and turned, facing the enemy. He glanced at Gerber and grinned, as if pleased with himself.

Gerber nodded and turned his attention toward the trail. The AKs had stopped firing. Gerber stood up, his left shoulder against the rough trunk of the tree. He looked out over the short bushes and grass and between the trees. As far as he could tell, there was no movement from the enemy position.

"Sweeping in!" Fetterman yelled.

"Go!" Gerber replied.

He watched as the first of his men broke cover, moving forward toward the enemy's position. Gerber covered them as he scanned the forest. Fetterman stopped, stooped, then straightened. He held an AK in his left hand, which he smashed and tossed away into the forest to deny it to the VC. He then continued on.

Gerber moved then, leaving his cover. He saw the medic working on a wounded striker and said, "There's another man with a shoulder wound back there. I put a bandage on him, but he'll need some help."

"I'll find him," said the medic.

As Gerber moved forward, the sound in the forest changed. First there had been firing, a roar that had wiped out all other sounds and overwhelmed the mind. It was more than the firing of dozens of different weapons. Somehow the sound was magnified, echoing through the trees, feeding on itself until it was one long roar. Then there was complete silence as the shooting ceased. But in only a few seconds the steady buzz of flies drawn to freshly spilled blood could be heard.

Gerber crouched by the body of a dead NVA soldier. The khaki of his shirt was wet with blood. There was a single bullet hole in his stomach from which blood had poured, covering his belt buckle, hiding the red star there, and soaking the crotch of his pants. There was another wound on his face. The bullet had plowed a furrow of skin, then ripped away his nose, allowing Gerber to look down into the nasal cavity.

The captain pulled the weapon out of the dead man's fingers. He slung it over his shoulder and moved on until he found Fetterman crouched over the body of another dead man.

"NVA," he said.

"Obviously," said Gerber. "Uniform tells us that."

"As does the haircut and the weapons. Not highly trained, but NVA nonetheless."

Staab appeared then. "What have we got?"

"Regulars, all armed with AKs."

Staab looked at the body, then crouched beside it. He pulled at one pocket, couldn't get it open easily, then took out his knife. Slitting the pocket, he spilled the contents onto the forest floor. Carefully he sifted through everything, tossing aside anything of no value to him as an intelligence officer.

"Tony, let's get our people taken care of. We'll want to get into the open to get a chopper in to evac the wounded. Lieutenant Staab and Sergeant Coats can check the bodies."

Fetterman moved back into the forest where the majority of the strikers had been left as security. As Staab and Coats hopped from body to body, taking documents and searching for intelligence data, Gerber moved east in the direction the enemy had retreated. He found a blood trail that led toward Nui Ba Den. There were also broken plants and bent branches. Men had obviously fled through the area.

He followed one of the blood trails for twenty yards and then stopped. Although he was still in sight of the strikers, to go much farther would put the trees between him and the other men, so he retreated.

"Sir," said Staab, "we've found a few things—unit insignia, some badges of rank and some documents, all of them in Vietnamese."

"Can't you read them?"

"No, sir."

Gerber took the documents from Staab and glanced at them. He couldn't understand much of anything himself. One item was a small book, perhaps a diary, that looked as if it had been started several months earlier. The other documents looked like rosters. As he handed the "diary" back to Staab, he said, "Hang on to this. It'll tell you a lot about the everyday life of the man who kept it."

"Not much in the way of military information, though," said Staab.

"Don't be too sure. A list of his daily activities might reveal more than you'd think. Any details in that journal could tell a great deal."

Fetterman approached. "Got two dead and three wounded. Wounds not life-threatening yet. In the shoulder. Tore up the muscle and probably broke bones. Painful but not deadly."

"You about done?" Gerber asked Staab.

The lieutenant stood and searched for his sergeant. Coats was kneeling by the last body, cutting the pockets free on the enemy's khaki shirt. As Coats got to his feet, Staab said, "We're ready."

"Tony, let's get the men organized and get out of here." Gerber pulled out his map. "There's a good LZ about five hundred yards to the south. It'll take us twenty minutes to get there and establish security."

"Got it, Captain."

Gerber moved to the radio operator and took the handset from him. He checked the frequency, changed it and said, "Black Hawk Six, Black Hawk Six, this is Zulu Rover. We're ready for pickup at PZ Hotel."

There was a moment of silence, then, "Understand, Papa Zulu Hotel."

"Roger that."

"Inbound your location. ETA in three five minutes."

"Roger that," said Gerber. He gave the handset back to the RTO. "Let's move it. We don't have a lot of time to fuck around."

7

NEAR NUI BA DEN

The trip down the mountainside was easier in the daylight. Thanh could see the pitfalls now, the ravines, the boulders and the fallen trees. In the dark they had been vague shapes and shadows that masked the danger. He led his men around them, staying in the cover provided by the thin vegetation that clung to the mountain. It was necessary to avoid the paths through the trees, bushes and meadows. They were obvious in the sunlight, and he knew that following them could be a fatal mistake. Even with that, in a matter of minutes, they were off the mountainside and on the relatively flat land that surrounded Nui Ba Den.

They stopped for a moment at the base of the mountain, forming a loose security circle. Thanh knelt in the center of it, the makeshift map held in his hand. He studied it, trying to place the few visible landmarks. When he thought he could find the ambush site again, he ordered Ngo to take point and head southwest. He stressed the necessity of sticking to the cover of the trees. Although there were no American helicopters overhead at the moment, they could appear in seconds.

Travel through the thin forest was simpler than the long hike from the North. Even though the Ho Chi Minh Trail had been well-defined and well-worn, it had been a long, grueling walk up and down hills and across mountain streams and wide rivers. There had been portions that had been little more than game trails, and they had detoured to the west a couple of times to stay out of range of artillery in South Vietnam. Not all of the Ho Chi Minh Trail was paved with pea gravel, and some of the branches and detours on it led through thick, almost impenetrable jungle that made life miserable.

Now, in the South, the terrain was easier to navigate. Nui Ba Den, rising behind him, told him all the time where he was and where safety lay. The light scrub of the Boi Loi Woods was easy to push through. Sunlight, streaming from overhead, baked the land and the men, but Thanh was used to the warm weather and the high humidity. He ordered Ngo to stop often so that the men could rest. They had all day to travel a couple of kilometers. There was no need to hurry.

Once, in the distance, they heard helicopters, and they dived for cover, but the aircraft never approached them. Instead, they fluttered to the ground a couple of kilometers to the west, stayed there, then climbed out, turning farther to the west. When the sound from the helicopters was gone, Thanh ordered his patrol forward again.

They moved, rested and moved again. They drank water from their canteens and shared food from their plastic bags containing rice and fish heads. Thanh wasn't in a hurry, figuring that he could take all day to get to the site. That wouldn't be the smartest thing, but he could do it if he felt like it.

They walked through patches of light forest with sunlight streaming down in shafts. There were patterns of ragged shadow and splotches of sun. They wove their way through them, looking right and left, but seeing no sign of the Americans.

Thanh pushed his way to the front of the patrol to order Ngo to turn right. As he approached the sergeant, there was an explosion behind him. The lieutenant whirled, thinking at first that one of his men had stepped on a booby trap. Dirt mushroomed and cascaded down. From the right came the single ripping of a weapon on full-auto. Bullets snapped through the trees. Then, quickly, others began to shoot, and Thanh realized they had walked into an ambush.

He leaped forward, diving for cover as more of the enemy began to shoot. One of his men screamed, the sound overpowering the noise of battle.

"Shoot!" ordered Ngo. He pushed the barrel of his AK forward and pulled the trigger. "Shoot!" he yelled again. He didn't care that he had no target. At the moment it was only important to get the men shooting. They had to start putting out rounds or they'd all die.

Firing erupted all along the line then. Thanh rolled to his side and looked at his men. There were a couple sprawled in the short grass that marked the trail. Blood stained their uniforms; he knew they were dead, cut down before they had a chance to fight back.

Anger boiled through him. He wanted to leap up and attack the Americans, shoot them all in the face. He wanted to kill them and mutilate the bodies. He wanted to smash and stomp their stinking intestines into the ground.

But instead he lay still, his face pressed into the rotting vegetation, and listened to the growing firefight. He felt the hardness of his weapon, clutched tightly in his hand, and knew he should be firing it. But he couldn't move. He was afraid motion would draw attention to him.

More explosions ripped the air, as grenades detonated. Dirt rained down around him. There was more shooting,

AKs against M-16s. Men were shouting—American voices calling out orders as he lay motionless, trying not to wet his pants.

Then Ngo was crouched close to him, shouting, "Are you injured?"

Thanh looked up dumbly and shook his head. "No, I'm not hurt."

"We've got to get out of here."

Thanh stared at him dully as if he had just heard the dumbest thing ever uttered.

"Lieutenant, we've got to get out or die."

Thanh glanced to the right where the body of one of his men was visible. Part of his face had been ripped away, exposing the gleaming white bone. Already flies were swarming around the wound, diving into the blood.

"Yes, we've got to get out."

Ngo jumped up and ran to the rear. Firing increased and the bullets seemed to follow him, slamming into the trees behind him. Bark and wood splinters exploded from the trees. Leaves, stripped from their branches, sprayed the ground.

And then Thanh was up and moving. He dropped near a tree and opened fire, holding down the trigger of his weapon. He didn't aim it. He just fired blindly into the jungle, fighting the kick of the weapon as it scattered 7.62 mm rounds. When the bolt locked back, the weapon empty, Thanh scrambled to his feet and ran.

The explosion of a grenade ahead startled him. He dived to the right but was unhurt. Rolling onto his back, he tugged a fresh magazine from his chest pouch. But, staring up into the sky through the gaps in the canopy above him, he completely lost track of where he was. No longer was it a forest in South Vietnam; for a moment he was in his training camp in the North. The rounds being fired were blanks. No one was dying, and in minutes the fight would end.

He jerked the empty magazine free and slammed a fresh one into the well. Yanking at the bolt, he let it slide home. Again he looked out into the jungle. Smoke hung in the air, obscuring the American position.

Suddenly he was on his feet, his weapon jammed against his hip, braced there. He screamed at the top of his voice and fired at the American position. Spotting a man move in the trees, he turned and hosed down the forest. There was a shout and the movement stopped.

Then the world around Thanh seemed to explode. Bullets whipped past his head. He dived for cover and rolled onto his stomach. Without thinking, he began to crawl away, moving rapidly.

He came to the body of one of his men—a private who had joined them as they'd marched down the Trail. A man whom Thanh didn't know that well, a young man with a girlfriend who would never see him again. All of these thoughts flashed through his mind as he looked at the body and noticed that the private hadn't bothered to shave. The stubble would never be shaved now. For some reason that bothered Thanh a lot. Stubble on the chin of a dead man. He couldn't pull his eyes from the dead man's chin.

"We've got to go!" shouted Ngo. "There are too many of them."

Thanh saw Ngo on his feet. The sergeant dodged right, then left, and vanished into the forest. Around Thanh the firing tapered off. His men were either running or were dead. No one was staying behind.

Thanh stood, the thick trunk of a palm protecting him. He glanced around it, saw no one, then took off. He ran away from the firefight. He leaped a small bush, splashed through a shallow stream and then turned. He ran as fast as he could move, forgetting everything he had learned in the North. He ran right, then he ran left, his legs pumping, his AK clutched tightly in his hand.

And he kept on running as the sounds of the battle faded behind him. He ran until his lungs burned and the air whistled in his nose and mouth. He ran as the pain spread from his chest and into his arms. He ran north, away from the Americans, suddenly, blindly, completely afraid of them.

They took on mythical proportions. They were the creatures of nightmares, coming out of nowhere to kill him, indestructible men who were afraid of nothing and no one, giants who would drive the North Vietnamese from the South, killing thousands in the process.

He stumbled once, sprawling to the ground. For a moment he didn't move, even with the sounds of the fight ringing in his ears. Then fear got the better of him and he was up and running again.

Thanh ran faster than he would have thought possible. He ran past a number of his own men who had lost their weapons and confidence. He caught and passed Ngo, running for the side of Nui Ba Den where he was sure he would be safe. Stumbling again, he fell heavily to the ground. This time he didn't move right away. The shooting had stopped. The only sounds now were the pounding of blood in his ears, the hammering of his heart and the wheezing of his breath, which made him sound like an old man.

He rolled onto his back and closed his eyes. His body was suddenly soaked in sweat, heat radiating from him. Blackness descended, then lifted. He opened his eyes and stared into the bright blue of a cloudless sky. A bird shrieked and a monkey called. A kilometer away, outside the woods, a water buffalo bellowed.

Slowly Thanh recovered from his run. He sat up and realized he was all alone in a forest he didn't know. Alone except for the Americans, who were somewhere behind him, wanting to kill him.

Again rage took over, bubbling through him and making him sick. Twice he had faced the Americans and twice he had fled from them. Twice he had gone in search of them and twice he had found them. His record against them wasn't impressive. He hadn't managed to cover himself in glory as he had dreamed of. Instead he had shamed himself.

He got to his feet and turned in a complete circle. The members of his patrol who had survived were nowhere to be seen. He rubbed a hand over his face, then wiped his sweaty palm on his khaki shirt.

He was a coward.

The word hit him with the physical force of a bullet. It threatened to knock him from his feet. It threatened to drop him to the ground so that he could burst into tears.

Coward.

There was nothing else to be said. He had faced the enemy twice and he had run. Not at first. He had fired his weapon, but it hadn't been the coordinated fighting of a trained soldier. It had been the effort of a scared, cowardly man who didn't deserve the uniform he wore or the respect his men had given him.

As he stood there, wanting to cry, wanting to scream, wanting to die, he heard a noise behind him. A quiet sound. A boot scraping on a log. Without thinking, he whirled, dropped and fired—a single, quick burst that tore into the forest.

As he dived to the right, he saw movement and came up to fire again. Then he recognized the face of Ngo and stood up again.

"What in hell..."

Thanh didn't know how to respond. He shrugged helplessly. "You shouldn't sneak around."

Ngo glanced over his shoulder then, as if the Americans were close to him. "We'd better get moving."

Thanh stared at the sergeant. He saw the fear in the man's eyes. He saw the stains on the sergeant's clothes and realized the man had run first. Thanh had stayed behind longer than anyone else. He had run past them, but they had left him first.

Taking control again, Thanh said, "We need to find the rest of our men."

"They're dead," said Ngo.

"Not all of them. They're scattered in the trees. We've got to find them."

Ngo glanced longingly at Nui Ba Den. He wiped an arm across his forehead, leaving a ragged wet stain on his sleeve. "Find the men?"

Thanh nodded. "We'll move back, see if we can locate any of them."

"How far?"

"A couple of hundred meters. A small search and then we'll return to the mountain."

"What are we going to tell the commander?"

Thanh smiled then. It was the first time he had smiled in hours. "We'll tell him the truth."

"The whole truth?"

"Of course. We ran into a superior force of Americans, fought them and were finally forced to flee. We inflicted great casualties on them."

Ngo was silent for a moment, then asked, "What if they want to see the battlefield? Count the bodies and collect the weapons?"

"You know how these Americans are. They clean up the battlefield, taking their dead with them. They fight battles to reclaim the bodies of their dead. They leave nothing for us to find and count. We can only estimate."

Ngo nodded and grinned. "That's correct. I know that we killed fifteen or twenty of them before they called for reinforcements."

"More," said Thanh. "Many more. Maybe fifty of them. I had two weapons, but had to abandon them."

"Yes," said Ngo, his voice suddenly strong.

Thanh looked at the sergeant and realized a truth in warfare. It was much easier to be brave when there was someone around to see the bravery. It was easy to be a coward when you were left alone with nothing but death as a companion and no one to witness the cowardice.

"Come," said Thanh. "Let's see if we can locate any of our fellows."

Ngo nodded and fell in behind Thanh.

8

NEAR NUI BA DEN

While the medic worked on the wounded and Staab tried to retrieve documents, insignia and diaries for any intelligence they might contain, Gerber and Fetterman worked their way from the ambush site to an open field not far away. They checked the tree lines, looking for signs of the enemy. But there were no signs. The ground was undisturbed and there were no bunkers. In the thicker jungles to the north and the west, the possible landing zones were so few that Charlie had ringed some of them with bunkers, but here, south of the heaviest forests, the LZs were plentiful. Charlie hadn't tried to second-guess the Americans.

They met on the northern side, and Gerber said, "We're clear here."

"And here."

"Okay," said Gerber. "Let's get the men moved in and call for the choppers."

"Yes, sir."

Gerber pointed at two of the strikers with quick, stabbing motions. "You men set up security on the north. Challenge anyone you don't recognize."

"Yes, Captain," said one.

As the men moved off, Gerber retreated, walking through the center of the LZ and checking the ground carefully. Charlie sometimes booby-trapped the ground, figuring he could take out a helicopter with a mine, but there was no evidence of anything like that.

When Gerber reached the trees on the far side, he waved the RTO over. He used the radio to contact the helicopters and told them the LZ had been secured.

"Roger, Zulu. Can you throw smoke?"

"Ah, negative, Black Hawk," said Gerber. "We'll need one zero minutes to get into position."

"Understand," came the voice. There was a burst of static and then, "Call when ready."

"Roger that."

Gerber gave the handset back to the RTO, then moved off to where the majority of the men waited. He saw that the medic had finished. Two men were nearby, hacking at saplings with their combat knives. They cut two trees down and sliced the branches from them so that they were left with two skinny poles about six feet long. As one spread his poncho liner on the ground, the other placed the poles on it. Then they folded over the poncho liner to make the stretcher. The weight of the body would hold the poncho liner in place.

They helped the medic load one of the wounded onto the stretcher and then began carrying the man toward the LZ. As they did that, Staab appeared. He had three AKs slung over his shoulder and carried a couple of chest pouches that held spare banana clips.

"I think we've gotten everything from the dead that we can," said Staab.

"Then get your sergeant and head toward the LZ."

"Captain, I still want to take a look at the Ho Chi Minh Trail."

"Overlooking the fact that it's in Cambodia, what do you think you'll learn by spying on the Trail?"

"Get a feel for the flow of traffic."

Gerber turned and stared into the forest to the west of them. "I think we can say the traffic on the Trail is heavy."

"How can you say that?"

Gerber glanced at Staab, then wiped the perspiration from his face. The humidity was so high that standing was enough to work up a sweat. "I can say that because of what's going on around here. Three weeks without contact and then contact twice in less than twelve hours in the same place. You check the night reports and you'll find that there was more contact around here last night. That'll tell you what you want to know without having to see the Ho Chi Minh Trail."

"Still," said Staab.

"Besides, we've got to get the wounded out of here," said Gerber.

Fetterman appeared then, the RTO trailing behind him. "Choppers are inbound."

"Then get the loads arranged and throw smoke."

"Yes, sir." He started to move but then turned back. "What about the wounded?"

"We'll take them to Tay Ninh first. Then we can drop the rest of the strikers back on Nui Ba Den before returning to Saigon."

"I'm not ready to return, Captain," said Staab.

"Then don't."

Fetterman moved in and ordered the men into loads for the choppers, telling them to find the group they had flown in with and to make sure everyone was there. No one was to be left behind. They had the wounded on stretchers and the bodies wrapped in poncho liners, which were brought out from the trees into the brightness of the LZ.

Fetterman stood at the front edge of the LZ, a smoke grenade in his hand. He yanked the pin and dropped the grenade at his feet. It popped in a flash that threatened to set the grass on fire. As he stomped on the spreading flames, the grenade began to billow green smoke.

Over the radio came "ID green."

Gerber took the handset. "Roger green. LZ is cold."

"Roger cold."

Gerber turned, facing south where the sound was coming from. Over the trees he saw the flight, small, noisy aircraft that grew quickly as the roar from the turbines drowned out all other sounds. He put a hand to his head as the choppers crossed the edge of the tree line, no more than fifty or sixty feet above the ground. The door guns began to fire, the muzzle-flashes dim in the bright sunlight. Tracers lanced out, struck the ground at the base of the trees and bounced, dancing off, into the sky.

Gerber dropped to one knee and turned away, facing the tree line, looking for signs that the enemy had sneaked into position to shoot at the choppers. As he did, a single ship broke away, flying along the trees, its skids no more than a yard above the branches.

The wind in the LZ picked up and dust flew outward in a huge, expanding cloud. Loose grass swirled around them and the air was suddenly hard to breathe. An instant later the wind died as the helicopters touched down.

Gerber whirled. Two strikers lifted a stretcher and ran to the first chopper. One of them climbed into the cargo compartment and his partner followed. Two others carried the body of a man to another chopper. Slowly the remaining men worked their way to the waiting aircraft.

When all the men were loaded, Gerber leaped aboard the lead helicopter. Touching the shoulder of the pilot, he yelled, "Hospital at Tay Ninh!"

"On the way."

They lifted then, charged the tree line and popped up. Gerber glanced out the cargo compartment door as the tree line and the LZ fell away. On the ground there was nothing left to see. The enemy had gotten clear of the fight. No one was moving in the trees or toward the LZ.

To the right was Nui Ba Den, but there was no movement on its slopes. Smoke poured from the Special Forces camp on top, making it seem as if the mountain were about to erupt. The smoke was from the camp dump, not enemy action. For the moment everything looked peaceful.

The flight to Tay Ninh didn't take long. They landed at the hospital and two men with a gurney came out to pick up the wounded. Once the wounded were gone they took off and stopped at the top of Nui Ba Den to leave both the survivors and the dead. Gerber held a hurried conversation with the camp commander, Captain Gallagher, telling the American officer that he would provide a full report later.

Then they took off again and descended to fifteen hundred feet, flying along the south side of Highway One. Avoiding the huge American base at Cu Chi, they flew over the village of Trang Bang, then dropped to the ground to avoid the active runways at Tan Son Nhut. Once past that they popped up to five hundred feet and circled Hotel Three. A few moments later they landed, hovering close to the chain-link fence that separated the helipad from the rest of Tan Son Nhut. Once they were on the ground, Gerber leaped out. He stood there for a moment, looking, then turned and ran across the grass toward the terminal under the tower.

Short of the door, he stopped and turned. Fetterman caught up with him, as did Staab and Coats. The roar from the helicopter faded and the rotors began to slow, as the pilot shut down the engine. Now the noise was coming from the airfield proper, where fighters were beginning to take off for their afternoon sorties against the enemy.

"Now what?" asked Fetterman.

"I think Staab should find someone to translate the documents. Then we can decide what to do."

Fetterman looked at the captain for a moment. "You have something in mind already?"

This wasn't the place to talk about anything, Gerber knew—too many ears around. The Vietnamese weren't supposed to be inside the fence at Hotel Three, but sometimes they managed to get close. Some of them were prostitutes, interested only in how much money they could make off GIs returning to their camps, fire bases and forts. But others were VC who were interested in picking up a few scraps of information along with the money they could make. "I think we need to head over to MACV to report in."

Staab shook his head. "We need to get back up to Bien Hoa as fast as possible."

"Not yet," Gerber said. "I want to know what those documents say first."

"Probably nothing of interest," said Staab.

"Probably right," Gerber agreed, "but we can have someone over at MACV take a quick look to see if there's anything for us to pursue."

Staab still hesitated. He stood facing the airfield, a hand to his eyes as if shading them. Finally he looked at Gerber. "My loyalty is to the MI people at Bien Hoa."

"I have no quarrel with that," said Gerber. "But we're all in the same Army. I think we should share the information rather than piecemeal it. I might know something that will fit with something you know, which will give us the whole picture."

"Yes, sir."

Fetterman disappeared, heading out the gate at the far end. He stopped on the road, then walked past the world's largest PX, which contained a movie theater at one end and the PX at the other. He walked through the gate there.

"Where's Fetterman going?" Coats asked Gerber.

"Knowing Tony, he's in search of transportation. And he'll find it."

They started past the terminal and went through the gate. Walking down the road paved with crushed gravel, they reached the end of the heliport and turned again. As they drew close to the theater, Fetterman appeared in the gateway next to the Air Force policeman guarding it.

"Shit," said Coats, "I was hoping for a chance to visit the PX."

"There anything special you wanted?" asked Staab.

"No, sir. Just thought I'd take a look around. I don't get down here that often."

"If you play your cards right," said Gerber, "you can fly back to Bien Hoa from Hotel Three, and that'll give you the chance to inspect the PX."

They made their way toward the gate, and the guard stopped them. "Can't take your weapons out with you."

Gerber stared at the man. "When did they start this chickenshit?"

"New regulation, sir," said the man. "We've had too many armed GIs running loose in Saigon."

Gerber laughed. "With the VC attacking everywhere, including downtown Saigon, don't you think it's a good idea to have the men armed?"

"Not up to me, sir. I'm just here to tell you that you're not supposed to travel off the base with your weapons."

Gerber glanced over his shoulder. "Just what in hell do you suggest we do with them?"

"There are lockers by the PX. You can lock them in there until you return."

"This is the dumbest thing I've heard so far today," said Coats.

"I agree," said Gerber. Then, eyeing the guard, he asked, "And what do you plan to do if we refuse?" Gerber saw that Fetterman was now sitting behind the wheel of a jeep, grinning broadly, his weapon visible beside him.

"My orders are to make sure everyone leaves his weapon, sir," the guard insisted.

"Well, I'd much rather lock them up at the SOG building," said Gerber.

"Oh, you're not going into Saigon?"

"No, we've got briefings to take care of."

"Then forget what I said, sir." The guard moved to the right, out of the way.

As Gerber approached the jeep, Fetterman told him, "You have to know how to handle these people. He knew better than to question me about my weapon."

"Fine," said Gerber. He pulled the passenger seat forward so that Staab and Coats could get into the rear. After they were in, he climbed in too, laying his weapon between the seats where it would be handy. "What did you say to that clown?"

"Told him I knew how to handle my weapon and no Air Force puke was going to take it away from me. He didn't say a word."

"I don't think we should antagonize our Air Force counterparts," said Gerber.

"Whatever," said Fetterman. He shifted into gear and twisted the steering wheel. Backing up, he worked the lever and the jeep lurched forward, heading for the main gate.

Before they got there, Gerber said, "They're going to want our weapons again."

As the jeep slowed, a large man wearing a white helmet liner and jungle fatigues approached it. He spotted their weapons, then noticed Gerber had replaced his boonie hat with his green beret. The man saluted and waved them through into the streets of Saigon.

They came to a stop, then turned into a Saigon street. The traffic was heavy—trucks, jeeps, taxis and military staff cars. Hondas weaved in and out of the traffic, along with Lambrettas, each of them carrying passengers, civilian and military, Vietnamese and American. And everywhere pedestrians filled the sidewalks—thousands of people moving in huge masses, imitating the ebb and flow of ocean tides.

Fetterman joined the crowd, steering the jeep in behind a taxi that held its position for a moment and then shot off. A deuce-and-a-half slipped in front of the jeep, belching black clouds of partially burnt diesel fuel.

That odor mixed with dozens of others. The heavy humidity, which threatened to crush them, hung in the air, trapping the stench of open sewers. The omnipresent smog stained the tropical sun a dull orange in the evening.

Gerber wiped a hand across his face, surprised to find it was covered in sweat. All he was doing was sitting in a jeep, and he was still perspiring. He shifted, put a foot on the dashboard and closed his eyes, trying to drive the sights and smells of Saigon from his mind. They always depressed him.

The sounds of the city overwhelmed them. Horns from trucks, cars, Lambrettas and scooters. Music from countless clubs and bars. Shouts from men arguing with one another, shouts from others begging for money and shouts from hustlers selling everything from genuine Ho Chi Minh sandals to the latest in "virgin" female flesh.

Gerber opened his eyes and glanced down the wide boulevard that led to the presidential palace. Halfway down the block sat an American-made tank manned by an American crew, protecting the leader of the South Vietnamese. Near the tank was a sandbagged bunker, also manned by Americans who had a Browning M-2 .50-caliber machine gun and three M-60s. Their job was to hold out until reinforcements, probably from the 716th MP Battalion, could get across town to save the South Vietnamese leader.

They drove by the president's bodyguards and entered another street that was narrower and more crowded. Slowing down, the jeep moved along at a crawl. A boy, no more than twelve, approached them, holding on to the hand of a girl who might have been a year older. He weaved through the traffic until he was walking alongside the jeep. Looking up at Gerber, he asked, "Hey, GI, you want my sister?"

"No, kid. I don't want your sister."

"Hey, GI, she numbah one. She do what you like. Two hundred P. You like."

"Christ," said Gerber, sickened. Two hundred P was less than two dollars.

"Hey, you, GI," said the kid, addressing Staab now. "You want my sister?"

"Take off," snapped Staab. He swung at the boy, missing him on purpose.

The boy stopped walking and stood in the middle of the street, the cars parting around him and his sister like a river flowing around a boulder. He put a hand to his mouth. "Hey, GI, you stink. You numbah ten."

"Yeah," Staab mumbled, "but I'm not selling my sister for a lousy two bucks."

Fetterman downshifted, hit the accelerator and slipped into a hole in the traffic that had just opened. He touched the brake, found another hole and shot through it. In seconds they were off that street and shooting down another, the traffic thinner and moving faster.

"Didn't like that street," Fetterman said.

Gerber nodded. Soon after, they pulled into the parking lot outside MACV Headquarters. Fetterman found a parking spot and bent down to retrieve the chain bolted to the jeep's floor. He looped it through the steering wheel, then used a brass padlock to secure it.

Gerber got out and picked up his weapon. He shouldered his webgear and stared at the building, a lawn leading up to it. Flagpoles, flying the South Vietnamese and American flags, rose before the double doors of the entrance.

Staab pointed at the South Vietnamese flag. "They got the colors right for that one. If they're not yellow, they're red."

Gerber took a deep breath and was about to say something but didn't. Sadly Staab was more or less right. The majority of the South Vietnamese were corrupt cowards who wouldn't fight to protect themselves. There were a few good ones. Gerber recalled a Vietnamese captain named Minh, who was one of the bravest men he knew. "Let's go," he finally said.

They left the parking lot and walked toward the building. Fetterman opened the first of the double doors and Coats got the second. They stopped just inside, where the coolness from the air-conditioning washed over them.

"I wonder if the American taxpayer knows about this?" asked Staab.

"I don't think the American taxpayer cares about it," said Gerber. He looked at Fetterman. "Let's find someone to translate those documents so we can get into town and change into some clean clothes."

"Yes, sir."

Gerber looked at Staab. "And you can get up to Bien Hoa, where they'll bury everything we have because no one there will know what to do with it."

Staab didn't say anything to that. Instead he pulled the diary from his pocket and flipped it open. There was a ragged rust-colored stain on the outer page—blood from the man who had involuntarily surrendered it earlier that morning. "Let's just get it done," he finally said.

"Right," Gerber agreed.

9

WASHINGTON, D.C.

Julie Drake stood on the sidewalk outside her apartment and waited for the limousine that had been sent to pick her up. No more than twenty minutes earlier, Halpren had phoned her to say that they were leaving for Saigon in twenty minutes. The Pentagon, which had been reluctant to clear civilians, no matter how high-ranking, into the war zone, had suddenly caved in. Halpren had said he suspected that the President, as commander in chief of the military, had called a general and made his wishes known.

Another woman might have been caught off guard by the short notice, but Drake wasn't. She'd been around long enough to know that some things happened suddenly and that those who weren't prepared to go with the flow found themselves standing on the outside looking in, wishing they'd been faster on their feet.

She'd finished her packing in five minutes. Figuring there would be no fancy balls but there might be receptions, she'd included a few nice dresses along with some practical clothes, underwear and a few personal articles. Anything else could be purchased or borrowed once she got there and discovered what she would need.

Now, as she looked at her watch, thinking that Halpren had made her jump through hoops for no reason other than making her jump through them, a car turned onto her street and glided to the curb beside her. The driver leaped from the limousine, hurried around the front and picked up her suitcase. Without a word to her, he opened the trunk and stuffed the case in, then opened the rear door. Drake got in.

Halpren grinned at her. "Made it."

"You're late."

He looked at the clock built into the small bar in the back seat, next to the telephone and the tiny black-and-white television. "Not much."

"Still·late," she said.

The driver got in and Halpren raised the partition that separated the chauffeur from the passengers. When it was in place, sealing them off, he asked, "You sure you still really want to do this?"

"Of course."

Halpren plucked his briefcase from the floor and opened it. He sifted through the papers and files and found a flimsy yellow page. "Casualty list for the past week."

"So?"

"So we lost nearly fifty men in ambushes and another twenty in rocket and mortar attacks."

She was silent for a moment, then said, "Again, so?"

"Julie, this isn't going to be a cakewalk. Those rockets and mortar shells can fall on anyone at any time. No one's safe in Vietnam. And as Americans we're going to be even bigger targets."

She laughed. "If I was going over to fight the war, I'd be worried. But the men on that list were soldiers. They knew what they were getting into before they went, and they were out in the field, not in Saigon."

"See, you don't understand. Those killed in the ambushes were in the field," he explained, "but the rocket and mortar attacks were on our largest bases. Even Saigon was hit by rockets again. No one's safe."

"Okay, how many nurses were killed?"

"What in hell does that have to do with anything?"

"The nurses are on those bases, and I'll bet that not one nurse was killed last week."

"Only because they didn't happen to be on the bases where the rockets fell. Next week it could be different. It's a crapshoot, and anyone in Vietnam could be killed by a rocket or a sniper, or caught in an ambush. Anyone."

Drake turned and looked out the window at the crowds surging over the sidewalks, at the cars that filled the streets and at the buses that seemed to be everywhere. She studied the crowds and the traffic for a moment, then said, "If you're trying to frighten me, you're doing a poor job of it. They're not going to let anything happen to a congressional delegation."

Halpren dropped the paper back into his briefcase and snapped it shut. "You're probably right."

"Besides, even if I was a combat soldier, I'd be safer than I am here. More people die in car accidents than are killed in Vietnam."

"That's the dumbest thing I've ever heard. There are millions of people riding around in cars and no one's trying to kill them on purpose."

"Still," said Drake, "nothing's going to happen to me unless I'm dumb enough to let you talk me out of this. Then I deserve anything I get."

Halpren glanced at the front. Through the smoked glass he could see the chauffeur's head. The man's attention seemed to be focused on his driving. Halpren took Drake's hand and squeezed it. "It's just that I don't want anything to happen to you."

"And if I don't go, you'll have the inside track for the next promotion."

"Shit, it's not like that at all."

"Can't you tell when I'm teasing?"

Halpren looked at her and then smiled. He let go of her hand and touched the nylon that protected her thigh. Slowly his fingers crept higher, up under the hem of her short skirt. He expected her to grab his wrist and protest that they didn't have the time and that the back of the limousine wasn't the place, but she didn't. Instead, she moved her knees slightly, spreading her legs.

"Teasing?" he said.

"Yes," she said, leaning back and closing her eyes. "A little joke."

Halpren felt the fabric of her panties, and still she didn't try to stop him. He was wondering what it would be like in the back seat of a limousine, driving around the streets of Washington in full view of anyone who cared to look.

Just as he decided to find out, the phone buzzed quietly and the little light on it began to flash. "Talk about timing," he said.

"Don't answer it," she said, her voice low and husky.

Twenty minutes later they arrived at Andrews Air Force Base. The Air Force policeman at the front gate stepped out of his glass-enclosed booth, glanced at the black limousine, at the license plate identifying it as a Senate vehicle and then at the windshield. Only the driver was visible, but the guard knew not to stop an important member of the government. He waved the car through and then came to attention, saluting.

Halpren sat up when the car slowed, saw the military guard at the gate and said, "We're nearly there."

Drake twisted around and put her feet on the floor. She lifted her hips and tugged at the hem of her skirt, pulling it down to cover her to midthigh. Quickly she buttoned her blouse. Then, raising one of the panels set in the bar near the TV, she was delighted to find a small mirror. Leaning forward, she frowned at her tousled hair, fumbled through her purse and extracted a comb. As the car stopped, she dragged the comb through her hair a couple of times, repairing most of the damage done by Halpren. Just before the door was opened, she dropped the comb into her purse and turned to Halpren. "How do I look?"

"Perfect." He reached down and put a hand on her knee, squeezing gently.

When the chauffeur opened the door, they were the perfect picture of innocence. He reached in to help Drake out. He stared at her legs as she tried to climb out without revealing anything.

Before Halpren could get out, Bishop was standing there, scowling. "Nice of you two to join us."

"Yes, sir. Traffic was bad."

"Well, come on," he said. "We don't have all day."

As the driver took the suitcases out of the trunk, Halpren and Drake followed Bishop across the tarmac to the operations building. It was a large air-conditioned structure with a glass front. They were conducted past a counter where two clerks worked, past white scheduling boards with aircraft tail numbers written in black, past desks where pilots filled out the paperwork necessary to get their planes off the ground, and past weather maps. Eventually they found themselves in the VIP lounge, which reflected the status of the people using it.

Unlike the waiting areas at other Air Force bases, this one reeked of luxury. The thick pile carpeting was powder blue. The walls were paneled with dark wood, and although no one could tell, they were also soundproofed so that visitors wouldn't be annoyed by the roar of jet engines as planes landed and took off. A number of large couches, each a different color, complemented the carpeting. In one corner sat a console TV, and above it a bank of three smaller sets, one for each network. A single large window looked out onto the airfield, allowing visitors to watch aircraft operations. However, the window was tinted so that sunlight wouldn't heat the interior of the room. Near a corner wet bar a hostess, an Air Force captain in a tightly tailored uniform, was on hand to assist visitors. She was a petite woman with short blond hair and a huge smile.

Bishop pointed to one of the couches along the opposite wall. "Sit."

He didn't bother to introduce either Halpren or Drake to the others in the room. There were two other senators, both of whom Halpren recognized, and three congressmen. Each had brought two or three aides. While the senators and congressmen stood near the window, drinks in hand, talking about the trip, the aides sat quietly, waiting for an opportunity to be of service.

Drake leaned close and whispered, "All this for a trip to Vietnam?"

Halpren looked at the other people in the lounge. All were young men with longish hair. Some wore business suits; others wore bush jackets, complete with loops on the breast pockets for large-caliber bullets. Their garb suggested that they viewed the trip as a holiday safari into the jungle, while those in suits seemed to see it as just one more business trip.

"Aren't any other women going?" Drake asked.

Halpren shrugged. "It's like I told you. This isn't an environment especially appealing to women."

Then, almost as if to make a liar out of him, the door opened and two women entered. One of the senators, talking near the window, turned, held his drink high and announced, "There we are. Everyone's here."

"So there *are* other women going to Vietnam," Drake said.

Halpren shook his head. "If either of them sets foot in South Vietnam, I'll be surprised."

"So what'll happen to them?"

"They'll wait somewhere else and join us again once we're out of Vietnam."

The door opened again. This time an Air Force officer entered. "Gentlemen," he said, "and ladies. We're almost ready for boarding. If anyone has any luggage still to be loaded, now is the time to take care of it."

When no one said anything, he retreated. Bishop walked over and said, "We'll be making the flight in stages. First to Hawaii, then to the Philippines and finally into South Vietnam." He glanced at Drake. "If you'd like to remain in the Philippines while we're in South Vietnam, that option's available to you."

"No," she said. "I want to make the whole trip."

Bishop grinned broadly and glanced at the other men. He patted Drake's knee, letting his hand slide higher. "Good for you."

A moment later the door opened once more and a different officer appeared. "If you'll follow me, please. Bring your drinks if you want."

He turned and walked away. The people filtered out of the room and walked outside to a blue Air Force bus. They climbed in and discovered that they weren't in a typical Air Force vehicle. It was new, with wider aisles and high-backed seats upholstered in soft cloth. Carpeting covered the floor, and the windows were tinted to keep out the glare. The air was cool and they could hardly hear the diesel engine.

When everyone was seated, the driver closed the door and the bus moved slowly toward the aircraft. He maneuvered the vehicle so that its door was close to the stairs leading into the plane. The passengers filed out and up into the large Air Force jet.

The plane wasn't a typical Air Force transport. It contained wide airline-type seats and had soundproofing on the bulkheads and fuselage, carpet on the floor, a brightly lit interior and lots of windows.

An Air Force officer, almost a carbon copy of the woman they'd left in the VIP lounge, stood at the top of the stairs. Like a stewardess on a commercial flight, she greeted the passengers with a smile and waved them to the rear of the aircraft. The only thing she didn't do was ask for a boarding pass.

As they moved along the aisle, Bishop asked, "This how all Air Force planes are set up?"

One of the other fact-finders shook his head. "If they are, the military appropriation is way too high."

Drake slipped into a window seat and looked out as Halpren sat next to her. Men in fatigues were working on fighter planes as well as transports. Blue crew vans slipped among the aircraft. Beyond was the runway, and as she watched, two fighters roared down it and lifted off, leaving a trail of thick black smoke.

"Phantoms," said Halpren.

"What?"

"The planes that just took off. They're F-4 Phantoms. That's the kind of plane doing a lot of fighting in South Vietnam."

Drake and Halpren sat in silence for several moments. The lights flashed once and as the pilots started the engines, a certain whining could be heard, but it never got louder than an annoying buzz.

The officer who was supplementing the staff of stewardesses came through, asked them to buckle their seat belts, then inquired if they wanted anything.

"How about a bourbon?" asked Halpren.

"No problem, sir. Is there a brand you'd prefer? We've got a fully stocked bar."

"Nope. Anything you have will be fine."

"Yes, sir," she said, smiling. "I'll bring it around just as soon as we're airborne."

"Thanks."

A moment later the plane moved, stopped, then taxied out onto the active runway without delay. The only traffic that could have caused a delay would have been the aircraft of the President or of the head of state of a foreign nation. Since the Andrews command post had not been alerted about any such flight, the most important one they had was that of the fact-finding contingent.

In seconds the plane was racing down the runway. Through the window Halpren watched the ground slide by and become little more than a green-brown blur. The jet leaped into the air and began a steep climb, the ground falling away rapidly as Halpren was pushed back into his plush seat.

Drake reached out, grabbed his hand and grinned at him, the smile a little sickly. "Takeoff's the worst," she said through clenched teeth. "That's the most likely time for a plane to crash."

"What about landing?"

"Not as bad," she said. "Then you've burned off so much fuel that the plane is lighter, also less fuel to explode. Takeoff is the worst."

Halpren didn't know if she was right, but figured it wasn't important enough to argue. He leaned forward to look past her out the window. All he could see was the cloudless blue sky.

"Going to be a long flight, isn't it?" she asked.

"Yeah," said Halpren. "A few hours to fly across the States. Then the leg to Hawaii will take several hours. If we did it nonstop, we'd be in the air about twenty hours straight."

She shifted in her seat, crossed her legs and said, "Twenty hours."

"Except that we'll stop in Hawaii and then the Philippines. It'll be a couple of days before we're in South Vietnam."

"Couple of days," she said.

"Hey," said Halpren. "It won't be as bad as all that. We'll sleep in regular beds, eat good food and have a chance to see part of the world."

She turned and looked toward the rear of the plane, where a bulkhead separated the seating from another compartment. Although she hadn't been through the door in the partition, she knew what lay beyond the barrier. Five or six small bedrooms, each not much wider than a single bed, were back there, along with a shower.

A stewardess started to hand out drinks. One of the senators had left his seat and was heading toward the rear of the aircraft. One of the other women, a long-haired brunette in a knee-length skirt and a white see-through blouse, followed him.

"You want anything," said Halpren, "you ask. You'll be surprised at what's available on one of these flights."

Drake settled back in her seat and shook her head. "No, I don't think I'd be surprised. Not at all."

10

MACV HEADQUARTERS
SAIGON

"I think the solution to the problem is to visit Jerry Maxwell," said Gerber.

"Who's Jerry Maxwell?" Staab asked.

Gerber saw that there was no one standing in the hallway near them, not that it would make much difference. Maxwell's job wasn't that big a secret, no matter what he thought about it. "Local spook," said Gerber.

"Then let's go see this Maxwell."

Gerber moved down the hallway, stopped at the top of the stairs and then descended into the lower level. At the base of the stairs was an iron gate and behind it an armed guard sat at a small desk. Gerber walked up to the iron gate. "I'd like to see Jerry Maxwell."

The guard, a young MP dressed in new jungle fatigues, looked up but said nothing.

"Maxwell?" prompted Gerber.

The guard turned his attention to the book sitting in front of him and then lifted the receiver of the field phone. He spun the crank, spoke into it and sat back, staring at Gerber. He studied the captain's dirty, sweat-stained uniform, then shifted his eyes to Staab, Fetterman and Coats. All four men were dirty, and armed.

Again he spoke into the phone, then put it down and leaned forward. Pulling a ledger toward him, he said, "Mr. Maxwell will be out to see you in a moment."

"You know," said Gerber, "if you'd bothered to ask a name, you could have saved yourself a lot of hassle. You'd have found we're cleared."

At that moment Maxwell appeared and shouted, "Christ, Gerber, what do you want?"

"Afternoon, Jerry," said Gerber. "Nice to see you again."

Maxwell came forward. He was a tall man whose skin was deeply tanned by the tropical sun. His hair was beginning to recede, something Gerber hadn't noticed before. Maxwell's face looked drawn and there were dark circles under his eyes. As usual he wore a white suit, a white shirt and a thin black tie. It was almost as if he was trying to fit the image of the Ugly American. A man who knew how to solve all the world's problems if the world would just listen to him.

Maxwell reached the iron gate. "Afternoon, Tony. Now, who do you have with you?"

"Lieutenant Staab and Sergeant Coats from MI up at Bien Hoa. We've got some things we'd like to show you and to talk to you about."

"I don't have a lot of time today."

Gerber reached out, grabbed one of the iron bars of the gate and moved closer. "Jerry, what is it with you? I come down here, I'm in a good mood, I have good info and you don't want to listen to anything. I'm not asking you to buy me a Coke."

Maxwell looked at the guard. "I'll vouch for these men."

"Yes, sir." Then the guard addressed the visitors. "Sign in, please." He got up and unlocked the iron gate.

When the ritual was finished, each of the men having written down his name, the date and the time, Maxwell led them down the hallway. The green tile on the floor was stained with rust, showing where metal filing cabinets had been stored and then moved. The cinder-block walls were painted light green. Condensation dripped down the walls, creating a musty smell, while fluorescent lights glowed overhead, making the hall as bright as an operating theater. There were a few pictures on the wall, mainly Army prints depicting great battles of the past.

Maxwell stopped at his door. "I normally don't let people in here I don't know."

"Christ, Jerry," Gerber said, "Staab and Coats are standing here in their official U.S. of A. uniforms. I tell you they're cleared and you make speeches. Just who in hell do you think they're going to squeal to?"

"Just letting you know the favor I'm doing for you," said Maxwell tiredly.

"Hear that, Tony?" said Gerber. "The spook's doing us a big favor."

"Maybe we should just forget this whole thing and find someone who'll be interested in the data we have," Fetterman suggested.

"If you guys have finished your normal comedy routine..." Maxwell said. He opened the door and stepped back, letting Gerber walk past him.

The captain entered the tiny office and took the visitor's chair, which was old and covered with vinyl that had been repaired half a dozen times with electrical tape. Next to it, shoved into the corner, was a large desk, its top awash in papers and files, the edge next to the wall lined with empty Coke cans. Maxwell's chair, which looked uncomfortable, had casters, and his weapon in a shoulder holster was draped over the back.

Opposite the desk was a bank of filing cabinets, the tops covered with more paper. The cabinet in the corner was a massive affair with a combination lock on the middle drawer. There was a metal folding chair near the files, which Staab took. Fetterman stepped to the corner so that he could lean against the filing cabinet. Coats tried to get out of the way as Maxwell closed the door behind him.

As the CIA man moved to his desk, he asked, "What can I do for you?"

Gerber pointed at Staab. "We've got a book, a notebook, a diary or a journal, something, that we'd like translated."

"Shit, Gerber, you don't need me for that."

"Jerry, I want someone to look at the journal who can keep his mouth shut. We don't want it to get out that we've got our hands on this."

"Let me see it."

Gerber glanced at Staab. "Lieutenant."

Staab handed over the book but didn't speak. Maxwell took it and said, "If you're MI, you have people to translate this."

"That's right," said Gerber, "but whatever MI knows, the South Vietnamese know and therefore the VC know. There are no secrets where the South Vietnamese are concerned."

"It's not that bad," Staab said.

"Anyway," said Gerber, ignoring Staab, "I want it translated."

Maxwell flipped through it quickly. "Doesn't look like a military document."

"Christ, Maxwell, just get someone down here to read it for us."

Maxwell closed the book and set it on top of the papers on his desk. He reached for the field phone and spun the crank. "Have someone find Major Shorack and send him down here." He cradled the receiver. "Be a couple of minutes. You want to tell me what this is all about?"

Gerber glanced at Staab and then at Fetterman. "We hit a small patrol this morning, and that was one of the documents we recovered as we swept the field."

"Then you have other things?"

Staab dug through his rucksack and produced a handful of papers. "Standard military stuff."

"Why in hell do you want to read some guy's private journal?" asked Maxwell.

"I'll tell you, Jerry," said Gerber. "The military documents won't be worth much. Hell, Charlie and the boys aren't dumb enough to be carrying anything of value from a military source—"

"That point's debatable," Maxwell interrupted. "We've captured documents that have mapped out whole plans of attack."

"Not from soldiers in the field. Those have come from finding and attacking enemy bases and breaking into tunnel systems. So I don't think we'll get much from the documents, but men write the damnedest things in their private journals. Who knows what we might learn?"

There was a knock on the door. Maxwell got up to open it. "Ah, Major Shorack. Come on in."

Shorack was a small, pale man with hair so blond that it was nearly white. His skin was reddish, almost as if he had been burned, but he wasn't peeling. There was no sign of facial hair. He had clear blue eyes, sharp, almost delicate features and a pointed chin. He looked to be about twelve years old, a kid pretending to be a soldier.

Maxwell pushed Shorack toward the old vinyl chair and had him sit down. Then, hovering over him like a mother hen, he gave him the journal. "Tell us what it says."

Shorack flipped through it, glancing at several of the pages and running his fingers along the lines of writing. He turned, faced Gerber and then looked at Staab. "This is the personal record of a private named Dien Minh Thuy. He left the North some five months ago to participate in a great adventure here in South Vietnam."

"Tell us what the last few pages say," Gerber said.

Shorack turned to the last entries. He read them quietly and then looked up. "Nothing for the past week or so. He misses his home and wants to return to the North as soon as he can. He hates it in the South. Complains about the heat, humidity and people. He's watched the farmers, who don't pay any attention to them. The farmers ignore them, pretend to see right through them."

"That does us no good," Maxwell snapped.

Shorack read another entry. "He complains about the darkness. They have lanterns but aren't allowed to use them much. They live in semidarkness, eat cold food and are treated poorly by soldiers who have been fighting in the South for months."

"Still does us no good," said Staab.

"It tells us that he's living underground," said Gerber. "It tells us that there are a lot of them around, and it tells us there's dissension in the ranks."

Shorack continued. "He came down the Ho Chi Minh Trail with a company—"

"Probably about a hundred men," said Coats.

"Came down with a company," repeated Shorack. "Saw lots of men and equipment on the Trail. Other soldiers, all going to the South. Trucks moving along the Trail, hundreds of porters with bicycles. Lots of men and equipment. Much of it bright and shiny and from the Soviet Union."

"And once they got here?" Gerber asked.

"Shit," Shorack said. "I don't believe this." He looked up at Gerber and then turned to study Maxwell. "They were loaded on trucks just over the border in Cambodia and then drove into South Vietnam."

"That's a load of crap," said Maxwell, the disgust obvious in his voice. "Guy's writing fiction."

"No," said Gerber, "I don't think so. I've heard rumors about this for a couple of weeks. That's one of the reasons Sergeant Fetterman and I were at Nui Ba Den."

"What in hell are you talking about?" asked Maxwell.

"Simply that there have been rumors of unknown convoys in the area. Trucks that come from Cambodia and drive straight into Nui Ba Den. A helicopter pilot told me he spotted a convoy one night but couldn't get permission to open fire. Everyone thought it had to be an American convoy, or more likely a South Vietnamese convoy. The enemy doesn't have trucks."

Shorack tapped a fingernail on the journal. "According to this, they do have trucks. Not all that many in South Vietnam, but they do have trucks."

"Anyway," said Gerber, "rumors are that there's another buildup of forces in the Tay Ninh area."

Maxwell waved his hands. "Wait a minute. How'd we get from the diary of a dead soldier to a buildup of enemy forces in Tay Ninh Province?"

"Easy, Jerry," Gerber said. He glanced at Fetterman and waited, but the master sergeant didn't say a word. "After the Tet offensive, we know the enemy was wiped out. Their losses were catastrophic, and—"

"I'm not sure about that," said Maxwell.

"I am," said Staab. He turned and faced the CIA man. "I've seen the reports from every conceivable source. In no case did the enemy gain and hold any of their objectives. The government of South Vietnam didn't collapse, and the peo-

ple didn't rise up to help the VC. Even in areas considered
to be VC strongholds, the people didn't revolt. Add all that
to losses of over fifty thousand men and you've got a catas-
trophe.''

"Regardless of that,'' Gerber interjected, "the important thing is what that diary tells us about men and supplies
moving down the Ho Chi Minh Trail in large numbers.''

"The implication is there,'' agreed Maxwell, "but this
isn't hard intelligence.''

"Oh, for Christ's sake,'' snapped Fetterman, "we've got
information from a source that's unimpeachable.''

"No source is that good.''

"Damn it, Jerry,'' Gerber said, exasperated. "No man is
going to lie about something like that in a diary that no one
but he himself is going to see. A journalist might embellish
the account to make it more interesting, a historian might
punch it up to make it better reading, but a man writing for
himself, describing what he sees, isn't going to lie about it.''

"Not to mention,'' said Fetterman, "that we have some
supporting evidence.''

"Whatever,'' said Maxwell. "What else have you got
there?''

Shorack read a couple of pages. "He talks about caves.
Not tunnels, but caves stacked with equipment, trucks,
guns, ammo, mortars, machine guns, quite a list of stuff.''

Gerber sat forward. "Where?''

"Doesn't say exactly,'' said Shorack. "Somewhere
around Nui Ba Den.''

"Captain,'' said Fetterman, "there have been rumors for
years that the mountain is honeycombed with caves and
tunnels. Story is that we hold the top and bottom and Charlie controls the middle of it.''

"This is getting ridiculous,'' said Maxwell.

"Staab, why don't you show the major some of the other things you picked up?" Gerber suggested.

"Yes, sir." He handed over a stack of documents.

Shorack worked through them quickly. "Not much of interest here. A paper explaining how to tax people for portions of rice and other food, a paper along the order of the stuff we get from Hanoi Hanna, stating how we're about to collapse and all they have to do is hang on. Propaganda, a roster, the beginnings of a CQ list, who has what duties for the next week and so on."

"How long is the list?" asked Gerber.

"About thirty names."

"A platoon then. And the man talked about a company. So we know there are other men in the region. Another seventy or so."

"Enough for me to mention it to my people at Bien Hoa," said Staab.

"Jerry?" prompted Gerber.

"Hell, I can't do anything with this. It's just not solid intelligence. You're basing everything on a diary, assuming that the man wouldn't lie in it."

"That and observed data from the vicinity," said Gerber. "Things that I've seen or that Tony's seen. Charlie's infiltrating Tay Ninh, and the only target that would gain international attention is Saigon."

"Oh, come on, Gerber."

The captain turned his attention back to the major. "Anything else of significance there?"

"I'd have to take a long, hard look at the documents, but I think that covers it."

"Thank you, Major," said Gerber.

Shorack looked at Maxwell, and when the CIA man didn't speak, he handed the dairy and papers back to Staab.

"You know, of course," said Gerber, "that this is classified."

"Of course."

As Shorack left, Gerber said, "I think that takes care of everything down here. Jerry, I'm going to be real unhappy if I read about any of this in tomorrow morning's intelligence briefings. The South Vietnamese have access to those, and what they know, Charlie soon knows."

Maxwell reclaimed his seat now that Shorack was gone. He picked up a file folder, tossed it aside and then rocked back so that he could put his feet up on the desk. Lacing his fingers behind his head, he said, "I'd be embarrassed to put any of this in a report. Not without something a little more substantial to go with it. I'm afraid that one VC private's diary just isn't that great a source."

Gerber stood. "Then we're out of here."

"Mack," said Maxwell, "I know you think I'm not very good at this, but believe me, you're being taken for a ride. Charlie is setting you up. This is a decoy of some kind. The enemy want to draw us into a battle where they control everything, so that they can wipe out an American unit. This could easily be the first step in that plan."

Gerber sighed. "Maxwell, you refuse to see the trees because of the forest. Charlie isn't that subtle. We have to exploit this, just as we should exploit all the intelligence we get."

"When you get back," said Maxwell, "I'll buy you a steak and say I told you so."

"When I get back," said Gerber, smiling, "I'll let you buy me that steak, as long as you'll buy Sergeant Fetterman one, too."

"Of course."

"Of course," echoed Gerber. "Anyway, thanks for the help." He opened the door and walked out.

The others followed him, and when they stopped at the iron gate to check out, Staab asked, "Now what?"

"I guess you can head on back to Bien Hoa with your data. I'd be careful about who sees it for the next few days. We don't want the spies in the South Vietnamese army letting the NVA know what we know."

"Yes, sir."

Once the guard let them through the gate, they headed up to the ground floor. For a moment they stood near the double doors that led out into the heat of the tropical afternoon. The sunlight was bright, and the men picking up cigarette butts and scraps of paper on the lawn looked hot and miserable.

"Can you give us a ride back to Tan Son Nhut?" asked Coats.

"We aren't going back there," said Gerber. "We're heading into Saigon. Besides, it's not that hard to get there from here."

"No, sir."

Gerber looked at the sergeant and changed his mind. "Hey, it's not that big a deal. We'll drive you out to Tan Son Nhut."

"Thanks, sir."

Fetterman moved to the right and scooped up a copy of the *Stars and Stripes* from a pile set inside the front door. He flipped it open, studied it, then turned it over.

"Anything of interest, Master Sergeant?" asked Gerber.

"No, sir, just the usual nonsense." He dropped the paper back onto the stack and then picked it up again. "Well, goddamn it all anyway."

"What?"

"We've got a fucking congressional committee coming to look into the Tet disaster."

"Christ," said Gerber, "that's all we need. Another group of know-nothings trying to figure out a disaster that didn't happen. Does it really say disaster?"

"Yes, sir. It says disaster."

"Then it's not even an unbiased search. They already have the answers. They're just coming here to make it look good for the paper."

"Well, maybe they won't do anything to hurt us," said Staab.

"Yeah," said Gerber. "And there weren't any Indians at the Little Bighorn."

"The only good thing," said Fetterman, "is that we won't have to talk to them."

Gerber looked at his watch. "Let's get out of here. I want to get something to eat before anything else can go wrong today."

11

ON THE SLOPES OF
NUI BA DEN

Thanh and Ngo waited in the forest, hoping that other members of their attack squad would appear. They searched the forest around them, moving carefully, quietly, stopping frequently to listen for sounds that the Americans were after them. Sitting in the shade of the palm and coconut trees, they listened to the birds screaming at one another and watched the clouds as they formed and dissipated. Thanh spent twenty minutes watching a spider spin a web between the leaves of a small bush, and when it was done, he touched the web with a blade of grass. When the spider attacked, Thanh squashed it with his rifle butt.

They let the morning slip away as they watched the American helicopters in the distance, knowing that the men who had attacked them were now getting out of the forest. The sound was far away, and they could only see the helicopters when the sunlight glanced off the windshields. As the Americans got out, Thanh and Ngo heard the distant firing of machine guns, then nothing.

When they found no sign of the rest of the squad, they decided to return to the interior of the mountain. Ngo led the way through the Boi Loi Woods, ignoring the trails and the direct path back to Nui Ba Den. The Americans were gone, the helicopters had proved that, and the longer they stayed out, the more likely their story would sound, the more believable their tale of a big fight with the Americans.

Ngo stopped after twenty minutes, crouching near the freshly turned earth of a shell crater. Dirty water covered the bottom of it, and the stench of death was everywhere. While there, Ngo pulled the last magazine from his chest pouch and tossed it into the water, watched it disappear.

"What did you do that for?" asked Thanh.

"If we fought the Americans all day, we wouldn't have any ammo left."

Thanh nodded and took the magazine from his weapon. He stripped ten rounds from it, leaving about half the magazine. He then threw his chest pouch into the water, figuring there was no reason to carry the extra weight of the empty pouch.

Ngo leaned forward, dug both elbows into the mud and smeared some of it on his chest. He then crouched in the mud, covering his knees. When he finished, he moved closer to Thanh, and without a word of warning, hit him in the face.

Thanh came up, his rifle pointed at the sergeant, his finger on the trigger. He felt blood trickling down his face, mingling with the sweat and dirt.

"We have to look like we've been in a fight," said Ngo quietly. "A small physical injury will help convince them."

"Don't hit me again," said Thanh as he released the pressure on the trigger.

Ngo ripped his shirtsleeve. Then, with his knife, he slashed his pants and, gritting his teeth, cut his leg. He pressed the wound, forcing the blood out, making it look much worse than it was. Finished, he said, "Now they'll see that we didn't escape unhurt. Minor wounds, true, but wounds nonetheless. They'll assume we were hurt in the fighting.''

Thanh sat back, his AK cradled in his arms. He looked up at the sky and suddenly felt like crying. The depression bubbled up from the pit of his stomach and threatened to overwhelm him. War wasn't supposed to be deception of his comrades. It was supposed to be a glorious fight to drive the American invaders from his land, just as his people had driven out the French. It was supposed to be great battles that would live throughout history and that would be topics of discussion for generations.

Instead, it was moments of terror when he fired his weapon because he didn't know what else to do. It was fleeing from the onslaught, praying a bullet wouldn't strike him in the back as he ran. It was mind-numbing terror as men died all around him, their blood staining the ground, their guts spilling out of their bodies.

If anyone had told him what war was really like, he would have deserted and stayed in North Vietnam. Instead, the political officer had come to the village with stories of glory to be won in the South, and he had believed. He had seen the looks on the faces of the girls as the political officer had talked about great battles, and he had been all too ready to join the troops.

He shook his head and stared at the ground. Death was all around him. Rotting vegetation recycled itself, animals preyed on one another endlessly, and the Americans stalked the Vietnamese, wanting to kill them. It wasn't glorious.

The roar of a jet broke into his thoughts. He looked up and saw the plane flash overhead, no more than forty meters above him. He rolled to the side and covered his head with his hands, but the noise faded quickly. The jet was on its way somewhere else.

"We should go now," urged Ngo.

Thanh got to his feet. "Yes. Now we go back to the caves. I'm tired of this."

Ngo turned and moved deeper into the forest. Thanh followed, stepping gently, afraid of the booby traps sprinkled throughout the area. He had been told where they were, but there was always the chance that he had forgotten one of them, or that another company, another battalion, had planted some he didn't know about. The booby traps were sometimes as deadly for the VC and NVA as they were for the Americans and the puppet soldiers from Saigon.

They worked their way north and then turned east, beginning the climb up the mountainside. Staying in the trees, they used the shadows to conceal themselves, stopping frequently and listening for sounds of pursuit or the roar of aircraft engines. As they continued along, they saw dozens of helicopters working the areas around the mountain, but all of them stayed several kilometers away. If one came close, there were plenty of hiding places on the mountain. The enemy helicopters were nothing more than tiny objects buzzing around the ground like so many annoying insects.

Halfway to the entrance to the tunnel, they stopped a final time. Ngo knelt close to Thanh and once more they talked their way through the story of the great firefight. Ngo didn't want them to agree on everything, because in a real battle men would witness different things. They had to be close on the major points but not on the details.

Thanh drank the rest of his water and then punched a hole in his canteen, telling Ngo it was a bullet that had nearly killed him. Then they started up the mountain again, ducking for cover as a helicopter flew over them. When it was gone, they started off again, hurrying toward the cave entrance.

Just as another helicopter passed over them, they found the trapdoor. When the aircraft was gone, they opened the door and dropped inside. As Thanh closed the door, Ngo collapsed on the tunnel floor. "We made it."

"Yes," said Thanh, "we made it." Thanh slumped against the wall and closed his eyes. Sweat covered him, staining his clothes and making his skin itch. In the darkness of the tunnel he couldn't see. There were sounds, some of them coming from outside, others from deep inside the mountain. He focused his attention on the noises, letting them drive everything else from his mind.

Ngo found a lantern, lit it and held it up. "We should be going."

"Yes," Thanh agreed, but he didn't move. He stayed there, clasping his AK in his hands, not wanting to see anyone else.

Ngo moved off down the narrow corridor, stooping to avoid bumping his head. Finally he was forced onto his hands and knees. He slung his weapon and held the lantern out in front of him to light the way.

Thanh watched the sergeant as he walked away. When he could no longer see the man, he could still see the light playing on the tunnel walls, swaying as Ngo moved. Finally Thanh forced himself up and followed the sergeant. He hurried on before Ngo got too far in front of him.

The two of them worked their way through the tunnel around a ninety-degree turn designed as a defensive point, eventually emerging into a larger tunnel that opened onto a cavern. There was plenty of light in the cave, the lanterns and even the electrical lights having been turned on.

As Thanh appeared, Captain Nhuan walked over and looked at him carefully. "Where are the bodies you were sent to retrieve? Did you fail in your mission?"

For just an instant Thanh hesitated. If he started to tell lies now, there would be no going back. He would never be able to retract them. And then the story that he and Ngo had devised tumbled out, almost on its own. He didn't have to think about it. "American ambush," he said. "We were caught in an American ambush and were forced to fight our way clear of it. Most of the squad was killed, but we managed to escape. Before we escaped I saw the bodies of fifty dead Americans."

The company commander stared hard at Thanh. He rubbed a hand on his chin, as if considering the information just given to him. Then he turned his attention to Ngo. "Is this true?"

"Yes, Comrade. We were fortunate to escape with our lives. The Americans were reinforced."

"Why is it that we heard none of this?"

Thanh suddenly realized they hadn't considered the noise a major battle would make. Hundreds of weapons, along with artillery and helicopters, would be heard for kilometers in all directions. The NVA had outposts on the mountain that opened to the surface. A pitched battle, even ten or twelve kilometers away, would have been obvious to the officers remaining in the tunnels and caves. "I don't know, Comrade," he finally said.

"Where's the booty from the battle?"

"We were forced to leave it behind," said Thanh. "There were too many Americans, and they kept arriving in their helicopters. We fought as long as we could."

"Sergeant, is this true?"

"Comrade," said Ngo, "it's all true." He pointed at his leg and added, "I was wounded myself."

The company commander crouched and studied the wound. "It's not very bad."

"I took a round through my canteen," said Thanh, holding up the damaged piece of equipment.

"Doesn't look like a bullet hole," said Captain Nhuan, examining it carefully.

Thanh shrugged. "We have told you the truth. There's nothing more to be said."

"Well," said the company commander, "come and let's talk to Tuyen Duan. He returned an hour ago."

Thanh felt his head spin. He hadn't thought of that. He'd believed that all his men had been killed or captured and that there would be no one left to offer another story. Frantically he thought about trying to change his story, to bring it into line with what had really happened, but he knew that anything he said now would just prove that he was a liar. All he could do was go with the company commander and hope for the best.

They crossed the chamber, crawled through a tunnel and came out into a larger room set up as a hospital. Wooden racks, two and three tiers high, were covered in straw and served as beds for the wounded. Shelves carved in the wall of the cavern were lined with bottles and packages of medicine stolen from the Americans or donated by students in the United States. There was a table at one end where four people sat. A nurse stood slightly to the rear as a doctor worked on a slightly wounded man. There was a bright light at the far end, but most of the chamber was wrapped in gloom.

They moved to a bed where Tuyen Duan lay, his eyes closed. "Private," said the company commander, "I understand you ran into a large force of Americans."

Duan opened his eyes and saw Lieutenant Thanh and Sergeant Ngo. He blinked rapidly, wiped a hand across his face and nodded. "Yes. Many Americans."

"Lieutenant Thanh claims you killed, you all killed, almost fifty Americans."

Again Duan glanced at the lieutenant. He squirmed uncomfortably, propping himself on his elbow so that he could see better. "Maybe fifty, maybe more. There were so many of them, with more arriving every moment."

"Ah," said Captain Nhuan, "I thought you said you didn't know how many Americans were there."

Duan fell silent for a moment. He turned toward Thanh, but the lieutenant offered no help. Finally he said, "There were many Americans there, all of them shooting at us. I don't know how many there were. Too many for us. We had to leave or all of us would have been killed."

"Very well, Comrade," said the company commander. "You can rest now." He turned to face Thanh. "Many Americans. Not much of a description."

Thanh felt his confidence return. Any of his surviving men would support the story, because it made them all look brave. It would do no good for a man to refute what was being said if it made him look like a coward. Here was a valuable lesson, one that he would have to remember. "It was a combat situation. No one had time to make accurate counts."

"Yes," said the company commander. "There are questions to be answered about this, but not now. Let's return to the first chamber."

"Excuse me," said Ngo. "Could I have the nurse take a look at my wound?"

"Of course."

Ngo touched Thanh on the back, as if to say, "See, we pulled it off." He moved toward the other end of the chamber and spoke to the nurse. She crouched, looked at his leg, frowned and then moved to the shelves, searching them until she found a brown bottle. Returning to Ngo, she crouched again and worked on his leg for a moment. Then she bandaged the wound swiftly and resumed helping the doctor.

As Ngo approached them, he said, "No big thing. Just a scratch really."

"How about you, Lieutenant?" asked the company commander. "Would you like medical attention?"

Thanh touched his cheek where Ngo had hit him. The skin was tender and ached. "No, Comrade," he said. "We have important work to do."

"Most commendable," said Captain Nhuan.

They returned to the main chamber and crawled into another tunnel that twisted upward. The floor was rough, hacked into the stone of the mountain. It curved, dipped suddenly and then began another climb. Each of the turns and dips was designed to thwart invaders or to protect the men in case the enemy threw grenades. Elaborate blast doors weren't necessary, because grenades weren't that powerful and large satchel charges would bring down the ceiling, effectively sealing off the blast.

They crawled through a large chamber that served as sleeping quarters for some of the men, then passed another room used as a storage area for weapons and ammunition. Turning once, they bypassed a dead-end chamber whose terminus was booby-trapped in case the Americans got into the system.

Finally they came to a conference room, a small chamber that contained several chairs stolen from the Americans, a few charts, a low slit that let in light and fresh air and a wooden table constructed from scrap lumber. They were very close to the surface. Thanh crossed the chamber and looked out the slit. He was high up on the mountain, looking out on a tiny valley.

"Please be seated," said Captain Nhuan.

Thanh sat down and folded his hands. Ngo dropped into another chair and waited. A moment later Sergeant Vinh entered and sat down without a word.

Captain Nhuan stood facing the slit, looking out over the trees, his hands clasped behind his back. He stood there for a long time, as if trying to think of something to say. Then, as he turned, another man entered. Thanh hadn't seen him before, and although his clothes had no badges of rank, the company commander bowed to him. Looking at him closely, Thanh realized he wasn't Vietnamese, but Chinese, one of the many advisers the Chinese had sent to the South to help in the war.

"Welcome, Colonel. We'll start now."

The stranger sat down. "Please do."

The company commander picked up one of the charts. It showed the positions of the American camps, their fire bases and their outposts. It showed the areas they patrolled most frequently, the routes those patrols used, and it contained the locations of the VC and NVA strongholds around them. He dropped the map onto the table. "The recent *Tet* offensive didn't accomplish much for us."

Thanh shot a glance at the unknown officer, waiting for words of protest, but the man didn't speak. Although everyone knew Tet had been a disaster for them and a victory for the Americans, no one had said so out loud. At least no one had until that moment.

"We have an opportunity to recover some of our lost face," the captain continued. "First, we're planning another assault on the enemy capital. The Western press was disturbed by our infiltration into the heart of Saigon. They made much of our attack on the American embassy, even though our sappers died before they could accomplish their mission."

"Please, Comrade Captain, hurry. We're not interested in history," the stranger said.

"Certainly, Comrade Colonel." The company commander pulled out a copy of an American newspaper and held it up for all to see. "One of our men who works with the Americans at Dau Tieng has provided us with this interesting document."

Thanh sat forward and looked at the newspaper. It contained strange symbols, the names of soldiers and dozens of pictures, obviously a very valuable intelligence resource if they had access to it on a regular basis.

"This will provide us with the information we need to score a big victory. It gives all the facts we need to plan an assassination of important Americans, assassinations that will spark more dissent in the United States and encourage more support for our cause here. A successful assassination will prove that we are all-powerful."

Thanh continued to study the newspaper, although it made no sense to him. The company commander dropped it onto the table and Thanh pulled it toward him.

"We've been provided with enough information to plan the mission. An attack on the convoy that will carry the leaders from the aggressor United States will show our strength. We'll be able to kill a number of high-ranking officials from both governments. With luck we'll have the opportunity to capture a couple of them."

"When will this take place?" asked the colonel.

"In the next week to ten days. We have yet to learn the exact itinerary, but we know they're coming. If we begin to prepare now, we'll be ready when they arrive."

Thanh nodded, thinking that it was a good plan. He then glanced at the newspaper, at the crossed American flags at the top of the page, not realizing he was looking at the latest copy of *Stars and Stripes*.

12

CARASEL HOTEL
SAIGON

Gerber sat at a table well away from the door, his back to the wall, and watched everything that was going on around him. He watched the waiters and waitresses as they served food and drinks. He watched the men in their business suits, or uniforms, no one in fatigues, and the women in their dresses, light summer dresses that were cut low on top and high on the bottom. The people circulating seemed to have no awareness of the war raging all around them.

Across the table from Gerber sat Fetterman, wearing khaki pants and a Hawaiian shirt that was mostly white with large blue birds on it. A light film of perspiration made Fetterman's face shine.

Sitting between Gerber and Fetterman was Robin Morrow, a journalist assigned to one of the Saigon press bureaus. She was a tall, slender woman, with light brown hair bleached by the sun. She was an ace reporter, one of the few who got out of Saigon to learn what was happening in the field. She was also one of the few who wrote unbiased accounts of the war.

Morrow was a good-looking woman with the brains to understand what was happening around her. Her features were sharp because she had lost weight during her stay in-country. That alone attested to her trips into the field. Journalists who stayed in Saigon put on weight because of all the good restaurants serving top-quality food. In the field there were C-rations that kept people alive, but no one gained weight eating them.

She finally put down her silver fork, which was crafted in the ornate and expensive style of the Old World, and asked, "What's going on with you two?"

Gerber glanced at Fetterman. "Something's going on here?"

"You know what I mean. You're gone for several days and suddenly show up in Saigon and want to go out to dinner." She put a hand against her chest. "I'm flattered, but I figure something must be going on."

"Not that I know of. Master Sergeant?"

Fetterman picked up his napkin and touched his lips. He glanced at the salad sitting in front of him and then up at Morrow. "Nothing's going on."

"When you two start that innocent routine," she said, "I suddenly get suspicious."

Gerber pushed his salad away from him. "Did you ever think that we just wanted to have dinner with a pretty lady? It might not be anything more nefarious than that."

"Sure," she said, sitting back in her chair. "Just what in hell is going on?"

Gerber looked out over the table at the restaurant. It was a large, quiet room with white tablecloths, fancy wallpaper and carpeting. The room was brightly lit by a huge chandelier supplemented by wall lamps set between the windows. Ceiling fans circulated the air, but sometime in the past the management had installed air-conditioning, which sucked the heat and humidity out of the room with a vengeance. Gerber turned his attention back to Morrow and studied her face. "You think something's going on?"

"You two always have something going on. Now, why don't you just share it with me and we can attack the problem? Why continue to play coy?"

Gerber shrugged. "What do you know about this congressional party coming in? Something about learning more about the Tet offensive."

"Just what I read in the papers," Morrow answered.

The waiter arrived with the main courses: steak and potatoes for Gerber and Fetterman, swordfish for Morrow. He took away the salad plates and left his customers alone, sipping the wine that Fetterman had insisted on ordering. When he was gone, Gerber asked, "Is there going to be a press briefing for these people?"

"There always is."

Gerber nodded. "Here's the problem as I see it. We have a bunch of journalists who don't know a thing about military operations talking to a bunch of congressmen and senators who don't know a thing about military operations. Then the politicians decide what went wrong at Tet. It doesn't seem to have occurred to any of them that nothing went wrong."

"Captain," said Fetterman, "you're overstating the case."

Gerber waved a hand. "Robin knows what I mean."

"Yes," she agreed. "But what does that have to do with you and me?"

Gerber didn't speak for a moment. He worked at putting butter and pepper on his potato. Finished with that, he cut into his steak, decided it was cooked properly and took a bite. "Robin, these people are going to be hanging around with the brass, colonels who want to make general, generals who would like another star or two or who want to protect pensions. They're going to be hanging around with political animals who will say whatever's convenient. There'll be men who'll say what the politicians want to hear regardless of the validity of those statements.''

"Mack," she said, "even if I could get you into the press briefing, there isn't going to be an opportunity for you to speak. There'll be one man up there talking, and then the congressmen and senators will ask some questions. That'll be it. It's all scripted in advance.''

Gerber cut some more steak. "So, the press, which doesn't know shit, is going to tell Congress what happened during the Tet offensive. That way Congress won't know shit, either.''

"I'm not sure I like your tone.''

"Miss Morrow," said Fetterman, "look at it from our point of view.''

"I'm suddenly demoted to Miss Morrow?'' she asked, raising an eyebrow at the master sergeant.

"Robin, then. It's just that we've listened to press reports that suggest the enemy won the battle. They had their asses kicked from here to next week. The Vietcong have ceased to exist as an effective fighting force. The levels of fighting throughout the country have fallen off sharply, with a few notable exceptions. How is that a defeat for us?''

Morrow cut into her fish and then put down her knife. "Tony, I didn't say it was a defeat.''

"No, ma'am, you didn't, but your colleagues have. In no way was it a defeat for us.''

"There are those who say that the fact the enemy was able to field such a force suggests that American policy in Vietnam is failing,'' Morrow said.

"A force that we knew they were putting together and that we hoped would come out for an all-out fight,'' said Gerber. "What difference does it make if Charlie or the North Vietnamese can field a hundred thousand men if half of them die inside of a week?"

"Mack, I'm not the one you should be arguing with. I'm on your side."

Gerber fell silent and took another bite. He chewed and swallowed. "A congressional committee to examine the disaster of Tet." He laughed. "That'll be a fair hearing. They already know it was a disaster because they saw it on their TV screens. Nothing is as important as the image on the TV, no matter how misleading that image is."

"Saigon in flames isn't misleading."

"Come on, Robin," said Gerber, his voice rising. "When in hell did you see Saigon in flames, other than on your television screen?"

She thought about that and said, "Point taken."

"So what do you plan to do about it, Captain?" Fetterman asked.

"I don't know," said Gerber. "I just don't like the idea that this congressional committee is going to show up here and get fed the same thing by the media that they've already seen on their TVs. The press here is responsible for what was seen in the World. I thought that maybe we could suggest that Tet wasn't the disaster everyone outside the military is making it out to be."

"A single voice of dissent among all those yelling disaster isn't going to be heard," Fetterman said.

Gerber put down his fork and took a deep drink of his wine, then rocked back in his chair. "I just can't sit here and do nothing. Hell, Tony, you saw it and know exactly what happened."

"Yes, sir," said Fetterman. "But then I also know when to strike the colors and get the hell out. This is going to be a no-win situation."

"Robin . . ." said Gerber.

"I'm afraid Tony is right on this one. You're not going to be listened to because you don't have enough clout. If you were so good, you'd be a general."

"But—"

"Makes no difference what the reality of the situation is," continued Morrow. "All that matters is the perception of the situation. On television perception becomes reality." She took a sip of wine and put down the glass carefully, staring at its stem. "As a kid I grew up thinking that George Custer had been made a general by accident during the Civil War."

"For Christ's sake, Robin," said Gerber.

"No, hear me out. Everyone said that it had been a mistake, an order written in two pieces that had made him a general. Everyone I knew believed it, but it isn't reality. It came from a fictionalized account of his life. From a movie. It made no difference that it was a movie. People believed it. That was fiction. Television news is supposed to be fact, so the facts are as reported, even if they're wrong."

"Maybe if we make enough noise," said Gerber, "someone will listen to us."

Fetterman grinned. "If you make enough noise, you know someone will slap you down."

"Of course," said Gerber.

"Then there is only one thing to do," said Morrow. "Get drunk and say fuck it."

"Well, I can't get drunk tonight," said Gerber, "leaving only the other option."

Fetterman looked at the remains of his meal and stretched. "I think I'd better get going now. I've got a big day tomorrow."

"You don't have to run off, Tony," said Morrow.

"Oh, yes, I do," said Fetterman. "I've got a little work to do and I want to get a good night's sleep."

As Fetterman disappeared out the door, Morrow said, "He didn't have to leave."

"He thinks he did. He's being clever about the whole thing, giving us an opportunity to arrange something for later if we want to."

Morrow put an elbow on the table, cupped her chin in the palm of her hand and smiled. "And are we going to arrange something?"

Gerber used his napkin, then tossed it onto the table. "I suppose we could."

"You know, Mack," she said, "I've been waiting for you to say something for the past hour. You're treating me like a relative you're not sure you like. A rich relative."

He looked at her for a moment. "I'm sorry about that. I've got a lot on my mind."

"I'm not sure that's sufficient."

"Maybe not, but that's the only excuse I have. We've been in the field and we'll probably be going out again tomorrow."

"Hey," said Morrow, "we'd better hurry."

Gerber waved a hand, signaling the waiter to get the check. He paid the bill with a handful of military script, the Monopoly money handed out to soldiers to help keep the inflation rate down. As they left the restaurant, Gerber said, "That might be a story you'll want to look into."

"What?"

"The military payment certificates. They say they're issued to hold down the local inflation rate, but I wonder if it isn't something more. It's not real money and we can default on it, meaning if someone shows up with a boatload of it, we don't have to redeem it for actual currency."

"I don't think I'm interested in the MPC right now," said Morrow.

They left the restaurant and walked toward the elevator at the far end of the lobby. Morrow stopped short and asked, "My place or yours?"

"Better make it mine," said Gerber. "It's closer."

They entered the elevator, a gilded cage that rose along one wall, letting them look down on the marble lobby where a fair-sized crowd circulated. They reached the fifth floor and Gerber opened the door. As they stepped out, Morrow stopped suddenly. "You don't have to go through this if you don't want to, Mack."

"I don't know what you're talking about."

"Your level of enthusiasm seems to be way down."

"I'm sorry." He was going to say more and then stopped. Everything he could say would sound lame. He had been in the field and he was tired, but she deserved more than that. He was worried about the things he'd seen and heard in the past twenty-four hours, especially the firefight.

He laughed. A firefight that morning and yet it seemed to have been a week ago. So much had happened. They had been in the field, sweating and fighting, then suddenly they were in Saigon trying to analyze everything they had seen and heard.

"Mack?" said Robin.

"Sorry," he said again, shaking his head, trying to drive the thoughts from it.

"Look, Mack, I can go back to my own room. You don't have to do anything you don't want to."

"And how would that look? Why, I'd be laughed out of the Special Forces."

"If your only concern is your image in the Special Forces, then I'm leaving."

"That didn't come out the way I wanted it to, Robin," he said. "I meant it as a joke. You used to be able to take a joke, even if it was in bad taste."

"Maybe it has something to do with your running off without a word. You know that I'll respect the secrecy of your missions. You can trust me."

Gerber shrugged. "I'm sorry. I would like you to accompany me to my room."

She softened. "Well, then, if that's how you feel, I'd love to go with you."

At last they stopped at the door to his room. He fished out his key, unlocked the door and pushed it open. Morrow entered and Gerber followed, hitting the light switch as he slammed the door.

The room was small, large enough for only a single, worn chair, his neatly made bed and a wardrobe against the wall that held his clean uniforms, civilian clothes and the little he owned that didn't belong to the army. The air conditioner, built into the wall under the window, had been turned off, and the room was uncomfortably hot and humid. Gerber moved to the air conditioner and hit the button. The motor started, the compressor rattled, and cool air began seeping into the room immediately.

Morrow joined him at the window, opened the curtains and looked out onto the lighted streets of Saigon. Neon blinked colorfully below them. People, thousands of them, walked up and down the street, with hundreds more in cars and Lambrettas. It certainly didn't look like a city at war. She turned and glanced at Gerber. "Has it been very rough?"

He shrugged. How did you answer a question like that? Anything you said sounded like a line. Yes, terribly rough. No, not really. A play for sympathy, or an act of bravery.

Instead, he dodged the question. He took her and kissed her once, feeling her lips under his, her body against his. Finally he broke the kiss and moved away so that he could close the curtains. He stood there for an instant and looked down into the Saigon streets. It was always the same down there. Thousands of people out hustling under the cover of darkness. Everyone pretending there was no tomorrow because for some of them there wouldn't be.

Morrow moved to the bed and sat down. "I don't know what you want me to do."

"That's the thing," said Gerber as he turned from the window. "I don't know what I want you to do, either. My mind seems to have stopped functioning."

"Well, thanks," she said.

Gerber moved so that he was standing with his back to the air conditioner, letting the coolness blow on him. He studied her. "It's not you. I'm tired and I've got a lot on my mind. More, with this damn congressional committee showing up."

"That has nothing to do with you," she said. "They come and go and have nothing to do with you."

"No, they don't, at least not directly. But it will affect me one way or another."

"Meaning?"

"You really want to hear this?"

Now she grinned. "Of course not. But you seem to want to talk about it."

"You want a drink? I've got some Beam's."

"Sure."

Gerber disappeared into the bathroom and returned with two glasses. He unlocked the wardrobe and took out the bottle sitting there. After holding it up to the light, as if inspecting it, he opened it, poured two fingers into a glass for himself and took a deep drink. "Smooth," he said. Then he sloshed some into a glass for Morrow.

She took a drink, then set the glass on the floor near her feet. "I can go if you'd prefer."

"No, Robin, I want you to stay here."

"So, what would you like to do then? Talk about the congressional committee?"

"Not really. I just get tired of all these people who don't understand the nature of war, who don't want to understand it and then make pronouncements about it or direct it. I wish they'd let us get on with the business of fighting it."

"Civilian control of the military is mandated by the constitution," said Morrow, wondering why she was prolonging the debate. It was one of the last things she wanted to talk about.

"I'm not asking for control of the military to be switched into the hands of the general staff or the Pentagon. I'm saying that once we're caught up in a war, let us do the job we're paid to do. Now more civilians who refuse to understand are going to try to learn something about a disaster that didn't happen."

"I've heard this tune before."

Gerber took another sip of the bourbon. "Yes, you have."

She leaned back and crossed her legs, letting her skirt ride higher. "So let's talk about something else, since we've exhausted that discussion."

Gerber finished his drink and set the glass on the floor out of the way. "All right. You pick a topic."

She reached up and began to unbutton her blouse. "How about us?"

Suddenly Gerber felt the tension drain from him. His worries about the congressional committee and the news media evaporated. All he could think about was Morrow. He moved toward her and said, "Good topic."

13

IN THE AIR
OVER THE PACIFIC

The layover in Hawaii was only eight hours, long enough for everyone to rest and get a decent meal at the hotel. For rest aboard the aircraft, the senators and congressmen used the bunks in the rear, but the seats were wide, well spaced and could be reclined so that they were almost as good as beds.

Halpren sat next to the window and watched as the sun disappeared in the west. For a long time it seemed to hang on the horizon, a glowing orange ball that was reluctant to set. The sky around it was a red-orange that tapered into violet and finally black as the stars popped out.

When the sun finally disappeared, leaving them cruising through the night, Halpren turned, but Drake had already gone to sleep, using a pillow and an OD green blanket a stewardess had supplied.

Halpren sat up for a moment and looked around the interior of the aircraft. There was a group of four people near the front, a single light burning above them. They had a deck of cards and were using matchsticks for chips as they gambled. Halpren thought about joining them and then decided against it. He'd have to crawl over Drake and would probably wake her. Instead, he pulled his briefcase off the floor, opened it and took out a paperback novel. He read for a few minutes and then realized he was tired. Putting down the book, he turned off the small overhead light and pushed the seat back.

Sunrise woke him hours later. He opened his eyes, glanced around, then closed them again. He was still quite tired. Quiet conversation issued from the front of the plane. He rolled onto his side, couldn't get comfortable, then flopped onto his back.

"You awake?" asked Drake.

"Yeah."

"We're going to be landing in about forty minutes or so. We're getting close."

Halpren groped with his fingers, found the button and raised the back of his seat. He opened his mouth, then closed it. Blinking, he rubbed his face and felt the stubble on his chin and cheeks. "Won't be soon enough for me."

Bishop appeared then, leaning in toward them, a hand on the back of the seats in front of them. Smiling, he said, "You two look awful."

"Thank you," said Drake.

"You can use the bathroom in the rear to clean up," the senator told them.

Drake pulled her blanket off and stood up. "I will, thank you."

Bishop moved out of her way, and as she disappeared beyond the bulkhead, he sat down next to Halpren. "So, how's it going?"

Halpren shrugged. "A few aches and pains, but it wasn't as bad as I thought it would be."

"You got something going with Drake?" he asked.

Halpren took a deep breath, then exhaled slowly. "Not really. We've had a couple of dinners, that sort of thing. But nothing serious."

"If you've got something going, I don't want to step on any toes."

"Well, sir," said Halpren, "we don't have anything serious going on. I doubt we'll ever have anything serious."

"Then I won't worry about it," said Bishop. "Just wanted to check things out."

Bishop got up and moved away. Halpren turned and noticed that the poker game was still going on. Just what in hell was he supposed to have said to Bishop? he wondered to himself. The senator wanted to know if Halpren had possession of Drake. The man didn't want to step on toes, so he followed the old male ritual of asking the competition to get lost. As Bishop's employee, there was nothing Halpren could say except that he and Drake had nothing going on. Then he had to take a step back to let the boss through. Any other course would be suicide. If he made waves Bishop would eventually find a reason to get rid of him.

He stared out the window at the bright white clouds. There was nothing he could do, he told himself, even though he really did want to spend more time with Drake. She was an intelligent woman, who didn't want to go shopping all the time or talk about soap operas. Oh, she did do those things, but she could also talk about the war in Vietnam, the space race and the Great Society. And when they tired of that, she even knew who the Washington Redskins were and why they hated the Dallas Cowboys. Halpren wished he was as well versed in soap operas as she was in football.

She returned then and sat down. Grinning broadly, her breath smelling like mint-flavored toothpaste, she said, "I guess it's your turn."

"Yeah, my turn." He moved down the aisle and walked back into the opulence that was the domain of the senators and congressmen. One of the women was sitting in a chair, wearing only her panties. She didn't seem concerned that everyone could see her naked breasts. Since she didn't care about it, Halpren tried to ignore her, but failed. He had to stare. She smiled at him.

Inside the little bathroom he found a disposable razor, a toothbrush wrapped in cellophane, toothpaste and shaving cream. Towels were plentiful, and surprisingly, there was hot water, too.

He shaved, washed his face and brushed his teeth. Finished, he felt better, though he had a dull ache in the back of his head, probably from sleeping in the seat. A big breakfast on the ground, a nap, and he'd be as good as new.

Leaving the bathroom and the rear compartment, he saw that Bishop was sitting with Drake, talking to her quietly. He thought about interrupting, playing ignorant, but knew that would gain him nothing. Instead he walked to the front where the poker game was running out of steam.

"New blood," said one of the players. "Too bad we're about to break up."

"Maybe on the next leg," said Halpren.

"Some of us are running a little too low on money for another session."

Halpren turned just as the pilot announced they were beginning the approach to Clark Air Force Base. He asked everyone to sit down and buckle up.

Halpren returned to his seat, slipping past Bishop and Drake. As he sat down, Drake smiled at him and rolled her eyes. Bishop didn't see the expression. She then turned back, facing the senator, a smile pasted on her face. "I don't know," she said. "I'm very tired. What all is planned for today?"

"I think we've got a briefing on the situation in Vietnam and on what we'll need to know while in-country," Bishop told her.

"I'm really tired."

Bishop patted her knee. "We'll leave it open for now, depending on what has to be accomplished here. I do know that we've arranged a couple of tours, and I'll want to talk to the boys from back home."

"We'll have to see," said Drake.

Bishop got up and walked to the bulkhead, disappearing into the rear. As he did, Drake looked at Halpren. "What in hell's going on now?"

"What?"

She glanced at the rear, as if looking for Bishop. "He swooped in on me and wanted to know if I'd have dinner with him tonight. Said something about a small reception for the congressional committee and their personal guests, but not for the whole staff. Thought I'd like to go with him."

"Maybe you should."

"What? How can you say that?"

Halpren shrugged. "Well, it's only a single dinner and he's in a position to do a lot of good for you in your career."

"You suggesting I sleep with him so that I can advance my career?"

Halpren glanced out the window and then back at Drake. "No, I'm only saying that a dinner won't hurt you."

"I thought we were going to eat together tonight."

"It's not that important. We can have dinner some other time."

She stared at him, the anger unmistakable. "You pimping for him now?"

"Jesus, Julie, there's no reason to get angry about this. I didn't mean anything, except that one evening with the senator isn't going to kill you. I wasn't telling you to sleep

with him or anything else. I was just saying that you should
do this if you want."

"Well, I don't want."

"Fine, then tell him you don't want to." Halpren turned
to look out the window again. Now there was land underneath the aircraft. He could see trees, buildings, cars and
people. They were getting close to touchdown.

"I will," she said.

As they fell silent, the plane slipped closer to the ground
and landed with only a single, almost imperceptible bounce.
The engines roared and the aircraft slowed rapidly, turning
from the runway and proceeding along the taxiway. In only
a few minutes they were parked on the concrete ramp and
one of the stewardesses had opened the door, letting in the
tropical heat, humidity and odor.

A moment later a man appeared at the front and said,
"Gentlemen, and ladies, we'll have a bus out here in a few
seconds to pick you up. There'll be a quick reception in the
VIP lounge in base operations, and then an opportunity to
get something to eat and head for your quarters to catch a
nap or to clean up."

The bus arrived and they were escorted off into the heat
of a tropical morning, the sky to the west gray-black and
boiling. There was a breeze from the ocean, smelling of salt
and fish. It was stiff enough to bend some of the trees and
nearly knock people off their feet as it gusted around them.

As soon as everyone was on the bus, the officer who had
greeted them took his place at the front again and grinned.
"Should have warned you about the wind. It's gusting up
to about forty miles an hour now and blowing steady at fifteen to twenty. Worst it's been in about a month."

He touched the driver on the shoulder and the bus headed
toward a low building at the edge of the airfield, pulling up
near a single door away from the expanse of glass that

marked the operations area. "Please follow me," their guide said.

The bus driver opened the door and the officer conducting them dodged out to the building. He opened that door, holding on to it with one hand, but leaning his hip into it so that the wind couldn't catch it. His other hand held his flight cap on his head.

The fact-finding party filed out of the bus and into the VIP lounge. It wasn't as posh as the one at Andrews, because the prestige of those who usually visited it was less. Rarely did anyone as important as a senator fly into Clark. A few generals, government employees, a Hollywood star on a goodwill tour, but rarely congressmen or senators, and never the President. Still, it was a pleasant lounge with wood paneling, comfortable couches and chairs that were just a little worn and dirty, a refrigerator in the corner, a TV sitting on a table, and a rack of magazines and paperback books. No one was assigned to wait on the VIPs.

A general came forward, his hand out, and said, "I'm General McWhorter. Welcome to the Philippines."

Bishop pushed his way to the front and offered a hand. "Thank you, General."

McWhorter made his way around the room, shaking hands and introducing himself. "We have a breakfast laid on at the officers' club for those who'd like it. After that, we've got a briefing prepared by a couple of men who have flown combat missions over Vietnam, and with a Green Beret who was in the hospital recovering from wounds received in the fighting. That is, if everyone's agreeable."

Bishop didn't wait for the others to decide. "Let's get at it, General."

McWhorter smiled and waved a hand. The door opened again and the officer guiding them said, "Please. This way to the bus."

They all trooped back out toward the bus, but Bishop stopped short and asked, "General, is someone taking care of our luggage?"

"Don't worry about that. You'll find your suitcases in your quarters."

"Very good."

Once they were all on the bus, it left the flight line, driving through the gate of a high chain-link fence and onto the base. They drove down streets lined with buildings, some of them partially hidden by thick growths of palm trees or tropical bushes. There were lacy ferns, the leaves delicate, and rubber trees with large, flat leaves that looked plastic, and there were flowering bushes covered with bright flowers. Sunlight filtered down through the growing cloud cover. The blackness in the west was spreading toward them rapidly.

They pulled into the parking lot of a low, sprawling building with a stone facade. Gardens, tended by Filipinos in khaki, surrounded the building. An American flag on a high pole flapped violently in the wind. The building's overhang shaded the glass double doors that led into the building.

McWhorter, who had ridden the bus and had stayed up front with the senators and congressmen, was off first, opening the door. He held it as the politicians walked through and then turned the duty over to another officer, letting him hold it for the aides who followed.

"Not exactly the royal treatment for us peons," said Halpren.

"What did you expect?" asked Drake as she pushed past him.

They entered the club and found themselves in a foyer with a ticket booth at one end. Stairs rose to the left and a hallway extended to the right. They headed down the hallway, decorated with pictures of Air Force planes, ranging from World War I fighters to the most modern bombers.

Eventually they came to brown double doors. Inside, the table, covered in white cloth, was long and U-shaped. There were chairs at the bottom of the U for the general and the senators. The congressmen would flank them, then a couple of colonels who were already there, waiting, and finally the congressional aides. Off to one side, near a bank of windows that looked out on the base and the greenery all around, stood a line of waiters. They were Air Force enlisted men, who wore clean, newly pressed white coats and dark pants.

Halpren stood behind a chair as far from the head of the table as he could. Drake got the one next to him. She leaned over and asked, "You trying to ditch me?"

"Never," he said.

As soon as the senators and congressmen were all there, they sat down, and as soon as they were seated, everyone else sat, too. The servers broke ranks and moved among the guests, pouring juice into the waiting glasses. Then they brought plates of food. Eggs, scrambled, fried and poached, were set on the table, followed by potatoes, toast, rolls, jam, bacon, ham and sausage. Cold or hot cereal, as well as coffee and tea, were also available.

Everyone dug in, passing the food around, and when a serving plate was nearly empty, a waiter moved in to replace it with another. Glasses were refilled before they were empty, and cups were kept brimming with steaming coffee.

At first conversation was quiet, as people concentrated on their meal. But toward the end, as the plates were emptied, two men carrying equipment entered the room. At the open end of the U, they set up a screen. A slide projector was positioned near the table with a remote control hooked into it.

The room lights were dimmed and the projector was turned on.

McWhorter stood. "If no one has any objections, we'll get started with the briefing."

"Please," said Bishop.

Two officers walked in and stood together. A third man, wearing a khaki uniform with stripes on the sleeve, followed them and took up a position behind them. The third man was the Green Beret who would tell them what was happening in South Vietnam.

"Gentlemen, and ladies." McWhorter bowed in the direction of the female aides. "With your permission, we'll give you a quick overview of the situation in Vietnam. Once the briefing is concluded, Captain Anderson, Lieutenant Davis and Sergeant Bocker of the Army's Special Forces will take questions."

One of the men moved forward and picked up the remote control. He hit the button and advanced the slides so that a map of Vietnam was visible. Then he grinned at everyone. "There's one thing everyone should know about Vietnam. It's something that sort of defines the whole place and brings it into focus for those who know nothing about it other than that it's a country in Southeast Asia."

He touched the button again and the slide changed. It showed jungle, but in the center of the frame was a small black-and-white snake. "There are a hundred varieties of snake in Vietnam. Ninety-nine of them are poisonous." He hesitated, letting that sink in, then added, "The other one will swallow you whole."

"Well, shit," said Bishop.

"Yes, sir," said the briefer. "That about covers it."

14

BIEN HOA COMPLEX

Staab sat in his bunker, his feet propped on the rough table, and stared at the dim light bulb hanging from a wire. The interior was cooler than outside, but still hot and humid, and to make matters worse, everything smelled musty. Coats had compared the odor to rotting garbage, a mildewed basement or an open grave. Staab had pretended not to hear the comment about graves.

Finally he looked over to where Coats sat reading a magazine. "You know, we didn't accomplish much by our little trip into the field."

Coats closed the magazine. "We learned that Charlie's alive and well in Tay Ninh Province."

Staab dropped his feet to the floor and leaned forward, his elbows on the table. "But now we have to act on the information. We gather intelligence, we pass it up the chain, but we never act on it. We've gotten our hands on some very good stuff, and once again we're not acting on it."

"Those Green Berets said they'd take care of it." Coats tossed his magazine onto the table. "They didn't want the information contaminated by allowing it to leak out to the South Vietnamese."

"So they claimed. But I think we could get the intelligence into the hands of the Twenty-fifth at Tay Ninh or Dau Tieng and have them act on it. It would keep the South Vietnamese completely out of the picture and allow us to do something positive for a change."

"I don't know, sir."

"Think about it, Tom. We bust our butts learning things. We risk our lives to get some of the information and then we report it through channels. What happens to it then?"

"Well, sir, the commanders of various units analyze the data we provide, see how it impacts on their specific assignments and act on it."

"Or not, as the mood moves them," said Staab. "And to make it worse, we never see any results. Hell, everything we do here might end up in the dumpster."

Coats didn't say a word.

"If I thought we were accomplishing anything here, not just at Bien Hoa, but in Vietnam, I'd stay on, extend for another tour, but I don't see that. I see us fucking around, playing at war, while handing all the advantages to the enemy. We accomplish nothing."

Coats got up and walked around, first toward the table and then back, deeper into the bunker, as if to hide in the shadows.

"Now we know something we can force into the forefront. We can go to a battalion commander or a brigade commander and say, 'Sir, we've got some hot intel. We've got some really hot shit. Let's act on it.'"

"That's not our job," said Coats.

"So what? If everyone had that attitude, nothing would ever get done. We all have job descriptions, so we stick close to them. We never venture out. We do nothing heroic or historic. We sit in our bunker—" Staab waved a hand around the room "—and say it's not our job."

"But it's not, sir. We provide the intel and send it up channels so that others can act on it."

"Then we'll make a recon into the field to gather more data. That's part of our job."

"We've done that already."

Staab stood. "I think we should take steps to see that this intel is acted upon. Hell, we know where Charlie is and we know what he's doing. We should go out and get him. Find him in his camps and kick his ass."

Coats took a deep breath and knew he was about to ask the question that shouldn't be asked. It would encourage the lieutenant to carry on with his fantasy. "Just how are you going to do this?"

Staab waved him over and pointed at the chair, but the sergeant stayed on his feet and paced. "Easy. We approach one of the battalion commanders who has people out in the field looking for Charlie, and tell him we can lead him to an enemy nest. Tell him we've got good intel about Charlie."

"Then we come back here?" asked Coats hopefully.

"Hell, no! We go with them in search of the enemy. Gives us more intel, and let's us see how the intel we provide is used. Makes the whole job worthwhile."

"I don't know, sir. Seems like we're moving in a direction we don't need to. Most guys in the field would pay good money to sit back here in this bunker and analyze the data. Keeps us out of the shooting."

"You want to tell your grandkids you sat in a bunker during the war?"

"At least by doing that I know I'll have grandkids. Besides, sir, what's this sudden desire to get the hell out of here? Used to be you were content to sit in here, read the documents, draw on the charts and never go outside."

Staab stood and faced Coats. "I don't know what it is. Maybe I just don't want to tell my grandkids I stayed in the bunker for the year I was here. Doesn't sound right."

"I say again, sir, at least I'd be around to have the grandkids." He grinned broadly. "Besides, by the time I have grandkids, nobody's going to know what the fuck happened here. I can make up some good stories and the grandkids will be happy."

Ignoring the lecture, Staab said, "I think it's time we catch a ride to Tay Ninh or Dau Tieng and see what we can do there."

Coats decided to try one last time. "Those Green Berets said they were going to do something."

"And if they do, fine, but if they don't, then our hard work will have gone down the drain. Besides, you want to live forever?"

"No, sir, I just want to live long enough to DEROS."

It didn't take Staab long to arrange a chopper ride out to Tay Ninh. They had to detour to Song Be, where the Special Forces camp needed some critical supplies, but then the helicopter was heading for Tay Ninh. Staab was told they could ride along if they didn't mind the detour.

They flew out to Song Be, strapped into the rear of the chopper, the jungle spread out under them like an unbroken sea of green. Rising in the south was the black shape of Nui Ba Den. Staab stared at the mountain until the aircraft turned and he lost sight of it.

They landed at Song Be on a long, red slash in the green vegetation. On the northwestern side of the strip was the camp, a star-shaped affair with a raised redoubt in the center. Opposite it, on the eastern side of the runway, was a village, and on the south side of that was a dump filled with cardboard boxes, paper, old tires and anything else the

Americans no longer wanted and the villagers had yet to take.

They were on the ground for only a few seconds. The swirling cloud of red dust kicked up by the chopper hadn't had time to settle before they were off again, climbing out to the south. Staab watched as the camp fell away, glad he wasn't stuck in the middle of a jungle surrounded by six strands of wire, with only a couple of hundred Montagnards to help in the defense if Charlie made a push at the camp.

Keeping to policy on ash-and-trash flights, they climbed to three thousand feet and headed southwest toward Tay Ninh. The city of Tay Ninh, to the east, contained over a million people, and the American base next to it was one of the largest. They approached the camp from the north. Staab could see the main runway with revetments on both sides for the aircraft based there. South of that, inside the perimeter, was the refueling point, which contained giant black tanks that held jet fuel. They were a target for enemy gunners and had once been hit. Flames had leaped 150 feet into the air. Fire fighters hadn't been able to put the blaze out, and it had burned until all the fuel had been consumed.

The rest of the camp was a series of dirt roads and one-story hootches. Some were long and narrow, the rusting tin on the roofs reflecting the blazing tropical sun. Sandbagged bunkers, all the dull green of the rubberized sandbags now in use, were omnipresent. There were also jeeps and trucks on the roads, hundreds of them, kicking up clouds of red dust that blew around the camp and settled on everything, making the place look like an enormous bleeding wound.

They hovered over the runway, then turned east and touched down near the control tower where there was a makeshift terminal. Staab and Coats hopped out. Once Staab was outside the rotor disk, he turned and held up a hand to thank the pilots for the ride. As he did, they pulled pitch, which increased the wind and created a huge cloud of red dust.

When the chopper was gone and it was quiet, Coats turned and asked, "Now what?"

Staab shrugged. "We find a ride over to the Twenty-fifth's area and then try to talk one of the battalion commanders into listening to us."

"Not much of a plan," said Coats.

Staab turned and walked over to a Spec Four sitting in a jeep, looking as if he wasn't sure what he was supposed to be doing. Like almost all of the soldiers in South Vietnam, he was young. "Need to get over to the Twenty-fifth's area."

The man opened his eyes, wiped the sweat from his forehead with the sleeve of his jungle fatigues and looked at Staab. His uniform was dirty, rust-colored from the coating of dust on it. He pointed down the road. "Just walk along there."

"I don't suppose you could give us a lift."

"Nope. Waiting for the first shirt. I miss him and he'll have my ass."

"I'm a lieutenant," said Staab.

The soldier looked at him. "But you ain't my first sergeant."

Staab laughed. "Good point. Down this road, you say?"

"Yes, sir. You'll come to the First Battalion's area and then Brigade Headquarters."

"Thanks." Staab waved a hand.

Coats shouldered his weapon and the two of them walked down the road, which had ditches on either side choked with gray, sickly weeds. They walked along under the hot sun, and were sweating before they had gotten very far. A jeep raced by and one of the men in it held up a hand, the middle finger raised.

"Now why would he do that?" asked Staab.

"Telling you he's got a ride, so fuck you."

"Nice attitude," said Staab.

The dust settled on their wet skin, turning to mud, then caking. It covered their uniforms and got into their mouths and noses, making the walk even more miserable.

"Why don't they spray something on the roads to reduce the dust?" asked Staab.

"Lieutenant, we didn't have to come out here. We could have stayed at Bien Hoa, sitting in our bunker and not worrying about such things."

Staab took the hint and shut up. A few minutes later they reached the First Battalion area. A main building, larger than the rest, sat near the road, along with a parking lot filled with jeeps. A white sign near the door announced the headquarters of the First Battalion, Third Brigade, Twenty-fifth Infantry Division, Lieutenant Colonel Homer P. Stanwick, commanding. The first sergeant was Billy Joe Renfield.

"Looks like a good place to start," said Staab.

"Sir, how's it going to look to these guys when we just drop in out of nowhere? There's no reason for these guys to believe us."

"And no reason for them to doubt us." Staab walked up to the door and entered.

It was typical of the hootches in South Vietnam—a dirty plywood floor, one-by-tens set at an angle to make a wall that reached halfway to the ceiling, and then screen to let the air circulate. A desk stood near the door, with one man in a sweat-stained OD shirt sitting behind it. Behind him were

OD green filing cabinets, a badly dented wall locker and a footlocker topped by a fan roaring at full speed.

"Yeah?" said the man at the desk.

"I'd like to see Colonel Stanwick."

"Colonel's not here."

Staab looked down at the young man. He had light blond hair, a scar on his forehead and the beginning of a mustache that marked him as a new arrival in Vietnam. Around his neck he wore dog tags, the chain threaded through a thin plastic tube that was supposed to keep the chain from leaving a mark on the neck.

"When will he be back?"

"Later. Went over to Brigade. Said he'd be back later."

Staab was about to give up when a man entered the building. He glanced at the man sitting at the desk. "Hobbs, I'll be in my office."

Hobbs got up. "Sir, this man would like to see you."

Stanwick looked at Staab. "Do I know you, Lieutenant?"

"No, sir."

"You assigned to me?"

"No, sir."

"What do you want?"

Staab glanced at Coats and then back at Stanwick. "It's something we should discuss in private."

"I have a lot of work to do." He hesitated, then said, "Come with me. I don't have much time." He turned and headed toward his office.

The office was completely enclosed, plywood from floor to ceiling. An air conditioner, built into the wall, pumped out cold air. A desk sat in the corner, facing the door, and along one wall was a bright orange settee. One end of the room, the conference area, held a table with six chairs.

Stanwick unbuckled his pistol belt and took off the harness. He dropped it on top of his desk. His uniform was stained with sweat in the places the harness had covered. He turned, rubbed a hand over the salt-and-pepper bristles of his short-cropped hair, then sat down. With a bullet-shaped head, a thick neck and broad shoulders, he looked like a defensive lineman just beginning to turn fat. "Now, what can I do for you?"

"Colonel Stanwick," said Staab, "it's more what I can do for you."

"Sit down," said Stanwick, gesturing at a chair, "and stop sounding like a salesman."

"Yes, sir. A little background. I'm an intelligence officer assigned to Bien Hoa, but in the past few days we've picked up indications that something is building around here. Specifically we've learned of a buildup around Tay Ninh and in the vicinity of Nui Ba Den."

"I've seen nothing to indicate anything going on around Nui Ba Den. Seen more activity around here."

Staab shrugged. "The activity's inside the mountain. We think there's a camp in there."

Stanwick leaned back in his chair and looked up at the ceiling. Plywood had been nailed to the rafters, enclosing the office for the air-conditioning. He tented his fingers under his chin. "I'm not convinced my men are equipped to handle an attack on an underground system."

"Colonel, you spend days in the field looking for the enemy. You search villages, jungle and forest. You chase intelligence reports, all to find and make contact with the enemy. I'm telling you where they are. We need to go get them."

"Show me on the map."

Staab shrugged. "I don't have a map with me."

Stanwick stood and moved to the door. He opened it, peeked out and said, "Hobbs, get us a map of Nui Ba Den." Stanwick stood in the doorway for a moment, took the map from Hobbs and returned to his desk after shutting the door. He unfolded the map and spread it out. "Now tell me what you know."

Staab got up and moved to the desk. He bent over it, examined the map, then pointed at the western slope. "I was in contact with a small NVA unit here yesterday. Given the direction the enemy came from, coupled with observations, some of them from the Twenty-fifth, and some of the documentation we captured, we know the enemy has a stronghold on the slopes of the mountain."

"Hell," said Stanwick, "we all know that. It's been a rumor ever since I got here. We hold the top and bottom and Charlie has the center."

"Now we know for sure. I have in my possession a document that proves Charlie has a base hidden in the mountain. Quite a large base."

Stanwick held out a hand. "Let me see it."

"I don't have it with me," said Staab. "It's classified. It's an individual diary, but the information contained in it is credible."

"Can I see it?" asked Stanwick.

Staab hesitated, then said, "I suppose, except that will just eat up more time. We need to hit the field before any more of the enemy get out of Cambodia and into the mountain."

"I won't be stampeded into a decision, Lieutenant. You say I can see this diary."

"Yes, sir. It's in Vietnamese. We've had part of it translated in Saigon. That told us what we had. When Special Forces finished with it, they gave it back to me and I took it to Bien Hoa. We've got it locked in a safe there."

"Who all saw it in Saigon?"

"Is that important?"

Stanwick shrugged. "You've asked me to commit my people to a fight where some of them will get hurt and others will die. You want me to do that on my faith in you, a lieutenant I've never seen before this afternoon."

"We talked to Jerry Maxwell at MACV. Translation was done by a Major Shorack. I don't know who he's assigned to."

"You wait here," said Stanwick.

"Yes, sir."

Stanwick left the office. Staab sat quietly for a moment and then stood. He walked over to the conference area where weapons were mounted on the wall, AKs and SKSs captured in various fights with the VC and NVA. They weren't all that interesting to someone who saw the results of such firefights on a daily basis. He walked around, searching for something interesting, but didn't want to snoop.

He grinned at the thought. Technically his job was to snoop. As an intelligence officer, he should be reading everything in sight, trying to fit all the pieces of the puzzle together, although it was hard to justify snooping on his own side.

He sat down, crossed his legs and forced himself to relax. He knew what Stanwick was doing. He was calling MACV to see if he could locate Major Shorack or Jerry Maxwell. If he found one of them, he would, by talking in circles to maintain security, learn if he, Staab, had been there with a diary. Once he had the answers to his questions and was satisfied with them, Stanwick would return and start to plan the mission. All Staab had to do was remain calm and not fuck up.

It didn't take as long as he'd thought it would. Stanwick was back with two other staff officers, carrying a load of charts. As the colonel entered, he snapped his fingers at Staab. "Over here, Lieutenant."

Staab walked to the conference area as the other officers sat down. Stanwick didn't bother introducing them. Instead, he spread out the maps, close-up charts that showed the slopes of Nui Ba Den in great detail.

"Now, where did you run into that enemy patrol?" Stanwick asked.

Staab moved so that he could see the map. He pointed. "In this general area."

"And you say the enemy was moving from the north toward the south?"

"Yes, sir, when we sprang the ambush."

"Do you know where the entrances are?"

Staab looked up into Stanwick's face. "No, sir, not exactly, but given what we know about the mountain slopes, enemy operations and the placement of our own forces, I suspect they're in this general area, no more than two, three hundred feet from the surrounding ground."

"Do you know what to look for?" asked one of the seated officers.

"If you mean, do I know how the enemy conceals the entrances to the tunnel systems, the answer's yes. I know what to look for."

Stanwick straightened and wiped a hand over his face. He stared at Staab. "I don't have to tell you that I made a few inquiries and I learned a few things about you. If I hadn't been sufficiently impressed, I'd have thrown you out. Since I didn't, it means I want to look for this enemy stronghold."

"Yes, sir."

"I'm doing it for two reasons. One is that the information looks good and I'm told you're reliable."

"Thank you, Colonel."

"The second is that we want to beat Special Forces to the punch. Those people are always getting the good press and all the glory. They think we grunts can't do anything right. They believe we aren't soldiers, just screwups who can't get real jobs in the civilian world. If it wasn't for Special Forces, they say, there would be no Army today. Just once I'd like to show the press that the regular Army can do something right. Show the press *and* Special Forces."

Staab laughed. "Yes, sir."

"We'll hit the field just after dawn tomorrow."

Staab nodded. "Might I suggest we hit the field a little earlier than that. Use the darkness to get into position."

"All right," said Stanwick. "Tomorrow morning we hit the field. Gentlemen, we have a lot of work to do tonight."

Staab pulled out a chair and slipped into it. As he watched the men begin to work, he realized it had been easier to convince someone to take the mission than he'd thought it would be. Show up, tell the commander where the enemy is hiding and the next thing you know, the mission's on.

Yeah, he thought. Real easy.

15

THE CONTINENTAL
SHELF, SAIGON

Gerber got out of his hotel room and then out of the hotel, figuring that if no one with the exception of Fetterman could find him, they couldn't give him bad news or assign him to a dirty detail. Morrow was still sleeping in the room, the noise from the air conditioner's compressor covering the little sound that Gerber had made as he'd showered, shaved, dressed and escaped.

He thought about eating in the hotel, but it would be too easy to locate him there. Instead, he stepped into the muggy heat of the morning, surprised that the night hadn't brought relief. But then, in Saigon, there was rarely any relief from the heat. The stone, concrete and buildings trapped the heat the way a greenhouse did, holding it close to the ground and baking everyone. And the humidity didn't help. The moisture made life in Saigon more uncomfortable, more miserable than anything else.

Even though he had showered, and just left an air-conditioned room, he was sweating before he walked a block. He wiped a hand over the back of his neck, which was soaked already.

Finally he came to the Continental Shelf, an outdoor café outside the Continental Hotel. Gerber entered it, found an empty table with a brightly colored umbrella shading it and sat down. A copy of the *Stars and Stripes*, left by the last customer, lay on one of the chairs.

Picking up the paper, Gerber saw that the congressional delegation had arrived in the Philippines for initial briefings and a layover before they proceeded to Vietnam. That was nice, Gerber thought. Let them rest and eat well in a safe environment while soldiers rode jammed together in commercial airliners that flew almost nonstop to Vietnam.

The waiter appeared and Gerber ordered a big breakfast, as he did every time he found himself in Saigon with a little time to himself. He ordered orange juice, steak, fried eggs, hash browns and coffee, a big breakfast to make up for the meals he missed when in the field.

Crossing his legs, Gerber looked out at the street filled with people. Pedestrians. Americans, Vietnamese and Europeans. Thousands of people, with only a handful of them involved in the war. The rest made money off the fighting. First there were the prostitutes, who worked hard for their cash, and then there were the profiteers. Men and women who were in Saigon because of the conflict and the opportunities it generated. American manufacturers who supplied hundreds of products. Men and women who ran the fancy equipment, technicians who installed it, salesmen with samples.

The waiter brought the orange juice and Gerber took a drink. It tasted bitter. He knew why. Although it was freshly squeezed, the hotel tried to wring every last drop from an orange, grinding it down to the rind. It gave the juice a slightly bitter taste.

The rest of the food arrived. Gerber glanced through the newspaper, when he wasn't watching the traffic. The din from the street covered the noise around him, and the odors that swirled through the air were masked by the smell of diesel fuel and exhaust fumes. It wasn't the best environment to eat in, and he suddenly wondered why he had decided on a sidewalk café. Maybe it was the prestige of eating there.

A shadow fell across his table. Had he been in the field, he would have dived for cover. Instead, he turned. "Morning, Master Sergeant," he said.

Fetterman pulled out a chair and sat down. "Morning, Captain. Didn't expect to see you for a couple of hours. Figured you'd be busy."

Gerber picked up a piece of toast and buttered it carefully. He took a bite, then asked, "Why did you figure that?"

"Well, you were with Miss Morrow."

"So?"

Fetterman shrugged. "So nothing. I went by your room, but no one answered the door."

"I left her there."

"Anyway, got a call a little while ago." Fetterman stared at Gerber for a moment. "Well, actually, I checked in with MACV a little while ago."

"Ah, Tony," said Gerber, "you know that will only get us both into trouble."

"Yes, sir, and it has."

Gerber groaned audibly and rolled his eyes. "Now what's happened?"

"I talked to Maxwell, who told me there was an inquiry about the validity of the data provided by one Lieutenant Staab. Maxwell replied that the information was good, and the party thanked him."

Gerber sat up. "Maxwell just passed out information like that?"

NO COST! NO OBLIGATION TO PURCHASE!

PLAY "LUCKY 7" AND GET AS MANY AS FIVE FREE GIFTS . . .

HOW TO PLAY

1. Get a coin and scratch off the silver area at the right. This makes you eligible to receive as many as four free books and a surprise mystery gift, depending on what is revealed beneath the scratch-off area.

2. You'll get hot-off-the-press Gold Eagle books, never before published. Send back this card and we'll send you the books and gift you may qualify for absolutely free!

3. And afterward, unless you tell us otherwise, we'll send you six action-packed books every other month to preview (two Mack Bolans, and one each of Able Team, Phoenix Force, SOB's and Vietnam: Ground Zero). If you decide to keep them, you'll pay only $2.49 per book—11% less than the suggested retail cover price—plus 95¢ postage and handling.

4. You must be completely satisfied, or you may return a shipment of books, at our cost or cancel at any time simply by noting so on your shipping statement.

GET YOUR FREE GIFTS NOW! MAIL THIS CARD TODAY!

PLAY "LUCKY 7"

Just scratch off the silver area above with a coin.
Then check below to see which gifts you get.

YES! I have scratched off the silver area above. Rush me any Free Books and Free Surprise Gift I may be entitled to. I understand that I am under no obligation to purchase any books. I may keep these free gifts and return my statement marked "cancel." If I do not cancel, then send me 6 brand-new Gold Eagle novels every second month as they come off the presses. Bill me at the low price of $2.49 for each book—a saving of 11% off the total suggested retail cover price for six books—plus 95¢ postage and handling per shipment. I can always return a shipment, at your cost, or cancel at any time. The Free Books and Surprise Gift remain mine to keep forever.

166 CIM PAP5

NAME _____

ADDRESS _____ Apt No _____

CITY _____ STATE _____ ZIP CODE _____

7 7 7	WORTH FOUR FREE BOOKS AND FREE SURPRISE GIFT
🍒 🍒 🍒	WORTH FOUR FREE BOOKS
● ● ●	WORTH THREE FREE BOOKS
🔔 🔔 🍒	WORTH TWO FREE BOOKS

GOLD EAGLE NO-BLUFF, NO-RISK GUARANTEE
- You're not required to buy a single book—ever!
- Even as a subscriber, you must be completely satisfied, or you may return a shipment of books, at our cost, or cancel anytime.
- The free books and gifts you receive from the "Lucky 7" offer remain yours to keep—in any case.

If offer card is missing, write to: Gold Eagle Reader Service, 901 Fuhrmann Blvd., P.O. Box 1867, Buffalo, NY 14269-1867.

GET YOUR FREE GIFTS NOW! MAIL THIS CARD TODAY!

BUSINESS REPLY CARD

First Class   Permit No. 717   Buffalo, NY

Postage will be paid by addressee

GOLD EAGLE READER SERVICE
901 Fuhrmann Blvd.
P.O. Box 1867
Buffalo, NY 14240-9952

NO POSTAGE
NECESSARY
IF MAILED
IN THE
UNITED STATES

Fetterman nodded. "Well, in all fairness to Maxwell, he merely indicated that Staab was reliable."

"Which means," said Gerber, "that someone's going to use the information."

"Yes, sir."

"Shit. If it's not handled right, it's going to be worthless."

"Thought you'd want to know."

Gerber looked at his breakfast. He hadn't made much of a dent in it, but there was no time to worry about things like that. "I think we'd better get over to MACV and see what happened. Then we'd better be prepared to move out into the field today."

"That mean we alert Captain Gallagher?"

"Not yet." He rubbed a hand over his chin. "Besides, Gallagher doesn't have enough men. We'll need a company of strikers." He glanced at the people in the restaurant around him and realized he was saying too much. He took his napkin, wiped his mouth and tossed it onto the table.

"Let's go."

"I've got a jeep," said Fetterman.

"Tony, I don't know how you do it. Everywhere you go you manage to promote transport."

"Easy, sir. We enlisted pukes have to take care of one another. You officers won't do it."

Gerber pulled out his wallet, opened it and tossed a ten-dollar MPC bill on the table. He was overpaying by five dollars, but he didn't care. "I'm right behind you."

They left the Continental Shelf, walked along, dodging the pedestrian traffic, and turned a corner. Fetterman's jeep sat parked in front of the Old California Bar of Exotic Delights. A GI sat on the hood and a dozen kids were standing around it, screaming at the man.

Gerber ignored the soldier, who looked as if he was too drunk to stand. He climbed into the passenger seat and waited.

Fetterman walked up to the man. "We're taking off now."

"Fine."

"You'll have to get off the hood."

The GI looked confused. "Oh, sorry." He leaped to the sidewalk and stood there, swaying back and forth. Hiccuping once, he giggled inanely. The kids pressed in close, their hands waving as they demanded money, candy or cigarettes.

"Where you going?" Fetterman asked the GI, ignoring the kids, knowing they would quickly spot another mark and take off.

"To the barracks. On my way there to get some sleep. Couldn't sleep downtown." He pronounced his words carefully, as if having trouble forming them.

"Come on," said Fetterman. "I'll give you a ride." The master sergeant grabbed the man's elbow and steered him to the driver's side of the jeep.

"I don't think I should drive," said the GI.

"Neither do I," said Fetterman. "You climb into the rear and I'll drive."

"Fine."

"Where are you going?" asked Fetterman.

"Tan Son Nhut."

"Perfect," said Fetterman. "The wrong direction."

"Why not let him sleep in the back while we take care of business," said Gerber. "We take him to Tan Son Nhut and some smartass MP is going to arrest him."

"Good point, sir," said Fetterman. "Hell, maybe some of you officers take care of the enlisted pukes, too."

"The old cavalry," said Gerber, "used to make sure the horses were fed and watered, then the men were cared for and finally the officers were allowed to eat. Heaven help the trooper who neglected his horse or the officer who neglected his soldiers.''

Fetterman unlocked the steering wheel and dropped the chain onto the floor. ''Sounds like the perfect system to me.''

He started the engine, checked the traffic and pulled out. They raced through Saigon, staying with the traffic, which had gone berserk. It was as if someone had decided to evacuate the city with only five minutes to spare. Fetterman kept both hands on the wheel, his eyes on the road, watching for someone trying to drive into him. Gerber held on to the handle on the dashboard and didn't say a word.

In the back, the GI was thrown around by the bumps in the road and the wild drive. He bounced off the seat, tried to scramble back up on it, then whooped, waving a hand over his head like a rodeo rider trying to stay on a bronco.

Finally they came to a side street, and Fetterman turned, getting them out of the rush. As they drove down the wide boulevard, he glanced over his shoulder and asked, ''What in hell was that?''

''Who knows?'' said Gerber. He released the handle and sat back in the seat, putting a foot up on the dashboard. ''Let's just head over to MACV.''

From the rear the GI asked, ''We going to slow down now?''

''I'm afraid so,'' Gerber told him.

Fetterman wound his way through a maze of streets, some of them residential, where the houses were little more than cardboard shacks and open sewers filled the air with the stench of human waste. Naked kids chased one another, while adults sat around doing nothing. There were wires overhead, tacked to poles, but none of the wires seemed to be connected to the houses. They had no electricity, indoor plumbing or telephone service. It was a temporary area that would wash away when the first monsoons came.

"Christ, what is that stink?" asked the GI.

"You know where you're going, Tony?"

Fetterman pointed to the left. "I know that the heart of the city is over there. I turn here, and we're back on track."

A few minutes later they rolled into the MACV parking lot. Fetterman looked at the man in the rear. He had slipped to the floor again and had his head tilted back, using the seat for a pillow. The man gasped once, then emitted a loud, buzzing snore.

"Fucker's asleep," said Fetterman.

They got out of the jeep and walked up to the double doors. "Maxwell?" asked Fetterman.

"Good place to start," said Gerber.

They walked downstairs, signed in at the iron gate and worked their way back to Maxwell's office. He answered their knock and waved them in.

"Figured you two would be here quickly." He returned to his desk and dropped into the chair behind it.

"All right, Jerry," said Gerber, taking the visitor's chair. "What in hell's going on?"

Maxwell picked up a file and made a production out of examining it. Finally he closed it. "Got a call from a Colonel Stanwick at the Twenty-fifth. Wanted to know if your young Lieutenant Staab was on the level."

"Over an insecure land line?" asked Fetterman.

"More or less," said Maxwell. "I merely told him that Staab had good information."

"But no one asked what that information was?" said Gerber.

"Mack, we know what it was. Stanwick was asking if the data you brought in was solid. I told him it was. Told him I had reservations because it was from a single source who couldn't be rated, but that Staab was reliable. Told him I didn't think Staab would lie about anything or overrate his data. He thanked me and that was it.''

"Meaning," said Fetterman, "that some leg is going to try to penetrate the tunnels on Nui Ba Den. He's not going to have a clue about what he's getting into, but he's going to try it anyway.''

"Shit," said Gerber.

"So what are you two going to do about it? What *can* you do about it?" asked Maxwell.

"You have any more on this? Anything that might have come in from other sources?" Gerber asked.

"On what?"

"Nui Ba Den. On what the hell's supposed to be going on in there.''

Maxwell shook his head. "We've got rumors, of course, just as you have. The rumors suggest the whole mountain is honeycombed with tunnels and caves, but we've got nothing positive, other than what you brought in.''

Fetterman, who was leaning against the filing cabinets, said, "I'd say that Stanwick will have his people in the field inside of twenty-four hours.''

"Shit," said Gerber again.

"Yes, sir. I would guess he'll field a company, probably two, and hold a third in reserve.''

"Jerry, I don't suppose you could do anything to stop this before it starts?''

"What would you have me do? I'm not in the chain of command, as you so often remind me. Any plea I make to the generals would be ignored.''

"This hasn't done us much good," said Gerber.

"What did you expect?" asked Maxwell.

Fetterman straightened. "I think the real problem is our young lieutenant. He didn't want to see his information go to waste, so he's out drumming up support."

Maxwell shifted around and looked at Fetterman. "So what are you going to do about it?"

Fetterman looked at Gerber. "Captain?"

"Head back out to the camp on top of Nui Ba Den," answered Gerber, "and try to get something organized before Staab and the legs fuck the whole thing up."

"That going to be possible?" asked Maxwell.

"Somehow," said Gerber, "I don't think it will be. I think we're in trouble on this."

16

EN ROUTE BETWEEN
THE PHILIPPINES AND
SOUTH VIETNAM

Halpren couldn't believe he was back on the plane. It seemed as if he had only been on the ground a few hours, though they had spent the afternoon and night at Clark. They had been shown the base, had toured the command post and flight line and had even been taken to Subic Bay to see one of the aircraft carriers, an impressive sight all by itself.

Now he was back on the airplane, making the relatively short flight to Saigon. He glanced to the left, where Drake had been sitting for most of the flight. Now that space was empty. She was sitting on the other side of the jet, refusing to speak to him, even refusing to look at him. She was pissed off. Her words. So pissed off that she couldn't see straight, and she didn't want anything to do with him now.

He turned and stared out the window at the swirling clouds below him and the sunlight blazing overhead. Cool air blew on him, and there was the constant, quiet roar of the jet engines. He was uncomfortable and unhappy.

He tried to force his mind from last evening's mess with Drake. She had dressed up, putting on her finest, waiting for him to call for her and escort her out for the evening arranged by the Air Force to impress the politicians.

But he'd never arrived. Instead, Bishop had shown up at her door. Halpren had hoped she would realize he hadn't had much of a choice, that she would spend the evening with the senator and then call him the minute she was free.

He'd seen them together in the officers' club where he had gone to eat dinner. It wasn't the special fare set aside for the senators, congressmen and their guests; the Air Force had arranged the party to keep the underlings happy. It would have worked, had Drake been there.

There had been dancing, with the young female officers and some of the locals who worked on the base. There had been an open bar, and liquor had flowed abundantly. Free food and free booze to the peons was the easiest way to make the big boys happy while they got the first-class treatment.

Bishop and the other politicians had put in an appearance, had a free drink and danced with some of the ladies. Halpren had used the opportunity to ask Drake if she wanted to dance.

"Why should I?" had been her response.

He had pulled her off the floor toward a darkened corner of the ballroom, where the sound of the music wasn't quite as deafening and where the shadows obscured them. A large rubber plant hid them and a fern in a basket made it seem as if they were in the jungle.

When they were alone, he asked, "What the hell kind of question was that?"

"You're a great one to ask."

Halpren studied her. Even in the half-light he could see she was angry. Her lips were pressed together in a thin line. Her face was flushed and her eyes flashed.

"I thought we had arranged all this," said Halpren.

"Great," she said. "You really are pimping for him."

He realized then that the argument that had begun on the airplane had never actually been resolved. He'd thought she would go out with the senator, make him happy and they'd all benefit from it. Now he fully realized he'd been happy with the solution, but she hadn't.

"I'm sorry about this misunderstanding...."

"I'll just bet," she said. She pushed past him and returned to the dance floor. He watched as she was stopped by one of the Air Force officers in a dress uniform. She smiled, then nodded, and they moved off to dance.

"Well, shit," he muttered, and headed for the bar, where he ordered a triple bourbon on the rocks and then decided he didn't want the ice.

She didn't call that night, and in the morning, in the VIP lounge where they were given doughnuts and coffee, she avoided him completely. Childishly she refused to speak to him when he finally maneuvered himself into a position that prevented her from fleeing. Instead, she pretended there was no one around until he gave up and walked over to the coffeepot for a refill.

When they boarded the plane, she stayed away from him, finding an empty seat far enough away that she wouldn't have to look at him.

"So," he said now, addressing the window, "I'd send her flowers if I could, but she'd probably just pull them apart."

Bishop slipped into the seat next to him. "Julie has it in for you."

"I was afraid of that," said Halpren.

Bishop grinned. "She didn't say one nice thing about you last night, though she didn't say anything particularly nasty, either. What did you do to her?"

"It was a misunderstanding that she won't let me explain." Halpren shrugged, then smiled weakly.

"Well, son, I'll tell you one thing. She's not a cooperative young lady. Ate the food, drank the booze and danced, but then insisted she was tired."

"We all are," said Halpren.

"You know what I mean. Don't pretend you don't. Anyway, there's no reason to pursue those who aren't interested when there are so many who are. Why, there was one little nurse last night, pretty little thing, who just threw herself at me. Real cute little blonde, but at the time I thought we had arranged for Miss Drake."

Gulping, Halpren decided to get a few things straight. "Excuse me, Senator, but I believe a real mistake has been made. I never talked to Julie about anything other than having dinner with you."

"Ah," Bishop said stiffly, "that explains it then. Well, I'm glad we had this little talk."

Before Halpren could say anything else, Bishop was on his feet. There was no time to try to explain to him and no chance to explain to Drake. Now he realized that not only was Julie mad at him for setting her up for a date with Bishop, but also the senator was mad at him because he hadn't done an adequate job of setting up the date. He'd tried to do a favor, and it had blown up in his face. Not exactly fair, but now that he knew the situation he'd be able to talk to Drake about it when she got over being mad. He wasn't sure he'd ever be able to explain it to Bishop.

Morosely he watched the world float under him. The clouds broke and he saw the ocean. There were some islands below, but he had no idea what they were. Then the clouds moved in and shut off the view.

Finally he picked up the paperback novel he had started the day before. So much had happened in such a short time that it seemed more time had passed. A week maybe. But when he concentrated, he knew it had been little more than twenty-four hours.

A short time later the pilot announced they were getting close to the Vietnamese coast. "There will be no danger to us until we approach Tan Son Nhut in Saigon. Danger at that point will be minimal. For safety I suggest you exit the aircraft as quickly as possible."

Halpren waited for more, but apparently the pilot had said everything necessary. Halpren closed his book and looked out the window. The coastline flashed past, and suddenly they were over South Vietnam. There was nothing interesting to see except the greens, grays and blacks of the landscape, but it was South Vietnam, a land that had taken on almost mythical proportions, given the amount of press coverage it had received. South Vietnam, land of America's current great experiment. He was minutes from touching down there.

The stewardess circulated and made sure everyone was sitting upright and that seat belts were fastened. Satisfied, she disappeared into the cockpit.

"Ladies and gentlemen, we're preparing to land in Saigon. The temperature is ninety-five with a humidity of eighty percent. Winds are from the east and are light. Currently they're reporting light mortar shelling with occasional bursts of machine gun fire." There was a second of silence, then, "Only kidding about the last."

"Great," said Halpren. He watched as the landscape changed slightly, coming into view as if his eyes were just beginning to focus. The greens of the hills and the rice fields gave way to the browns, tans and grays of the city. He saw Saigon in the distance, a giant smudge, a blemish on the otherwise beautiful green land. They continued down, and then, after they had passed the city, they seemed to fall out of the sky. The jet was aimed at the long parallel runways of Tan Son Nhut. This wasn't a careful, shallow approach into a friendly airfield, but a steep dive toward the ground to confound enemy gunners, if there were any around to be confused.

The engines roared and the passengers laughed bravely, but Halpren knew they were all scared. They hadn't expected to dive for the ground. He wondered if there was something going on that the pilot hadn't told them.

The plane hit the ground hard, bouncing once before it settled onto the tarmac. The engines roared, and Halpren was thrown against the seat belt. Then, just as suddenly, the pressure was gone and the engines were quiet.

"Welcome to Tan Son Nhut," said the cheery voice of the stewardess. "Our last stop."

The plane rolled to a halt, and Halpren unfastened his seat belt, wanting to get off the target just as quickly as he could. Up front the stewardess opened the door, and once again, as in the Philippines, the tropical air came rolling in. As Halpren pushed his way toward the front, he was quickly covered in sweat.

Everyone hurried from the aircraft and onto the waiting bus, except for the politicians. Staff cars with armed, uniformed drivers waited for them. Halpren got onto the bus and fell into the first empty seat. The vinyl was hot and sticky. The windows were open and there seemed to be no breeze. Heavy screens with a wide wire mesh covered the windows.

"Won't keep the bugs out," someone said.

"Meant to keep out the hand grenades," said the driver, without looking around.

"Fucking great," said the voice.

An officer got on. He was dressed in sweat-stained jungle fatigues that looked as if they had started out the day pressed and starched. Behind him was an MP, who wore a flak jacket and steel pot and carried an M-16.

"First thing," the officer said, "we'll be heading toward your quarters here on the base. You're surrounded by high fences, machine guns and guards. There isn't anything to worry about."

"I heard that the VC were inside the wire during Tet," said the man who had worried about the screens.

The officer took off his boonie hat and wiped away the perspiration on his forehead. "Tet was a different story. Even with the attacks, they didn't do that much damage here, and they never approached the VIP quarters."

"That's not the way I heard it," said the man.

"Well, then, you must have been reading the newspapers or watching television. Anyway, if no one has any other questions, we'll get going."

The driver closed the door and started the engine. A black cloud of diesel smoke blew by them. Halpren leaned forward and saw the first of the cars drive off, bypassing the operations building and heading toward the interior of the base.

"Well," someone said, "here we are in Vietnam."

Halpren glanced out the window, and except for the palm trees in the distance, the backbreaking humidity and the roar of jet fighters carrying huge loads of bombs, he wouldn't have believed it. Then he noticed the revetments for airplanes, sandbagged so that only the tail sections showed, and the buildings with their stacks of sandbags around the lower floors. Armed men, wearing flak jackets and helmets, walked along the perimeter of the base. There were bunkers and machine guns, and, of course, the guard at the front of the bus, armed against enemy attacks. Maybe it wasn't so hard to believe he was in Vietnam, after all.

The bus pulled up in front of a low building with a large picture window and a row of air conditioners, one for each room window. There were awnings over the windows, but the roof was tin, as were all the roofs on the base.

"These are the VIP quarters here on base," the officer told them.

"I thought we'd be staying downtown?" one man wondered out loud.

The officer grinned. "You'll be safer on base than in one of those hotels downtown. But if you'd like, arrangements can be made for that. Certificates of nonavailability will be provided for those of you who desire a hotel room."

Halpren stood. "I'll stay here."

"Good."

As Halpren moved to the front, others joined him until there were only two men sitting on the bus. One of them shrugged. "Oh, hell, it's not that bad." He stood up.

Inside it was dark. A ceiling fan turned overhead and an Air Force clerk handed each man a packet with his name on it. Next to each name was a room number. When the clerk finished with the men, he glanced at the three women and shrugged. "Don't know what to do with you."

The officer moved forward. "Arrangements have been made over at the hospital to put each of you up in the nurses' quarters. Your accommodations will be as pleasant as those here and, of course, there are the hotels downtown."

When everything was taken care of, the forms signed and the luggage delivered, the officer announced, "A briefing will be held at the officers' club."

"Now what in hell could they tell us that we need to know?" someone asked.

"The senators and congressmen will be there," said the officer.

"We'll have transportation?"

"There's a bus outside." With that, the officer turned and opened the door, gesturing to the women. He led them out. Halpren watched out the window as Drake climbed into the bus. So far he hadn't had a chance to talk to her in private. Maybe later. He turned, pulled his suitcase out of the pile and headed down the hallway toward his room.

The briefing was just like all the others Halpren had been to in his years of government service. The important people sat up front, and a man in uniform flashed slides on a screen. Halpren had a funny view of the latter. He visualized a half-dozen young guys sitting around creating slides for the general's briefings. What made it funny was that they were in Vietnam doing it, not at the Pentagon, or some base in the United States, but in Vietnam. They'd been ordered to Vietnam so that they could make pretty slides for generals pretending to fight a war.

The officer at the front droned on, showing slides of Saigon, Bien Hoa, the beaches at Vung Tau and Cam Ranh Bay, the rice paddies and cornfields, and finally the jungle. And, yes, he told them, there were cornfields in Vietnam. He talked about what it was like in Vietnam, talked about the men in the field chasing the elusive enemy, the fighting that had raged a couple of weeks before, and then alluded to the goals of the American war machine.

That last one surprised Halpren. In all the two or three years he'd worked for Bishop, he'd never heard anyone talk in terms of goals. Vietnam was something that was done, a year of something akin to on-the-job training. The goal was to survive the year and return to the States. Now an officer was talking in terms of overall goals.

When he finished, Bishop asked him, "Who established these goals you mentioned?"

The officer set his pointer on a desk. "They're merely long-range items suggested by Administration policy, such as Vietnamization, so that the South Vietnamese take on a larger role in their self-defense, a training program for the local inhabitants to improve their economy so that it provides a living wage for them, and finally a reduction in the American commitment to South Vietnam.''

''Fine, Colonel,'' said Bishop, ''but those aren't military objectives. Not like, say, the invasion of Germany during the Second World War. Not like crushing the Japanese so they'd be forced to surrender.''

''No, sir. Not goals like those.''

''I see,'' said Bishop. ''Militarily what do we need to win this thing?''

The colonel stood there for a moment, shifting his weight from one foot to the other. ''Militarily,'' he repeated.

''Come on, Colonel. That's not a difficult question. What do you need to win?''

The colonel rubbed a hand over his short-cropped hair and stared at the row of officers sitting to the left of the congressional delegation. ''That's something that I'm . . . that we've . . . that isn't germane to this briefing.''

''Won't wash, Colonel,'' said Bishop, folding his arms to wait for an answer.

''Excuse me, sir,'' said the colonel. ''The problem is that such a policy is dictated at a higher level. My job here has specific goals, but they're not designed to lend themselves to answer your question.''

''Double-talk,'' snapped Bishop. ''Like everyone else, you don't have an answer.''

The colonel started to speak but then didn't. He stared at Bishop and shook his head.

''All right,'' said Bishop. ''Let's move on to more important things, unless someone else has a question on this topic.'' When no one spoke, Bishop said, ''Now, what can you tell me about this Tet fiasco?''

"That will be covered tomorrow during the briefings at MACV."

"You don't have an opinion, Colonel?"

"No, sir. My role during Tet was a minor one."

Bishop picked up a pen and rolled it between his palms. "Already starting your alibi? Your role in Tet was minor, so that you can't be held responsible for anything that happened during the attacks."

"No, sir," said the colonel. "Actually, I was caught in my quarters during the first few hours, and we were all told to stay put. By the time I could get clear, the situation had stabilized."

"Yes," said Bishop. "I imagine it had."

The colonel stood there quietly, his eyes roaming over the people seated in front of him. Sweat had beaded on his face, and he wiped at it nervously. "If there are no questions concerning the current situation here, I'll turn you over to Major Machelles, who will brief you on tonight's activities."

As that man took over and began to drone, Halpren shifted around and tried to spot Drake. She was sitting with the other two women, trying very hard not to see him. Finally he turned his halfhearted attention back to the briefing. Nothing important was going to happen until morning. Then they would begin to learn about the Tet disaster, and he would have a chance to talk to Drake. All he had to do was remain patient. That was the key.

17

INSIDE NUI BA DEN

As he had done before, Thanh crouched in the darkness of
the tunnel that would take him out onto the surface. A cool
breeze blew in from vents hidden in the vegetation. There
was no light, other than that created by a lantern stolen from
the Americans at Dau Tieng several months earlier.

Thanh knelt at the foot of the trapdoor, his eyes focused
on its underside. He was aware of the smooth walls of the
tunnel, scraped out with steel and stone tools. Roots from
bushes on the surface poked through, looking like icicles in
the dark. He reached up with his left hand and touched his
lips. He wasn't thrilled about another trip to the surface, not
after what had happened to him in the past, but he was ready
nevertheless.

Ngo moved toward him. "We should move in a few minutes."

Thanh nodded and looked up at the trapdoor again. They
were only making a recon, to see if the Americans had more
men in the field now that the congressional delegation was
getting close, to see if there were any special preparations
being made to protect the delegation as it inspected the
camps around Nui Ba Den.

The strategy meeting had been strange. His company commander had given them the whole itinerary of the American politicians. It had been printed in the *Stars and Stripes*, but it had also been posted on various bulletin boards in a half-dozen different camps where VC spies could see it. The Americans talked about security and then did everything in their power to alert the enemy to their plans. The newspapers reported what the Americans were going to do. Their own officers wrote memos and orders, posting them where anyone who could read could see them. And then they allowed the Vietnamese free access to everything in a camp.

So Thanh and Nhuan had talked about the American politicians, where they were going and when they would be going there. They had plotted it all out on a map stolen from the French. They had studied everything, noting that the congressional delegation would be within a dozen kilometers of any number of Nui Ba Den cave exits.

"When we learn where the Americans are patrolling," Captain Nhuan had said, "we'll know where to attack."

And now Thanh was waiting to go out on patrol again, despite his recent failures. Everyone was doing something, preparing for the attack that would stun the Americans, and his task was to spot American patrols.

"It's time," said Ngo.

Thanh nodded but hesitated. He didn't want to leave the safety of the caves. He didn't want to go out where he would have to make decisions that could kill men. He wanted to hide in the tunnels where no man could see that he was frightened in battle, where no one would know he trembled at every sound in the jungle or that he shook when he heard the distant boom of American artillery. He wasn't a brave man; he had learned that during the earlier firefights. Put plainly and simply, he was a coward.

"Are the men ready?" he finally asked, knowing full well that they were. Every delay was welcome.

"Yes. Everyone's ready," Ngo replied.

"Then let's go."

Ngo pushed past Thanh and stood up, one hand on the underside of the trapdoor. A rope loop hung there and Ngo grabbed it. He then pushed the trapdoor out of the way, easing it down by using the loop. The half-light of dusk filtered in as one of the men turned out the lantern. Ngo stood up and checked out the surrounding terrain, turning slowly in a complete circle. Naturally there were no Americans or South Vietnamese around them.

As Ngo scrambled out of the tunnel, Thanh moved up so that he could get out next. He wanted to let everyone else get out first but knew he had to lead. If he stayed behind, if he was always the last out and the first in, the men would notice it. There would be talk. He had to perform, or he would find himself deserted in the field.

He lifted himself out of the hole and crawled around to the north, staying low, listening to the sounds. Helicopters in the distance. Jet planes high overhead. Artillery booming everywhere. The Americans were making their presence known to everyone who could hear.

He found a fallen tree, the trunk rotting into softness. Slipping under it, he turned and slowly got to his knees so he could look down the mountain. In the growing blackness that hugged the ground, he could see vague shapes: trees, huts, bushes and rice paddies. A single light bobbed across the ground, then went out suddenly.

The rest of the men crawled out of the tunnel system and spread out around the trapdoor. They secured the hatch, then waited. Thanh took a deep breath and moved back to them. He found Ngo, touched the sergeant on the shoulder and motioned to him.

Ngo understood. He hesitated, letting all the men around him get used to the darkness and to being outside. Then he stood and followed the trail. The rough path wound through vegetation that had been cut down by monsoon rains as the water rushed downhill. There was a tangle of scrub and light grass, as well as rocks, potholes and pitfalls. It was rough terrain that could conceal a hundred enemy soldiers. Or a thousand. Or a whole army.

After ten minutes Ngo stopped and slipped to one knee. He closed his eyes and listened to the growing night sounds. Behind him he heard the rattle of equipment that hadn't been tied down properly, the scrape of a foot on a rock and the rustle of clothing against the branches of a bush—little sounds that were almost lost in the normal jungle noise. He heard them because he was listening for them, and if the Americans were out there, they would hear them, too. The Americans weren't deaf, or stupid.

But he heard nothing to suggest that the Americans were around. He sniffed at the wet tropical air but couldn't detect any cigarette smoke, after-shave or insect repellent. Finally he stood and began to move again, figuring there would be no danger from the Americans until they reached the bottom. The Americans never climbed the mountain.

It didn't take them long to get to level ground. Ngo hesitated, then moved off fifty meters. He came to a log lying on the ground and halted again. Sitting behind it, he looked at the men as they followed him.

They spread out silently, and when they had finished establishing security, Thanh moved toward the sergeant. He crouched next to him, his lips close to the man's ear. "How about staying here?"

"Our orders are to patrol and search for signs of the Americans," Ngo said.

Thanh nodded. "We rest for fifteen minutes, then move south, staying under the cover of the trees." He then stepped back under the protection of a palm and knelt, his shoulder against the rough bark.

When the time was up, Ngo got to his feet and waited. Without a word the others pulled back until they formed a rough line behind him. He moved then, first deeper into the forest and then to the south, avoiding the trails. They skirted a farmer's hut. From inside came music on a battery-powered radio, but also the sounds of a man and woman making love. Ngo stopped, held up a hand and then worked his way closer to the hut. He crouched under the window, his head cocked to the left as he listened to the couple. When the woman screamed once, Ngo grinned and moved away from the hut.

He veered deeper into the forest, dodging around the thickest growth, followed a path for twenty or thirty meters and then slipped into the trees again. Moving slowly, he searched for signs of the enemy. But the night was quiet, the sounds of the insects gone and the noise of the animals reduced. Then something fled from him, and Ngo was angry that he had startled whatever it was. He was supposed to be able to walk up to anything in the jungle. It shouldn't hear or see him. It should remain in place until he grabbed it, if that was what he wanted to do. If it ran, then he wasn't moving quietly enough.

As the sergeant slowed down, Thanh caught up to him, touched his shoulder and pointed. They were skirting a pathway, the ground charcoal against the surrounding blackness. There were shapes of trees and bushes and then small plants that came right down to the edge of the trail. With the thin canopy overhead, it looked as if they were walking through a cave, as if they had never left the interior of Nui Ba Den.

"We stop here," said Thanh.

Ngo nodded. He didn't say that they were supposed to patrol. Instead, he dropped to the ground.

Thanh moved off deeper into the trees and then came back out. Silently he moved the patrol into position, setting up an ambush. They lined the trail, seven meters back from it. Two men were split off from the group as rear guards and two more set out as flankers on either side. There would be no one sneaking up on them this time.

That done, Thanh settled in for the night. At first he knelt, one knee on the soggy vegetation of the forest floor. Water seeped into the slight depression caused by his weight, soaking his pants. Insects buzzed around his face, darting in and out to taste the salt of his sweat. Mosquitoes came, hovered, but didn't bite.

After thirty minutes, with no sign that anyone else was in the forest, Thanh relaxed. He sat down but kept his back straight, telling himself he would remain alert. He would search the forest for the enemy, and if they came, he would be ready.

Thanh hunched over slightly, the strain of sitting upright without something at his back becoming too difficult. Holding his rifle in his right hand, the butt against the ground, the barrel pointed up into the trees, he shifted, but that, too, became too much of a strain, so he set the rifle across his legs and leaned back, one palm on the wet ground. Finally he achieved some comfort.

The forest around him wasn't frightening. He'd spent his whole life near jungles and had never been worried about them. There were snakes, rats and tigers, but they didn't bother him if he didn't bother them. It was only since he had arrived in South Vietnam that the jungle had become dangerous. Now there were soldiers in it who meant to kill him. There were random bombings and artillery barrages designed to frighten men. And frighten him they did. He could see the snakes or hear the tigers. With his AK he could easily kill even the largest, deadliest tiger, but there was nothing he could do about the bombs and artillery shells. Until the first one fell, there was no warning. The jungle erupted around you, killing friends and ripping their bodies to shreds.

He didn't like his line of thought. It frightened him to think about the power the Americans could employ without risking themselves. Fighting men in the forest was one thing, but bombs falling out of the sky was another. He couldn't shoot at the bombs and he couldn't run from them. One moment it would be quiet, peaceful, and the next, men would be dying without a chance to defend themselves.

He felt a cold lump settle in the pit of his stomach. Chills rippled along his spine. The Americans were coming; he knew it. They were going to drop bombs and kill him, and that angered him. There was nothing he could do about it. There would be no warning, just a sudden, deafening roar, a blast of heat and a whir of shrapnel. Death falling out of the sky.

He changed position again, started to lie down, then realized what he was doing. He was about to go to sleep, unconcerned with the job he had to do or why he was out in the forest.

Thanh sat up abruptly, then stood. He moved among his men, walking carefully, slowly, so that he didn't disturb them. He found two of them asleep and most of the rest sitting on the ground. No one was alert. No one believed the Americans would come out in the night. The enemy loved the daylight and feared the night. They hid in their camps behind rows of wire and walls of sandbags during the night. But there was nothing to fear in the night, or so Thanh's men believed.

The lieutenant woke up the careless men but didn't say anything. He worked his way along and found that the rear guard had gone to sleep. Suddenly angry, he kicked one of them. With the rear guard asleep, the Americans could sneak up and kill everyone. If the Americans were out there...

He returned to his spot and again bent to one knee. Carefully he listened to the sounds of the forest as the night slipped away. The heat had faded a little, but the humidity stayed high, coating everything with a thin, sticky film.

For hours he crouched in the forest, waiting for the morning and the Americans. At dawn he was going to pull back and return to the mountain. There would be nothing to report because he had seen nothing. He'd fib a little in the report, suggesting they'd ranged farther than they had, but no one would challenge him. Then they could spend the day resting safely in the caves and tunnels where the Americans never ventured, and where the Americans could never find him.

He felt sleep tugging at him and thought of the comfort of lying on straw with nothing to worry about. He thought of the coolness that circulated throughout the tunnels and caves and how good it felt as the air worked its way deeper into the cavern. Darkness and coolness and nothing to worry about, because even the biggest American bomb couldn't penetrate the mountain.

As the first faint signs of dawn began to creep into the eastern sky, there was also the distant beat of helicopter rotor blades. At first Thanh didn't hear them, and when he did, he didn't realize what was going on. As the sound built, from just a tiny noise on the edge of perception to a riot of whining turbines and popping rotors, he knew the Americans were coming. Not at first light as they always did, but before first light when they could catch the VC and NVA napping.

Thanh was on his feet instantly, his AK in his hands. He snapped off the safety but didn't move. Turning his head right and left, he tried to figure out where the helicopters were, but the sound vibrated and echoed, making it impossible to tell.

"Americans," said Ngo, sliding up beside him.

The blacks of the forest had changed to grays. Monkeys and birds screamed. The insects were gone now and there was a light, warm breeze. Fog from the low-lying areas drifted in, making it seem as if part of the forest was on fire.

Thanh turned in a slow circle. He lifted a hand and wiped his face. The noise from the aircraft was louder now, coming right at him. He wanted to run but didn't. It seemed safer to stand where he was.

"What do we do?" asked Ngo.

It was a good question. A dandy question. Thanh glanced at the brightening sky and then to the rear. He couldn't decide what to do. Run or stand? Fight or hide?

And then the solution was thrust on him. The helicopters roared overhead, no more than two hundred feet above him. He felt the rotor wash as the choppers low-leveled past. Looking up, he saw the dim glow of the lights and the black shapes of the helicopters.

"We stay," he said.

Ngo nodded but didn't move.

Thanh listened to the receding sounds of the helicopters. A thrill bubbled through him. The Americans had passed him and were on their way to attack someone else. The enemy hadn't seen him or his men as they clung to the ground, trying to avoid contact. If he stayed where he was, made no noise, he would be safe.

Ngo stared at the sky. "When do we return to our camp?"

"Later. After we learn what the Americans are going to do. Then we go home."

"Maybe we should try to find out where they went. Find out what they're doing."

"No," said Thanh. "There are others to do that. Our job is to remain here and see if there are more Americans in the area."

"Yes, Comrade."

As Ngo turned, Thanh knew he had made the right decision. The war had passed over his head and there was no reason to run out and try to find it. His assignment had been to locate the Americans and determine if there were more of them in the vicinity of Nui Ba Den. He could tell his company commander that the Americans were out in force. He didn't have to attack them to prove it.

Thanh settled back on the forest floor to wait for the opportunity to return to the tunnels with his report. He was almost happy.

18

TAY NINH BASE CAMP
RVN

It didn't take Colonel Stanwick long to be convinced and it didn't take him long to design a plan of action. Staab stood in the corner conference area and told the officers, company commanders and their operations officers what he knew about enemy fortifications inside Nui Ba Den, not that he knew all that much. The important points were that the enemy seemed to be moving into the area of Nui Ba Den in large numbers and that many of them, along with their supplies and weapons, were staying right there.

The plan was relatively simple. There would be a movement of troops from the staging area along the runways at Tay Ninh out to the forests and rice paddies around Nui Ba Den. Then two companies would sweep upward, searching for the hidden entrances into the mountain, with one company to stand by as reinforcements in the field. A fourth company would stand down, but would be available in case things went terribly wrong and help was needed quickly.

The biggest hassle was arranging the aviation assets. Every commander in Vietnam wanted helicopters to move his troops from one area to the next. No one wanted to walk when he could ride and no one wanted to ride when he could fly. The scheduling of helicopters had become a nightmare, with some companies logging twelve hours of flight time a day when Army regulations dictated a maximum of eight.

But somehow Stanwick got the aviation assets assigned to him and he got his soldiers out, forming along the runway by four in the morning. The helicopters, from the 187th Assault Helicopter Company across the runway from the battalion's area, picked up the first company.

Staab was assigned to the lead aircraft; Coats in the trail. Stanwick wanted them to act as scouts. They had been in the Boi Loi Woods recently, had run into the enemy there and were considered to know more about the area than anyone else.

The choppers, their navigation lights on bright flash, hovered into position, then set down at the side of the runway. Staab climbed in, carrying a CAR-15 and two bandoliers of ammo and wearing a pistol belt holding two canteens. He sat on the troop seat, his back against the soundproofing of the bulkhead that separated the transmission from the cargo compartment, and watched as the other soldiers got in.

When the chopper was loaded, it just sat there, engine whining and blades popping. Staab leaned forward and touched the company commander on the shoulder. "What the hell's happening?" he shouted over the noise.

"Colonel's up in the C and C now, looking at LZs. Once he finds something satisfactory, we'll be airborne."

"Shit. We fuck around too much and we're going to lose the element of surprise."

The captain grinned. "Going in helicopters kind of eliminates the element of surprise. We make so much noise, Charlie knows we're on the way."

Staab shrugged his answer and stared out the windshield. Now that the sun was rising, he could see the end of the runway better. Beyond that was the bunker line, a wall of sandbags and fighting positions to keep the NVA out of the camp. At the moment they were gray-black lumps slowly taking shape.

He closed his eyes and wondered if he had done the right thing. Gerber and the Green Berets had been trained to handle this kind of operation. He was about to fly out with infantry troops who had no special training. They were kids plucked out of college, or between college and high school, young men who hadn't thought about what they wanted to do with their lives but who were now sitting in Vietnam with sophisticated weapons, kids who should have been sitting at home watching friends play football or baseball, or playing it themselves on scholarships.

That was the funny thing. While he had been home, on orders for Vietnam, he'd watched a college basketball game where the commentators had talked about the pressure placed on a teenager to perform in the arena of big-time college sports—teenagers, eighteen and nineteen years old, who displayed a great deal of courage while trying to throw a round ball through a hoop.

Then he looked at the men in the chopper with him. If any of them, including the pilots, was over twenty-one, he would have been surprised. There were no commentators here to talk about courage, pressure and performance. If one of these kids failed, people would die. If one of these kids failed, *he* might die. Looked at from that perspective, there was no pressure on kids playing basketball in college. They were getting a free ride and a pass on the draft because they could throw a round ball through a hoop.

The sound from the turbine changed as it became louder. One of the pilots turned and glanced into the rear as the chopper lifted, becoming light on its skids. A soldier whooped, his voice rising with the whine of the turbine.

They lifted off, hovering three feet over the runway for a moment. Then the nose dipped and they began racing toward the perimeter. As they gained speed, they began to climb, the nose coming up. They crossed the bunker line and the concertina wire, then climbed out to the north over open fields. Off to the right was a small village. To the south was the city of Tay Ninh.

They continued the climb into the brightening sky. Out the door he could see the other choppers, the lights no longer as bright as they had been. He could just see the shapes of the choppers as the sun rose. Not much to see yet.

They turned east toward Nui Ba Den, which wasn't that far from Tay Ninh, but not much more than a black smudge in the distance. There were lights at the mountain's summit, where the Special Forces camp was located, and now, early in the morning, there were lights around the base—farmers getting ready for a day in the fields.

The captain, a young man like all the others, snapped off the safety of his weapon. He kept the barrel pointed upward, just in case it fired by accident. His men followed his lead.

Staab didn't bother with that yet. He kept his eyes focused on the terrain. It was all dark, some of it black, some of it gray. He could see stands of trees and open rice paddies. There was some movement down there—farmers and water buffalo. He waited for the strobing of muzzle-flashes and the climbing string of glowing green tracers, but they never came.

The crew chief leaned around from his well. "We're one minute out."

The men moved closer to the doors, one of them sliding out his feet to touch the skids. In his left hand he held his weapon and with his right he held on to the fuselage of the helicopter.

As they lost altitude, the door guns opened fire. The muzzle-flashes, nearly three feet long, stabbed out into the darkness. Ruby-colored tracers flashed, hit the ground around the trees and disappeared or bounced up, tumbling into the sky.

A gunship rolled in, its rockets firing in blasts of light near the doors. Sudden bursts of orange-yellow exploded, engulfing the tree line. The firing increased as all the machine guns in all the helicopters began to shoot.

Staab put on his steel pot, faced one of the doors, ready to hit the ground as soon as possible. As they descended he could see trees, dark shapes taking form now that the sun was higher.

They touched down and the first men leaped into the grass. Staab slipped across the rough deck, stepped on the skid and jumped to the ground. He crouched there, the helicopter behind him, the rotor wash flattening the grass and stirring up a cloud of dust and debris that swirled around him.

Seconds after he was out the chopper lifted. The aircraft behind it flew over him, their skids only a few feet above. As soon as they had cleared the LZ, the door gunners opened fire again, raking the tree lines to the north. And then, suddenly, it was quiet.

Without a command, the men were up and moving. Staab headed toward the east where Nui Ba Den dominated the surrounding territory. They entered the trees, passed through the finger of forest quickly and found themselves facing a series of rice paddies. The company commander didn't hesitate. He moved forward, stepping over the eighteen-inch-high dike and into the murky water on the other side.

The company followed him. Staab almost stepped up onto the dike, then remembered that it was the dike that would be booby-trapped. He knew they should avoid dikes unless they saw farmers moving along them.

They made their way forward, the lukewarm water splashing around their knees. A stench rose from the water, not unlike that of the outhouses that dotted the American camps. They moved rapidly, the only sound coming from the water as they sloshed through it and the sucking of the mud as they pulled their feet free. Some of the men stepped on the rice plants, using the stems and roots to support their weight so that they didn't sink into the muck.

Staab halted about halfway across the rice paddies to rest. Even without the sun up, he was sweating heavily. The humidity remained high and perspiration poured off him, soaking his uniform and turning it black. He had thought the rough part of the mission would be climbing the mountain, but now he wasn't sure. Walking through ankle-deep mud that sucked at his feet was hard going. The muscles of his feet, ankles, calves and thighs ached. His knees burned with the strain. Looking across the rice paddies, he felt he would never be free of the mud.

He knelt with one knee against the paddy dike. Breathing heavily, he could feel moisture soaking through his fatigues, not that it mattered now. In front of him the company had spread out, moving toward the tree line that curved away from them about thirty yards out.

Just as Staab looked up he saw flashes lighting the trees and ground in front of him like the strobe from a camera. At first he thought someone was trying to photograph the trees as a souvenir for the World. Then the noise reached him—a sudden burst of staccato firing that sounded more like firecrackers in the distance than an enemy weapon. The men in front of him began falling or diving for the cover offered by the short dikes around them.

A round whipped by his head, the sonic crack from it scaring hell out of him. He dived for cover, and the water rushed up to his shoulder and soaked his entire uniform. The smell seemed to close in, threatening to gag him. He inched his way higher so that his nose was well out of the slime.

Firing erupted around him, M-16s shooting into the trees. Red tracers slashed through the burgeoning light of morning. Men shouted orders to one another. One man screamed in pain, his voice high, unnatural.

The machine gun in the trees fell silent, and then another opened fire. Green tracers lanced out, looking like basketballs thrown at his face. Staab pushed the barrel of his weapon higher over the top of the dike, but didn't shoot. He had no target and was worried about hitting the men in front of him.

More weapons opened fire then. By inching higher he could see into the tree line where the muzzle-flashes were as numerous as fireflies on a summer evening. Tracers slashed overhead. Most of them were green. The sounds grew, too, until he felt as if he were participating in a Fourth of July celebration gone berserk.

A voice rose from the rice paddy then. "Open fire! Open fire!"

"Move it up. Jones, on the right."

"Medic!"

"Valenzuela, hit that machine gun. Valenzuela!"

"He's down."

"Somebody with a grenade launcher, hit that damn machine gun in the trees."

Staab slipped lower then and rolled onto his back. Staring up, he noticed that the sky was brighter than it had been.

The stars were completely gone, and he could see the dirty gray shapes of clouds. He worked his way to the left toward a corner of the rice paddy.

"Hey, watch it!"

"Sorry," he said. He stopped moving and looked at his weapon. There was mud on the butt and barrel, but he didn't think he'd stuck it into the water. He checked, found it clear and rolled back onto his stomach.

Spread out in front of him was the infantry company. The men were stacked up against the dikes like tumbleweeds against a fence. A few were shooting, the muzzle-flashes of their weapons reflected by the water around them. Two men were using M-79s, launching grenades that landed in the trees with dull thumps and flashes of orange.

Firing from the trees slowed and then stopped again. One man stood and ran forward, leaping a dike and then falling into the water with a big splash. A second man tried it and then half a dozen were up, running forward in a strange, bent-over fashion, like old men fighting a wind.

A single RPD fired, and one of the men snapped upright and fell. The others dived for cover. The wounded man floated facedown, but no one made an effort to get to him. If he was still alive, he would quickly drown.

Staab sat there, his eyes on the man. He wanted to get up and run to him, but his arms and legs wouldn't obey. He checked the safety of his rifle, hoping that in the second he looked away something would change in the paddy. He looked back, but the man still lay facedown.

"Damn it all," he muttered. The machine gun in the trees kept firing.

Then, suddenly, another man was up and running. He took long, graceless strides, weaving right and then left. Others popped up and started shooting, pouring rounds into the trees. One man screamed and stood, throwing a grenade like a centerfielder trying to nail a base runner. As he released the grenade, he fell forward onto his face out of the line of fire.

The running man took a long step and then dived, stretching out prone. He hit the water with a big, wet splash. Water and mud flew up, hiding him for a moment. When it cleared, he was next to the man who had been wounded. He had flipped him over so that he could breathe.

Staab wanted to stand up and cheer. He wanted to rush forward and slap the man on the back for his act of bravery. Instead, he lay there, his face in the mud, and wondered how they were going to get out of the rice paddies.

"Let's move it!" someone yelled.

"Let's kick some ass."

Then a voice cut through. "Hold your positions. Put out some rounds. Open fire now."

An M-60, set in the corner of a rice paddy, began to shoot. The muzzle-flash was washed out, almost impossible to see now that the sun was higher. The tracers, once a bright red, were now pinkish. But the machine gun continued to fire, concentrating on the trees in front of it.

Then, overhead, came the sound of a freight train, a flat, wobbling sound, and an instant later a bright flash. The ground just short of the trees erupted into a geyser, the water, mud and rice plants leaping high into the air. The detonation came an instant later.

Staab turned and looked. Fifty feet in front of him the company commander lay on his back next to the RTO. The CO had the radio handset pressed against his ear. He was gesturing with his left hand, which held his M-16.

There was a second explosion in the trees, not more than fifty yards from them. A moment later there were more as the artillery began to rain down. Loud explosions ripped through the air. Trees crashed. Trees disappeared. The firing from the forest tapered and then stopped. But the artillery didn't. It worked its way from one end of the finger of forest to the other, ripping out trees and bushes and stripping bark and leaves with volleys of deadly shrapnel.

There was a momentary silence. Then the CO was on his feet, waving an arm. "Let's go!"

He started forward. Other men got to their feet and ran toward the trees. They fired from their hips, screaming at the tops of their voices like Rebels hitting the Union lines at Gettysburg.

For a moment Staab watched the attack with detached interest. How could the captain get his men to their feet to attack the trees? And suddenly he found himself up and running along with them. He screamed like everyone else, burning off the nervous energy of the adrenaline pumping through him. It wasn't a conscious act. He moved through instinct, afraid he would be left behind and thought a coward.

As he ran forward, the mud pulled at him, trying to trip him. He saw the body of one man lying on his back. His uniform was wet, but Staab didn't know if it was blood or water. There was no expression on the GI's face. He looked as if he had gone to sleep in the paddy.

Staab swept by him, leaped a dike and dropped to one knee. Firing erupted in the trees. AKs against M-16s. He could hear the difference in the weapons. There was an explosion, not the gut-shattering noise of an artillery round, but a fainter noise. Someone had thrown a grenade.

Staab got to his feet and ran forward. He leaped for cover at the edge of the forest, rolled once and stopped at the base of a tree, its roots sticking up through the ground like bony fingers. He wanted to fire but couldn't see a thing. The sun was higher, backlighting part of the forest, creating shifting, shimmering shadows.

He got onto his knees, his rifle against his shoulder. Turning his head right and left, he saw a shape rise from the forest floor—a small, slight man holding an AK. Staab didn't hesitate. He pulled the trigger and saw the rounds strike the man, who fell, tossing his weapon to the side.

With the enemy soldier down, Staab jumped to his feet. He leaned against the rough bark of a coconut tree. Around him was more firing. Single shots. Bursts of machine guns. Screams. A whistle and a shout. A man ran by, head down, roaring. He leaped a small bush and disappeared. There was an explosion nearby. Staab dived for cover, rolled and heard the shrapnel whirl overhead.

He got to his feet again and ran to the right, where he heard the hammering of a machine gun and saw muzzle flashes as the rounds shot into the forest. There were screams. A man stood and ran.

Staab reached the machine gun and dropped down beside it. One man lay behind the weapon, his shoulder into the stock as he fired short bursts. The assistant gunner crouched next to him, feeding the linked ammo into the weapon. They worked well together.

To the left was more movement, not the rushing of the Americans as they ran into the trees searching for the NVA, but a tentative movement, like a hunter on the prowl. Staab turned and crawled toward it, waiting it. There was a flash of sunlight reflecting from the barrel of a weapon. Then he saw the curved banana clip of an AK-47. He aimed and pulled the trigger, putting a burst into the enemy's rifle. Trying to hit the man, he let loose with another volley. There was a scream of pain and a crash as the man fell.

Staab waited there, figuring he'd done everything he should. He had attacked the trees, fired at the enemy and killed one of them, maybe more. Now it was time to sit still

After all, he was an intelligence officer, not a combat infantryman.

The lieutenant slipped to the rear, where the machine gun had fallen silent, though the gunner still searched for targets. The man glanced at Staab. "Pushed the fuckers out of here."

"Sure did," Staab agreed.

Another shape appeared, but it was a tall man holding an M-16. Staab got to his knees and yelled, "Come ahead!" He wanted the man to know he was there.

The man, a big black sergeant who had lost his helmet and whose head was covered in sweat, waved a hand. "You get this gun out of here and fall back to the paddies," he told the gunner.

"Yes, Sergeant."

"You, too, Lieutenant."

Staab was on his feet then. "What's going on?"

"We're falling back to regroup. Let Bravo Company have the lead while we take care of the wounded and get them evacked."

"We don't have a lot of time," said Staab.

"Hell, Lieutenant, we got all the time we need. We take care of our own first, then we worry about the shit you boys from MACV dream up."

Staab moved to the edge of the forest but didn't walk out into the paddies. In front of him were wounded men lying on the dikes, out of the filthy water and where the medics could work on them. Three poncho-covered bodies lay fifty yards away from the wounded. Men were scattered around, providing security.

The company commander appeared and stood next to Staab. "Those were NVA regulars we ran into, not VC."

"How do you know?" asked Staab.

"Not one swinging dick was wearing black pajamas, they all had AKs and they all have those white sidewall haircuts. Hard-core."

Staab nodded, because it confirmed what he had believed all along. And he knew the media would report that they were VC, since they thought the two forces were interchangeable. The American armed forces had eliminated the VC as a fighting force, but the media hadn't noticed, because they couldn't tell the difference between a guerrilla and a well-trained soldier.

"What's the plan now?" asked Staab.

"Get the wounded evacked and the dead picked up, then rotate to the rear as the company in reserve. Bravo's taken up point now, and Charlie will be advancing."

"Shit, I need to get over to Bravo then."

"No way. They're a klick from here and moving already. You'll just have to stick with us."

Staab looked back at the wounded men, one of them screaming as if his guts were on fire. He saw the dead men again and decided he was happy to be right where he was. "Yes, sir," he said. "I'll stick with you."

19

It seemed as if a lifetime had passed since he had been at the camp on Nui Ba Den, but Gerber realized it was only a couple of days. He stood at the perimeter wire, using the big Navy binoculars that someone had stolen while on a destroyer, and watched the helicopters working close to the southwestern slopes of the mountain.

"You think that's Staab?" asked Fetterman.

"Who knows?" replied Gerber. "I suspect it's him, but can't tell."

"Going to hurt us?"

"I wouldn't think so. If anything, he'll draw off some of the enemy support and end up helping us."

Fetterman held out a hand, and Gerber gave him the binoculars. As he studied the flatlands below them, they heard firing—machine guns and small weapons.

"Stepped into it already," said Gerber.

"Just a small action. No mortars yet. Just a squad or two."

Gerber turned and looked back up the slope toward the command post where the company of strikers stood. Gal-

lagher and two of his NCOs were walking among the South
Vietnamese troops, inspecting them, ensuring that they al
carried the equipment, supplies and ammo they woul
need.

"Let's get this show on the road," said Gerber.

Fetterman made one more pass with the binoculars an
watched as the second lift was brought in and dropped of
at the LZ a klick north of where the first one had landed
No one seemed to be firing at that point.

Gerber hesitated, and when Fetterman was done, h
walked up the slight rise, stopping short of the company o
strikers. There were just over one hundred men, split int
three platoons with a headquarters squad. Gallagher ha
assigned one of his NCOs to each of the platoons and ha
assigned himself to the headquarters squad. Gerber had tol
him it wasn't necessary, but Gallagher had insisted.

"Have to prove to the troops that I'm as willing to go wit
them as I am to send them."

"That's your decision, Captain," Gerber had said.

Now Gallagher left the formation and walked down t
Gerber. "We're set when you are."

"Who's going to take point?"

"Sergeant Klein. He's made a few recons on the slope
and seems to have an idea of where to look for some of th
entrances. We don't find anything, we can be back here b
noon."

"Yeah," said Gerber.

"We find anything," said Gallagher, "it's going to b
rough going in."

Gerber shrugged but didn't speak. He'd figured that ou
himself. He knew the enemy was in there, and if they foun
an entrance, it was going to be dangerous, maybe deadl
trying to use it. All the advantages were on the side of th
VC and NVA, but there wasn't much that could be done. I

the intelligence estimates and his guesses were right, the enemy had a real stronghold inside the mountain.

"If you're ready, then," said Gallagher.

"Let's do it."

Gallagher returned to his men and said something to them quietly. Klein broke away from the group, heading down the path toward the wire. Klein was a short, stocky man with black hair barely visible under his boonie hat. He had a round face with thick features, his eyes close-set, his nose long and sharp. Like most of the others, he was heavily tanned. He was followed by three strikers, shorter, thinner men who wore fatigues that looked as if they had been styled after those of the Americans.

Klein reached the gate, a flimsy frame crisscrossed with barbed wire and topped with concertina. He opened it and moved through. In seconds he was heading down the rapidly steepening slope of Nui Ba Den.

The rest of the company moved out then, following the path made by Klein. Gerber and Fetterman were near the head of the column as they passed through the gate. Just outside the wire the red dust vanished, and there was a light cover of short, soft grass, which was coated with dust, giving it an unreal look. As the men walked, a cloud rose from the grass, making it seem as if it were burning.

There was a narrow plain outside the wire and then a slight ridge of dark volcanic-looking rock that dropped away over the edge of the mountain. Klein walked to the ridge, found an old pathway through it and then descended. The rest of the men reached that old pathway through it and then descended. The rest of the men reached that point and saw that Klein was moving down a trail that snaked its way lower in a series of switchbacks.

"I don't like following a path," said Fetterman.

Gerber knew exactly what the master sergeant meant, but if they were going to walk off the mountain, they would have to use one of the few trails. The terrain was too steep not to use them, unless everyone was skilled in mountain climbing. There were outcroppings of rock, steep cliffs and very little in the way of easy trails. They were forced to stick close to the paths. The only real worry would be booby traps, because there was no way the enemy could set an ambush. There wasn't enough cover for an ambush.

Gallagher moved forward so that he was walking next to Gerber. "We try to sweep the trail frequently and we rarely find anything."

"Great," said Gerber.

The trail became steeper, making the footing treacherous, and then flattened out as they came to a meadow about a hundred yards long and half that wide. There was a carpet of dirty grass and no evidence that anyone had walked through it in the past week. Klein stopped and pointed, and the strikers with him raced across the remainder of the meadow, falling to the ground next to a couple of boulders that looked as if they had been erected as a gate to the rest of the path. The men spread out in the meadow, taking up security. The headquarters squad moved away from the trail and fanned out in a rough circle inside the perimeter.

"This is one of the areas where we suspect there'll be an entrance," Gallagher said. "It's either concealed in that outcropping of rock there near the face of the cliff, or opposite it near the point where the meadow drops off and where that vegetation could hide it."

The strikers fanned out, poking into crevices, suspicious bushes and rock structures. They chased out animals, lizards and a couple of snakes. Several of the men yelled and ran when they found the snakes. One of Gallagher's NCOs chased one of the serpents and lopped off its head with his machete. The other snake found safety in another rocky area, and no one felt the urge to chase it out.

It took them thirty minutes to search the meadow carefully. Just when they thought there was no trapdoor leading into the mountain concealed there, one of the strikers found it. He jammed his knife into the ground, twisted and saw the woven bamboo mat used to hold the dirt and roots of the plants in place as the trapdoor was opened.

Gallagher moved a squad into position, surrounded the trapdoor, and then backed off ten or twelve yards. "How do we handle this?" he asked.

Gerber crouched and stared at the trapdoor. "Jerk it open and drop a grenade down it."

"Tells the enemy we're coming," said Fetterman.

"They already know it," said Gerber.

Gallagher didn't wait for anything more to be said. He moved toward the door and, with the help of several strikers, ripped it up and out of the ground. Three men stood around the newly opened hole, their weapons pointed into it, but there was no movement at the bottom. Gallagher took a grenade and pulled the pin. He held the explosive up so that everyone could see it, threw it into the tunnel entrance and flattened himself on the ground, a hand over his head. An instant later the grenade exploded, the noise filtered by the tunnel walls. Smoke and dirt came boiling out of the hole in the ground.

Gallagher scrambled forward and peered into the swirling dust and smoke. He reached out, as if he could part the curtain of dirt, and saw nothing of interest.

Fetterman and Gerber were there in an instant. "Tony?" said Gerber.

"We've got to get someone in there," Gallagher said.

"Sergeant Fetterman has explored tunnels before," said Gerber.

"You volunteering me, Captain?"

Gerber grinned. "Of course."

"Then you'd better plan to be my backup."

"Of course." He pointed at Gallagher. "We'll want a squad to follow us, but not too closely. And the rest to cover us so that Charlie doesn't come up from other areas and follow us into the tunnels."

"We'll keep this whole area covered," said Gallagher.

Fetterman shrugged his way out of his harness and rucksack, dropping them onto the nearby grass. He took out his knife and slipped it into his boot, then put grenades in his pocket and pulled out the Browning M-35 pistol he carried. The staggered box magazine held thirteen rounds, with an extra one in the chamber. He pushed spare magazines into different pockets so that he would always be in a position to get at one of them. Finally he took a flashlight, removed the red lens and turned it on. The beam was bright and steady.

Gerber followed suit, except for the knife. He was worried about the blade cutting his foot. Instead he taped the scabbard to the side of his boot, then slipped the knife in. Unlike Fetterman, he left the red lens on the flashlight and clipped it to the front of his fatigue pants. Then, with a pistol in one hand and a grenade in the other, he was ready to go.

As Fetterman moved to the edge of the tunnel entrance, Gerber looked at the men going in with them—South Vietnamese strikers who weren't familiar with the tunnels or fighting in them. Gerber suddenly wished they had a squad of Kit Carson scouts. The former VC might be very helpful in the tunnels. It was one of those obvious things that no one thought of until they were on the verge of making a move and it was too late to do anything about it.

"Ready, Captain?" asked Fetterman.

"Hang on, Tony." Gerber studied the men. "No one panic down there and no one fire unless it's absolutely necessary. You all understand?"

There were nods from the strikers.

"Okay, Tony, we're ready."

Fetterman shifted around, sitting on the edge of the tunnel entrance, his feet dangling. He knew that in some places the only way to enter the tunnels was headfirst, slithering in like a snake after a gopher. He turned on the light, shone it down and then launched himself like a kid dropping off the dock of a bay.

As soon as he did, Gerber took his place. He could see Fetterman crouched in the bottom of the hole. The master sergeant was pressed up against one side, squatting, his head turned so that he could see down the tunnel that led away from the entrance. Fetterman glanced up at Gerber and waved.

When the master sergeant crawled forward into the tunnel, Gerber dropped into the hole. As he landed, he leaned back against the dirt wall, surprised at the consistency of it. It was almost as if the wall had been sprayed with concrete, forming a rough, solid surface. It was an impressive feat.

He entered the tunnel proper. The floor was fairly flat and sloped downward. The walls were curved and in places the roots of plants stuck through. But the dirt on the walls was compressed, solid.

Almost immediately they came to a turn in the tunnel that was designed as a blast wall. Fetterman halted there, lay flat on his stomach and peeked around the bend. He turned, glanced over his shoulder and then moved forward again.

Gerber followed on his hands and knees, the Browning clutched in his right hand. He put the heel of his hand on the hard dirt of the floor, keeping the weapon up, away from it. Behind he heard the scrambling of the men and wondered what good they would be if a fight broke out. Such a fight would be between the men at the head of the column, Fetterman against a VC or NVA. There was no way to mass a force.

They continued down for a while and then back up. There were tunnels off to the left and right, but Fetterman stayed out of them, almost as if he knew they were traps for intruders or escape hatches. He stayed on the main route as it moved deeper into the mountain.

Then suddenly the tunnel opened up into a wide chamber, a small hole and then a domed room that had to be fifty feet wide and more than a hundred long. Fetterman stopped, then crawled forward. Gerber caught up, glanced around and followed Fetterman.

''Good God!'' said Fetterman. He had turned off his flashlight but could still see due to the electric lights strung along the ceiling.

Gerber touched the back of his hand to his lips and realized he was sweating, but not from heat and humidity. It was cool in the cavern. He turned and saw stacks of supplies, ammo in boxes, food in big burlap bags, uniforms and military equipment.

''Now what?'' asked Fetterman.

Gerber scratched his head. They couldn't leave it and they didn't have the explosives to blow it up. They had confirmed beyond all doubt that the enemy was using the interior of the mountain as a base camp. It had to be an extensive network if they had this much stored this high in the mountain and this close to the surface.

The others began to crawl out of the tunnel. As they did, Gerber spread them out in a defensive ring with the hole at the center of the semicircle. ''Let's continue on,'' he said. ''Move deeper and see if there's more of this.''

''Come on, Captain, you know there will be.''

"Sure," he said. He took a step, then stopped. The magnitude of the discovery overwhelmed him. He had known that Charlie stored a lot of equipment and weapons underground. Fetterman had once described a fully assembled ZSU-23 that he had found in a tunnel, but Gerber hadn't expected anything like this chamber, even knowing that Charlie had driven trucks into Nui Ba Den. "Let's go," he finally ordered.

Fetterman moved off slowly, using the cover on the cavern floor—a boulder that had once been part of the ceiling a century or more ago, stalagmites growing toward the roof. A pool of water was at one side of the room, and a pathway crossed the cavern floor. Fetterman followed it about halfway, then stopped. He dropped to the ground and held up a hand. When Gerber got close, the master sergeant said, "Someone's coming."

"That's all we need," Gerber muttered. The captain turned and waved a hand. The men scattered, hiding behind the rocks and equipment. Gerber moved to the right, off the path and toward the pond where there was a depression and a large rock. He crouched behind the boulder and snapped off the safety of his pistol.

The enemy soldiers burst from the other side of the cavern, talking to one another, laughing at some unspoken joke. The sound of their voices echoed throughout the cave, bouncing off the walls and reverberating across the floor. One of them stopped, pointed and then walked toward where Gerber hid. They moved slowly, easily, unaware that the Americans had penetrated their stronghold. The man stopped, stooped, cupped his hand and dragged it through the cold, dark water. He lifted it to his mouth and drank. When he finished, he straightened and laughed.

The NVA soldiers moved toward a stack of equipment, walking past both Gerber and Fetterman, seeing neither man. One of them stopped at the crates, touched the wood, read something and pointed at a higher crate. As he did, he turned and saw Fetterman lying on the cavern floor.

He pointed and shouted. As he did, a shot rang out and the man grabbed his chest. He took a staggering step and collapsed. The second man screamed something and there was a burst of firing. He took the rounds high, spun and fell, his head spraying blood.

Gerber was up and moving. "Shit!" he rasped as he ran to the downed men. Grabbing the AK lying near the fingers of the first dead NVA, he tossed it away. Two of the strikers came up to him, both grinning. "You jerks," he growled. "You shouldn't have fired."

"Captain," cried Fetterman, "coming up behind us."

"Take cover."

Four men ran from the tunnel entrance. They fanned out and dived for cover. As two more ran out, Gerber, now lying on the cavern floor behind a rock, aimed and fired. The crack of the shot echoed throughout the cave, sounding like a volley. One of the enemy soldiers fell, while the others began to shoot. In seconds it sounded as if there were a thousand men shooting instead of the handful who were there.

Gerber rolled away from his rock, closer to the equipment. He picked up the AK. As he moved, he saw one of the enemy soldiers stretched out behind a rock. Aiming carefully, Gerber pulled the trigger. The man leaped as if he had been burned. As he did, a dozen rounds shredded his body. He collapsed and died quickly.

More of the enemy began to pour from the tunnel at the far end. First one or two men, but then more and more, fanning out and firing as they came. Gerber used the AK then, firing into the mouth of the tunnel on full-auto. He emptied the weapon and turned to look at the dead men.

Neither of them had spare ammo. "Stop them from getting clear!" he yelled. "Aim at the tunnel."

The firing was concentrated there. Rounds bounced off the rock, setting off sparks. Bullets ricocheted around the cavern. The water in the pool became agitated as bullets struck it, and the echoing increased until it was a continual roar, as if a giant hurricane had gotten inside the cavern.

Gerber crawled to the right and stopped. Bullets whipped by him, kicking up dirt on the floor. He fired with his pistol, saw the bullets slam into the rock near an enemy soldier, then fired again.

For two minutes it stayed like that—everyone firing as fast as they could pull their triggers, weapons on full-auto, chugging out rounds. Then there was a single explosion as Fetterman threw a grenade. The orange-yellow blast was blinding, and shrapnel slashed through the air.

Then, in rapid succession, there were more explosions as the strikers gave up on their pistols and M-16s and used their grenades. The detonations rolled through the room like the thunder of an overhead storm.

Firing from the enemy tapered off, and one man tried to duck out the tunnel. Gerber put a round into his back, dropping him in the entrance and partially concealing it. The firing slowed as the enemy soldiers died. One of them threw out his weapon and stood, hands over his head. A burst from an M-16 cut him down. He flopped onto the ground and was still.

Then Gerber realized there were no AKs firing, just the pistols and M-16s. He rolled onto his back and shouted, "Cease fire! Cease fire! Cease fire!" until the strikers heard him and one by one stopped shooting. When the last of the echoes died away, Gerber said, "Tony, check the bodies. Take two men with you and plug that fucking tunnel."

"Yes, sir." Fetterman was up and moving.

Gerber got to his feet and ran around the edge of the pool to the body of one of the dead. He saw a huge hole in the man's head, exposing brain tissue. Grabbing the corpse's weapon, he slung it and moved to the next body. He caught up with Fetterman near the tunnel entrance. The master sergeant was down on his hands and knees, peering into it over the piled-up bodies. "What do you think?" Gerber asked.

"They know we're here now," said Fetterman laconically.

"Then maybe it's time we got out."

"Yes, sir." He hooked a thumb over his shoulder and asked, "What about all that?"

"We can blow it up as we get the hell out."

"There's a lot more to see in here," said Fetterman.

"Yes," agreed Gerber, "but not now. We have to get out while we still can."

20

Morrow rolled over and reached out, forgetting for the moment that Gerber was gone, off on one of those secret assignments he refused to talk about. She knew that once he had been in North Vietnam and once he had been in Laos, but she didn't ask and he didn't tell. Had she reported some of the things she had learned from him her byline would have made the front page, but understanding the war better than some of the civilians around, she knew the danger such reports would mean for him. It was a dilemma that sometimes woke her in the middle of the night, her stomach knotted tightly and her body covered in cold sweat.

She sat up and looked at the bars of morning sunlight on the ceiling. Although her eyes were heavy and she didn't want to get up, she threw the covers back, letting the air from the ceiling fan cool her. Rolling to the right, she stared at the face of the traveling clock on the night table. At first the time didn't register. She studied the hands, then realized it was almost nine o'clock. The press briefing Gerber had wanted to attend before he went into the field was only thirty minutes off. She'd have to hurry in order to make it herself.

By skipping breakfast and taking a shower instead of a bath, she could hit the briefing around the time it started. She decided she'd stand at the back, listen to everything that was said and take notes. Though she was one of the few reporters who had been caught in the street fighting in Saigon, she'd stay out of the discussion and learn as much as she could about Tet. Morrow had seen the assault on the American embassy as the MPs and Marines had kicked the sappers out, and she had been in the crowd that had cheered as the American flag had been raised on the building a mere five hours later than usual.

She got up, went into the bathroom and looked at herself in the mirror. Not bad-looking for an old bag of thirty-one, she thought. The only problem was a network of lines around her eyes caused by squinting in the bright tropical sun. She refused to wear sunglasses; she just didn't like them.

After brushing her teeth, she turned on the water for the shower, holding her hand under the spray so that she could adjust the heat. When she had the desired temperature, she closed the curtain and twisted the shower knob. Quickly she slipped into the tub and turned her back, moving to the rear and letting herself get used to the water.

Finished, she got out and toweled herself. Back in the main room, she put on a bush jacket, matching skirt and black boots. Before she left she picked up a notepad, a couple of pens and her small tape recorder. That was the thing about being stationed in the Far East. She could buy a small tape recorder cheaply and tape the whole interview. Her notes could then guide her so that she missed nothing.

Out on the street she found a cab and rode over to MACV Headquarters where the briefing was to be held. She paid the driver and ran up the sidewalk, stopping only long enough to flash her press pass at the MP at the gate. He grinned at her as he opened up to let her in. She then hurried to the building, through the double doors and into the green-tiled hall.

The briefing was in the main conference room, not far from the office used by General Westmoreland. As she arrived, she noticed an armed MP stationed at the door. He wore combat gear, a flak jacket and a steel pot and was armed with an M-16 and a pistol. Such security wasn't normal during press briefings.

She approached and held up her press pass. "Robin Morrow."

"You're a little late, Miss Morrow. I'm supposed to keep everyone out of there."

"Including members of the press?"

"Everyone who's late."

"There other reporters in there?"

"Yes, ma'am, there are. A whole passel of them, along with a bunch of civilians from the embassy."

"Then there's nothing being discussed in there that's all that secret. You're out here for show, to prove how serious we are and to remind everyone we're in a combat zone with the enemy all around us."

The MP used a thumb to push back his steel pot. The chin strap hung down so that he looked like John Wayne in *The Green Berets*. He grinned then and nodded. "I suppose you're right about that."

"Then there's no reason not to let me in. I can mention your name in my story."

"I think it would be better if you didn't mention my name in your story."

"Don't you want your folks and your girlfriend to know how good a job you're doing?"

"No, ma'am," the MP said, grinning broadly. He had nearly perfect teeth. "I told my mom that I wasn't going to get anywhere near Saigon. She thinks all the fighting goes on in the capital, because all the news reports are filed from here.''

''All right,'' Morrow said, laughing. ''If you don't let me in, I'll have to mention your name.''

''Then by all means,'' he said. He leaned to the right and opened the door for her.

Smiling her thanks, she slipped in and felt the door close behind her as she turned to look at a forest of heads. The room, a long, narrow affair with a conference table in the middle, had been changed. The table was gone and now, at the far end, a stage had been set up, where five men sat. Morrow didn't recognize any of them and assumed they were the members of the congressional delegation.

She slipped along the wall and saw a table in front of the stage. Behind it, facing the politicians, were those being questioned: one military officer she didn't recognize, three newsmen and a civilian employee of the embassy.

Behind that table were rows of folding chairs filled with spectators. The congressional aides sat in the first rows, then other civilians, probably members of the ambassador's staff, more reporters, many of whom she recognized, and then a few military men. Stuck in one corner was the local CIA representative, Jerry Maxwell. He was leaning against the wall, a bemused look on his face.

There was a single empty chair on the far side and Morrow moved toward it and sat down. She opened her notepad, turned on her tape recorder and looked around quickly. The walls were the same shade of green as always, but the watercolors of Saigon scenes had been taken down. An American flag adorned one corner, a South Vietnamese in the other.

Morrow leaned forward to read the hand-lettered sign in front of the center politician. It identified the man as Senator Bishop. He was sitting with his elbows on the table. "Why is it that no one suspected the enemy would be able to put as many men into the field as they did?" he asked, staring at the only military officer on the panel.

Morrow turned and got a look at the officer. He was an older man, a brigadier general who had arrived in Vietnam after Tet. She wondered why he had been selected to represent the military's point of view. There were a thousand other officers in Saigon who would have been better choices, though most of them weren't even field grade, let alone generals.

One of the newsmen leaned close to the microphone. "If I may, Senator?"

"Please."

"I think one of the major problems was that the staff in Saigon, on orders, purposely underestimated the strength of the Vietcong so that they could look good in the reports filed back in Washington."

Morrow grinned and waited for the general to explode. She'd heard members of her bureau say the same thing, and she knew that it wasn't true. Gerber had explained to her how the military had changed the accounting system, because an untrained man with a weapon wasn't the same as a soldier. Five untrained men who were given weapons weren't worth one trained soldier. Giving people rifles didn't make them soldiers.

But the general didn't say a word. He let the reporter continue to analyze the state of the Vietcong and the North Vietnamese Army, talking about how the enemy had swooped into Saigon and surprised everyone completely.

"Then there was no indication that the enemy was planning anything until the VC were in the streets of Saigon?" Bishop asked.

"No, Senator. No one had a clue about it. It was a real failure of the military intelligence systems. And we saw how well the VC did, overrunning the American embassy."

Now he would speak up? Morrow thought. But the general just sat there quietly.

One of the soldiers in the back wasn't content to sit and listen quietly. He said, "This is a busload of complete and total bullshit."

Bishop banged his gavel sharply. "No more of that in here."

The reporter looked around, then faced Bishop. "We had the enemy in the streets of Saigon for five days, gunning down people. They were in the American embassy. They took the imperial capital at Hue and held it for thirty days. All this from an enemy who was supposedly being defeated at every turn by the American Army."

Bishop turned to the man sitting beside him, then looked at the reporter. "You were here for Tet?"

"Yes, Senator. I arrived in-country last September, so I've had the opportunity to observe the situation for the past several months."

"Did you attend any of the press briefings?"

"Yes, Senator, every one of them. During that time there were no indications that the enemy were planning anything. Each night the Army briefers said the enemy were being beaten on every front. We were told the enemy didn't have any good soldiers and that the American Army would have no trouble dealing with anything thrown against it."

"And yet the VC overran a large section of Saigon?"

"Yes, Senator. In a matter of hours the situation was turned upside down, and portions of Saigon were on fire. The Communists ran amok, and the Army was powerless to stop them."

There was a groan from the audience, and Bishop banged his gavel again. Morrow felt herself getting sick to her stomach. Gerber had been right. This wasn't an investigation into Tet; it was a witch hunt. Bishop knew what he wanted to hear, and Morrow wondered if he had handed out a script. The reporter seemed to know what to say to maintain center stage.

She looked at Maxwell, who just shook his head. He didn't look as if he was going to say anything. And the few soldiers in the room weren't allowed to speak. It was a one-sided fact-finding tour with the facts already found. Bishop was there to learn that the Army had lied to Congress, the Administration and the American people.

"What do you think led to this disaster?" asked Bishop.

One of the other civilians pulled the microphone over and said, "If I may, Senator."

"You are?"

"C. Noble Howell, Jr. I'm an assistant to the chargé d'affaires."

"Proceed."

"Yes, sir. I think a careful examination of the facts reveals an answer. At the very top of the military structure there was a desire to see the conclusion of the war. Therefore, the accounting systems, those that dealt with the capabilities of the enemy, the numbers of the enemy and the quantity of equipment were refigured to give the impression we were winning. The military commanders wanted to have some positive numbers to send to the President, and this led to underestimating the enemy's resources."

"Interesting," said Bishop, "but I don't see the connection to the disaster."

"Simple, sir. The military underestimated enemy strength, and by doing so, contributed to a false sense of security. That made everyone believe the war was winding down and that we'd all be going home soon. Put simply, the enemy couldn't field an army."

When the man stopped talking, there was another outburst from the military men in the room. A couple of them looked at the brigadier general, waiting for him to speak his piece, while the others yelled at the front of the room. Bishop banged his gavel several times but said nothing until the room fell silent. He glared at the audience. "You'll have a chance to speak your piece if you respect the dignity of this inquiry. If you insist on these outbursts, I'll have the room cleared."

Morrow shook her head in disbelief. She couldn't believe that the inquiry had been so poorly rigged. She didn't know who had sought out the witnesses, but apparently those who had an ax to grind had been called. The questions weren't very probing, and the answers were little more than surface rhetoric.

To the uninformed, the Tet offensive might look like a disaster. To those who didn't look below the surface, it might seem as if the enemy had scored some kind of victory. To those who hadn't listened—and the press was as guilty of that as anyone—it might seem the enemy had pulled off an attack that no one was ready for. But Morrow knew all that to be completely wrong.

She had been in the city room when reporters had interviewed one another about Tet. In their stories, they had quoted informed sources, though those sources, other reporters, were nowhere near as informed as the soldiers in the field, whom no one had bothered to interview. When the journalists had no facts, they made them up from their observations inside their press bureaus. They analyzed the few facts they were getting over the wire, interpreting those facts until they were distorted. And when they had no facts, they made guesses based on what they had heard earlier. What was happening in the field was different from what was reported in the newspaper.

She knew all that. She had tried to get stories published, but they had differed significantly from what the others were reporting, so they had been killed. The press didn't want to undermine its own credibility by reporting conflicting points of view, not when the vast majority of the reporters in Saigon knew what was happening at Hue, Song Be and Khe Sanh without ever seeing one of those places.

And now the politicians had arrived to investigate the disaster manufactured in the press. Unlike the press, which was supposed to be objective, Bishop and his pals had made up their minds and were out to further their political careers. The facts got in the way, so the inquiry was stage-managed, just as Gerber had feared it would be.

Now she wondered if Gerber's sudden deployment in the field had anything to do with the press conference. Maybe all the officers who had something to say had been moved out of Saigon while the politicians were around: make no waves and don't provoke the attention of Congress being the rules of the game.

There were questions she wanted to ask, but if she stood up to shout them, she could lose her press credentials. That had happened before: irritate the big boys and they suddenly didn't call on you and ignored your questions. After a while the bureau would send you home because you were useless to them, and all because you had had the gall to ask a question a senator didn't want asked. So she sat there, waiting for the soldiers in the room to have their turn to speak. Every time there was an outburst, Bishop quieted it by telling the men they would have their turn.

And then, suddenly, the press conference, the inquiry, whatever it was, ended. An aide moved to the front table, whispered something in Bishop's ear and then disappeared. The senator banged his gavel. "I've just been informed that our time here has expired," he announced.

Cries of anger erupted. Two men stood up, their hands next to their mouths as they shouted at Bishop. He banged his gavel twice, then saw that it would do no good. Shoving his chair back, he banged the gavel several more times while aides shouted for order. Finally he shook his head and tossed aside the gavel. He retreated from the conference room, using the rear door through which Westmoreland and his aides entered for a briefing when the military used the room.

As the door slammed, the congressional delegation gone, the noise in the room began to drop off. The soldiers turned to talk to one another, while those who had been interviewed sat still, not wanting to call attention to themselves.

Maxwell slipped into a chair next to Morrow. "What did you think of that?"

"What were they trying to accomplish?"

"Bishop wants to run for higher office and is trying to make a name for himself. Tet's the perfect opportunity because no one knows that much about it yet. It'll take a couple of months before the damage can be assessed."

"Were we hurt by it?"

Maxwell grunted. It was more of a laugh than anything else. "I was referring to how badly the enemy was hurt. The damage done to us was done by the press and the Administration."

"What's on the great agenda for Bishop and his people now that they're out of here?"

"They're moving into the field, going out to Cu Chi or Dau Tieng to talk to some of the men there and learn how they handled the Tet offensive."

Morrow scratched the top of her head, a puzzled look on her face. "Did I miss something, or did I just witness a managing of the news?"

"Hell, Robin, everyone's been managing the news since the dawn of time. Where in hell have you been?"

Morrow stared at Maxwell and wondered the same thing. Where in hell had she been?

21

OUTSIDE NUI BA DEN

After the American helicopters flew overhead, and with the sound of distant firing drifting toward him, Thanh decided he had seen and heard enough. The Americans were swarming all over the western face of Nui Ba Den as well as the Boi Loi Woods. He didn't know why they were there, but he had procured the data he'd been sent into the field to gather. It was now time to retreat.

He slipped from cover and moved down the ambush until he reached Ngo, who was anchoring one leg of it. Before he crouched he checked the field in front of him, seeing nothing unusual there. He leaned close to the sergeant. "We must leave."

Ngo agreed. "But we can't get back to the mountain the way we came."

"Then we head south and find our way in there."

Ngo looked in that direction, but there was nothing to see except the trees, bushes and vegetation of the Boi Loi Woods. "That will take us a while."

"And keep us away from the Americans."

Ngo crawled off, alerting the rest of the patrol as Thanh recalled the rear guard. When they were ready, Ngo took point, moving due south, away from the place where the Americans had landed not long ago. He stayed inside the trees so that American pilots wouldn't see them as they tried to escape.

A single helicopter did fly over them. Thanh whistled once and the men scattered, diving for cover and then freezing solid. The lieutenant knew that movement on the ground was the easiest thing for pilots to see. A man in the open, if he didn't move, might not be noticed, but a man running through the jungle could be spotted.

Thanh sat with his back against the rough bark of a tree, his legs next to the roots that seemed to reach from the trunk outward and anchor themselves to the ground. He saw the helicopter in the distance and watched it as it flew straight at him, as if the pilots had already spotted him.

He didn't think much of that. There was no way he could have been seen moving through the forest from that distance. But the flight path of the aircraft didn't change. The helicopter grew steadily, changing from a distant spot in the sky to a roaring insect, then finally into a huge machine of destruction, coming right at him.

Slowly he reached to the left for the comforting weight of his AK. Moving it, he dragged it toward him as he stared up at the helicopter. He listened to the beat of the rotors as they thrashed the air, the whine of the turbine as it washed out all other sound.

Lifting his AK, he snapped off the safety, wanting to shoot the helicopter out of the sky. He wanted to see it change into a flaming hulk and fall to the earth. But then he remembered the one that had been filled with lights. It had been a simple thing to shoot out the lights, but then the hidden aircraft had shot back at him, changing the quiet night into a hellish morning of death.

Now, before he could act, before he could think about acting, the helicopter flew over him. He looked up at the bottom of it, not understanding the message painted there. In seconds the sound faded and there were no other helicopters around him.

Thanh got up and pointed to the south. Ngo understood and began to march in that direction. The rest of the patrol fell into position. Thanh hung back and then started off. He glanced up at the sun, thankful that it hadn't risen very high yet. By noon it was going to be very hot; the humidity was deadly already.

They marched on for thirty minutes, avoiding open areas, sticking to the forest, even when it meant walking an extra kilometer. If they were caught in the open, there would be no help. An American patrol caught in the open could call for artillery, for air support, for reinforcements, even for rescue by helicopter, but Thanh's only course was to fade away. A Vietnamese patrol caught in the open couldn't fade away. It could only die.

They stopped once to rest. Thanh drank from his canteen. He screwed the cap back on, wishing for something cold. The water inside the mountain tasted sweet and was ice-cold, much better than the stuff from outside streams.

Ngo took off again, leading them around a small village. Through gaps in the trees, Thanh saw farmers sitting around cooking fires, their women hovering to serve them. They all should have been in the fields working, but the activity—Americans in helicopters, jet aircraft—and the occasional sounds of fighting kept them at home. If the combatants were at it in the fields, the best place to be was at home, out of the line of fire.

Thanh's platoon halted again and fanned out. The lieutenant listened carefully, but no one was chasing them. There was shooting to the north, there was artillery firing somewhere, but there was nothing directed at him or his men. When they started again, Ngo turned north, heading for the southern face of the mountain.

As they walked toward it, Thanh thought that it was strange that the Americans hadn't attacked it. They fought around it, and once or twice there had been patrols on the slopes, but there had never been an American attempt to penetrate the mountain. They had to know it was being used as a base. It was a visible sanctuary. Cambodia was protected by an invisible line on the ground that the Americans sometimes ignored, but Nui Ba Den was a visible haven, one that was almost inviolate. It rose in front of him, calling to him, offering him hope, protection and safety. He couldn't wait to get there. He wanted to order Ngo to speed up, but didn't want to make any mistakes that would cost him his goal.

They came to a small village of grass-and-mud huts. A single street, filled with pools of water, wound through the center of the hamlet. An old woman sat outside a hut, staring up at the mountain. There was no sign of anyone else.

Ngo avoided the hamlet, sticking to the thick vegetation on the western side. Once beyond that, they reached the slopes of Nui Ba Den. Ngo halted there and rested. Thanh moved up to where the sergeant crouched. "You stopped."

"Yes, Comrade. We must rest before we begin the task of climbing."

"We have to find an entrance," said Thanh.

"There's one not too far from here, not too high on the slopes. I've seen it before."

"Then let's go."

Ngo waved a hand, indicating the rest of the patrol. "The men need to rest. They're tired. A few minutes here won't make any difference."

"They can rest once we're safe."

Ngo shrugged and stood. He slung his rifle, then wiped a hand over his face. He was bathed in sweat. The sun, much higher now, was baking the ground.

Thanh didn't care. He pointed at the slopes. "It'll be cooler in the caves."

"Of course, Comrade," said Ngo.

He started forward again. The men responded slowly, sluggishly. They stumbled on, dragging their weapons, forgetting about noise discipline. They wanted to rest, but Thanh wouldn't let them, not outside where the Americans could find them. Once they were safe inside Nui Ba Den, they could sleep for all he cared, but now they had to get up to the sanctuary.

They came out of the forest and entered an area of low scrub and tall grass, some of it higher than the men. Now they would be visible from the air. They had to hurry. Noise discipline was a secondary consideration.

"Hurry," said Thanh, trying to get Ngo to move faster. "Hurry."

The NCO turned, glanced over his shoulder and broke to the left. He moved to a clump of trees and disappeared. The patrol followed, with Thanh in the rear. When he reached the trees, the lieutenant noticed that half of his men were missing. Ngo was standing near an outcrop of rock, and as Thanh watched, another of the men slithered into the rocks, disappearing.

"Sanctuary," said Ngo.

"Very good," said Thanh. He retreated to the edge of the trees and looked out. In the dusty grass he could see their winding path leading right to where they were. An enemy pilot would see the trails and know someone had been walking through the grass. He would discover the hidden tunnel entrance. But there was nothing Thanh could do about it now, except get his men out of the tunnels and or der them to climb higher on the mountain so that there would be paths leading out of the trees—a dangerous game given the activity to the west of them.

"Comrade Lieutenant, it's time," Ngo urged.

Thanh nodded and took a final look at the grass. A little rain, a strong breeze or a day or two, and the evidence of their passing would be wiped away. He turned and moved to the rocks. Ngo was lying on his belly. He grinned at Thanh and then pulled himself into the tunnel.

When Ngo was gone, Thanh did the same. The tunnel dropped away, and he pulled himself into it. The light faded quickly so that he was hauling himself through darkness. The odor of dirt filled his nostrils, and the sounds from outside seemed to be magnified. The slightest noise could be heard easily as it reverberated on the tunnel walls.

The tunnel went down, turned upward, then descended again. Thanh turned a corner and saw a light not far away. Scrambling toward it, he heard a babble of voices echoing down the chamber toward him. As he pulled himself out of the tunnel into a chamber of the cave, Ngo spun around. "The Americans have been in the system!"

"What?"

"Americans were in the upper level. They came right into the caves." He stopped talking, glanced around, then in a calmer voice added, "They've been driven out now, but they entered the tunnels for the first time."

Thanh looked at one of the other men in the chamber, an officer who wore khaki and had his shoulder tabs on. "It's true," he said. "The Americans were in here."

"Then what are we going to do?" Thanh asked.

"Draw them away from us."

Thanh peered into the dim light of the cavern. Lanterns were set up on boxes and rocks, putting out harsh white light, but there were only a few of them. His men were standing around, looking tired and scared. "How do we do that?" he asked.

"First," said the officer, "what did you see while you were out there?"

Thanh turned and looked at the tunnel entrance, as if he could see something that would remind him. He shrugged and told the man they had seen many American helicopters, had heard firing from many guns, but they hadn't seen many men. They knew that something big was going on out on the western side of the mountain.

"Some of our men have run into trouble. The Americans are coming for us."

"What are we going to do?" wailed one of Thanh's men.

"We're not going to panic," snapped the officer. Then, speaking calmly, he said, "Panic will kill you. This isn't the first time the Americans have pushed into a tunnel complex. A first for us here, but not into the tunnels."

"It's not?" asked Thanh.

"No. They've penetrated the upper reaches of tunnels before, but they never crawl deep enough. They give up and use hand grenades, telling themselves that the explosions will collapse the tunnels and seal us in."

"So what are we going to do?" asked Ngo.

"Draw them away from us," the officer said again as he grinned. "First, we have more of our men in the western area, moving to meet the American advance there. A sniper can hold up a column. Wound a man and the Americans spend an hour, two hours trying to get him out by helicopter."

Thanh felt fear grab his stomach. His testicles drew up tightly, causing him pain. He tried to keep his face blank but failed. "We're going to be snipers?" he asked.

"No. We have men trained for that. They're outside now, harassing the Americans. No, we must do something big to keep them away from us."

Thanh glanced at his tired men. They were standing around, pretending not to listen. "Then what are we to do?"

"Go back outside and join the other units in place to attack the American convoy."

"Convoy?"

"The one carrying the American delegation reviewing Tet activities. Word has come from our allies in Saigon that the American delegation is about to leave the area. We'll go out and ambush them."

"When?" asked Thanh. He wanted to sit down. He wanted to drink water. He wanted to run from the tunnel and hide in the caves.

"You must rearm, taking extra ammo with you, and then move to the eastern side of the mountain. The American itinerary has been changed slightly, but they have been kind enough to provide us with the information. They'll fly to Dau Tieng, then drive in convoy to Go Dau Ha to look at the bridge there. We'll be ready."

Thanh nodded but didn't move. Ngo turned and said, "Let's get going."

Shortly after, Thanh, Ngo and the whole platoon crowded together at the end of one of the tunnels. Two men had crawled forward to open the trapdoor that led outside. Thanh shifted nervously from one foot to the other.

The first month, after the walk down the Ho Chi Minh Trail, had been calm. They had stayed inside the tunnel and cavern system, sometimes listening to the sounds from outside, filtered down to them by the tunnels. They had moved toward the surface and stood in spider holes and bunkers, watching as the Americans patrolled the rice paddies and the forest far below, but no one had had plans of going out to engage the enemy.

Now the situation had changed radically. He had been out three days in a row, and he had run into the Americans three days in a row. Now he was going out again to face the Americans, and this time it wouldn't be a small patrol, but a company-size force. Reinforcements would be close, as would death for the NVA. The Americans would swoop down with guns blazing to protect the congressional delegation.

Thanh told himself he wasn't a coward. A coward ran and refused to go out on any mission again. He just wasn't a brave man. He didn't want to die in South Vietnam, hundreds of miles from his home, fighting for a cause he didn't believe in. He wanted to stay in the caves until it was time to return to the North. He didn't want a hero's welcome; he just wanted his family there, saying that they were happy to see him.

One of the men who had scouted the tunnel returned and looked up. He smiled. "We're ready to go out now."

Thanh waved a hand and Ngo crouched, crawling into the tunnel that led to the surface. Thanh envied Ngo's bravery. The sergeant didn't seem to be frightened by anything. He wasn't like Thanh, who wanted to stay in the rear all the time. Ngo forced his way to the front to lead. Ngo should be the officer and Thanh the sergeant.

Thanh had forgotten that Ngo had been among the first to flee when the initial ambush had collapsed. All he could think about now was how Ngo was always in the front, charging ahead.

"Comrade, it's your turn," said one of his men.

"Of course," said Thanh, getting down. He hesitated for a moment, wishing there was a way he could escape, but he could think of nothing. He glanced over his shoulder and then began crawling along the tunnel, wishing he could believe he wasn't wriggling toward his death.

22

THE AIR AMERICA PAD
TAN SON NHUT, SAIGON

Halpren stood under the blazing midmorning sun and wondered why they had to travel around South Vietnam. There was no reason to go into the field, other than for pictures of Bishop wearing new jungle fatigues and pretending to learn what had happened during Tet. He wiped his hand over his forehead and studied the moisture there, surprised that he could perspire so quickly. It was as bad as stepping out of the shower.

The Army CH-47 helicopter sat off to one side. It was painted a dull OD green that contrasted with the bright silver of the old DC-3s. There were two guards on the ramp, both armed with M-16s. Their jeep, with an M-60 mounted in the back, sat parked near the hangar.

One of the other aides walked up. "Going to be a hot one."

"I'd forgotten how hot it can get in the tropics," Halpren said, wiping his face again. "This is brutal."

"Yeah. We've got about twenty minutes before takeoff."

Halpren turned and saw Drake standing outside the door, talking to an Army officer. "Excuse me," he said.

"Of course."

He walked across the ramp, squinting in the bright sun. Moving up behind Drake when the officer left, he said, "Julie, can we talk?"

She whirled and stared at him. Sweat was beaded on her forehead and upper lip. She blinked rapidly. "What?"

"I don't like the way things have developed here."

"Tough." She started to turn.

He grabbed her arm. "Wait."

She jerked her arm free and yelled, "Don't you touch me! Just don't touch me!"

"What are you so mad about?"

"Oh, for Christ's sake, David, what do you think? Palm me off on Bishop to further your career. Set the senator up with the little chippy so that he'll think of you when it's time to hand out promotions."

Halpren took a deep breath and shook his head. He was going to tell her that it must be nice to be perfect, then realized she'd only get madder. Instead he asked, "You don't want to hear my side of it?"

"I don't see what you could possibly say to change my mind. You urged me to go to dinner with Bishop, and he seemed to think that everything was arranged then. It was all supposed to be straightforward."

"Except I just suggested you have *dinner* with him. That was it. I didn't know he was going to assume anything more. I'm innocent."

"Right, Halpren. You're innocent."

"It's a misunderstanding."

"I've got things to do. Is there anything else?" She didn't wait for an answer but turned, opened the door and disappeared inside.

"Well, I tried," he said to himself. He then followed her into the building, walking down a narrow hallway to a waiting room.

A man in starched jungle fatigues stood at the front of the room. He wore a pistol belt holding a regulation-issue Colt .45, canteen and first-aid kid. Pushed back on his head was a steel pot, which made him look like the all-American soldier from every war movie ever made in Hollywood. He held a short wooden pointer in one hand and there was a map of Vietnam on the wall behind him.

"In the next few minutes," he said, "we'll take off and fly out to Dau Tieng, which used to be a French plantation. It's still a plantation, but the main buildings have been taken over by American forces and we have a camp there. From there we'll board trucks and make the ground tour, heading from Dau Tieng south toward Go Dau Ha, staying to the east of Nui Ba Den, the Black Virgin Mountain."

"Why's it called the Black Virgin Mountain?" asked one of the political aides.

"I think that's the English translation of Nui Ba Den. Now, once we reach Go Dau Ha, we can tour the ARVN facility there, and we'll be picked up by a helicopter and taken to Tay Ninh base camp for the night. Once there, you can eat in any of the various mess halls and tour that facility. There's a USO show scheduled for the evening at the Third Brigade, Twenty-fifth Headquarters officers' club, and we can attend that. Are there any questions?"

"What about an escort from Dau Tieng to that other place?" asked Bishop.

"A full company is being provided by the Twenty-fifth Infantry Division, the Tropic Lightning Division, with a battalion on standby. There'll be a road watch performed by the helicopters and a platoon of MPs will precede us. It's going to be an uneventful ride."

"Let's do it then," said Bishop.

The briefing officer eyed the room. "If there are no other questions, the chopper's waiting."

They turned and filed out slowly, the level of conversation rising as they moved. There were questions about what to expect in the field and questions about the safety of flying in helicopters.

They filed down the hall and back out into the stifling late-morning heat. The helicopter sat on the ramp, the heat shimmering up from the tarmac. The rear ramp was down, and there were two men standing at the base of it. Neither of the men wore flight helmets, but each had one in his hand. They were dressed in Nomex flight suits, not jungle fatigues.

The delegation walked up into the helicopter and were surprised. The interior wasn't as clean as it could have been. There were red troop seats along both sides of the fuselage. At the front of the chopper, just aft of the bulkhead that separated the cockpit from the cargo compartment, there were hatches in the fuselage for M-60 machine guns.

Halpren climbed the ramp and slipped along the troop seats, finally taking one near the front. Bishop followed him, grinned and sat down next to him. "On our way," he said.

"Yes," said Halpren, not sure how he felt about the senator now that he had learned that Bishop expected to be serviced regularly. "On our way."

Bishop fumbled with the seat belt and buckled it. "That Drake," he said quietly, shaking his head and laughing, "doesn't understand the nature of power."

"I guess not," said Halpren, wanting the conversation to go in another direction. "Just what are we doing?"

"About to make a flight into the heart of VC country."

"What?"

"Don't get your bowels in an uproar. From what I understand, Dau Tieng is surrounded by a number of VC and NVA units, but that's on paper. Makes everyone look brave. It's a loose ring that doesn't bother our boys much."

Halpren shifted around and looked at Bishop. "What are we doing in Vietnam?"

"We're trying to learn the truth about Tet," said Bishop, exasperated. "Learn why we were so poorly prepared and how we could let a second-rate army beat us so badly."

"I thought we were here to determine if that's an accurate picture. The military maintains that it was a defeat for the Communists, pointing at the one-sided casualty figures and the fact that the enemy didn't hold on to any of the gains they made during the offensive."

Bishop snorted. "That's an old Army trick. They won because they still held the field at the end of the battle. Let me tell you, back during the Indian Wars, just before the Custer massacre, the Army ran into Sioux and Cheyenne on the Rosebud, more than a hundred miles from the Little Bighorn. After a day of fighting, the Indians retreated and the Army claimed a victory. But if it hadn't been for the Shoshone scouts, the Army would have been chopped up into little pieces. They counted it as a victory, though, because they held their ground. The Indians didn't give a shit about holding ground. They knew they'd whipped the Army."

"The situation's a little different here. The enemy took some heavy casualties."

"Son, don't let them fool you with that nonsense."

"Then what are we doing here if we already have the answers to the questions?"

"We don't have all the answers yet. But we're getting them. And it looks good to say we were investigating on the spot. Makes a good story for the network news, provides them with some good visuals."

Obviously the truth was no more important to Bishop than it was to the military men leading the war effort. Tet wasn't a disaster because of anything that happened in Vietnam, but a disaster because Bishop wanted it to be. Now he was in Vietnam to prove his point, which explained the rigged investigation in Saigon. No one was allowed to speak except the people who had been carefully screened in advance. Halpren looked at the senator and wondered why he had been excluded from the inside track. Before the trip Halpren should have been in the know. Bishop shouldn't have held back anything. Now he had to ask questions.

He'd made a simple mistake regarding Drake and the senator, a misunderstanding, and his career was in ruins. He glanced across the deck of the chopper to where Drake sat talking animatedly with two men. She laughed at something, shot a glance at him, then turned her attention back to the men. A simple misunderstanding, and he had to find a new job because the one he had was a dead end.

His thoughts brought him right back to Bishop's crusade in Vietnam. Somehow, somewhere, Bishop had been snubbed by the military, and now he had a golden opportunity to get even. The facts of Tet were unimportant to him; Vietnam represented an opportunity to get even.

Halpren suddenly wanted to get off the aircraft. He wanted to stay in Saigon until the fact-finding tour was over. He didn't want to be associated with the tour, with the trip into the field or with Bishop.

But the engines began to whine. The crew chief circulated, making sure everyone was comfortable, even though the temperature inside the aircraft was climbing rapidly. As the ramp came up, and with the rotors spinning rapidly, the sound inside increased, making conversation almost impossible. The roar of the engines and the pop of the blades vibrated throughout the chopper, shaking everyone down to the fillings in their teeth.

Halpren was happy about the wall of noise around him. He didn't have to be polite to a man he now despised. He could sit there, lost in thought, and pretend he couldn't hear if Bishop talked to him, and he was isolated from everyone else.

They lifted off and climbed rapidly. There was no inane conversation from the pilot about what they were doing and what they were flying over. There was just the ever-present pounding of the rotors and the shrill scream of the twin turbine engines.

The aircraft reached altitude, and the crew chief brought a flight helmet around for Bishop. He donned it, hooked into the helicopter's intercom system, unbuckled his seat belt and went roaming the length of the CH-47, peeking out portholes and buttonholing crewmen like a man running for mayor.

Halpren finally unfastened his own seat belt and headed for one of the portholes. He stared down at a scraggly forest of stunted trees, bare bushes and dried grasslands. Grabbing the sleeve of one of the door gunners, he shouted, "Where's the jungle?"

"North," said the man. "To the north about fifty miles. All the jungle you can handle."

The answer was difficult to hear over the roar of the engines. He nodded his understanding and turned back to the window, where he saw a couple of villages, some roadways, the huge, oval-shaped camp at Cu Chi and then the Saigon River. Off in the distance, it looked as if a portion of the Hobo Woods had caught fire. He pointed that out to the gunner.

"No, sir. Artillery prep. They put in artillery to keep the enemy out and to detonate any booby traps that might be strung on the ground."

Halpren nodded. He watched the arty prep, saw flashes of bright orange as the last of the rounds were detonated, then returned to his seat. There was nothing else that interested him on the ground in South Vietnam.

The crew chief circulated again, telling everyone to sit down. Bishop found another seat across from Halpren. As the senator sat down, the sound in the aircraft changed dramatically, and they began a rapid descent. Halpren worked his jaw, making his ears pop, wondering if they were about to crash. Drake's words about takeoff being the worst came back to him then. He sat quietly, leaning back into the red webbing, and waited for the noise of the engines to die and the chance to get out of the chopper.

They touched down on the side of the runway near a stand of trees. As soon as the wheels hit the ground, the pilot dropped the collective and shut down the engines. After the ramp was lowered, the passengers got to their feet. Halpren followed Drake off the aircraft but didn't speak to her. Instead, he walked off to the side and took in the surroundings.

There were soldiers everywhere, but unlike those in Saigon, these men weren't dressed in crisp, starched uniforms. They wore old jungle fatigues that were slightly faded, and each man carried a weapon. Some had M-16s, while others carried the older M-14s. There were also a couple of pilots, obvious because they wore baseball-like caps or boonie hats instead of helmets, as well as pistols in Old West holsters.

Unlike Saigon, Dau Tieng was quiet. There was the buzz of helicopters at the refueling point, but they soon took off so that there was no noise, just a quiet that filtered down on the runway. There were no vehicles, no loud music, no shouting, nothing but the silence of a small camp in the middle of a forest and a rubber plantation.

As they stood there, a tall military officer walked over to them. He didn't look thrilled with the idea of hanging around with the congressional delegation. "Mr. Bishop?" he said as he approached.

The senator strolled over to the officer, who pointed southward while they talked.

Halpren saw Drake standing off by herself and walked over to her. As he approached he grinned at her. "Well, I think you can consider yourself even."

"How's that?"

"I'm out in the cold. Bishop's made that pretty clear. I'm through with him."

"Couldn't happen to a nicer guy," she said.

Halpren stared at her for a moment, then said, "What's the use."

As he crossed the runway, wondering what the other side of the base looked like, the officer who had been talking to Bishop called out, "Ladies and gentlemen, we have a meal set up for you near the headquarters building. Once we've eaten lunch, we can board the trucks and head out to Go Dau Ha."

Halpren wasn't sure he liked the way the man shouted out the destination, but he turned and joined the group walking toward the headquarters. As they approached the building, he saw that the Army had set everything up like a picnic. There were large containers with hot food, servers dressed in jungle fatigues but wearing thin white coats, and a stack of metal trays. A meal in the field so that the delegation could feel like real soldiers in a real war.

"Now all we need," said Halpren, "is for someone to shoot at us."

"Don't say that, even if you're joking," said one of the other aides.

"Why not? Might liven things up." But Halpren knew he didn't mean it. He just wanted to get this whole thing over and return to Washington so that he could look for a new job. When he reached the serving line, he picked up a tray and a handful of silverware. ''God, I wish I was home.''

23

ON THE SLOPES OF
NUI BA DEN

While Fetterman worked to plug the tunnel entrance to keep
the enemy bottled up, Gerber and the strikers pulled down
the stacks of equipment, kicking the wooden boxes into
kindling and creating piles of trash to burn.

Fetterman suddenly stopped working, stuck his head
close to the tunnel entrance, then turned and ran back toward Gerber. "There's someone coming. A lot of them. And
they're making one hell of a racket."

Gerber looked at the equipment stored in the cavern and
knew they couldn't destroy it all. They could stay, trying to
get it all, or they could set fires and escape. "Let's get going.
One of you men take point."

Two of the Vietnamese strikers ran across the cavern
racing to the tunnel that would lead them out of the cave.
The leading man leaped, dived onto his stomach and
crawled forward, trying to enter the tunnel. The second man
grabbed the foot of the first and hauled him out.

Fetterman sprinted after them. He grabbed the shoulder
of the second man and pushed him back away from the tunnel entrance. "Wait right here."

The first man used the time to get deep into the tunnel. Fetterman knelt and called, "You wait there."

Gerber watched as the rest of them continued to pull down the equipment, scattering it on the floor of the cave. Finally he could hear the enemy in the tunnel, coming up from deeper in the mountain. That meant it was time to get out. "Go!" he ordered the men. "Get out!"

One by one they stopped and took off across the cavern floor. Gerber took a smoke grenade and pulled the pin. When ignited the grenade would release a cloud of colored smoke, as well as shoot flames from the bottom that could be used to set fire to the equipment, wood and clothing. He tossed the grenade into the closest pile and ran.

Catching up to Fetterman at the far end of the cave, he turned and saw flames eating at the first pile and spreading to the second. Not the best way to destroy the equipment, but the only one they had. "Let's go, Tony."

"Yes, sir." Fetterman got down and entered the tunnel, crawling quickly.

As the master sergeant disappeared, Gerber checked the tunnel opposite them. There was no indication that anyone was there, though the noise was increasing. The fire spread rapidly, the blue-white smoke combining with the red from the grenade.

Gerber then got down and crawled into the tunnel. In front of him he saw Fetterman scrambling along. The master sergeant slowed, glanced back, then hurried on.

Gerber yelled, "Hurry it up!" He noticed that the tunnel was beginning to fill with smoke. At first there was just a hint. Gerber could barely smell it, the dampness of the tunnel, the odor of the dirt, overwhelming it, but then he started choking.

They worked their way back along the tunnel, turned the corner and hurried forward. Finally, up ahead, Gerber could see a shaft of sunlight. The smoke filled the tunnel, making it increasingly hard to breathe. Gerber flattened himself against the floor, but that didn't help.

He waited there, trying to hold his breath. Then, easing his way forward until it was his turn to get out, he slipped out of the tunnel and stood at the bottom of the shaft. He reached up, grabbed the top of the hole and pulled himself out. As he rolled clear, he said, "Use some grenades. Roll them in there."

Gallagher, who had been crouching near the entrance, moved forward. He took two grenades and looked down. Leaning forward to balance himself, his hands on the other side of the tunnel, he dropped down. He knelt, pulled the pins and threw the grenades. Then he scrambled up and out, rolling away from the tunnel entrance. A moment later there were two explosions, and a cloud of dust rolled out.

"I don't think that did it," said Gerber.

"I'll get my demo man down here and we can seal it off for good," Gallagher suggested.

"That won't do it," said Fetterman. "It's too extensive. You'd need to find every single entrance, and I don't think we'd ever have that kind of luck. Besides, even if we did, the men trapped inside would be able to dig their way out. It's impossible to believe the size of the tunnel system down there or the number of exits in it."

"Not to mention the equipment they've got stored down there," Gerber asked.

Klein put in an appearance then. "Captain, we've got smoke coming up out of the ground in seven or eight different locations."

"That's from the fires we started," said Gerber.

"What do you want to do about it?" asked Gallagher.

"Hell," said Gerber, "they're going to know we're running around out here and trying to get into the tunnel system. They'll be waiting with every trick in the book. We've almost got to pull back."

"What about Staab and the legs below us?" asked Fetterman.

"Christ," said Gerber, "I don't know. We needed to make a move without alerting the enemy. It's too late for that now."

"We could plot the locations and then call in air strikers to take out the tunnels," Gallagher suggested.

"Wouldn't work," said Gerber. "They're too deep, and they're designed to absorb everything but a direct hit."

"Then what?"

Before Gerber could respond there was a single rifle shot. An AK round snapped through the air. Gerber dived left and Fetterman went right.

"Anyone see where that came from?" Gallagher shouted.

A striker pointed to a clump of trees about a hundred yards downhill. Gallagher got out his binoculars and swept the terrain with them.

"That's one of the places we were getting some smoke," said Klein.

"You know," said Gerber, "conventional wisdom is to call in artillery and take out the sniper that way. Let the artillery kill him and then we go out and pick up the pieces, if there are any to pick up."

"Shit, it's probably one guy," said Gallagher. "Let's just go get the son of a bitch."

FARTHER DOWN THE MOUNTAIN, on the western side, Staab and three companies of the First Battalion of the Third Brigade were having no luck with the enemy. There were snipers hiding everywhere, taking potshots and then disappearing. Squads sent out to find the snipers found where the enemy had hidden, but no signs of the men. They had taken off and vanished. Then, before the Americans could move on, another sniper would take a shot or two to slow them down.

Staab tried to get the Americans to move faster, sure that the NVA were moving their equipment away from the mountain somehow. He wanted to get at them before there was nothing left to get. He couldn't believe how slow the progress was.

After they had gotten the wounded evacked from the rice paddies, and with one of the other units in the lead, they had moved only a hundred yards before the sniping started. Since then they had moved fifty yards farther. Most of the time the wounded were being moved to the rear, which meant everyone had to wait until a helicopter arrived to evac whoever had been shot.

Staab finally found Stanwick, who had landed and was advancing with Bravo Company, though they weren't moving very fast. He stood with the company commander, examining the map. "We've got to put some pressure on the enemy," said Staab, "and keep it on them."

"And just how do you suggest we do that, Lieutenant?" asked Stanwick.

"Stop letting one man hold you up. We've got to get to the tunnels."

Stanwick waved a hand. "Then why don't you take point and we'll follow you."

"Yes, sir," said Staab, understanding.

Coats came up. "I think we've got the guy spotted. There's a squad moving up on him."

"There," said Stanwick, "that fast enough for you?"

They heard a distant shot, one round, a scream of pain, then a man shouting, "Shit! Shit! Shit!"

"Let's go!" yelled Stanwick. He took off, dodging in and out of the trees, head down, one hand up to secure his helmet.

Staab followed but stayed back. As they approached the area where the wounded man lay, Staab dived for cover. In the distance the wounded soldier was on his back, one hand holding his thigh. He lay in a patch of sunlight, easily visible. Staab knew why the VC hadn't finished him off. He was the bait.

Crawling forward, Staab came to where Stanwick knelt, one shoulder against the rough bark of a palm tree. Staab snapped the safety off his weapon.

Stanwick looked at him. "Got one squad working their way east and another west. We'll outflank him that way."

Staab got to his feet and used one of the tree trunks as cover. He took out his binoculars and scanned the trees for the enemy sniper. There was a flash of light, and Staab saw the outline of the man in the branches of a tall, slender tree, almost hidden by the foliage. "Got him."

"Where?" asked Stanwick.

"Across the clearing. There are two tall trees side by side and then a short one with a white trunk."

"Got it."

"Okay, he's up in the tall tree to the right. Up in the crotch, about fifty feet off the ground. Can't see him now, but you will when he moves."

While Stanwick watched the enemy soldier, Staab searched for the men on the ground. Movement caught his attention: a half-dozen Americans with M-16s and M-79s were advancing. It was a scene out of a war movie—actors heading into battle.

They spread out, all of them looking up into the trees. One of the Americans waved a hand and pointed at the ground near him. A man broke cover, ran to that spot and knelt. The first man handed off his M-16 and then waved his fingers. Keeping his eyes on the tree where the enemy soldier was hiding, he held out his hand. The second man put the M-79 into it.

Now the soldier broke open the weapon, checked the 40 mm grenade, then dropped it back into the weapon. Leaning against a tree, his left shoulder braced, he aimed and fired. The grenade detonated low on the tree.

As it went off, another soldier darted into the clearing where the wounded man lay. He snagged the soldier's arm and began dragging him to safety. It didn't look as if he would make it. Then a machine gun opened up to the right, the bullets shredding the leaves of the tree where the NVA sniper hid. As that happened, a second soldier ran out to help the first. They returned, heads down, pulling the wounded man between them, his feet dragging behind. When they reached the safety of the trees, there was a shout. A single man cheered, but then he was joined by others until it sounded as if the home team had scored the winning run.

In the field there was one more shot from the sniper, and then the jungle erupted. The M-79 fired again, the round missing the tree and exploding behind it. Another machine gun, from the other side of the clearing, began to shoot. It was joined by M-16s.

The firing tapered off then, as if each man had emptied his weapon at the same time. The AK used by the sniper fell out of the tree, and an instant later his body joined it. As the enemy hit the ground and lay still, three men broke cover. They hurried toward the body. One of them detoured long enough to pick up the rifle. The others ran toward the dead sniper, grabbed him and dragged him into the open.

"Now we can move," said Staab.

"You bet," agreed Stanwick. He ran to the right where the wounded American lay, and Staab followed him.

Stanwick knelt by the wounded soldier. His face was covered with sweat and his skin color looked bad. Blood stained his uniform from the crotch to the knee.

"How you doing?" asked Stanwick.

"Christ, it hurts."

Stanwick patted the man on the shoulder. "Of course it does, but look at the bright side. You're out of here. Out of this operation and out of Vietnam."

"Still hurts," said the man through clenched teeth. "Burns like a bastard."

"We've got a chopper coming in for you." Stanwick looked at the medic. "Did you give him morphine?"

"Just now, sir. It'll take a moment to work."

"Hang on, soldier," said Stanwick.

"Sorry about this, Colonel," said the wounded man. "Didn't mean to hold up the operation."

"We're moving on now," said Stanwick. "Listen, you get back to the World, you write to us. Let us know how you're getting along."

"Yes, sir."

Stanwick looked at the medic. It seemed that the wounded man was beginning to relax a little. The medic nodded. "We can move him out now toward the LZ."

"Then do it."

Staab looked at his watch and saw that most of the morning had bled away. The plan had been to get into the field early, move rapidly to Nui Ba Den and catch the enemy napping. Now the morning was gone and they weren't getting any closer to Charlie. There were enemy sniper and pickets all over the place slowly giving ground, probably while hundreds of enemy soldiers slipped away. "Colonel."

"Lieutenant, you have got to be patient. We're making good progress."

"But the enemy's going to be gone."

"If they have as much equipment as you claim, it won't matter because they won't be able to move it all. Take a soldier's weapon from him and he's no longer a soldier."

"Yes, sir," said Staab. He felt frustration knot his stomach, threatening to double him over. No one wanted to do anything; they just wanted to move at a snail's pace until it was time to go home.

THANH CAME UP out of the tunnels for the fourth time. He moved rapidly to the tree line ten meters away, dropping to the ground next to Sergeant Ngo. As they waited there, more men joined them. First just a squad, then a platoon and finally a company.

Captain Nhuan joined them and waved a hand, ordering them to get up. Without a word he pointed, and a man ran off to take the lead. The unit formed into single file with flankers on either side and four men forming a rear guard.

Around them were other companies, men advancing from the eastern side of Nui Ba Den through the surrounding forests to the road where the congressional delegation would appear. While snipers and sappers stayed on the mountain, slowing the Americans there, Thanh and his men moved off to find the delegation.

The pace was rapid as the men hurried through the low forest at the base of the mountain. They didn't worry about noise discipline or leaving telltale signs. They were interested only in covering the ten kilometers from their tunnel exit to the road the American delegation would be using.

Thanh had a hard time keeping up with the force. They were nearly running through the forest. The rapid pace sapped his strength and filled his mouth with cotton. Sweat poured from him, soaking his khaki shirt and making it hard to hang on to his rifle thanks to his slippery hands.

But Thanh wouldn't slow down and drop out as some of the others did. Stragglers had a way of disappearing in South Vietnam. Sometimes the enemy caught them and sometimes they got lost. The random artillery could kill them, or a helicopter could spot them. To be alone and armed in South Vietnam was one of the fastest ways to get killed.

Thanh stayed with the company, feeling safe, even though he was running toward a battle. He breathed through his mouth, sucking in the hot, humid air. A pain in his shoulder radiated outward. The air seemed to burn his throat, but he refused to slacken his pace.

They ran on through the trees, splashing through a shallow stream, across a rice paddy and into the forest again. They dodged right and left, missing the trees and the huge bushes covered with sharp spines and orange flowers. They ran onward, the noise of their running drowning out the sounds of monkeys and birds overhead. Thanh couldn't hear helicopters or jets, or the firing where lone men worked to pin down enemy companies and battalions.

For thirty minutes they kept it up. And then, suddenly, they stopped. The point man held up a hand, and the company scattered into the trees for security. Thanh stood, leaning forward, his elbows on his knees. His weapon was clutched in his left hand, the butt on the ground. His breath was rapid, audible, and sweat had turned his shirt into a wet rag. He thought he was going to pass out.

Then they were off again, but this time they walked, moving cautiously. They worked their way through the forest until they came to a place where the trees had been cut back and the bush had been chopped away. In the center of the open area was a dirt road, high and wide, with drainage ditches on either side. It was a road constructed by American engineers, linking Dau Tieng with Highway One near Go Dau Ha, and then on to Cu Chi and Saigon.

Thanh dropped to one knee and studied the area. The edge of the forest was as straight as a wall, the brush, trees, grasses and vegetation that had formed that part of the forest having been cut and then burned. The theory was that it made ambushing the convoys that used the road more difficult because of the seventy-five meters of open ground.

With the others, Thanh moved to the very edge of the forest and looked out. The road was a red slash in the center. There was a small bridge, constructed of metal tubes covered by dirt and then surfaced. To the south, fifty meters from the bridge, was a turn and then another bridge.

A group of men ran from the forest and bent double as if trying not to be seen. They headed for the bridge, and as they approached it, they threw themselves down. One of them scrambled under the bridge, and in that moment, Thanh knew why the site had been chosen. They could stop the convoy and keep it from driving away in either direction by taking out both bridges. Then they would have the opportunity to capture the American delegation at their leisure.

Ngo moved over, sat down and fiddled with the safety on his AK-47. "It'll be a most interesting afternoon."

Thanh looked at his sergeant and nodded. There was nothing to say to that. He was thinking more of the ambush and the American response to it. They had to act fast because the Americans would come swarming in like angry wasps. They wouldn't fool around or approach cautiously. They would run in with guns blazing, killing everyone in sight.

"If we don't capture them quickly," said Thanh, "we're going to have to kill them. No other choice."

"Yes," agreed Ngo. "I thought of that, too. Capturing them gives us a lever, and killing them gives us a stick. I don't know which is better for us."

"Killing them," said Thanh. "Then we can get out of here without having captives to slow us down."

"But the captives give us a bargaining chip."

"Not us," said Thanh. "Our leaders in Hanoi, but not us. It does us no good."

Ngo nodded but didn't speak.

The men in the field near the road finished and began to work their way back to the forest. Now they moved slowly, one of them holding a wheel as another pulled wire from it. Naturally the mines would be command-detonated. That would be the only way to ensure they would explode when it was most advantageous.

"Looks like we're getting close to being ready," said Thanh. His voice had risen slightly as fear clutched his stomach. He felt a chill on his spine, and the back of his neck tingled as the hair stood up.

"Yes," agreed Ngo. "Close." Again he checked the safety on his AK. "Very close."

AT DAU TIENG Bishop and his fellow politicians finished their tour of the base. Halpren watched as the men drove up in two jeeps, having seen everything there was to see. While they had driven around, Halpren and the others had been fed and then told to relax. Three trucks had been brought in for the politicians and their aides to ride in. It was the beginning of the convoy.

Halpren stood in the shade of a large tree, watching as the soldiers checked the three trucks, one parked behind the other. A machine gun was mounted in each right behind the cab. A soldier stood near each weapon, checking it and the ammunition.

Other troops came out of the trees, moving toward the trucks, but no one seemed inclined to board. The politicians and their aides approached the trucks, too, but no one bothered to get in.

Halpren strolled over to the jeeps and asked Bishop, "Is this trip necessary?"

"You keep asking that, David," said Bishop.

"I'm not convinced that a drive through the country is the smartest move to make. Why not fly?"

"Because," said Bishop slowly, as if lecturing a backward child, "we have to show our support for the ground troops. If we can order them into battle on the ground, we can show that we're not afraid of a simple ride on the ground ourselves."

Halpren wasn't sure he understood Bishop's reasoning. The vast majority of politicians and women stayed out of the war zone altogether. Now, in some kind of grandstand play, Bishop was arranging a convoy when a helicopter flight would be so much faster and safer.

"You better get on one of the trucks," said Bishop. "You don't want to get left behind, do you?"

Halpren shook his head, but he wasn't sure he believed the answer. Maybe getting left behind was the thing to do.

He walked over to one of the trucks as a soldier dropped the tailgate with a loud clang. Two civilians climbed in. Halpren grabbed the side and hoisted himself up, moving along the side of the truck bed to where there were wooden seats. It didn't look like a comfortable way to travel.

Within minutes all three trucks were loaded. Another couple of jeeps pulled up behind them and then a helicopter came in low. As it climbed out, taking the noise of its rotors and turbine with it, the MP behind the machine gun turned. "We'll be moving out now. If something should happen, stay with the truck, hit the floor and let us handle the problem.''

"Excuse me," said one of the aides. "There aren't very many of you.''

"At the gate we'll be joined by three more trucks containing another fifty men. We've got people on alert and helicopters on standby. There are plenty of men available, should we need them.''

"Somehow that's not very reassuring," said the aide, although the MP had moved off and couldn't hear him.

Halpren leaned forward. "I know what you mean. I'm not convinced this whole thing is a good idea.''

"What can you do when the senator decides it is, though? Looks good for his hawkish image to be seen in the combat zone, riding in a jeep with a machine gun in the back.''

A man in the lead jeep turned and waved a hand over his head, giving him the appearance of a wagon master from the Old West. There was a whining from the ignition and then a belch of black smoke from the stack just behind the cab, and the engine rumbled to life.

When all the trucks were running, the lead jeep lurched forward, turned and headed off, following a dirty track cut through the grass at the side of the runway. They turned onto another road and then headed straight for the gate. Three trucks, each loaded with armed men, sat there as promised.

An MP ran from the guard shack, opened the gate and then stepped back out of the way. A jeep drove through, followed by a second jeep and then the first of the trucks, the one in which Halpren was riding. As they cleared the gate, the trucks with the soldiers joined the convoy. They raised a cloud of dust that swirled upward and then hung in the air.

Halpren closed his eyes for a moment and felt as if he were beginning a walk down a narrow corridor to the tiny room where he would be executed. He couldn't shake the feeling that something bad was about to happen. He wished he had missed the truck when he'd had the opportunity. Now that chance was gone, all he could do was hold on and hope for the best.

24

EAST OF NUI BA DEN

Thanh hoped the wait would be a long one. He hoped they would sit in the forest in the shade of the trees, hidden from the road for several hours, and then head back to the mountain. He hoped the American convoy would be canceled, rerouted or ambushed somewhere else. That was what he wanted almost more than anything else in the world at that moment.

He ate a cold lunch of rice and fish heads, washing it down with weak tea. Then he sat quietly and waited for the Americans. The forest was relatively quiet. It wasn't the thriving, bustling place the jungle was. There were no monkeys, and although there were birds, they weren't present in the numbers the jungle boasted. Besides, these were dirty gray swamp birds. And there were insects, thousands of them swarming around, disturbed by the humans who had moved into the edge of the forest. Thousands of insects drawn by the rotting vegetation at the edges of the road. Or the rotting bodies.

Thanh checked the safety on his weapon again and again, setting it and taking it off, not sure what he should do. When the Americans arrived, he wanted to get into the business of shooting right away. But he didn't want to accidentally shoot himself while he waited. What was best? Safest? On or off?

To his right were several other members of his platoon. One man lay on his belly, facing the road, his weapon by his side. Another sat upright, staring into the distance. A third was asleep. Thanh couldn't believe anyone could sleep. His own belly was alive with butterflies, and thoughts of death and pain danced in his head when he concentrated too much.

The sun continued to climb, baking the ground around him. Humidity hung in the air like a heavy, oppressive blanket. Time dragged. Birds flying overhead seemed to move in slow motion. The world had changed since he had run down from the mountain. Everything had slowed down and Thanh was convinced the wait would never end. It would continue until he found himself an old man with nothing left to live for.

He moved slightly when he noticed that his left leg had fallen asleep. The tingle crept up to his groin and clutched his balls. He wiggled his toes and felt the pain shoot from his foot upward. Gritting his teeth, he tried not to move until the blood started flowing again.

He was just beginning to hope that the information had been wrong or that the Americans had changed their plan when the word came down the line: the Americans were on their way. A spy outside the gate at Dau Tieng had seen the jeeps and trucks leave the camp; they would soon be at the first bridge.

Thanh felt his head spin as the news circulated. The lieutenant listened as the whispering swirled around him. Then there was a rustling in the forest as the men shifted, preparing for the Americans. The man who had been asleep was now awake and the man who had been lying on his belly was now on his knees, watching the road.

Thanh checked his weapon again, found the safety on and took it off. He checked the magazine and worked the bolt, ejecting a live round. He wanted nothing to go wrong when the shooting started.

In the distance he heard the first faint sounds of the approaching trucks. It was a quiet sound, barely loud enough to penetrate the forest and overpower that of the insects around him. But as he concentrated, he heard it grow, a single truck, then the sound of others. And in the distance, over the treetops on the other side of the road where it turned back toward Dau Tieng, was a light cloud of red dust, a faint smudge barely visible but there nonetheless. Dust was kicked up by the tires of the trucks as they drove along. The moment he dreaded was upon him.

Thanh touched his chest and felt the weight of the spare magazines there. On his hip were two Chicom grenades. He could shoot, throw his grenades and then hide. There were so many others that no one would see what he did. No one would know what a coward he was.

The rumbling of the trucks became louder, the dust cloud brighter. In the forest there was a scrambling as the men got into position to attack the convoy. Then, almost before anyone knew it, a helicopter appeared overhead, a single helicopter flying along the road, dodging from one side to the other in search of enemy soldiers. It pulled up, turned and retreated, buzzing the ground near the road, then turned again and came toward them. Thanh could see the faces of the pilots in the cockpit as the aircraft flew over him, but it didn't stop or fire. Apparently they had seen nothing of interest on the ground. The helicopter flew off, crossing the road again, then disappeared.

Now the truck engines were louder. Thanh got to his feet and stood behind a tree. He wanted to watch but could see nothing. The pop of rotor blades came again as the helicopter returned. He knew better than to move. Instead, he flattened himself against the tree as the men in the helicopter inspected the ground around them once more.

Finally the first jeep came into view about half a kilometer away near a bend in the road. Behind it was another and then the first of the trucks. They moved quickly, crossing the first bridge. There was no hesitation. They suspected nothing, and Thanh felt excitement swell through him, momentarily pushing aside the crippling fear. The Americans were on track as planned.

The whole convoy pulled into view, larger than he had expected it to be. Three jeeps were in the lead, then three trucks, another jeep and three more trucks. The last truck held soldiers, something Thanh hadn't expected, either though now that he saw them, their presence made perfect sense. Bringing up the rear were two more jeeps. There were a lot of soldiers and almost too many machine guns. Tanks were the only thing missing, and Thanh wondered why the Americans didn't have a couple with the convoy to protect it.

All the vehicles crossed the first bridge and headed for the second. The helicopter hovered over them for a moment then broke away toward the southwest. It disappeared within seconds.

The first jeep approached the second bridge. Thanh raised his weapon and aimed, but like everyone else, held his fire. Suddenly the ground in front of the jeep exploded. The bridge disintegrated in a cloud of dust and debris. An instant later, Thanh heard the detonation, a roaring explosion, not a flat, single bang. The ruined bridge flew upward, the debris cloud climbing twenty meters.

An instant later the second bridge disintegrated, followed by a second explosion, this one smaller, quieter, the debris flying only ten meters into the air. As that happened, the machine gun on the lead jeep began to chatter. The gunner stood behind the weapon, holding on with both hands and swinging the barrel around. The muzzle-flash was lost in the bright sunlight, and the tracers were pale, washed-out, pinkish. They came nowhere near Thanh.

He grinned, lifted his rifle, sighted and began to shoot. He didn't aim. He just put out rounds, feeling secure in the sound of the firing and the feel of the kick from his weapon. The Americans were trapped.

THE TRIP OVER THE DUSTY Vietnamese roads hadn't been the experience Halpren had expected. He had thought, as they drove along, that the wind created by their movement would provide some relief from the heat and humidity. But that wasn't the case. They weren't moving fast enough to create a breeze. The wind swirled over the back of the truck, bringing the dust from the vehicles in front with it, making it hard to breathe and harder to see.

They moved along rapidly, too fast to see anything easily through the dust, but too slow to be cooled by the wind. But then there wasn't anything to see, just open ground from the edge of the road to the jungle, where the undergrowth had been cut back. There were piles of trees, bushes and vegetation here and there that had been partially burned, but much of it had been left to rot under the hot sun.

Halpren held on to the rail behind him. Everyone bounced around in the back of the truck. Dust covered them quickly, and some of the men were sweating enough that they had mud on their faces and running into the collars of their shirts.

For the first few minutes Halpren was afraid the enemy
would be waiting for them. But as they moved out of sight
of Dau Tieng into the countryside, he relaxed a bit. There
was no way the enemy could know where they were, or the
route they were taking. And the helicopter overhead provided a certain comfort. Halpren was sure the pilots would
spot any enemy soldiers who might be in the area.

He relaxed and leaned forward, his elbows on his knees.
"Christ," he said, "it's hot."

One of the men pulled a giant white cloth from his pocket
and mopped his face with it. "I wonder if it's always this
fucking hot."

Another of the men stood and turned, then knelt on the
seat, a 35 mm camera in his hand. He focused quickly and
snapped a couple of pictures. They drove past a farmer's
hootch, a small structure made of mud and covered with
rusting tin. To one side of the building was a family bunker
and tied to a pole in the front was a water buffalo.

"Well, one thing about this," said Halpren, "we couldn't
see the land this way from a helicopter."

"I don't know about that. If the pilots of those Hueys flew
low and slow enough, we could. Not only that, but we'd be
in a position to get the hell out if something happened."

"What could happen?" asked Halpren. He didn't know
why he asked the question because he knew exactly what
could happen. A single rifle bullet was all it took.

The man shrugged. "Probably nothing. Still, I wish your
Bishop and my Creed weren't so hot on seeing this damn
country on the ground."

"The funny thing," said Halpren, "is that no one's arranged for press coverage of this. I'd have thought we'd have
reporters all over the place."

"Oh, you didn't know? There's a couple of pool guys in
the last truck. They're getting film of this, interviews and

the like. Have to share most of it with the corps in Saigon, but they can keep one or two things.''

''I would have thought,'' said Halpren, ''that they'd all want to be in on this.''

''Are you kidding? Who wants to ride around South Vietnam in a fucking truck when they can avoid it?''

''Good point.''

The man wiped his face again, then stuffed the handkerchief into his pocket. He leaned back and closed his eyes, looking as if he was going to be sick.

Halpren knew how he felt. The heat and humidity sapped your strength and threatened to kill. They crushed the spirit, made the head ache and turned the stomach over. Water helped, but he found that he tended to drink too much too fast, which made him feel sicker in the long run. It didn't help that they were riding along a bumpy, poorly maintained road, breathing in dust and diesel smoke. It was as if the Army wanted all of them to get sick to prove to them how tough the military was.

They rounded a corner and roared along a straight stretch of road. Halpren turned and looked over the top of the cab. He watched the jeeps as they raced along, kicking up clouds of the red dust that seemed omnipresent in South Vietnam.

Because he was looking ahead, he saw the first explosion, an eruption of dirt and debris, and his first thought was that he didn't want to drive through that cloud of shit. He didn't want to have to breathe it, so he glanced around to see which way the wind was blowing. That was why he saw the second explosion behind them. And then he heard the rumbling boom of the first detonation and the flat bang of the second.

''Oh, shit!'' he said, standing up.

One of the machine guns began to hammer suddenly. He saw the tracers slashing into the jungle at the side of the road, saw the rounds hit the ground at the base of the trees and bounce, tumbling into the sky.

"What the fuck?"

"Everyone get down!" shouted the MP.

"What's going on?"

"Down! Get down!" The MP swung his weapon around, saw nothing and spun again, searching for the enemy.

There were shrieks behind them, screams of panic from both men and women. One of the jeeps turned and slammed into the ditch, bouncing out and across the open ground. The MP in the rear hung on, firing the M-60.

There was confusion in the trucks. Everyone was shouting. One man leaped over the side and lay sprawled on the road. Others dived to the floor and tried to crawl under the seats. There were more shouts and screams.

The jungle erupted. Automatic weapons began to bark. Muzzle-flashes sparkled in the shadows. There were cracks as the rounds passed overhead. Shooting broke out from the column. Soldiers piled off the trucks and spread out. Some of them dived into the ditch, raised their weapons and fired. The sound built, the individual reports blending into a single, long detonation.

Halpren threw himself to the floor and crawled to the rear. He knew that the trucks would be the targets. To survive he had to get out and get away from them.

"Help me!" shouted a man. "Help me!"

"Get us out of here!"

"I'm hit! Help me!"

The man behind the machine gun had found his targets. He kept the weapon firing, the muzzle-flash leaping out nearly three feet. The ammo jerked from the can and rattled against the side.

Then there was a single, wet slap, and the MP staggered. He grabbed his shoulder and fell, sitting on the bench. He tried to stand up, the blood spreading across his shirt. He groaned, and the color drained from his face. Five men watched him slump to the floor, but no one moved to help him, and no one got behind the weapon.

Halpren leaped over the tailgate and fell into the dirt. Around him there was chaos. People were running, screaming, shouting, crying. The soldiers were out of their trucks and in the ditches, firing into the trees.

"Get down!" yelled a soldier. "Everyone get down!" He was running along the trucks, trying to get the civilians out of the line of fire.

Another of the jeeps in the rear pulled out. It roared along the side of the convoy, its machine gun firing into the trees. The passenger was hit suddenly. He stood up as if going to jump, then fell to the ground, where he rolled over and over, the dust wrapping itself around him as he skidded to a halt and didn't move.

Halpren saw the weapon the man had dropped. A black plastic M-16 lay on the ground undamaged. Suddenly it was important that he retrieve that weapon. Without it he would die. Leaving the cover of the truck, he ran forward, constantly aware of the shooting around him. Bullets kicked up the dirt near him, and one of the truck tires blew.

Halpren grabbed the M-16 and scrambled to the rear. He leaped into the ditch and slid down out of the line of fire. Studying the weapon, he checked it closely. There was dust on it and a magazine jammed into it, but he realized he didn't know how to cock it. He didn't know where the bolt was.

By rolling to the left he put himself in the shadow of the second truck. He crawled forward and peeked under it at the trees on the other side. Fascinated, he watched the battle rage.

Then the helicopter returned. The door guns fired as it swooped along the column and then disappeared. It turned and came back again. Halpren got up and ran toward the front of the column.

All the senators and congressmen were in the ditch opposite the shooting. There were a dozen soldiers around them. The machine guns had been taken out of the jeeps. One of them was firing, its rounds flashing out and slamming into the trees. The soldiers had the important people surrounded, protecting them. No one had yet thought about doing the same for the aides and other civilians.

The chopper came back then. Bullets ripped from the trees, slamming into the aircraft. The door guns responded as the pilots fought for control. Halpren could see the thin metal of the tail boom rip and pop as the bullets hit it. Smoke poured from the chopper and it began to wobble. It slowed, then hung in the air as more enemy bullets slammed into it, knocking it into a slow roll. The pilot fought for control. He dropped the nose, trying to gain speed, but the action failed. The chopper dropped, and at the last instant, the pilot tried to level the skids. Instead he hit the ground, nose low, about twenty yards from the road. The aircraft bucked and flipped over. As it did, the rotors smashed into the ground and splintered. Pieces of the rotors became shrapnel. A soldier was hit and fell, blood spurting everywhere.

"Oh, shit!" yelled someone.

"Hit the dirt!"

"Good Christ!"

The helicopter rolled over and the engine screamed as if it had been hit, then suddenly stopped. Fuel bubbled from the ruptured tanks. One of the men stumbled out of the wreck, and fell. Two MPs hustled toward the chopper.

"It's going to blow!" shouted someone.

"No. No fire yet. Get them out."

Then suddenly one of the officers was up and moving. He stopped and yelled, "Davis, get some fire on those trees!" Clark, get to the rear and get a platoon together. Move the civilians out of the trucks."

"Yes, sir."

"Where the fuck is the RTO?"

"He's been hit."

"I want that goddamn radio."

Halpren ran up, but before he could speak the officer demanded, "Where in hell did you get that weapon?"

"Off the road."

"You know how to use it?"

"No."

"Then give it to me." He held out his hand.

Halpren started to obey, then shook his head. "I'll just hang on to it if you don't mind."

"Halpren!" shouted Bishop. "Get down and shut up!" He looked at the officer, now crouched by the wheel of the jeep. "Get us out of here."

"Just as soon as I can," the man said.

"You better make it goddamn fast," said Bishop. "Real goddamn fast."

Halpren nodded his agreement. If they didn't get out soon, they were all going to die. He had been right; he should have stayed at Dau Tieng.

25

Two squads moved out and flanked the sniper. The rifle squad kept a stream of tracers flowing toward the man, and when the grenadiers got into position, they opened fire with the M-79s. The explosions ripped the vegetation apart, knocked down the saplings and killed the sniper. It took them ten minutes to get him.

When the sniper was dead, Gallagher turned to Gerber and asked, ''Now what?''

''Let's get some of these other tunnels located and identified and then we can begin to eliminate them.''

The RTO, accompanied by Sergeant Klein, approached. Klein said, ''Captain, I'm getting the strangest calls here.''

Gallagher took the handset and listened for a moment, then looked off to the east. ''You heard about that congressional delegation here to find out about Tet?''

''Yeah,'' said Gerber.

''Sounds like they've stepped on their dicks not far from here.''

''Maybe we should head in that direction then,'' suggested Gerber.

"Why not?" Gallagher said. He kept the handset pressed to his ear, then said to Klein, "Get the men assembled at the eastern end of the clearing. You take point."

"Yes, sir."

Gerber ran back to where Fetterman crouched near the tunnel entrance they had found. Smoke was still seeping out of it. When the captain arrived, Fetterman said, "Didn't get it sealed."

"Doesn't matter now. We're heading down the mountain."

"What happened?"

"Sounds like the politicians have been ambushed and we're going to pull their fat out of the fire."

"Choppers?"

"Before we call for aircraft we're going to check things out a little better."

Fetterman shrugged and stood. "Where do you want me?"

"Given the fact we've made contact, I think you'd better bring up the rear. Don't let anyone get close to us."

"Yes, sir."

There was a shout from the far end of the clearing where the strikers had formed into a long, thin line. Klein was at the front. He turned, saw that everyone was ready and took off, moving rapidly into the scraggly trees at the far end.

The column moved then, with Gerber and Fetterman having to hustle to catch up. When they entered the trees, they slowed slightly and then turned north on a path that descended rapidly. The footing was treacherous. They had to grab the branches of trees to keep from falling. Slipping and sliding on the smooth rocks and rotting vegetation, they found it impossible to maintain noise discipline.

After only a few minutes, they heard the sound of distant firing, a rolling, booming noise that echoed up the mountainside. Gallagher hurried to the rear to talk to Gerber. "Sounds like they're catching hell down there."

"Let's stop then and learn what we can. Unless I miss my guess, there's an American unit about three, four klicks west of here that could be airlifted in."

"What about us?"

Gerber stood up and tried to see through the gaps of the vegetation. "Strikes me," he said, "that if we can come in from behind the enemy without them realizing we're there until we open fire, it'll break the attack."

Gallagher rubbed a hand over his face. "Probably. If we have time to get down there."

"There's no way to get choppers in here. We have to move either up or down. The choppers will give us away. We move on our own and we'll fuck up the enemy."

"I suppose," said Gallagher.

Klein halted the men and hurried to the rear. "Getting tense down there," he announced. "A chopper's been shot down and a truck's burning."

"Shit!" Gallagher shook his head. "We'd better get moving."

"Keep the pace as fast as possible," said Gerber.

"I planned on that, but once we're off the mountain we're going to have to slow down." Gallagher turned and ran toward the front of the column.

"That was the old military tradition," said Fetterman. "Ride to the sound of the guns."

"That didn't always work," said Gerber.

"No, sir, but it got everyone into the fight."

STAAB HAPPENED to be standing near the RTO and Colonel Stanwick when the first of the messages came in, an almost garbled cry for help, the sound of firing in the background. One man, his voice high and tight, tried to make it clear that they were pinned down by a large enemy force and needed help quickly.

Stanwick took the handset from the RTO. "Unit calling, this is Lightning Six."

"Lightning Six, Lightning Six, this is Road Watch One Six. We're pinned down southwest of Dau Tieng on Highway 239. We need assistance immediately."

Stanwick pulled the handset from his ear and snapped his fingers. One of the men opened a map and held it up for the colonel to see. "Good Christ, that's twenty, twenty-five klicks from here."

"Choppers are on standby at Tay Ninh," said one of his officers. "We retreat a hundred yards to that clearing we just crossed and we can be picked up. Then a short flight."

"Road Watch One Six, say situation."

"Roger, Lightning Six, we have a large force of November Victor Alpha in the trees seventy-five meters from our location. We have burning trucks, one helicopter down and portions of the road destroyed."

Stanwick rubbed his face with his free hand and stared at the map as if there was some kind of answer printed on it. He saw Nui Ba Den, Tay Ninh and Dau Tieng. He saw the network of highways and the open areas around them. There was no easy way of getting in there. "One Six, we're on the way."

"Roger, Lightning Six."

Stanwick pointed. "Get the men moving back toward the clearing and set them up for pickup. I also want a rear guard in place." He moved to the right where he could see the numbers on the radio, then adjusted the frequency. "Hawk Six, this is Lightning Six."

"Go."

"Roger, we're ready for pickup at map reference two seven eight one on the Bailey grid."

"Roger that. We're on the way."

Stanwick gave the handset back to the RTO. He motioned two of the officers over. "Let's get the men formed and move on back to the clearing. Set up the loads for a staggered trail."

"Yes, sir."

"You going back to the C and C?" asked Staab.

"No, I'm going in with the first of the assault troops. Nothing for me to do in the C and C but sit on my butt while the boys on the ground fight."

The men came swarming up out of the trees, running to the rear. One man sprinted into the lead. Others fanned out behind him. There was shouting, orders given as the company reversed its course suddenly.

"Sir, I've got Lightning Alpha Six on the horn."

Stanwick took the handset, and without waiting said, "Pull back now. Set up for pickup in the first clearing that will accommodate the choppers."

"Yes, sir. There are bunkers around that site."

"Then clear them, but get in a position for a pickup to be executed in two zero minutes."

"Roger that."

The whole company turned then and hurried to the rear. The flankers were out, crashing through the jungle. Staab caught sight of them as they dodged in and out of the patterns of sunlight. He hurried to keep up with the soldiers, thinking they should be more careful. Booby traps and ambushes were still a reality.

And then, suddenly, they were in the clearing. The men spread out, several of them circulating among the trees, checking for the enemy. When they had cleared the site, they returned and reported to Stanwick.

"No one out there," said one lieutenant. Around his neck was an OD towel, which looked like an oversize go-to-hell rag.

The company then came out of the trees, forming into loads for the choppers. A couple of the men crouched, watching the trees, while one stood at the front of the loads, a smoke grenade in his hand, waiting.

Stanwick grabbed the handset. "Hawk Six, this is Lightning Six. We're ready for pickup."

"Roger. Can you throw smoke?"

Stanwick looked at the lieutenant. "Throw a smoke grenade."

The lieutenant did as instructed and the grenade threw off a huge cloud of bright red.

"ID red."

"Roger, red."

"Inbound your location. Say suppression."

"Negative suppression. We have other units in the area. I say again, negative suppression."

"Roger, negative suppression."

Over the treetops the helicopters appeared. Staab stood close to Stanwick in the lead group of seven soldiers. As the choppers crossed the tree line, they flared, their noses rising as their undercarriages came into view. A moment later the men on the ground were hit by the rotor wash, a blast of air that staggered Staab. He grabbed his helmet and closed his eyes as the choppers settled to the ground.

Without a word the men clambered into the helicopters, taking the troop seats or sitting on the deck. As soon as everyone was loaded, a matter of seconds, the chopper was up again, climbing out over the trees at the far end of the clearing.

They broke to the right and headed south. Nui Ba Den bulked black and broad off to one side, and then it was gone and Staab could see farmers walking behind water buffalo in the rice paddies. The farmers kept their eyes on the water buffalo or on the paddies where they worked. They pretended they heard and saw nothing. The only thing in the world was the dirty water of the rice paddies under their feet.

Stanwick leaned close to Staab, shouting over the sound of the engine and the rotors. "This is probably going to be a hot one. We touch down, you leap out and drop to the ground. You don't want to move until you know what the hell's going on around you."

"Yes, sir," said Staab.

Now Stanwick grinned. "I don't know what you had in mind, Lieutenant, but I've got to say you're a dumb fuck. Give me the chance to stay the hell out of the fighting, and I'd do everything in my power to stay out of it."

Staab bobbed his head in an exaggerated nod. But even as he did, he knew Stanwick was feeding him a line. The men in the field envied those who were in the relative safety of the base camps, but few of them would change places. Those left behind felt they were somehow less than real soldiers. Stanwick wouldn't be able to stomach an assignment in the rear. He'd find excuses to get into the field. That was obvious. Ninety percent of the commanders did their job from the back seats of helicopters with a dozen radios to assist them. Stanwick was on the ground with the troops, leading them rather than managing them.

"Anyway," shouted Stanwick, "it's probably going to be a hot one."

Staab touched the safety of his weapon and wondered what he had gotten himself into. He could have passed the information along as Coats had suggested and let someone else handle it. That was what everyone else did.

Then he pushed such thoughts from his mind, concentrating on the scenery flashing under him. The choppers hadn't climbed to their normal fifteen hundred feet, but remained low, screaming over the ground, low-leveling just ten feet above the rice paddies.

Stanwick leaned forward and tapped Staab on the shoulder.

"We're going in. Get ready."

Staab watched as something changed in the rear of the chopper. Normally the men didn't move as they approached the LZ. They sat back and watched the world at their feet, but not this time. They knew the enemy was out there, knew the NVA and VC would try to shoot the helicopters out of the sky.

The men weren't in the doorways. Instead, they tried to stay back, using the thin skin of the fuselage for protection. They were up on their feet, ready to spring from the chopper as soon as they could. And all of them had their helmet straps buckled. They didn't want to lose their steel pots as they hit the ground.

Through the windshield Staab saw the convoy. One of the trucks was burning and the wreckage of a helicopter lay on the east side of the road. Men were crouched in the ditches. Smoke and dust hung in the air as the two forces shot it out.

"Get ready!" shouted Stanwick unnecessarily.

The door gun suddenly opened fire and Staab jerked. It surprised and scared him. His heart pounded as the blood hammered in his ears. He turned and decided he was going to leap off the chopper on the side opposite the enemy in the trees. He didn't care how that looked.

The nose of the helicopter came up, hesitated, then dropped. The skids were level. There was a snap, and part of the windshield disintegrated. One man seemed to jump, then sprawled on the cargo compartment floor. Blood spurted, covering one of the men next to him.

Then they were on the ground. Over the sound of the rotors and the engine, Staab could hear the firing. Machine guns and rifles on full-auto. Grenades going off. Bullets slamming into the choppers, riddling them. Staab wanted to get out, but there was a man standing in front of him. He was aware of the bullets all over the place. Staab pushed the man in front of him, who leaped and fell into the grass. Then Staab jumped, feeling his feet sink into the ground as he dived for cover.

The chopped lifted off, the wounded man still lying in the rear. The door gunner tried to get from his well and over the troop seat so that he could help the wounded man.

When the helicopters were gone, Staab scrambled across the open ground toward the trucks. He could see people running around, using the vehicles for cover. One of them burned brightly, sending a cloud of black smoke towering into the sky. The firing from the enemy weapons, and from the Americans, filled the air.

He reached the ditch and threw himself down. Glancing to the right, he saw two dozen civilians lying there, using the trucks and terrain for protection. They were surrounded by a platoon or more of soldiers, who kept them down and protected them.

Staab crawled forward toward a knot of people. Stanwick knelt near one of the jeeps, a map spread out on the ground. One man was pointing to it. None of them seemed concerned by the proximity of the NVA.

"We've got to get the civilians out of here," said one of the MPs.

"Of course. You need to get those choppers back in," said Bishop.

Stanwick touched his lips with the back of his hand. He popped up, looked over the top of the jeep, then dropped back. "They're going to key on that. As long as the enemy's in the tree line and not using mortars or grenades, the civilians are safe here. We put some more people on the ground and we should be able to protect the choppers.''

"Just get us the hell out of here," said Bishop.

Stanwick looked at the MP officer. The man shook his head. "You've got the rank, sir. It's all yours."

"Thanks." Stanwick turned and stared at the civilian. "Well, Mr. . . ."

"Bishop. United States Senate."

"Bishop, the problem is that Charlie will wait for us to put your people on those choppers and then do everything he can think of to bring them down. As long as he stays in the trees, you're relatively safe."

"How can you say we're safe?" demanded Bishop.

"I said relatively safe."

There was a crash and dirt rained down. Stanwick turned and yelled, "Anyone get that spotted?"

"Trees to the south!" shouted one of his men.

"Put some fire into the trees there. Now. Do it now." He turned back to Bishop. "Anyway, as long as you keep your head down, you won't get it shot off."

"Fine," said Bishop.

"Staab, what can you tell me about this?" asked Stanwick.

"I'd say we've got a company, maybe more. NVA in the trees firing everything they have."

"Why NVA?"

"Fire discipline," said Staab. "They're not randomly firing but taking targets under fire. A few men shooting so that we know they're around, the rest standing by."

"Are they going to attack us?"

"I think we can expect that, and expect it shortly. Now that they've seen reinforcements arrive, they're going to know their time is running out. They'll hit us in a few minutes, and we'd better be ready.''

Stanwick spotted his first sergeant. ''Renfield, you'd better get everyone set for an assault.'' He pointed at the trees behind them where there was no indication of the enemy. ''And put a platoon in there so we don't get surprised.''

''Yes, sir.''

Stanwick wiped the sweat from his face. ''Now, if we can hold on for a few minutes, everything will work out.''

''If,'' said Staab.

''Yeah, if. That's always the word.''

26

AT THE BASE OF
NUI BA DEN

The run down the mountainside didn't take long. The path twisted back and forth, lengthening the distance to the base of Nui Ba Den, but it was all downhill, and neither Gerber nor Gallagher worried about an ambush. Both figured the enemy were near the convoy, attacking it, and they wouldn't have to worry about the enemy until they got closer to the highway.

So they ran down the mountain. They leaped over fallen trees and shallow streams and ran around obstacles or hurdled them, always trying to keep the force of gravity from knocking them off their feet.

When Klein reached the base of the mountain, he slid to a stop and let everyone else catch up. When Gerber and Fetterman, who brought up the rear, arrived, Gallagher said, "Now we can hear the shooting."

The sounds of the battle reached them easily—hundreds of rifles and machine guns firing in unison. The din originated in the east but echoed around them, punctuated by the blasts of a few grenades.

"I make it three klicks at most," said Fetterman.

"We can either take it easy, moving toward them carefully, or we can rush forward," said Gallagher.

Gerber nodded, understanding what Gallagher was saying. The enemy, when they had a large unit pinned down, usually set up to ambush the rescuers. Sometimes that was the goal of the mission: draw the Americans and South Vietnamese out into the jungle where they could attack them. Now Gallagher wanted to throw away some of the rules in favor of haste.

"Tony?" said Gerber.

"Speed's important, Captain, but it'll do those people no good if we get killed."

"There you have it, Gallagher. We follow good field technique. It'll take us longer, but we'll get there in one piece. Rushing forward, we might not."

"Yeah," said Gallagher, "that's what I thought, too. Just wanted to make sure we all agreed."

"I suggest," said Gerber, "that Sergeant Fetterman take point."

"Klein's a good man," said Gallagher.

"And he's had point all day. Time to get him out of there and let someone else have it."

"That suit you, Sergeant?"

"Fine with me," said Fetterman.

"Then let's do it."

All three hurried forward. Klein was crouched at the base of a tree, his rifle cradled in his arms. "Sir?" he said.

"Take the rear," Gallagher told him.

"Yes, sir. Thank you, sir."

"Tony," said Gerber, "we've got to move as fast as possible. There isn't much time."

"No, sir, not much." He turned and glanced in the direction of the firing. "Forty minutes with luck."

"Forty minutes," said Gerber. "Let's go."

Fetterman took out his canteen and poured some of the water into his hand, wiping it on the back of his neck. He slipped the canteen into the pouch, snapped it shut, then looked at his rifle, setting the safety. Next he held the rifle so that his thumb was against the selector switch, ready to shove it to single-shot or full-auto. "Now?" he asked.

"Now," Gerber said.

Fetterman moved off rapidly. He headed into the trees away from the path. Stopping once, he listened to the battle sounds as they filtered through the trees toward him. Then, satisfied that he knew where he was going, he headed off toward the fighting.

Gerber stayed close to the master sergeant. He kept his head moving from side to side, searching for booby traps. If they stumbled over one now, it would slow them down considerably, unless they left the injured man behind.

Fetterman broke out of the forest and into lighter scrub, increasing the pace. The flankers had to practically run to keep up. The rear guard fell farther behind, but Fetterman didn't want to let up. Speed was all-important.

After twenty minutes Fetterman stopped at the edge of the forest. He stared out of the trees at a farmer working a narrow strip of land between the tree lines. The clearing was no more than fifty, sixty feet across. Even so, it was the perfect place for an ambush.

Gerber crouched near the master sergeant and studied the terrain. He pulled his boonie hat off and wiped the sweat from his face.

"I don't like this," said Fetterman. "It's the perfect place to hit us."

Gerber looked right and left. There was no way to avoid the clearing. "We've got to cross."

"If they've got a rear guard, this is going to be where it is."

"You could take a squad and recon ahead. If we make a little noise here, they might let you reach the trees, hoping to catch us in the open."

"Or they might simply cut us down so that we'll have dead and wounded to deal with."

Gerber looked at his watch. "Three minutes and then we go. Take one squad and get across the clearing as quickly as you can."

"I don't know, sir."

And then Gerber saw something that made him grin. He pointed at the farmer in the field. The man wore black shorts and a coolie hat and carried a long, thin switch, which he waved in the air over the rear of his water buffalo, as if to frighten it. "If there was an ambush in the trees, do you think the farmer would be out there?"

Now Fetterman smiled. "If he wasn't very bright, he might be."

"Whenever you're ready, Master Sergeant."

Fetterman dropped back, selected a dozen men and headed for the edge of the forest. They lined up there, hesitated, then burst from cover, hurrying across the open ground. Halfway to their destination, they slowed, then broke into a run. In less than a minute they were in the trees on the other side. Gerber waited for a burst of firing, but it didn't come. Instead, Fetterman appeared and waved them forward.

They were twenty minutes from the ambush site.

THANH SAT AMONG THE TREES, firing his rifle at the trucks on the road. He couldn't believe the plan was unfolding as designed. One of the enemy jeeps came down off the road and bounced toward them. An MP stood behind the machine gun, firing, but was unable to aim properly. Bullets sprayed all over, some of them flying harmlessly into the sky.

As the jeep came closer, more of Thanh's brethren began to shoot at it. Bullets slammed into the metal, ripping off pieces. The windshield shattered and the headlights exploded. The vehicle bounced high once and then the front end fell into a hole. More bullets struck the radiator, and steam geysered into the air.

When the wind blew the cloud of steam away, the driver was gone, having dived for cover. But the machine gunner stood his ground. Now he was more accurate, aiming at the bases of the trees where the NVA had taken cover. Rounds slammed into the bark, splintering it.

More and more North Vietnamese aimed at the American. Bullets tore the seats apart, knocked out the rest of the windshield and punctured the tires. The jeep caught fire, but the American stood his ground, pulling the 7.62 mm ammo from the can attached to the weapon and firing it calmly.

Thanh felt his blood boil. How could the American stand there without the Vietnamese cutting him down? Thanh got to his feet, braced himself against a tree and aimed. He squeezed the trigger and felt the weapon fire, but the American remained unhurt. The enemy stayed where he was, screaming, his voice cutting through the sounds of battle with a bloodcurdling yell.

Thanh aimed again, the sights of his AK-47 on the man's chest. He could see the name tag, although he couldn't read it. He could see the black stripes sewed to the sleeve of the man's uniform. But before he could fire, the American let go of the machine gun and dived over the side of the jeep. As the American vanished, flames began to spread over the back of the jeep. Smoke obscured it for a moment and then blew away as the fire grew rapidly.

Then Thanh saw the machine gunner and the driver of the jeep. Both were running back toward the road and the safety of the trucks. The ground around their feet shuddered from the withering fire, but both men kept moving. Cheering arose from the trucks as the Americans urged their compatriots onward. Now the firing increased as they tried to protect the running men. Grenades arced out. Some of them exploded and others issued clouds of red, green and yellow smoke. The fleeing Americans were effectively screened.

A moment later there was a cheer as the Americans reached safety. Thanh dropped to one knee and turned his attention to the trucks where the rest of the Americans were. He aimed his weapon and fired on single-shot, trying to hit tires, figuring that would disable the vehicles permanently. Firing again and again, he burned through his ammo quickly.

The NVA still had the Americans trapped, though. He was sure. They couldn't drive out and they couldn't run. There were a few dead enemy soldiers sprawled on the ground where they had fallen. He was pretty certain the Americans wouldn't leave the bodies, either.

Thanh felt good. The ambush had worked very well. And then, in the distance, he heard the pop of rotors. Helicopters were coming. He turned and looked. Through the gaps in the vegetation he could see them—ten, twelve, not that far away, not that high. They raced out into the open and then flared. Door guns fired, and Thanh threw himself to the ground, listening to the crack of bullets as they flashed overhead.

The noise from the helicopters and the firing drowned out everything. Then Thanh heard someone screaming—a single man, his voice high, shrieking as if in terror. He looked around, then realized he was the one who was screaming.

He got onto his knees, jammed his weapon forward and began to shoot. Flipping the selector to full-auto, he held the

rigger down and ripped through the rest of the magazine.
As he fired, he screamed, even after his weapon was empty.

He fell back and scrambled around a tree. Leaning against
t, he pulled the empty magazine from his weapon, slammed
another one home, worked the bolt and then froze. Bullets
from the American machine guns smashed into the tree. He
felt them hitting it. Heard them hitting it. Bark and bits of
branches and leaves rained down on him.

Rolling to the right, he kept his face down, his weapon
pointed at the trucks. He peeked up and through the vegetation and saw the convoy again. But now there were helicopters beyond it. Men were pouring from them. Thanh
aimed at them, but as he pulled the trigger the helicopters
lifted off. They turned their tails toward him and shot across
the open ground, climbing when they reached the trees. In
seconds they were gone, and the only noise was the rattle of
rifles and machine guns.

Thanh held his fire and watched. The Americans had
taken cover and seemed content to stay put. Some of them
were firing. A few had machine guns, and M-79 grenades
were exploding all around.

Thanh slipped to the rear and hid behind a tree. He kept
his weapon aimed at the Americans but didn't see the point
in firing into the trucks now, not with helicopters in the area.
If the Americans wanted to escape, they would use the aircraft.

He leaned his face against his forearms and closed his eyes.
He hadn't realized how loud a battle could be. Everyone
firing and yelling. Explosions and helicopters. Cries of pain
and despair. Orders and bugles and whistles. Everyone
making noise.

And then Captain Nhuan was behind him. "Comrade,
have you been injured?"

Thanh lifted his head slowly and turned. "No, Comrade, I was resting."

"In the middle of the battle?"

"For a moment only."

"Ah, well, we're going to attack the Americans in a few minutes. Kill the soldiers and take the civilians prisoner, before more helicopters can return."

"There are too many Americans," said Thanh without thinking.

"Are you afraid of the Americans?" asked Nhuan. "They're no better than us. They bleed and die just like us. And they're not driven as we are. We will triumph over them."

Thanh nodded his agreement, but wondered what good triumph would be if he was dead, killed in a useless gesture against a relentless enemy.

"Ten minutes," Nhuan said. "Be ready then."

"Certainly, Comrade," said Thanh.

As Nhuan left, Thanh got onto his hands and knees. There was a dead soldier near him. He crawled to the body and pulled the man's chest pouch off, recovering the spare ammo. Slipping into the pouch, he pulled it round so that it covered his back. It wouldn't offer much protection from American bullets, but it might help. And it gave him additional ammo. He only had two full magazines left.

A bugle sounded, and Thanh knew it was the signal to get ready. The next sounding of the bugle would initiate the attack. He hoped it would never come but knew it would. They had to make the gesture.

THE AMOUNT OF FIRING surprised Halpren, or maybe it was the sound of the firing that surprised him. Educated in military matters by the Saturday matinee, Halpren associated shooting with background noise that allowed the actors to speak their lines bravely. Newsreel footage was almost the same: distant shooting, sometimes answered by a weapon close at hand while the reporter ducked close to the ground and whispered his story. It was impressive, and certainly looked good on TV.

Obviously he wasn't prepared for sustained firing: guns roaring on full-auto and grenades detonating. Nor was he prepared for all the shouting, screaming and shrieking. Armageddon had come with a vengeance.

Halpren lay on the ground in the ditch, his head down. He wanted to do something but didn't know what. The words of the MP officer still rang in his ears. The man had been right: he didn't even know how to cock the weapon.

But then he saw one of the soldiers reload, noticing how the man pulled at something behind the sight that resembled a handle. Now, using his middle and index fingers, Halpren pulled the charging handle to the rear and saw a live round eject. The selector switch was set on single-shot. He was ready to fire.

Rolling away he climbed up the shallow slope to the road. He peered between two trucks and saw the trees alive with the enemy. Then he thought of Drake. From the moment the ambush had begun, he hadn't thought of her. He had been concerned with getting out of the truck and then getting the weapon. Thoughts of others had been far from his mind. Glancing to the right now, he saw a group of civilians crouched in the ditch, protected by a number of MPs.

Halpren slipped down to the bottom of the ditch where there was soft earth and pools of foul-smelling water. He crawled along, keeping his head down and trying not to smell the water. An explosion startled him. He flattened, and felt the water soak through his clothes. Laughing at himself, he crawled on until he was in the shadow of the second truck, not far from the others. He moved into the group and searched it quickly. "Where's Drake?" he shouted.

One of the others pointed at the next group over. "There," he called.

Halpren moved off toward the next group, reaching it a moment later. He saw Drake cowering near the bottom of the ditch, her foot only inches from one of the pools. She looked strangely out of place, a young woman who should have been back in Washington attending a concert perhaps, rather than hugging the ground in South Vietnam, trying to avoid getting killed.

He crawled to her and shouted over the sound of the shooting, "Julie, are you all right?"

She looked at him, her hands over her ears. "Christ, David, I never thought it would be like this. How do the soldiers stand it?"

He held up the M-16. "At least they're armed. That helps."

She moved closer and hugged him. He felt her body against his and thought it odd. Bullets flying all around them, the enemy in the trees close by, and all he could think of was her body. He could smell her hair and perfume and feel her warmth.

"What happened to you?" she asked.

"Fell in the water."

And then they heard the sound of helicopters coming, a dozen swarming like hornets to attack the enemy. Halpren turned to the south where the choppers were crossing the tree line. They came forward, flared and settled. The rotor wash blew past them, snagging everything and swirling it up into the air.

The noise overpowered the shooting from the trees. Now he could hear only their own weapons firing as the Americans tried to keep the enemy from shooting at the helicopters. But it didn't work. Rounds slammed into them, punching through their fuselages, ripping at their engines and breaking the Plexiglas of their windows.

Soldiers tumbled out, a hundred of them dropping to the ground as soon as they were clear of the choppers. In seconds the aircraft took off, the enemy blazing away as the door guns returned fire. Then the choppers rotated and fled to the east.

"We could have escaped on those," wailed Drake. "They could have gotten us out."

Halpren shook his head. "No. Not yet. Too many of the enemy soldiers are shooting. Someone would have been killed."

"I'd take the chance," she said. "Get me out of here. That's all I want."

The soldiers who had been on the choppers scrambled forward, joining the beleaguered MPs. They filled in the gaps in the lines and some of them began to shoot.

"Things are looking up," said Halpren.

"How can you say that?" demanded Drake.

"The size of our force just doubled and there are helicopters close at hand."

STANWICK CROUCHED in the shadow of one of the trucks and used a pair of binoculars to examine the enemy positions across the open field. He tried to get a sense of the size of the enemy force, but each time he thought he had a handle on it, something new would happen. More weapons would begin to fire, or an enemy unit would appear where none had been before.

He scrambled back down into the ditch and snapped a finger for the RTO. The man crawled over and released the antenna so that it stood straight up. He gave the handset to Stanwick.

"Lightning Alpha Six, this is Lightning Six. Say status."

"Airborne and inbound your location. We're one five minutes out."

"Roger. Advise when zero two out."

"Roger."

Stanwick gave the handset back to the RTO. He slipped to the right, moved back to the top of the ditch and saw movement in the trees. The enemy was getting ready for something. Suddenly he understood what the movement meant. Charlie wasn't going to sit back and keep them pinned down, hoping for a chance to ambush the relief columns. No, he was going to come swarming out of the trees in the hope of overrunning the trucks.

Stanwick was up and moving along the line. "Get ready. They're coming." He reached the end of the column and started out again. "Steady. Fire on full-auto when they get close. Aim low. Keep putting out rounds."

He made it back to the lead jeep and dropped to the ground. Motioning the RTO over, he said, "I want the closest arty advisory. We'll need some artillery support."

"Yes, sir."

He put the handset to his ear and glanced at the trees. As the tuning squeal faded in the radio, he saw that he was too late. There was a rising wail of a bugle and the enemy came swarming out of the trees, shouting and shooting.

"Oh, Christ!" he said, as he tossed the handset aside and opened fire with his weapon. "Here they come."

27

ALONG HIGHWAY 239
EAST OF NUI BA DEN

Gerber and his relief column had worked their way closer to the convoy trapped on Highway 239 and were now moving through the jungle toward the road. It wasn't the thick triple-canopy jungle of the Central Highlands, but a thinner forest of middle-size trees and a thin undergrowth of small bushes. A carpeting of rotting vegetation covered the ground.

They stopped as the sounds of battle in front of them increased. Fetterman set up security and then retreated, finding Gerber and Gallagher. They crouched together near the thick trunk of a palm tree.

"I figure we're half a klick back now," said Fetterman. "You thought about how you want to handle this?"

Gerber took out his map, but it wasn't much help. It showed the roadway, the light forest and a notation that there were plantations in the vicinity. None of that was useful to him now that he was close to the fight.

"We need to filter through the trees toward the rear of the enemy formation," said Gallagher. "And we've got to let the men on the road know we're out here."

"They'll have a rear guard out, too," said Gerber. "I'd like to take that out quietly, so Charlie doesn't know we're back here. Then, when we pop up, we'll surprise the bastards."

"I imagine," said Fetterman, "they've got a platoon as the rear guard. There won't be any way to take them out quietly."

"We don't know that," said Gerber. "Maybe they were sloppy, figuring no one could get behind them this fast. Maybe it's only a couple of guys to spot helicopters, but we didn't use helicopters. So we go take a look."

"Me and Klein?" asked Fetterman.

"You, Klein and me," said Gerber.

"I don't like being left out of this," said Gallagher.

"Can't be helped," said Gerber.

"I know," responded Gallagher, "but I don't have to like it. Not one bit."

Gerber checked the time. "Thirty minutes to recon, find the guards and take them out. If there's a platoon back there, we'll have to get out and return with the strikers."

"And I'll wait here," said Gallagher.

"As our rear guard. And you can make contact with the convoy to let them know we're here."

"Got it," said Gallagher.

"Tony, you brief Klein. Make sure he understands we've got to move quickly but quietly."

"Yes, sir."

"Thirty minutes from now," said Gerber.

Gallagher set his watch and nodded. "In thirty minutes I move, whether I've heard from you or not."

"Right."

Fetterman peeled off and located Klein. He brought the Special Forces sergeant to the group. As they approached, Gerber stripped his rucksack and handed it to Gallagher.

When Fetterman arrived, both he and Klein followed suit so that each man had a weapon, a pistol and a knife. Gerber added a couple of grenades and Fetterman made sure he had a first-aid kit.

Gerber checked his pistol again and slipped it back into the holster. He put on the safety of his M-16, drew his knife and glanced at Fetterman. "Let's do it."

The master sergeant moved off slowly, working his way through the forest carefully, using the shadows for cover. He worked his way to the east, moving in slow motion, his head jerking right and left, as he searched for the enemy.

Gerber was five yards behind him, off to the right. He stepped over a log, went to one knee, listened and then moved on. There were hardly any animal sounds. The birds and monkeys had fled. The rattling of weapons from the battle ahead filtered through the trees. They were getting closer to the road. He reached out, touched a branch and then slipped around it, working his way east. Klein was on the other side, doing the same thing, moving slowly, listening for signs of the enemy and keeping his eyes open.

Fetterman halted, held up a hand and pointed ahead. Gerber saw a shadow move. An enemy was crouched there. He had shifted around, trying to get more comfortable, and in doing so had given himself away.

Gerber knelt on the soft, wet ground. Slowly he looked right and left and then, in the shadow of a large tree, spotted another enemy. This man was standing, leaning against the rough bark. His head was bowed as if he was sleeping, and his weapon was next to him, the barrel against the tree, the butt on the ground.

Gerber held up one finger and pointed. Fetterman nodded and turned toward Klein. He held up two fingers and then pulled one across his throat, telling Klein they were moving in for the kill. Klein nodded his understanding.

Fetterman moved first, easing his way through the forest. He stepped over a small bush and then got down on his hands and knees. Moving another five feet, he slipped to his belly and continued on his elbows and feet, hugging the ground. He circled his adversary, glancing at him but not staring at him. When he was four feet back, he rose to his feet and crouched, his knife in his right hand.

The enemy seemed to sense something. His eyes flicked open and he stared ahead, suddenly alert. He started to lift his AK and then froze. Fetterman struck, moving in a single, fluid, silent motion. He grabbed the enemy by the chin and lifted to expose the soft skin of the throat. Holding the man's mouth shut to keep him from crying out, he slashed with the knife. Blood spurted and splashed and the air around was filled with the odor of hot copper.

As the man sagged, Fetterman twisted and shoved the knife up into the back over the right kidney. He forced it higher, piercing a lung and the heart. There was a quiet groan and the man went completely limp. Fetterman lowered the body to the ground and then turned.

A second soldier, one he hadn't seen, was coming at him. The soldier had the bayonet of his AK extended and his head down. He was going to drive the bayonet through Fetterman's body and pin him to the tree. The master sergeant spun and grabbed the barrel of the AK, pushing it away from him. Stepping inside, he struck with the knife, plunging it up under the enemy soldier's breastbone. Blood poured from the wound. The NVA dropped his weapon, grabbed his chest and fell back into the jungle. He rolled over onto his belly, his hands under him.

Fetterman dropped with him, a knee in the man's back, holding him down, but the man was dead. The master sergeant stepped back, away from the body, and picked up the

AK. He stripped the bolt and dropped the gun into the dirt, stepping on it.

Gerber had no trouble. He moved toward the tree where the NVA soldier leaned. As he approached, he slowed and then stepped to the right. Moving to the tree, he slipped around to the side where he could see the enemy soldier. With his left hand he grabbed the man, jerking him to the side. As the head came up, Gerber cut, slicing through the neck nearly to the spine. There was a gurgle as blood poured from the enemy's throat and mouth. He fell to the jungle floor, kicked once and was still.

Gerber moved forward carefully and stopped. He picked up the AK and pulled the two Chicom grenades from the NVA's body. Leaving the dead man, he crouched near a flowering bush. Fetterman moved toward him, and Gerber saw the blood covering the side of Fetterman's uniform. "You okay?" he whispered.

Fetterman nodded. "Not mine."

Gerber checked the time and saw there were eighteen minutes left. Not much time to eliminate the rear guard if it was very large. He pointed to his watch.

Fetterman nodded and moved off. He kept the pace slow, creeping forward, using the cover around them as he searched for the enemy. Then he stopped again and pointed.

Klein saw the man and moved toward him. As he did, the man turned and looked right at the Special Forces sergeant. For an instant the enemy didn't move, surprised by the sudden appearance of the American. Before the NVA could react, shout or shoot, Klein kicked out and knocked him off his feet. He fell onto his side with a grunt of pain, and as he rolled to his stomach, Klein dropped onto his back, kneeing the NVA's spine. Grabbing the man's head, he jerked it up and cut his throat. The NVA bucked once, trying to throw Klein off and roll. But he spasmed instead and died.

Gerber moved up, touched Klein on the shoulder and pointed to the rear. Klein understood that they had run out of time and had to retreat. Fetterman joined them, moving close to Gerber. "Got one more," he said. "I think it was the sergeant."

Gerber nodded and wondered if they had eliminated the rear guard or only a small part of it. He tapped Fetterman on the shoulder, and the master sergeant took the point again, this time heading toward Gallagher and the strikers.

WITH ALL THE MEMBERS of his company, Thanh crouched at the edge of the forest, using the trees and rotting logs for cover. Firing from the Americans had fallen off, but they were still putting rounds into the trees. A soldier screamed suddenly, stood up, his arms outstretched, and then fell forward on his face. A second soldier grabbed his feet and pulled him to the rear. Someone else grabbed the dropped weapon.

There were others running through the trees behind him, men he'd never seen before, fifty of them, a hundred of them, filling gaps in the line and swelling their ranks. Thanh was impressed with the numbers. He'd had no idea that so many soldiers had been committed to the fight.

The officer Thanh had seen only once before moved down the line, stopping to talk to each group of soldiers. He didn't wear the uniform of the NVA but was dressed as a Chinese officer. The adviser, a taller, stockier man than the North Vietnamese, crouched near Thanh. "Don't shoot the civilians. They'll be unarmed and helpless. We want to capture them. Don't hesitate to kill the soldiers, even those who are wounded. They're our enemies. Kill them. Understood?"

When Thanh and the others near him nodded, the Chinese officer moved off to talk to the next group.

A bugle sounded a moment later, and the men began to get up. They checked their weapons, worked the bolts and snapped off safeties. Then they knelt, stood, then knelt again, filled with nervous energy they couldn't work off.

Thanh wanted to get up but was afraid to move. He could see through the vegetation and knew the enemy could see him, too. He didn't want to be a target before it was necessary.

And then the bugles came again, a dozen of them. With that came a shout that rippled through the ranks. At first it was a quiet one that built until it was a roar. Immediately the soldiers began to run from cover, flowing out into the open.

Thanh was on his feet, falling in with them. The shooting increased—American M-16s and Soviet-made AKs. Thanh burst from the forest into the open. The man beside him shrieked and grabbed his crotch as blood splattered the ground and the men around him. He fell to his knees and rolled onto his side, still screaming.

Thanh lowered his head and ran forward as he had been told to do. He fired his weapon once but didn't know where the bullet went. He didn't want to shoot his fellow soldiers.

He was aware of them falling around him. He saw them as they stumbled and fell. They were jerked from their feet. They screamed and moaned and rolled in the mud of the open ground. A dozen went down around him. Blood-drenched men, dying in the hot afternoon sun. There was screaming and shooting and bugles. Hundreds of men shouting and shooting.

He ran onward as the numbers of men attacking the Americans decreased. Ngo, who was out in front, stumbled, fell and didn't get up. Thanh was sure the sergeant had tripped, and ran to him. He crouched over the body, oblivious to the shooting around him. He pulled on Ngo's shoulder, but the man was limp. There was a stench around him, the foul odor of death.

Finally he rolled Ngo onto his back and saw the hole where his chest had been, a big, open wound, now partially packed with red mud. And then he realized it wasn't mud but Ngo's lungs and heart, open to the air, exposed for all to see, touch and smash.

"No," he screamed. *"No!"*

He leaped up and fired his rifle at the American position. The rounds hit a truck and bounced off. Wood splintered from the side and glass shattered.

But that didn't scare the Americans. Thanh saw them shooting back, the muzzles of their weapons strobing in the harsh tropical light. Tracers came at him. Bullets kicked up the dirt around him. Another struck the body of his dead friend.

Again he started forward, jerking at the trigger of his weapon. When it was empty, he stopped and yanked the magazine free, letting it fall to the ground. He pulled a fresh one out, jammed it home and began to shoot as he ran.

He was slammed in the chest, lifted from his feet and thrown to the ground. At first, as the breath whistled out of him, he didn't understand what had happened. Then the ache began in his chest and he thought of Ngo's ripped body. He put a hand to his stomach and worked it upward but there was no wetness, no white-hot pain. As his fingers touched the chest pouch and the single spare magazine left in it, he realized he had indeed been shot, but the bullet had embedded itself in the spare magazine. For some reason it hadn't set off the AK rounds. The chest pouch had saved his life.

For a moment he lay there, staring up into the bright blue afternoon sky. He saw a bird windmill overhead and thought that he had never seen a bird around a battle before. It was strange, but the birds and animals all seemed to flee before the shooting started.

Suddenly he wished he had been smart enough to do the same thing.

HALPREN HAD CRAWLED forward up the slope of the ditch so that he could see the trees where the enemy hid. The firing from there was tapering off. He glanced back at Drake and the other civilians. Smiling at her, he tried to reassure her, tried to let her know things weren't that bad yet.

And then the bugles started. First one and then more. There were shouts and whistles, and the enemy burst from the forest, running across the open ground and firing. Halpren sat there stunned, surprised the enemy would attack them, surprised at the number of men pouring from the trees.

Around him the Americans began to fire. Halpren watched, fascinated, as the VC ran toward him. The Americans returned fire. An officer ran along the bottom of the ditch, shouting instructions to the men, telling them to fire on full-auto, to aim low and put out rounds.

Halpren rolled onto his back, glanced down at Drake and then to the right. One man was hit by an AK bullet. He dropped his weapon and rolled down into the bottom of the ditch. Two men leaped to him, dragging him up out of the water. One of them tried to bandage the wounded man.

"We need a medic over here."

"Medic!"

"We need some help up here!" yelled another man.

"Ammo! I'm running out of ammo!"

"Coming at us on the end. Direct your fire over there," ordered an officer.

"Jesus, they're coming at us."

"Take the men in front first. Full-auto. Shoot low."

"Ammo."

"Shit! That was close."

A man rolled to the right. He jerked a magazine from the button of his M-16 and threw it away. Pulling another from his bandolier, he jammed it into the well. As he yanked on the operating lever, he grunted once, sat up and rolled over. Blood stained his back.

"Oh, shit! Oh, shit! Oh, shit!" cried one of the civilians.

Two men pulled the soldier toward them and began to work on him, trying to stop the flow of blood. As they worked, Halpren realized he had been a spectator. He was doing nothing to help the situation.

He scrambled upward, poked the barrel of his M-16 under the truck and opened fire, at first just pulling the trigger. But then he stopped. He watched the enemy swarming toward him. There were men falling. Men dying.

He aimed at one of the soldiers and pulled the trigger. The man kept coming at him. He fired again, and this time saw dirt fly from the uniform of the NVA. The man threw up his hands, lost his weapon and fell to the ground.

Halpren swung around and fired at another man. He shot at him until the NVA went down. Halpren saw him try to get up, so he shot him again. When the enemy soldier stopped moving, Halpren found a new target, but the weapon was empty. He looked to the right and yelled, "Ammo! I need some more ammo!"

One of the soldiers looked at him and grinned. He stripped off his bandolier and tossed it over. Halpren pulled it close, opened it and found another twenty-round magazine. He worked at it but couldn't get the old one free. Checking the weapon, he found a button, pushed it and the magazine fell out. Quickly he jammed another one in and worked the charging rod.

He opened fire again. The enemy was closer now. Halpren was stunned that men would run across open ground, their fellows falling around them, and that they would keep coming. He heard the screaming from the wounded, heard the hammering of the weapons, heard the shouts of the enemy.

He shot another soldier, and then the NVA were in the ditch on the other side of the road. Halpren knew they were all about to die. Bishop had wanted to see the war in Vietnam, and now that desire was going to kill them all.

STAAB CROUCHED near the front of the lead jeep and fired on single-shot as fast as he could pull the trigger. Enemy bullets slammed into the side of the jeep. One of the headlights shattered, spraying glass. Staab dived to the right and rolled down the slope out of the line of fire. "Shit," he said.

Coats crawled up to him. "Sure stepped on it here, sir," he said.

"Christ, Tom."

Coats popped up and fired three times. He dropped back, took a breath and did it again. As he hit the dirt a second time, he said, "We're not going to stop them. There are too many."

Staab nodded grimly. "Then we need to take as many with us as we can."

"Yes, sir!" Coats crept forward and fired.

Staab watched him for a moment, glanced at the civilians huddled at the bottom of the ditch and was glad he wasn't one of them. He had been ordered to Vietnam, but they had volunteered to come. He had a rifle in his hand and could kill the enemy. They could only hope the Army would put up a good fight and keep them alive.

He opened fire as the first of the Vietnamese made it into the ditch. Some of them rolled down, taking cover in the bottom of it. Others crouched there, firing into the trucks, at the machine gunners and at the soldiers. The noise seemed to get louder until it was one long, loud, drawn-out explosion.

Staab emptied his weapon, stripped the magazine and tossed it away. As he slammed another one home and used the charging rod, there was a shout on the other side of the ditch. Bugles sounded and there were screams in Vietnamese. Staab knew that it meant the final part of the attack was coming.

The Vietnamese suddenly appeared then, running at him. They came boiling out of the ditch, screaming and shooting. One of them leaped into the jeep and stood between the seats. Staab rolled to the left and fired without aiming. The rounds hit the man in the chest, flipping him out of the vehicle. He landed on his back in the dirt, his feet kicking, his arms thrashing.

Another came running around the front of the jeep. He had his AK at his hip, firing away, but not at anyone. Staab got to his knees and swung his rifle. The barrel hit the enemy in the stomach, knocking him off balance. As the man fell, Staab scrambled around and fired. Dirt exploded near the NVA's head as he tried to escape. Staab fired again and again, finally putting a bullet into the enemy's back. He shrieked, tried to scramble away and then collapsed, lying still.

Staab turned and saw two more enemy soldiers. He opened fire on them. One of them grabbed his side and dropped his weapon. The other fired, and Staab felt a pain in his leg. It would no longer support him and he started to topple. He tried to shoot the man but couldn't get his weapon around.

He knew he was about to die and there wasn't a damn thing he could do about it. He was too slow. He hadn't been paying attention.

The shot rang out, but there was no more pain. The NVA dropped to the ground without a sound. Staab, now lying on his side, turned and saw Coats standing there. Coats flipped him a salute and turned. A rain of bullets slammed into his chest and face, driving him back into the side of the jeep. He slipped to the ground, dead before he knew he'd been shot.

Staab fired then. He didn't aim. He just pulled the trigger. The enemy who had shot Coats was lifted off his feet and thrown back. He rolled over in the dirt and slipped into the ditch.

"We're not going to make it," mumbled Staab. "We're not going to make it."

28

ALONG HIGHWAY 239
EAST OF NUI BA DEN

Stanwick watched as the North Vietnamese ran across the open ground, and although his men took a high toll of the enemy, the NVA kept right on coming. They ran up to the ditch on the other side of the road, dived for cover and then came up, shooting. There were hundreds of enemy soldiers; they outnumbered the Americans two to one.

Stanwick shot at them, dropping enemy soldiers until his weapon was empty, then he grabbed the handset from the RTO and yelled, "Hawk Six, Hawk Six, this is Lightning Six."

"Go, Lightning Six."

"We need gun support now. Do you have guns?"

"Roger, guns. Heavy fire team."

"Hawk Six, the bad guys are in the field and coming at us. We need assistance."

"Roger, assistance. Guns inbound."

"Hawk Six, they're in our lines. We need help now."

"Roger," said Hawk Six. "Contact Talon Four Six on six six decimal five."

Stanwick, aware of the shooting around him, aware of the screams of pain of the wounded and the dying, reached over to dial the new frequency. He worked rapidly, thinking of the nightmares where he worked at dialing frequencies but could never get the right one. Somehow, in his dreams, he overshot or undershot it, or the numbers shimmered and changed. He was never able to hit it right, and that was with no one shooting at him. But that didn't happen. He dialed the frequency, listened as the turning squeal faded, then said, "Talon Four Six, this is Lightning Six."

"Go, Lightning Six."

"We have gooks in our lines. We have them coming out of the trees. You need to hit them from south to north, parallel to the highway."

"Inbound."

"Talon Four Six, you better hurry."

"Roger that. Can you throw smoke?"

Stanwick almost laughed at that. The enemy would be obvious as they came at the American position, but the pilots wanted smoke. "Roger that." He let go of the button on the handset and told the RTO, "Throw a red smoke grenade over the trucks."

The RTO grabbed a grenade and pulled the pin. He twisted and threw the grenade over the top of the truck so that it bounced toward the enemy position. "Smoke out."

The sound of rotor blades came then, blotting out the shooting going on around him. He turned and saw the first of the choppers as it streaked over the treetops.

"ID red."

"Roger, red. The enemy's in the smoke." He then tossed the handset at the RTO, grabbed his weapon, rolled to the right and began to fire. As he did, there were two explosions across the road. And two more. And two more. Splashes of brown dirt geysered into the sky. There were screams and yells from the enemy as some of them turned to fire at the attacking helicopter.

The chopper broke to the right then, the door gunners firing into the enemy lines. The second helicopter rolled in, but this one didn't use rockets. They opened fire with the miniguns. The muzzle-flashes from the rapidly rotating barrels looked like balls of fire at the side of the chopper and the sound wasn't that of a machine gun but of a buzz saw, starting quietly, then building to a roar. The stream of 7.62 mm rounds dug up the ground and chopped through the enemy lines.

The third helicopter rolled in, its rockets firing and ripping through the NVA soldiers. The fusillade from the American line increased. The men, who had crouched behind the trucks and in the ditch, scrambled forward, shooting. Bodies were scattered over the field. Dozens of them, some ripped to pieces, lined the ditch.

But the enemy attack had been broken. The NVA fled now, trying to get out of the open. They ran straight for the trees, seeking sanctuary. Stanwick got to his feet and ran down the line of jeeps and trucks, checking on his men. There were dead and wounded scattered behind them and lying in the ditch. Medics worked on the wounded. As he moved, he warned them, ''They'll be back. They've tasted victory.''

He could see the high-water mark of the enemy assault. They had reached the trucks and a few had penetrated the American lines. They had died for their bravery, but they had gotten there on the first attempt. Stanwick knew they would try again as soon as they could regroup. He had to get the second airlift in as quickly as possible. He had to hope the Special Forces men could get in behind the enemy though with them moving in the trees, he couldn't use artillery.

Stanwick ran past the civilians, who were cowering in the ditch. One of them came up to him and shouted, "You'd better get us the fuck out of here. Right fucking now."

Stanwick grimaced. "Sir, please stay down. The enemy's still close."

"Get the choppers in here now," ordered the man.

Stanwick recognized the hysterical man as Senator Bishop. "Senator, if you don't keep your head down, you're liable to get it fucking well shot off." The colonel moved away then, checking on his lines. When he reached the end, he rushed back to the front and grabbed the handset from the RTO. "Hawk Six, this is Lightning Six."

"Go, Lightning Six."

"We have civilians here and need to get them out."

"Roger that."

HAVING RECOVERED from the impact of the bullet that hit him, and from the moment Ngo died, Thanh was filled with rage. He screamed that anger at the enemy as he ran across the open ground and dived into the bottom of the ditch. He screamed it as he lay in the bottom of the ditch, listening to the firing all around him. Then, clawing up the other side, he was face-to-face with the Americans. He could see their white or black skin, their round eyes and white teeth. He could read the name tags of their uniforms and smell the odor of their after-shave. He was close enough to kick them. But he didn't kick anyone. He shot at them point-blank, the rifle held at his hip. He fired again and again, turning and twisting, spraying bullets everywhere.

He saw an American soldier lying on the ground near the tire of a truck. Turning, he fired at the man. The first round struck the frame of the vehicle, ricocheting off in a flash of sparks. Again he fired and again he missed, but the American didn't seem to notice. The third shot punched through the American's helmet and blood spurted from it. The man slumped forward and slipped to the rear.

Rockets exploded behind him. Thanh spun, heard the choppers and saw more rockets. He dived into the ditch, rolled to the bottom and scrambled through the weeds. The lead chopper turned, crossed over the trucks and climbed out away from him. As that happened, the second aircraft turned, its guns firing in a loud, continuous sound that ripped through the air. The vegetation was torn to pieces. Running men were cut down, their bodies exploding under the impact of dozens of machine gun bullets. Blood splashed and sprayed, creating a mist that drifted on the breeze.

Thanh turned his head and felt his stomach flip over. Bile exploded in his throat, but he gritted his teeth, refusing to throw up. He closed his eyes so that he could no longer witness the destruction of his comrades.

When the noise ended, he was up on his feet again, running as hard and fast as he could. The last helicopter rolled in, firing more rockets. They tore up the field to the left. More of his friends died, and as the detonations walked toward him, he threw himself to the ground. Somehow he survived that attack. Shrapnel whirled over him. Hot blasts of air rocked him. Others were hit and screamed. Some shot at the choppers to no effect.

As the last helicopter turned, Thanh leaped up and bolted. But now the forest seemed to be miles away. He'd never be able to reach it. He'd die on the remains of the trees and bushes cut down to protect the road. He'd rot right there with the vegetation.

He stumbled once, fell to his hands and knees and lost his rifle. But then he was up again, his AK in his left hand. The trees were closer now. The American choppers began another run, the rockets slashing through the air, but Thanh didn't stop. He ran as hard as he could, leaping the bodies of the dead, his eyes on the forest.

As the ground began to blow up again, Thanh reached the trees. He leaped at them, diving for the cover they offered, and landed hard, driving the breath from his lungs. He lay there among the branches and leaves of the forest, water dripping on his back as he breathed heavily. The helicopters worked the open field but didn't attack the trees. He was safe if he stayed where he was.

Slowly he rolled onto his side and then sat up. Turning, he looked out over the field. There seemed to be no living thing left. A hundred men had died crossing the clearing. They lay scattered around like a handful of corn thrown on the ground. Thanh shook his head. The attack had accomplished nothing.

He got to his feet, moving deeper into the forest. Around him the others who had escaped were doing the same thing. There was no communication among them as they tried to stay alive. No one was talking or issuing orders. Those who had survived the first attack were running deeper into the safety of the forest.

The first shot caught him by surprise. Thanh thought it was one of his comrades firing a captured M-16 as he hurried away from the road, but then the forest erupted around him. He heard the sonic snap as the rounds whipped past him. Diving for the ground again, he tried to figure out what was happening. How had the enemy gotten behind them?

Thanh lay on the forest floor, his face pressed into the moist mass of vegetation, and listened. There were shouts, shots and screams.

"The Americans have outflanked us!"

"Fire! Everyone fire!"

"We've got to get out of here."

"Split up. Run."

There was a stuttering blast from a machine gun. One man screamed, "Help me! I'm hit!"

Thanh didn't know what to do. He stayed where he was, trying to think but unable to decide. There was too much noise, too much confusion, to allow him to concentrate. He needed a few minutes of silence, but he couldn't get it.

He crawled to the right where there was a large tree. Using it for cover, he got to his feet and tried to see what was happening. There were shafts of light and patches of dark in front of him. The muzzle-flashes twinkled, creating an almost friendly sight.

Thanh pushed the barrel of his AK around the trunk and pulled the trigger. He fired a short burst that was answered immediately. A dozen rounds slammed into the tree, stripping the bark from it. Wood splinters sprayed his face and hands. He ducked back and dropped to his knees.

Crouching there, he tried to figure out what to do. The firing from the forest became more intense. The sound rolled outward toward him and beyond. He didn't think he could sneak through it.

Then there was a rising shout—American and Vietnamese voices in the trees. Shadows danced and swayed. Thanh fired at one, but nothing happened. It stayed where it had been, weaving back and forth. He spotted another and fired. This time someone shot back. The bullet zipped by him and he ducked.

The first bullet was followed by another and another. One hit him in the shoulder, spinning him. He lost his grip on his weapon as he fell back, landing on his wounded shoulder and shrieking in pain so intense that it burst behind his eyes and blackened the sky over him.

For a moment he couldn't move, the pain was so bad. But as it subsided, he felt light-headed, as if about to faint. He wanted to roll onto his side and get up, but he couldn't. He lay on his back, bent over the thick root of a tree. Blood pumped rapidly from his wound, pooling under him as he slowly lost consciousness. He wasn't aware he was dying quickly, only that the sky was darkening before it was time. For a moment he thought the sun was setting. He never realized he was a brave man, as brave as anyone else thrown into battle. He died believing he was a coward who had run every time he got into a fight with the Americans.

GERBER AND THE STRIKERS fanned out a hundred yards deep into the jungle, aware that helicopters were going to be working over the open field between them and the stalled convoy. The captain hoped the gunship pilots had been told that there was another American force in the trees, but he knew that in the heat of battle instructions sometimes got garbled. Gerber had no intention of becoming a casualty to friendly fire.

Once they had established a defensive line facing the enemy, with a rear guard whose orders were to shoot first so that they wouldn't be eliminated as easily as the NVA's had been, they settled down to wait. Gerber didn't want his men to fire until the enemy retreated into the supposed safety of the trees. The surprise of Americans and South Vietnamese would devastate Charlie and break his spirit. Gerber hoped the enemy would surrender without much of a fight.

As the helicopters rolled in, working the ditch and open ground with rockets and miniguns, the strikers got ready. The buzz-saw rip of miniguns came toward them. It was punctuated by the detonations of rockets and the screams of the enemy as they fled.

Moments later there was movement in the forest. Shadows danced and sunlight flashed as the NVA ran for safety. Gerber eased his rifle higher and waited. Then, seeing a man running right at him, he aimed and fired. That was the signal for the rest of them. There was a volley, a hesitation, then enemy soldiers went down.

Firing increased. Gerber watched two men turn to run. Both were hit and slammed to the ground. Off to the right a man threw down his weapon but was shot four or five times, the blood staining his khaki shirt, quickly turning it red.

There was return fire from the enemy but not a coordinated volley. A bugle sounded and the firing tapered off. Three men stumbled forward, their hands up, but were cut down by their comrades. The NVA didn't want anyone surrendering.

"Hold your fire!" yelled Gerber.

"We've got three of them over here," said Klein.

"Hold them there. Tony, how's it look?"

There was a wild burst of firing and then Fetterman said, "Got them."

"Bring it on in," ordered Gerber. "Hold your fire."

He stood up, moved forward and saw a man running through the trees. The man wore a pith helmet and khaki shirt and carried an AK. Gerber yelled for him to stop, but the man ignored the command. The captain aimed and fired once. The man disappeared, falling into the vegetation. The firing tapered off to single shots. More of the NVA came toward them, their hands raised.

"Let's get out of here," said Gerber. "Klein, get with the RTO and advise the grunts that we're coming out of here with prisoners."

"Yes, sir." Klein moved off toward the striker who was carrying the radio.

Gallagher appeared, grinning. "Wasn't much of a fight."

"Not for us," said Gerber. He wiped at the sweat on his face. "Not for us."

They moved forward cautiously, checking the bodies of the dead enemy soldiers. They picked up weapons, grenades and documents, and some of the strikers began taking souvenirs. Gerber ignored that, figuring they deserved it for their part in the fight.

They reached the edge of the forest and halted. In front of them was the open field where the enemy dead lay. Beyond that was the convoy, and overhead were four or five circling helicopters.

Gerber glanced at Klein and yelled, "Tell them we're throwing smoke." He took a grenade and threw it out of the forest.

"ID yellow," called Klein, relaying word from the grunts behind the trucks.

Gerber then stepped from the tree line into the opening. He walked out a few feet where he was visible to the men on the road. Right and left of him were the strikers, along with half a dozen NVA soldiers who had surrendered.

Gerber waved a hand and the line moved forward. As they did, there was a cheer from the road. The Americans there appeared, applauding, screaming and laughing.

They covered the open ground rapidly, walked through the ditch and up onto the road. Gerber looked at the men suddenly surrounding him and asked, "Where's Lightning Six?"

A man pushed through toward him. "Right here."

"MacKenzie K. Gerber. Happy to make your acquaintance, Colonel."

"I'm happier than hell to see you myself. What in hell were you doing in that forest?"

"Supporting you," said Gerber. He turned and looked to the west where Nui Ba Den dominated the sky. "We were running a mission there when we heard about the trouble."

"Christ, Captain," said Stanwick, "that was some feat, getting off the mountain and down here."

"Yes, sir."

A civilian appeared then. "I want my people taken out of here now."

"Captain Gerber," said Stanwick, "may I present Senator Bishop."

"Senator," said Gerber.

"Cut the shit, Colonel. You order those choppers in here now, before something else happens."

"If you'll excuse me," said Stanwick, "I have some things to do."

"Certainly, sir," said Gerber.

As Stanwick and the senator disappeared, Gerber spotted Staab kneeling near the body of Coats. He moved down to him and said, "A good man."

"Yes, sir. One of the best."

Gerber crouched down and looked at Staab. "I think maybe you should look into getting him a medal for his part in this. Bronze Star for valor at the least."

Staab nodded. "His folks would like that."

Gerber stayed there a few more seconds, waiting for Staab to say something, if the lieutenant wanted to. Finally the sound of incoming helicopters interrupted them. Gerber got up and said, "You get the citation prepared and forward it to me, I'll sign it, too."

"Thank you, Captain."

Gerber moved back up to the road. Gallagher appeared and said, "I'm going to get choppers to take us back up to Nui Ba Den. No sense in walking back up the mountain."

"All right," said Gerber. "I think Tony and I will catch a ride back to Saigon with the civilians."

Gallagher stuck out a hand. "Good to work with you, Captain."

"The same, Captain," said Gerber.

One of the grunts threw a smoke grenade out into the open field and the choppers headed for it, filling the air with noise and debris. Conversation ceased as everyone turned away from the choppers and the dust. When the aircraft touched down, the civilians moved toward them, Bishop leading the way.

Fetterman came up beside Gerber. "Fucking boondoggle," he said.

"One of the biggest."

He grinned and pointed at Bishop. "Think we taught the senator anything about fighting the war here?"

"Shit, no," said Gerber. "He knew it all before he got here. We taught him nothing."

"Yeah," said Fetterman. "That's kind of what I was afraid of."

"We all were."

EPILOGUE

Gerber had a seat in the back of the conference room. Morrow had gotten press passes for him and Sergeant Fetterman and had made them promise not to tell anyone where they had come from. The two Special Forces men now waited for Senator R. Turner Bishop and the other members of the congressional delegation to enter the conference room with their announcements.

Gerber leaned toward Morrow. "Have you got any idea what he's going to say?"

Morrow shrugged and opened her notebook. "I don't think you're going to like it."

"Why?"

"The rumblings are that he's using the attack on the convoy as a springboard to prove how inept the military is. Couldn't keep their itinerary a secret, that sort of thing. He's going to link the ambush with the mismanagement that cost us so much during Tet."

"Christ, we got his fat ass out of there with no one getting hurt."

"He claims it took too long, they were in real danger and the military failed to respond to the threat. He says the breakdown in intelligence was responsible for the enemy being there in the first place."

"And if it hadn't been for our intelligence, Fetterman and I wouldn't have been on that mountain and Staab wouldn't have been in the field."

"Hey, don't yell at me. I'm on your side."

"Right," said Gerber, but he wondered. The American press seemed to be one of the three or four enemies they were fighting in South Vietnam.

The rear door opened and Bishop entered. Gerber noticed a change in the man. He was no longer tired, dirty and scared. He was revitalized. Sweeping into the room, he took the center seat, pulled the microphone closer and unfolded his notes. "I have a brief statement and then I'll be ready for questions."

He fixed everyone with a stare. Here was a man back in his element. The terror of the afternoon in the fields of South Vietnam with the NVA swarming out of the trees was now in the past. He was in command again. He was the authority and everyone had better know it.

"The fiasco of which I was a victim three days ago was a demonstration of the ineptness of the American military effort here in South Vietnam. It was a classic example of everything that's wrong. The American forces were completely unprepared for the attacks, and it was only sheer luck that prevented an incident of international proportions."

"Shit," mumbled Gerber. "It was military skill that prevented it. We have to coordinate everything with the South Vietnamese, knowing full well the VC and NVA have infiltrated to the very highest levels. It was Bishop who insisted on driving from Dau Tieng to Go Dau Ha when he could have flown. Not to mention everything was in the paper."

"Shh," said Morrow.

Gerber rocked back and looked up at the ceiling.

"That demonstration of military failure has convinced me that all I've heard about Tet is true. It was a breakdown of American military policy that resulted in a defeat for the American forces."

Gerber couldn't let that pass. The truth had to be told before the whole story became distorted. For some reason the congressional delegation had arrived with a decision made and was now reinforcing that decision. It had no basis in fact. Political motivations had to be the reason.

Gerber stood up as Bishop said, "I came here to learn the truth about our military policies. I've learned that our policies are a failure."

"Bullshit!" said Gerber. "Tony, let's go."

"Yes, sir."

"You, sir," said Bishop, "halt right there!"

Gerber faced the senator. He knew how much trouble a senator could cause for a military man. With the right words in the right place Bishop could end his career. He could make sure there were no more promotions, no more choice assignments. He could make sure Gerber ended his career counting blankets in a supply depot in Utah. But Gerber didn't care. At least he didn't care at that moment.

"Excuse me," said Gerber. "I'm not going to stand here and listen to a man who has no knowledge of the military or the way it works malign it. I'm not going to listen to the creation of a myth. Facts show we won at Tet, but everyone seems to want to take it away from us. And if we were so bad, explain why no civilians were hurt in that convoy of yours. No, sir, I won't remain here."

Gerber pushed his way through the crowd, reached the door and was stopped by an MP. The sergeant looked into Gerber's eyes and then stepped aside without a word.

THE DOORS BURST OPEN and Halpren saw a single officer exit, followed by a sergeant and then a young woman who had to be a reporter. They hurried down the hall away from the meeting without looking back. When they were gone, Halpren said, "You know, Julie, when we get back to the States, I'm resigning."

Drake stood with her back to the wall. Neither had wanted to sit inside during the press conference. They'd had their moment in the sun when the choppers had landed at Tan Son Nhut. Now they were content to sit back and let Bishop and his colleagues have the spotlight.

"You're really going to quit? Why?"

"I can't work for a man like Bishop. Not with everything I've seen in the past week. He came to Vietnam knowing everything he wanted to accomplish. It wasn't a fact-finding tour, just a chance to grab headlines. He rejects everything positive about Tet and plays up the negative. Those who defend the Army's point of view are eliminated."

"That the only reason you're going to quit?"

"I don't know," said Halpren, shrugging. "I didn't like the way he acted in the field, the way he demanded they save his butt first. He's somehow more important than the rest of us."

"And what about that night on the way to Vietnam?" she asked.

"That, too," responded Halpren. Finally he was getting his chance to explain it all to her. "He asked me if we had a thing going and I said we didn't. I thought it was the best thing to say. I mentioned to you that you should, for your career, have dinner with him." Halpren shook his head. "It was an incredibly stupid thing to say."

"It made me mad," she told him. "It sounded as if you were trying to advance your career by sacrificing me."

"A misunderstanding."

She smiled. "You were so brave," she said, to change the subject.

"Yeah. Shaking like a leaf."

"No, I mean it. You were the only one who picked up a rifle. Everyone else stayed hidden in the ditch."

"I was lucky I didn't get my ass shot off."

She stared at him for a moment, searching his face, then asked, "What was it like? To kill that man?"

"You know, the funny thing is, I don't really remember the feeling. I pulled the trigger and he fell, but there was no emotion at that moment. Nothing. Then later we were so happy to be alive that I didn't think about it. The relief of getting on the chopper wiped out all thoughts."

"And now?"

"And now it's an act in the past. I wish it hadn't been necessary to shoot him, but then I'm glad it was him and not me. Do you understand what I mean?"

"No," she said. "You took a human life."

"But it wasn't as if I walked in and gunned the man down. I had to shoot, or I would have died. I don't want to have to do it again, but for that one moment I was really alive. Everything was so clear. So crystal clear. I heard everything distinctly. I saw everything. It was a life-or-death situation, and I'm the one who lived through it."

She didn't say anything.

"I'm sorry it happened, I guess, but as I said, it's something in the past." He realized he could never make her understand. If it had been a movie, he would have been devastated by the act, as if to justify it to the audience, but here in Vietnam there was no audience.

Just then there was a burst of sound from the conference room.

"Guess they're breaking it up," he said.

"When they're through," she said, "would you like to have dinner with me?"

Halpren nodded. He reached out and touched her shoulder, surprised that something good could come out of the Vietnam War. "I can't think of anything else I'd rather do."

GLOSSARY

AC—Aircraft commander. The pilot in charge of the aircraft.

ADO—A-Detachment's area of operations.

AFVN—Armed Forces radio and television network i
Vietnam. Army PFC Pat Sajak was probably the mos
memorable of AFVN's deejays with his loud and long
"GOOOOOOOOOOOOD MORNing Vietnam!"
The spinning Wheel of Fortune gives no clues abou
his whereabouts today.

AGGRESSOR FATIGUES—Black fatigues called aggres
sor fatigues because they were the color of the uni
forms worn by aggressors during war games in th
World.

AIT—Advanced Individual Training. The school soldier
were sent to after Basic.

AK-47—Assault rifle normally used by North Vietnames
and Vietcong.

ANGRY-109—AN-109, the radio used by the Specia
Forces for long-range communications.

AO—Area of Operations.

O DAI—Long dresslike garment, split up the sides and worn over pants.

P ROUNDS—Armor-piercing ammunition.

PU—Auxiliary Power Unit. An outside source of power used to start aircraft engines.

RC LIGHT—Term used for a B-52 bombing mission. Also known as heavy arty.

RVN—Army of the Republic of Vietnam. A South Vietnamese soldier. Also known as Marvin Arvin.

SA—Army Security Agency.

SH-AND-TRASH—Refers to helicopter support missions that didn't involve a direct combat role. They hauled supplies, equipment, mail and all sorts of ash-and-trash.

ST—Control officer between the men in isolation and the outside world. Responsible for taking care of all problems.

UTOVON—Army phone system that allows soldiers on one base to call another base, bypassing the civilian phone system.

DA—Bomb Damage Assessment. The official report on the results of a bombing mission.

SCUIT—C-rations.

ODY COUNT—Number of enemy killed, wounded or captured during an operation. Used by Saigon and Washington as a means of measuring progress of the war.

OOM BOOM—Term used by Vietnamese prostitutes to sell their product.

OONDOGGLE—Any military operation that hasn't been completely thought out. An operation that is ridiculous.

BOONIE HAT—Soft cap worn by a grunt in the field whe
he wasn't wearing his steel pot.

BROWNING M-2—Fifty-caliber machine gun manufa·
tured by Browning.

BROWNING M-35—Automatic pistol, a 9 mm weapo
that became the favorite of the Special Forces.

BUSHMASTER—Jungle warfare expert or soldier skille
in jungle navigation. Also a large deadly snake n·
common to Vietnam but mighty tasty.

C AND C—Command and Control aircraft that circle
overhead to direct combined air and ground oper·
tions.

CAO BOI—A cowboy. Refers to the criminals of Saigon wh·
rode motorcycles.

CARIBOU—Cargo transport plane.

CH-47—A Chinook.

CHINOOK—Army Aviation twin-engine helicopter.
CH-47. Also known as a shit hook.

CHOCK—Refers to the number of the aircraft in the fligh·
Chock Three is the third. Chock Six is the sixth.

CLAYMORE—Antipersonnel mine that fires seve·
hundred and fifty steel balls with a lethal range of fift·
meters.

CLOSE AIR SUPPORT—Use of airplanes and helicopte·
to fire on enemy units near friendlies.

CO CONG—Female Vietcong.

COLT—Soviet-built small transport plane. The NAT·
code name for Soviet and Warsaw Pact transports a
begin with the letter *C*.

CONEX—Steel container about ten feet high, ten feet deep and ten feet long used to haul equipment and supplies.

CS—An improved form of persistent tear gas, usually dispersed as a fine powder from grenades.

DAC CONG—Enemy sappers who attacked in the front ranks to blow up the wire so that the infantry could assault a camp.

DAI UY—Vietnamese army rank equivalent to captain.

DC-3—World War II vintage twin-engined cargo plane. Also called a C-47 or Gooney Bird.

DEROS—Date Estimated Return from Overseas Service.

DIRNSA—Director, National Security Agency.

E AND E—Escape and Evasion.

FEET WET—Term used by pilots to describe a flight over water.

FIELD GRADE—Refers to officers above the rank of captain but under that of brigadier general. In other words, majors, lieutenant colonels and colonels.

FIRECRACKER—Special artillery shell that explodes into a number of small bomblets that detonate later. It is the artillery version of the cluster bomb and was a secret weapon employed tactically for the first time at Khe Sanh.

FIRST SHIRT—Military term referring to the first sergeant.

FIVE—Radio call sign for the executive officer of a unit.

FNG—Fucking New Guy.

FOB—Forward Operating Base.

FOX MIKE—FM radio.

FREEDOM BIRD—Name given to any aircraft that too troops out of Vietnam. Usually referred to the commercial jet flights that took men back to the World.

GARAND—M-1 rifle that was replaced by the M-14. I sued to the South Vietnamese early in the war.

GO-TO-HELL RAG—Towel or any large cloth wor around the neck by a grunt.

GRAIL—NATO name for the shoulder-fired SA-7 surface to-air missile.

GUARD THE RADIO—Term that means standing by the commo bunker and listening for messages.

GUIDELINE—NATO name for the SA-2 surface-to-a missile.

GUNSHIP—Armed helicopter or cargo plane that carrie weapons instead of cargo.

HE—High-explosive ammunition.

HOOTCH—Almost any shelter, from temporary to lon term.

HORN—Term that referred to a specific kind of radio o erations that used satellites to rebroadcast messages

HORSE—See *Biscuit*.

HOTEL THREE—Helicopter landing area at Saigon's Ta Son Nhut Airport.

HUEY—UH-1 helicopter.

HUMINT—Human intelligence resource.

ICS—Official name of the intercom system in an aircraft.

IN-COUNTRY—Term used to refer to American troop operating in South Vietnam. They were all in-countr

INTELLIGENCE—Any information about enemy ope ations. It can include troop movements, weapons c pabilities, biographies of enemy commanders ar general information about terrain features. It is any information that would be useful in planning a mission.

KA-BAR—Type of military combat knife.

KIA—Killed In Action. (Since the United States wasn't engaged in a declared war, the use of the term *KIA* wasn't authorized. KIA came to mean enemy dead. Americans were KHA or Killed in Hostile Action.)

KLICK—One thousand meters. A kilometer.

LIMA LIMA—Land Line. Refers to telephone communications between two points on the ground.

LLDB—Luc Luong Dac Biet. The South Vietnamese Special Forces. Sometimes referred to as the Look Long, Duck Back.

LP—Listening Post. A position outside the perimeter manned by a couple of people to give advance warning of enemy activity.

LRRP—Long-Range Reconnaissance Patrol.

LSA—Lubricant used by soldiers on their weapons to ensure they would continue to work properly.

LZ—Landing Zone.

M-3—Also known as a Grease Gun. A .45-caliber submachine gun that was favored in World War II by GIs. It's slow rate of fire meant the barrel didn't rise. As well, the user didn't burn through his ammo as fast as he did with some of his other weapons.

M-14—Standard rifle of the United States forces, eventually replaced by the M-16. It fires the standard NATO round—7.62 mm.

M-16—Became the standard infantry weapon of the Vietnam War. It fires 5.56 mm ammunition.

M-79—Short barreled, shoulder-fired weapon that fires a
40 mm grenade. These can be high explosives, white
phosphorus or canister.

M-113—Numerical designation of an armored personnel
carrier.

MACV—Military Assistance Command, Vietnam, replaced MAAG in 1964.

MAD MINUTE—Specified time on a base camp when the
men in the bunkers would clear their weapons. It came
to mean the random firing of all the camp's weapons
as fast as everyone could shoot.

MATCU—Marine Air Traffic Control Unit.

MEDEVAC—Also called Dust-Off. A helicopter used to
take wounded to medical facilities.

MI—Military Intelligence.

MIA—Missing In Action.

MONOPOLY MONEY—Term used by servicemen in
Vietnam to describe the MPC handed out in lieu of
regular United States currency.

MOS—Military Occupation Specialty—A job description.

MPC—Military Payment Certificates. The monopoly
money used instead of real cash.

NCO—Noncommissioned officer. A noncom. A sergeant.

NCOIC—NCO In Charge. The senior NCO in a unit, de-
tachment or patrol.

NDB—Nondirectional Beacon. A radio beacon that can be
used for homing.

NEXT—The man who said it was his turn to be rotated
home. See *Short-Timer*.

NINETEEN—Average age of combat soldier in Vietnam,
as opposed to twenty-six in World War II.

NOUC-MAM—Foul-smelling sauce used by Vietnamese.

NVA—North Vietnamese Army. Also used to designate a soldier from North Vietnam.

ONTOS—Marine weapon that consists of six 106 mm recoilless rifles mounted on a tracked vehicle.

ORDER OF BATTLE—The list of units available during a battle. Not necessarily a list of how or when the units will be used, but a listing of who and what could be used.

P (PIASTER)—Basic monetary unit in South Vietnam, worth slightly less than a penny.

PETA-PRIME—Tarlike substance that melted in the heat of the day to become a sticky black nightmare that clung to boots, clothes and equipment. It was used to hold down dust during the dry season.

PETER PILOT—Copilot in a helicopter.

PLF—Parachute Landing Fall. The roll used by parachutists on landing.

POW—Prisoner of War.

PRC-10—Portable radio.

PRC-25—Lighter portable radio that replaced the PRC-10.

PULL PITCH—Term used by helicopter pilots that means they are going to take off.

PUNJI STAKE—Sharpened bamboo hidden to penetrate the foot. Sometimes dipped in feces.

PUZZLE PALACE—Term referring to the Pentagon. It was called the puzzle palace because no one knew what was going on in it. The Puzzle Palace East referred to MACV or USARV Headquarters in Saigon.

REDLEGS—Artillerymen. Derived from the old Army where artillerymen wore a red stripe on the legs of their uniforms.

REMF—Rear-Echelon Motherfucker.

RINGKNOCKER—Graduate of military academy. Refers to ring worn by all graduates.

RON—Remain Overnight. Term used by flight crews to indicate a flight that would last longer than a day.

RPD—Soviet-made 7.62 mm light machine gun.

RTO—Radio Telephone Operator. The radioman of a unit.

RUFF-PUFFS—Term applied to the RF-PFs, the regional and popular forces. Militia drawn from the local population.

S-3—Company-level operations officer. Same as the G-3 on a general's staff.

SA-2—Surface-to-air missile fired from a fixed site. It is a radar-guided missile that is nearly thirty-five feet long.

SA-7—Surface-to-air missile that is shoulder-fired and has infrared homing.

SACSA—Special Assistant for Counterinsurgency and Special Activities.

SAFE—Selected Area for Evasion. It doesn't mean the area is safe from the enemy, only that the terrain, location or local population make the area a good place for escape and evasion.

SAM TWO—Refers to the SA-2 Guideline.

SAR—Search And Rescue. SAR forces were the people involved in search-and-rescue missions.

SECDEF—Secretary of Defense.

SHORT-TIME—GI term for a quickie.

SHORT-TIMER—Person who had been in Vietnam for nearly a year and who would be rotated back to the World soon. When the DEROS (Date of Estimated Return from Overseas Service) was the shortest in the unit, the person was said to be next.

SINGLE-DIGIT MIDGET—Soldier with fewer than ten days left in-country.

SIX—Radio call sign for unit commander.

SKS—Soviet-made carbine.

SMG—Submachine gun.

SOG—Studies and Observations Group. Cover name for MACV special operations.

SOI—Signal Operating Instructions. The booklet that contained the call signs and radio frequencies of the units in Vietnam.

SOP—Standard Operating Procedure.

SPIKE TEAM—Special Forces team used for a direct-action mission.

STEEL POT—Standard U.S. Army helmet. The steel pot was the outer metal cover.

TAOR—Tactical Area of Operational Responsibility.

TEAM UNIFORM OR COMPANY UNIFORM—UHF radio frequency on which the team or the company communicates. Frequencies were changed periodically in an attempt to confuse the enemy.

THE WORLD—The United States.

THREE—Radio call sign of the operations officer.

THREE CORPS—Military area around Saigon. Vietnam was divided into four corps areas.

TO & E—Table of Organization and Equipment. A detailed listing of all the men and equipment assigned to a unit.

TOC—Tactical Operations Center.

TOT—Time Over Target. Refers to the time the aircraft is supposed to be over the drop zone with parachutists, or the target if the plane is a bomber.

TRICK CHIEF—NCOIC for a shift.

TRIPLE A—Antiaircraft Artillery or AAA. Anything used to shoot at airplanes and helicopters.

TWO—Radio call sign of the intelligence officer.

TWO-OH-ONE (201) FILE—Military records file that listed a soldier's qualifications, training, experience and abilities. It was passed from unit to unit so that the new commander would have some idea about the capabilities of an incoming soldier.

UMZ—Ultramilitarized Zone. Name GIs gave to the DMZ (Demilitarized Zone).

UNIFORM—Refers to the UHF radio. Company Uniform would be the frequency assigned to that company.

USARV—United States Army, Vietnam.

VC—Vietcong, called Victor Charlie (phonetic alphabet) or just Charlie.

VIETCONG—Contraction of Vietnam Cong San (Vietnamese Communist).

VIETCONG SAN—Vietnamese Communists. A term in use since 1956.

WHITE MICE—Referred to South Vietnamese military police because they wore white helmets.

WIA—Wounded In Action.

WILLIE PETE—WP, white phosphorus, called smoke rounds. Also used as antipersonnel weapons.

WSO—Weapons System Officer. The name given to the man who rode in the back seat of a Phantom; he was responsible for the weapons systems.

XO—Executive officer of a unit.

ZAP—To ding, pop caps or shoot. To kill.

ZSU-23—A multibarreled twenty-three millimeter antiaircraft weapon used by the communist forces.

In Bolan's never-ending war against organized crime, the hunter has become the hunted. But the battle is only beginning.

DON PENDLETON's

MACK BOLAN

BLOWOUT

Framed for murder and wanted by both sides of the law, Bolan escapes into the icy German underground to stalk a Mafia-protected drug baron.